Walking with Stingrays

MICHAEL WOOD

Pen Press

First published in Great Britain by Pen Press

All paper used in the printing of this book has been made from wood grown in managed, sustainable forests.

ISBN13: 978-1-907172-91-5

Printed and bound in the UK
Pen Press is an imprint of Indepenpress Publishing Limited
25 Eastern Place
Brighton
BN2 1GJ

A catalogue record of this book is available from the British Library

Cover design by Jacqueline Abromeit

Cover photograph – Wagonga Inlet, Narooma – by Jonathan Poyner
www.jonathanpoynerphotography.com

Then let your schemes alone
Adore the rising sun
And leave a man undone, to his fate

Robert Burns

Also by Michael Wood

THE FELL WALKER

Chapter 1

I HAVE FOUND IT! I HAVE FOUND IT! AT LAST, I HAVE FOUND IT.

After 30 exciting, absorbing, frustrating, liberating, testing, invigorating, freezing, stifling, fascinating years of searching I have found it.

Those of you who have read my travel books in the past will know that, while bringing you tales of far-off places, I have also been on a personal pilgrimage. I have been searching for the best place to live on this wondrous planet of ours. Now, at last, I have found it.

Of course the things that I personally seek and my opinions of the things that I find are entirely subjective. Yet I am sure I represent – with all humility – a few million other middle-aged, harassed and weary British subjects who dream of leaving their grey lives behind and finding something better. Most will never realise their dream, but I suspect that just reading that better places do exist, always brings them a glimmer of hope that one day they will be the ones to find their way to paradise.

Regular readers will know that in the past I thought I had found the best place to live, only to rescind my opinion at a later date. They will remember how I eulogised about a fishing village on the island of Majorca, and later a coastal settlement in Uruguay, only to find that after a few months living in those places reality did not match up to early impressions, and I ended up completing just another pair of travel books, albeit interesting ones I hope.

This time it is different. I have been living in this place for the past 11 months and time is not diminishing its appeal. On the contrary, as new scenes appear and new experiences unfold, I am growing more passionately attached to it.

It is not perfect – nothing can be. But it is the nearest thing to pleasant, comfortable, dare I say happy living that I have come across in all my travels. And guess what? The people speak English, they drive on the left side of the road, and they play cricket. However, when I say that the climate is wonderful, you will know that the similarities with Britain have ended.

I am, of course, talking about Australia – that vast, unique island continent that I have visited twice before. My previous books covered the enormous, beautiful wilderness that is Western Australia and the Northern Territory, a land so vast that most of Europe can fit into it, yet contains a population equal to one European city and the tropical state of Queensland where cowboys round up cattle by helicopter on farms (properties) as big as Wales, and the Great Barrier Reef plays host to the world's tourists and leaves them full of wonder.

My long-term plan was to pay at least another two visits to Australia, to cover the states of South Australia, Victoria, and Tasmania, after my current visit to the state of New South Wales. Although Australia is one country, such a vast and diverse continent could not, in my opinion, be accurately written about without numerous visits, just as you would not write about Spain, France and Germany in one visit.

However, this plan might not come to fruition for I am now so captivated by the south coastal area of the state of New South Wales that I might not venture further.

Lying in the south-east corner of the continent, New South Wales is about three times the size of the British Isles. With eight million people it is Australia's most populated state, but with four million of them living in the city of Sydney it still leaves most of the land empty by European standards. Most of the rest of the population can be found on the coast north of Sydney, taking in the industrial city of Newcastle, with the rest scattered in a multitude of small and medium-sized farming towns inland, beyond the Great Dividing Range, where the pioneers cleared the land of millions of trees and brought in their sheep and cattle (slowly giving way to vineyards as wool declines).

On the coast south of Sydney, after travelling 100 kilometres, you will find the large industrial town of Wollongong. After that the towns grow smaller and smaller until, with still 700 kilometres to go to reach the city of Melbourne in Victoria, you find yourself in a sparsely populated area of vast forests, multiform hills, glorious beaches, pristine seas and turquoise lagoons. This is the unspoilt, undeveloped south coast of New South Wales, and it doesn't get much better than this.

Amongst all this natural beauty a few small towns sit randomly scattered in forest clearings beside the sea, next to lagoons, beneath the mountains, allowing you to live a modern, civilised life in an ancient, pristine natural environment that white men first set eyes on only 150 years ago.

The area has been organised into shires, the central one being called Eurobodalla Shire. Anywhere along this Shire's wonderful coastline would be a great place to live, but my preference is the small town of Narooma – taken from the aboriginal 'Noorooma' – meaning 'clear blue waters'. How aptly named.

I arrived in Narooma travelling south on the Princes Highway, having travelled many miles down a corridor of tall eucalyptus trees. I turned a bend and was suddenly confronted by an expanse of brilliant turquoise water. 'WOW!' is what I said, and apparently what everybody else said when they first saw it. This is the Wagonga Inlet, named after the Wagonga tribe, and it is just the beginning of the glory that is Narooma – the best place on earth to live.

Before going into more detail, allow me to explain to new readers what criteria I use when looking for the best place to live. First of all

I am a country bumpkin, brought up running wild in the fields and hills of England, out in all weathers, swimming and fishing in the rivers, climbing trees, scrambling up the hills, observing the wildlife, building tree-houses, collecting conkers, sledging in the snow. As a result, cities and large towns are anathema to me. In the country, when you find an excess of species in close proximity you call it a plague – a plague of mice, of rats, of rabbits, of cockroaches – and you usually take steps to reduce their numbers. That is how I see cities and large towns – as plagues of people – and while it is beyond my understanding why so many people choose to live in them, I am not advocating the same drastic measures. I am glad that they do, as it leaves more space for the rest of us, those who enjoy freedom to move and closeness to nature.

But I do like the conveniences and comforts that only towns can offer – the speed of supermarket shopping, the relaxing coffee shop, the bank, the pubs and small restaurants, the doctor, the dentist, and most importantly – the library. So my ideal is a town just big enough to have at least one of all the above, plus some sporting facilities. As a general rule I have found that these towns have a population somewhere between 3-6,000. My final idiosyncratic requirements are that they should have no more than one set of traffic lights and no multi-storey car parks.

It is also necessary that I reside at the edge of such a town where I can see, hear, smell and touch the natural world, where I can go for rural walks from my front door yet be within walking distance of the town's conveniences.

It would add to its appeal if this town could be within a two-hour country drive of a place where an occasional symphony concert could be attended and of a mountain range where I can indulge my love of walking in high places.

Essentially, the town must be on the coast, and my house must have a view of the sea. (You will note that my two previous 'best places' were both by the sea.) Why? It is not about the view. I don't think a vast panorama of sea is particularly interesting, certainly not as entrancing as a beautiful mountain landscape. It is because it is another world, an alien world, a place of mystery, a place where man must watch out, take care, a place where he is not almighty. It is a constant reminder of the vastness and age of the planet, our insignificance in it, our split second of life on it. It puts our small troubles into perspective. It is humbling. It is an antidote to egoism – a trait noticeably missing from coastal dwellers.

This town must also be in an area where flora and fauna dominate the scene, where flowers and trees and fish and birds and animals are abundant, where man is at the margins. A place where nature rules.

Finally, and most importantly, my best place to live must have a climate that adds to rather than detracts from everyday life. A climate that is comfortable for a white man raised in England.

The small town of Narooma meets all the above criteria, then throws in world-class fishing, the most beautiful golf course I've ever played on, an Olympic-size swimming pool, oyster farms, lagoons where you can collect your own free prawns, good surfing, superb ocean swimming conditions, excellent yet inexpensive housing and restaurants, and a palpably calm, relaxed atmosphere that can only be exuded by people who know that they are blessed to live in such a place.

On my second day in Narooma, when walking to the post office, marvelling that such a mundane task could become such a pleasure as I took in the wonderful panorama, a small fat man of retirement age, dressed in the standard Australian outfit of hat, sunglasses, shirt, shorts, white socks and trainers, beamed broadly at me as we passed. Instinctively I smiled in return, wondering if he had won the lottery. He must have noted that small question in my smile for when I half turned to watch him pass, he also half turned and said over his shoulder 'just another day in paradise mate'. Need I say more?

6

I should point out that in my 30 years of travel writing I have seen every continent, every ocean, thousands of beaches, millions of trees, hundreds of mountains, rivers and estuaries.

I've seen numerous white beaches fringed with palm trees – the classic postcard paradise. I've seen staggeringly beautiful mountain scenery, jungles bursting with exotic flowers, and the exciting African, Indian and South American wildlife. They are all exquisite in their own way, but I have found that, though they are wonderful places to visit, they are not good places to live in permanently.

Many of them are within the tropical region, which almost automatically means extreme heat, monsoon rainfall, high humidity, and the inevitable disease bearing, biting insects. For this reason I do not subscribe to the cliché 'tropical paradise'. They are not for this white man from England.

So, I can say with some authority that although the south coast of New South Wales, Narooma in particular, does not have the best beaches I've ever seen, nor the most luxurious forests, nor the most enticing waterways, nor the most interesting wildlife, nor the greatest mountains, it is still outstanding in all these elements, and it doesn't have the negative aspects of the tropical regions. And, it does have one vital element in which it is supreme – a perfect climate.

This climate, averaging 24 degrees in the summer and 17 degrees in the so-called winter, with just enough rain to keep the trees tall, the fairways green, means that flowers blossom all year round, that you can grow tomatoes, citrus fruits, bananas in your garden, that you never see a leafless tree, fog or frost or snow or ice or mud, that you wear few clothes, that your car stays clean, that you need little fuel, that you can plan outdoor events ahead with certainty, that beautiful parrots and kingfishers share your breakfast at an outdoor table, that you are never hurried by inclement weather, that you can play outdoor sports almost every day, keep yourself healthy and relaxed. This climate adds to your life, it sustains your life; it allows you to choose what to do almost every day of your life. It is what I call a 12-month alive climate, compared with a 6-month alive climate in Britain where your outdoor choices are strictly limited and impossible to plan with certainty.

However, it is not a boring climate like much of inland Australia, where you can get long periods of cloudless, rainless skies, and the small towns appear to have no citizens as the unforgiving heat drives them to hide behind their shutters. Here, though blue skies are predominant throughout the year, they are rarely cloudless, with showers coming in short spells and thunderstorms bringing heavy downpours, all of which quickly dry up in an hour or two. The mornings are usually calm, with the afternoons bringing a gentle sea breeze that helps in summer, and sends the few flies and harmless mosquitoes back into the forest.

Put simply, it is like having the best imaginable English summer for eight months of the year with the other 4 months being like the best possible English spring. This, of course, is not to the liking of many born and bred Australians who are seasoned to high temperatures and find this area a bit on the cool side. This, and the 'Benidorm' attractions of the hot Queensland coast is why this beautiful coast, ideal for family holidays, has stayed relatively quiet and undeveloped, and as a consequence why it is so attractive to me.

Might the publication of this book spoil all this, bring the hordes, a plague of tourists? I doubt it. Most readers will reside on the other side of the world, and those that do visit Australia are unlikely to give Narooma priority over the Barrier Reef, Uluru, and other well-known icons during their short holiday visit. If it does happen to attract a few more tourists then I'm sure they will be very welcome to the Narooma businesses that cater for them.

James Ogle blinked. He took his glasses off and rubbed his eyes; they were getting tired and itchy. He took a deep breath and stretched his arms and yawned. He'd had enough for the day. He reached for the mouse and scrolled back to page one and started to read through the nine double-spaced pages he had just written. Not bad, he decided. I'll polish it up tomorrow.

He had become a lazy writer, always procrastinating, always finding a reason to stay away from the computer. It was usually the call of the outdoors – fishing, golf, walking, and in a place like Narooma these were irresistible.

At least he had made a start; after 11 months of pure outdoor indulgence he had made a start – he was back to the grind – his agent might give him some peace now. Her regular emails from her office in London had become tedious, though he appreciated that he needed to be pushed, and he admired her tenacity. His wife should also be pleased, but that didn't matter.

James knew he was lazy. At 54 years of age you should know yourself. He also knew he was quite a good writer. You don't make a living writing for 30 years unless you are. After the usual initial struggle for recognition, his books now sold in enough quantities to keep the wolf from the door. But he was always aware that it was a precarious existence, which is why he had made arrangements to provide himself with greater security, although this arrangement now felt like Coleridge's albatross around the neck.

He relied on quality rather than quantity. He kept his writing simple and true, avoiding the flowery adjective, the unnecessary simile. He tried to follow Hemingway's philosophy – 'prose is architecture, not interior decoration'.

He had become a travel writer because he had been born with a love of place. As a child, confined to holidays in the British Isles, he had fallen in love with the Scottish Hebridean islands – their wildness, their mystery. On a fine summer's day he would gaze in awe at the flat glass sheets of silent shimmering sea, separating them, holding them together. He would find that he had stopped breathing.

And later – the English Lake District – its mountains, valleys, lakes and forests coming together in scenic perfection. How could millions of years of haphazard nature produce such symmetry?

He had always hated it when his holidays were over, when he had to leave the wild magic places behind and return to the safe, overcrowded blandness of south-east England where his hard-working parents had become reluctantly trapped in a suburban world of job security and mortgage repayments. At school he had day-dreamed about one day living in the wild places. At university he had vowed not to get trapped like his parents.

He had spent two years as a junior reporter on a London daily, hating the city but learning the essentials of the job – about brevity, simplicity, accuracy. It was during this time that his girl friend persuaded him to take his first holiday abroad. She had tired of following his backpack up wet British mountains, had not totally shared his passion for the challenge.

He had gone to the South of France with some reluctance, expecting to be bored. And though he was a bit restless to start with, itching to be doing instead of just looking, slowly the relaxing effect of the consistent sun won him over and he started to enjoy simply being in its pleasant warmth. He came late to the realisation that the sun had the power to make an ordinary place desirable, an ugly place bearable, and was the reason why people who lived in the sun, no matter their circumstances, smiled more. Now he hankered for more.

While on that holiday he had made notes of the places and people and events that caught his eye, and on his return to work he wrote a feature article based on the notes. It was well received by the editor and published with few alterations.

The following year he had gone to the Mediterranean island of Menorca with a new girlfriend. Again he had enjoyed the pleasures that only the sun can bring. Again he made notes and produced a feature article. It was accepted with alacrity. He sensed that he might have found his vocation.

With the impetuosity of youth he resigned from the paper and set off for France, intent on working his way around the country, writing about it along the way, and completing his first travel book within a year. The fact that he wanted to part company with his latest girl friend also had a bearing on his decision.

He had wanted to go the whole hog and head for Africa, but a wise old head at the newspaper suggested he should try a civilised country close to home to start with, in case things didn't go according to plan. 'Never leap into unknown waters,' he had said, 'always dip your toes in first.'

For the most part, things had gone to plan. He had spent six months travelling around France's coastline, its rural hinterland and its Alpine regions, avoiding the cities. He had worked in cafes and bars and vineyards and warehouses and farms, and had compiled copious hand-written notes in four large, lined jotting pads.

Returning to Britain, he had rented a familiar old cottage at Blackwaterfoot on the Isle of Arran off the west coast of Scotland, spent every waking hour of six weeks turning his notes into a type-written manuscript, posted it off to an agent he had met at a party he had attended with his previous girl friend, then hung around the island, doing bar work, and playing golf, and fishing, while waiting for the agent's verdict.

He had called the book 'Ogling France'. He had inferred his name into the title so people would remember it. He knew that a successful author's name sold more books than the title, and he intended to be successful. Already he was planning a series of 'Ogling' books, and envisaged a pair of binoculars as the 'Ogling' logo. Each book's cover was to have the title 'Ogling (country)' with binoculars looking down on a cut-out shape of the country he was writing about.

The agent, Nicola Smart, had liked his first book, then come up with the 'brilliant idea' of doing a series of 'Ogling' books. Within three months she had sold the book and the idea to a well-known publisher, and signed him up. He had done it all within his 12-month plan.

For the next ten years he repeated the formula, slowly building up the sales of his books until he had a loyal following and general approval by the critics, some of whom started to talk about a country having being 'well and truly Ogled'. After ten gruelling but mostly enjoyable years, at the age of 35 he had arrived – made a name for himself. The cost had been an almost non-existent social life.

James pressed the 'save' icon, then switched off his computer. He slowly turned his well-upholstered swivelling chair to face the large window at his right elbow. A slight smile came to his lips and his whole demeanour relaxed as he looked forward to visual pleasure.

He had been very lucky. Furnished houses for rent were pretty scarce in Narooma, and his arrival in town had happened to coincide with two being available. The first had been too close to the town centre, but the second fulfilled all his criteria for a perfect location. On the northern, forest-fringed edge of the town a clearing had been cut in the forest, starting at the edge of a beach and travelling back up a long, steep hill – looking like a very wide fire-break. In this gap between the trees five individual houses and a road had recently been built up the hillside, each house far enough apart so that the one behind could see over the top of the one below. All the houses had wonderful views of the beach and the ocean. James's house was the third one up, about 200 metres from the beach, which he could walk down to through the forest at the back of his house. It was a typical modern Australian detached house, with a very large double garage built into the hillside, and spacious three-bedroomed, two-bathroomed accommodation on one level above it, with extensive decking on two sides, surrounded on four sides by lawned gardens containing flowers, shrubs, hedges and fruit trees. Exterior water hoses were mounted on all four corners of the house and a fenced-in area to the side of the house was clearly designed as storage for your boat. Overall it provided living space at least double that of a typical U.K. detached house. James had never lived in or fancied new property, but its ease of use soon won him over.

The house above him was occupied by a pleasant Swedish woman called Valdis. She was a widow whose husband had come to Australia many years ago to work on the massive Snowy Mountains hydro-electric scheme, completed in 1974. Like many women in the town she spent a lot of her day in the garden, attending to her all-year-round display of flowers and shrubs. When not gardening she sat out on her deck, wearing her wide-brimmed floppy white hat, watching the comings and goings of the abundant wildlife, and her few neighbours. The only thing that tempted her indoors was a televised game of cricket, for which she expressed a passion. She always gave James a wave whenever he left his house.

The house below, larger than the others, was occupied by a retired Australian couple whose two expensive cars and a very large boat complete with four-wheel drive to tow it, spoke of a healthy bank balance. James saw them occasionally as he drove past and waved, or at a distance as they drove out of their triple garage. He had never seen them walk down to the beach, or walk at all. He suspected, unkindly, that they might have two scooters indoors to get them around their mansion. He had yet to learn their names.

Within two weeks of moving in, James had started to think of his rented house as home, such was the appeal of its position and the sunny outdoor living on the large raised decks overlooking the ocean.

His bare feet came out from the shadows under the desk and placed themselves on the warm, sunlit carpet. Even the simplest routine of daily life became a pleasure in this wonderful place.

He looked out of the window, across the wooden decking, and saw the blue Pacific Ocean. Four boys were surfing on Carters Beach, a two-man boat sat not far out, fishing for flathead. A sudden big splash – the whales were still making their way north to the tropics.

His concentration on following the antics of the whales was suddenly disturbed by a flurry of parrots landing just in front of him, on the deck's railing. Eight lorikeets sat in a row. He loved these small, brilliantly coloured, garrulous birds. They were like cockney cheeky chappies, the 'Del-boys' of the parrot world, all twitching shoulders and heads, and restlessness, and full of vim. They had fierce red eyes that told you they were no pushover. They were afraid of nothing, chased off birds twice their size, landed on your hand to beg for food. What characters!

Assuming that the lorikeets had spotted some food, other parrots started to fly in. Three rosellas – beautiful, but slightly nervous – landed on the deck and started their comical bowlegged strutting. A pair of stunning king parrots arrived in their elegant green and scarlet cloaks, as though they had called in for breakfast after an all-night ball. They remained slightly aloof from the rest. Loud squawking and heavy wing flutters announced the arrival of a mob of cockatoos. Large, strikingly white, with formidable beaks, these beautiful birds were not quite so welcome as they usually came to eat the fruit in the garden.

The previous tenants of the house had left a garden full of tomatoes, grapefruit, oranges and passion fruit. Fortunately they had also left netting that covered the fruit and protected them from the cockatoos, although they were crafty enough to take a nibble here and there. That same netting had brought a mini drama to the house a week ago, when his wife had discovered a black snake enmeshed in the netting that protected the tomatoes. He assumed the snake was lying in wait for a bird or animal that liked to eat tomatoes, or perhaps it was just seeking a new hiding place.

He had telephoned the local volunteer organisation that dealt with these things. Two people came from W.I.R.E.S (wildlife, information, rescue, and education service) and slowly disentangled the snake, taking great care to avoid its venomous bite. They put it in a sack and said they would take it out into the bush a few miles away and release it.

All the birds and the snake had arrived on their doorstep from the 'bush', being the forest that bordered the property, only 10 metres from their garden fence. He loved the idea of living so close to potentially dangerous animals. It created a slight frisson in the air, made you think about the natural world, reminded you that man did not rule here. In contrast, he knew that back in Britain the greatest excitement that awaited him was finding a parking space free.

The forest thrummed with bird-song, mostly from the appropriately named bellbird, a small olive-green, rarely-seen bird that started its bell-like tinkling at dawn and didn't stop until dark. This gentle, happy-sounding tinkling was a permanent and pleasant background to all outdoor activity. Occasionally the bellbirds would provide a choral background as the whipbirds made their fantastic calls – the male making a long high whistle followed immediately by a sound like a whip cracking. These sounds made the temperate forest sound more exotic than it actually was.

The final arrival at the party was a kookaburra – the giant kingfisher, famous for its loud laughing call, which, when timed just after a bad golf shot, could sound alarmingly human. He knew this bird well. It regularly sat with its mate on a tree branch overlooking the house, and usually came down to check out the action. It was a regular visitor to their breakfast table on the deck. It would stand on the table and wait to be spoon-fed. With its blank expression, long beak, and a square head covered in small feathers that stuck up in the air, it reminded him of Stan Laurel. Kooky was his favourite.

James was about to go out to top up the bird seed feeder when his wife shouted 'are you there' from some distant part of the house. Elaine was back from her swim. He hated shouting. But it was only one of the many things he hated about his wife. He had been trying to get rid of her for years. Now that he was intent on staying in Australia, and she wasn't, he had decided to murder her.

Chapter 2

'Hard at it as usual.' She had come into the room quietly, probably also bare-footed. She was on automatic, her words thrown away in a flat, disinterested monotone. A reply was not expected.

James continued looking through the window. He did not turn around. He also found himself on automatic, the words tumbling out without thought while he continued to watch the wildlife. 'Yes, it is quite hard watching the whales. They take some following. Almost as difficult as following a soap opera plot.'

She made a slight noise with her nose, then left the room. Their late-morning skirmish was over. It had been brief, with honours even. She had delivered a small thrust, he had parried. The game went on.

He hadn't told her he had started writing because he didn't want to let her think that her nagging had finally succeeded. It had nothing to do with her. It was all to do with not letting his agent and publisher down, and his own sense of guilt at not working for so long. He was not yet entirely comfortable with his newly acquired laziness, the routine of work having become hard-wired into his system during his early years. He was also looking forward to the small, perverse pleasure of letting her continue to nag unnecessarily.

He heard the insect screen door of the living room slide open then slam shut, the light aluminium frame and surround coming together in a loud metallic whack! Now she was in front of him, on the outside deck waving her towel and swimsuit at the birds; all the birds except the lorikeets taking off. She didn't like the birds – 'noisy, messy'. She checked the railing for droppings, then lay her towel and swimsuit over it to dry. She turned around towards him and looked upwards, over his head, to the roof of the house or the forest beyond or the distant sky? Had she spotted an eagle or a flock of geese or pelicans? *Probably admiring the satellite dish,* he thought cruelly. But just for a moment, with her head tilted back tightening her neck, and the sun creating shadows emphasising her high cheekbones, he remembered how she had looked 20 years ago, and why he had fallen for her, and why she could still turn heads at 48.

Slowly, her absent gaze came down until she saw him watching her through the window. She stared at him and held his eye, while she flicked her dyed blonde hair back with her left hand, and reached into her shorts pocket with her right. She took out cigarettes and lit one, and blew the smoke up into the air with an exaggerated gesture of pleasure. She knew he hated smoking.

Not for the first time, James thought wryly, *I went to bed with Grace Kelly and woke up with Sybil Fawlty.*

They had met in that romantic place where most 30-somethings meet – the supermarket. Not one of the big town giants, but just about the smallest one able to allow itself the title, the only one on the Scottish island of Arran, in the small town of Brodick.

He had been on the island for two weeks, in his usual Blackwaterfoot cottage, typing up his eighth book 'Ogling Finland'. He had enjoyed his Finnish odyssey because it had allowed him to achieve one of his lifetime ambitions – to visit the home of one of his favourite composers – Sibellius.

He tried to visit the homes of the great composers wherever he travelled and write a few paragraphs about them in his books. He was unashamedly passionate about music. Although he admired the great writers and poets and painters, he knew that music was the greatest of all the arts, that the great composers were to be cherished. What was it about an arrangement of different musical notes and sounds that appealed so much to humans? Why should some particular arrangements move you to tears, reveal your soul, tell it stories it did not know it wanted to hear, make sense of things that are unspeakable? What incredible magic was at work that made him stop reading, stop driving, stop talking, stop everything when a favourite masterpiece started up? Though he might be familiar with every note, he could not listen casually. He was compelled to listen intently. It was wrong not to. He knew that if he could only capture in prose what Beethoven – whose music should be listened to on one's knees – captured in music, he would be immortal. It was, of course, impossible.

His routine on the island was well established by this time. On arrival off the ferry at Brodick on the east coast, he would stock up with supplies at the supermarket and drive across the island to his cottage on the west coast. Here he would work hard most of the day, occasionally jogging along to the village shop for fresh milk and the like, or, weather permitting, have two hours off to take up the challenge of the beautiful, quirky 12-hole golf course that lay along the shore.

Conditions in the small cottage were basic and conducive to working without distraction. By now he had progressed from a typewriter to a personal computer which sat incongruously on an old scrubbed wooden kitchen table he had pushed in front of the cottage's only front window.

At times, usually when struggling with word flow, he would look out across the calm waters of the Kilbrannan Sound to the distant coast of the Kintyre peninsula, another place he knew well. He would imagine himself crossing the peninsula to reach its western shore, there to gaze across the Sound of Jura to the mountainous Isle of Jura. Here, on Jura, he would walk north until he reached a remote old farmhouse called Barnhill. On entering the primitive farmhouse, he would find an angular, stern-faced man sitting at a table similar to the one in his cottage, writing feverishly with a fountain pen in an exercise book. His clothes would be 60 years out of date and he would introduce himself as Eric Blair. James would recognise him as George Orwell, the pseudonym he used when writing his ground breaking novel '1984'.

James would not always find inspiration in this imagined journey, but he did always find a strange kind of comfort and kinship in knowing that Orwell once sat out there and looked across the same expanse of clear Hebridean air when lifting his head from the page.

Every two weeks he would take a day off, drive over to Brodick, play golf on its sedate little course or fish from the rocks, have some lunch, then top up his supplies at the supermarket before returning to the west coast.

He was in good spirits as he pushed his trolley down the narrow supermarket aisle. He had struck the ball cleanly most of the round, and parred the last five holes. His eyes were on the shelves studying the tins of salmon – one of his fast, healthy meals – when a woman's voice shouted 'Jonathan'. He looked up to see a woman walking towards him pushing a trolley but with her head turned to look at a small boy of five or six loitering a long way behind her. 'Come on, Jonathan,' she pleaded as she continued to push the trolley until it collided with James's trolley.

He heard her gasp slightly before she said, 'Oh! I'm so sorry,' as she turned to face him. Their eyes met and continued to meet in what James had come to call a 'movie moment'. At 35, he'd experienced many similar moments, particularly in European bars and taverns after a day's work. He had always thought of the male as predator, but now he knew better. After ten years of roaming, he was like the proverbial sailor, with a girl in every town.

Now, in a supermarket in Brodick, he was looking into the light-brown eyes of an exceptionally beautiful woman who had long ash-blonde hair, smooth skin and high cheekbones. He had seen that split second of double take in the eyes many times before – the ploy used by Hollywood – the 'movie moment'. He knew that the attraction was mutual.

The boy, Jonathan, who was small and chubby, came running forward to see what was happening, tripped and hit his head on James's trolley. He started to cry immediately and looked to his mother for comfort. James bent down to examine the boy's head. There was a small red mark on his forehead and a tiny scratch. 'He'll be fine,' James said, straightening up, and smiling reassuringly at the woman. They continued to smile at each other as they disentangled their trolleys, during which James noticed that she did not wear a wedding ring. There was a moment of hesitation before they both went their separate ways.

Two minutes later, James had finished his shopping and arrived at the check-out. Shortly afterwards, the sound of sniffling and muffled crying behind him told its own story. He turned to find the boy looking theatrically miserable. The woman looked at James, shrugged her shoulders and gave him a resigned smile.

James checked his supplies through and waited outside for them, noticing that there was a coffee shop on the other side of the road that also sold ice cream. It had started to rain slightly.

She came out carrying two bags, Jonathan trailing forlornly behind. James stepped forward and winked at her, and said in a falsely raised voice, 'I think that wound on Jonathan's head might need a plaster. I can fetch one from my car if you like.'

'Yes…that would be kind,' she smiled, understanding his intention. 'Why don't we come with you,' she added quickly, 'get out of the rain.' James noticed a slight East End accent hiding behind the practised Oxford. They all walked the short distance to the adjacent car park where James retrieved the first-aid box he always carried in his Volkswagen camper van. He made an exaggerated fuss as he placed a dressing and then a plaster over the tiny scratch. When he had finished he stood up and said, 'I'll bet an ice cream would make your head feel better, Jonathan.'

The boy looked up at his mother and attempted a pleading smile. 'I'd like one as well,' she said, as she glanced a 'thank you' look at James.

They left all their shopping bags in the back of the camper van and crossed the road to the coffee shop. They found a place to sit. Jonathan had a large ice cream. James and Elaine Sampson introduced themselves to each other, ordered coffee, and sat in warm conversation for 20 minutes. In that short time he learned that she had been a widow for three years, that she lived in Buckinghamshire and that she was on holiday with her son for another week. She didn't read travel books or any other kind of books, only magazines. She had never heard of James. She explained this in an apologetic manner, exposing to James an insecurity only felt by those from a working-class background. But she made it clear that she was very impressed by anyone who could write one book, never mind eight.

When they got back to the car park, James retrieved her bags from his camper van and carried them to the vehicle she indicated – a new silver BMW four-wheel drive.

She got into the car and lowered the window. She looked him in the eye unwaveringly. 'Do you fancy a real cup of coffee? I make a good one at home. I'd like to thank you for calming Jonathan down.' She didn't end with a smile and this told James a lot.

'Where are you staying,' he said lightly.

'Sannox…it's about 20 minutes up the coast…'

'I know it,' James interjected in a frivolous tone, 'lead on, McDuff, and I'll follow.'

In spite of the rain, the drive up the island's east coast was a delight as always, the road hugging the shore, the silken sea always in sight. He knew the picturesque hamlet of Sannox well, nestling under the mountains, with its own little beach and rocks to fish from. It was one of his favourite places on the island.

Eventually, they drove past the few scattered cottages that he knew as Sannox, and she turned into the drive of what used to be a hotel. It had gone the way of many when Spanish sun took over the holiday trade. Now it had clearly been completely renovated and turned into a very large private home with neat lawns, gravel drive, and four garages. She parked her BMW outside the front door and, taking the keys from her handbag, went to open it.

Loaded in more ways than one, James thought as he pulled up beside her, wondering why she would rent such a huge house just for the two of them.

Inside, she put on the percolator, then gave him a guided tour of the house. It had a grand entrance hall, two huge reception rooms, a cellar bar and games room, six large en-suite bedrooms, a marble bathroom and kitchen with gold fittings, quality furniture and carpets, but tasteless décor, paintings and ornaments. It was as if two people with different ideas had been let loose on it and created a schizophrenic display of ostentation. 'What do you think,' she asked with a smile, as the tour came to an end back in the kitchen.

'Pretty awful, eh!' James said conspiratorially, raising his eyebrows, expecting her now to join him in a mutual condemnation of the owner's taste. The smile left her face, and she turned to the percolator. There was five seconds of silence followed by James speaking in an artificially loud voice attempting bravado. 'You own it, and I'm a bloody idiot. *Mea culpa, mea culpa.*'

She turned around, and started to laugh when she saw him standing with his hands raised in surrender, a look of penance on his face. 'Yes, you are an idiot, and please mind your language when children are about.'

'Sorry.'

'Black or white?'

'White please, and when can I put my hands down, please, Miss?'

She laughed again. 'Consider yourself forgiven.'

James bowed down before her. 'Bless you, Miss. I will spread the word of your munificence across the globe. Wizened Mongolian elders will speak of you to their grandchildren…'

'Shut up and drink your coffee.'

'Yes, Miss.'

'And stop calling me Miss.'

'Yes…Elaine.'

'That's better.'

While they drank their coffees in the lounge, with Jonathan watching television in the adjoining room, Elaine explained that her late husband, who had been twice her age and previously married, had owned an electronics company with factories in Kent and Ayrshire. She had been his secretary in the past, and after his death, in a helicopter crash, she had attempted to run the company herself, but had found it too much to cope with. She had sold the company to a large international electronics group who had previously been keen to buy them out. Her husband had used this house in Sannox both for holidays and for entertaining important Scottish clients; he would bring them over to fish and play golf and sup the island's whisky. He had also entertained clients at their Buckinghamshire home. James dare not ask how big that might be. Elaine hesitated before pointing out that they – she – also had a holiday villa on the Mediterranean island of Majorca.

As she went on telling him about her past, James got the feeling that she was very lonely and a bit unsure of herself and… 'You know you are in a very vulnerable situation, don't you,' he blurted out. 'It's a big bad world out there. Lots of unscrupulous people, mostly men. A beautiful woman like you, with money, will bring them running…'

'I meet them all the time,' she interrupted.

'I bet nobody blew their chances quicker than me,' James offered jokingly.

'At least you were honest,' she laughed lightly, and there was warmth in her smile.

Jonathan came into the room and demanded attention and the phone rang and routine domesticity took Elaine from the room. While she was out, James took a stroll around the large lounge. He paused to look at a framed photograph standing on the polished surface of an occasional table. It was a full-length shot of a couple standing on the steps at the front of the house. Elaine was smiling wanly, but the man beside her was beaming. He was an inch shorter than Elaine, much older, and clearly a businessman. He was of that universal type who have large rectangular heads, a mane of dark hair, no necks, and broad square shoulders; who have the knack of looking heavy with importance; who sound absolutely certain about everything they say, and give the impression that they were never, ever, children. *Probably daunting to live with,* James thought sympathetically. The man was carrying a baby boy, presumably Jonathan, who he rested on his considerable stomach. Clearly the late Mr Sampson had done lots of entertaining and not much exercise.

When she came back James interrupted her apology and announced that it was time for him to leave. She looked disappointed; she had clearly been expecting to spend more time together. James recognised the look.

Before leaving, he made sure she knew precisely where his cottage at Blackwaterfoot was, and casually invited her to 'pop in for a cup of tea and a microwaved scone if you're passing.' He remembered that she had only one week left on the island. If she called to see him during that time, he knew he was on to a winner.

As they said goodbye at the front door, he leaned forward and gave her a fatherly peck on the cheek. 'Thanks for the coffee. I'm off to the chiropodist now…see if he can reduce the size of my feet…bye.' He felt her hand touch his arm, as though she had been ready to embrace. When he turned to go, she stepped back, clumsily 'Bye…bye.'

Three days later, James was hard at work, checking his Finnish maps and reference books to make sure he had spelt 'Uusikaupunk' correctly, when he heard a car pull up on the grass verge in front of his cottage. He waited for the knock before opening the door and inviting Elaine and Jonathan in.

He was unshaven and he hadn't cleaned up for a week, but that was how it was when he was working. His very rare visitors had to take it or leave it. He waited until Elaine had taken in his primitive surroundings, then said, 'Well, what do you think?' He answered his own question at the same time she did and they both said together 'Pretty awful, eh!' and smiled knowingly at each other.

He removed some books from the two remaining chairs, positioned at either side of the table, and asked if they would like to sit down; somebody had painted these traditional wooden farmhouse chairs with white gloss, which was now chipping badly. As they shuffled themselves into the confined spaces, James put the kettle on, washed some cups, put three frozen scones in the microwave, got the butter out of the fridge, cleaned a knife under the tap, found three dinner plates (he didn't have small plates), and asked what they had been doing, while he proceeded to produce the tea and scones and a glass of milk for Jonathan.

Hunched together around the table, balancing plates on knees and trying to find space for cups among the papers and computer paraphernalia, swapping stories about the island, James explaining his work, Jonathan drawing on sheets of paper, it turned out to be a nice cosy get-together, and it had that surprisingly relaxed quality which happens when virtual strangers feel as though they have known each other for some time. James noticed that she had made a bit of an effort. It was quite subtle, he thought, but everything about her looked just a bit more shipshape than at their first meeting. He wondered what she now thought about him, now that he had revealed his normal scruffy self.

The answer came when, as he was rising to clear away the debris, she picked up her handbag, and when he returned from the kitchen area, she held out a key ring with three keys on it, offering them to him. 'These are the keys to the house at Sannox. You are welcome to use it when we are gone,' she paused to smile, 'assuming you can put up with its awfulness.'

'But I...'

'Only if you want to. No charge, no strings. You could make one of the bedrooms as basic as this if you wanted to, and work looking out at the mainland for a change, or you could just use it as a base for fishing or golfing or something.' She held up her hand when she saw him about to protest again. 'Honestly, I've been wondering what to do with the place, whether to sell it or keep it...it doesn't get used much now. And I like the idea that it would be put to creative use. I'm not creative as you can tell, so this whole writing business is a new world to me. I'd like to find out more about it.' She paused, and James knew she meant she would like to find out more about him.

They batted the subject around for quite a time, James needing it to get over his surprise, but in the end he could see no harm in taking the keys. Even if he only used the house as a fishing base, it would be nice to spend some time in Sannox.

She told him about the caretaker in the village who could fill him in on all the usual stuff about heating and bin days etc, and who also had a set of keys, and asked him if he ever got down to the London area. When he explained that he routinely headed for London from the island, to meet his agent and publisher, and sometimes do some publicity appearances and interviews, she gave him her address and phone number in Buckinghamshire and suggested that he might like to return the keys in person, when he was free from business.

Six weeks later, James found himself driving down a country lane west of High Wycombe, looking for the address Elaine had given him. The Chiltern Hills were looking their best, the lush late summer greenery enhancing the chocolate-box prettiness of the typically English scene – rolling hills, leafy lanes, pretty villages – an area sought after by the rich of London, escaping the city grime.

With some help from a village post office, he eventually found the country lane in question, and duly came upon the entrance to Elaine's house. Carved into the stonework to the side of the large cast-iron entrance gate was the name 'Hidden Gem'. James was to learn later that it had been built in the late 19th century by an adventurer who had made his fortune in South African diamonds, which made the naff name almost forgivable.

He drove up the long drive, through the private grounds heavy with oak and beech trees, dappling the sunlit ground with dark shadows. To call it a house was a misnomer; it was a mansion. But James was not surprised by its grandeur. While still on the Isle of Arran he had contacted an old colleague at the newspaper – the business editor – and asked him to find out how much Sampson Electronics had been sold for two years ago. The answer came back surprisingly quickly – 39 million pounds.

So began a relationship that got off to a mixed start. From his flat in an old cottage on the banks of the River Misbourne, on the outskirts of Little Missenden, that he shared with an old university mate, Simon Mathews, James made frequent journeys to call on Elaine. That they both lived in Buckinghamshire had turned out to be a useful coincidence. They did all the usual early together things – restaurants, village pubs, cinema, country walks. And soon it was holding hands, and warm goodnight kissing. But she always stopped any further advances, and always made it clear that he was expected to go back to his flat at night. James reckoned she was either arcane or archaic or both, or, heaven forbid, frigid. Being someone who had long ago moved into the modern world of casual sex, he found her behaviour disquieting, but not strange enough to make him leave the stage. In all other ways she was engaging – kind and affectionate in an overt manner, which did his image and morale no harm at all when witnessed by others. Wherever they went, heads turned to look at this stunning beauty and the man she clung to with such obvious devotion.

She started to buy him presents. Small to begin with, but gradually becoming grander and more expensive. And the notes attached to the presents followed a similar progression. 'To my dear James' became 'To my darling James' became 'With love from Elaine'. James's protests at her extravagance went unheeded. When she presented him with the latest, most expensive set of golf clubs on the market (he could change them to his own preference if he wished), with a note saying 'With all my love' he had little doubt that she was showing more than just kindness.

It became clear to James that she was making a bid for him, that she wanted a permanent relationship, probably marriage, and she was using all the means at her disposal. Judging from the photographs he had seen of her late husband, he concluded that Elaine had married for money, so she was well aware of its powerful attraction, and now she was using that power to achieve her aim.

James was worried. He knew that at 35 he couldn't keep up his present hectic lifestyle much longer. He was getting a bit old for sleeping in a camper van or a B&B, as he toured endlessly. Was it time to settle down, make a permanent home, start a family? (that thought surprised him). Was this the woman to do it with? Let's see – she's beautiful, very rich, kind, affectionate, a reasonable cook and easily pleased. 'What more do you want,' he heard a million men say in his ear. But he now knew that they were not on the same wavelength when it came to taste in all its aspects – politics, art, music, sport, the outdoors, nature; all those occasional but essential things that oil the wheels while bodies slowly rust.

They had so very little in common it was alarming. Elaine was 100% female. She didn't have a single male hormone in her makeup. She was indoors and fashion shows; he was outdoors and sport. She was soap operas and celebrity magazines; he was world politics and literary novels. She was Radio 2 and Madonna; he was Radio 4 and Maria Callas. *But she was rich.*

Should he wait until he found his soul mate? She hadn't turned up yet, so what were the odds that she would in the future? Pretty long, he reckoned. *And would she be rich?*

His deliberations brought some clarity to one of the questions. He did not want to settle down in the conventional sense. He wouldn't mind a permanent base, but he wanted to keep on travelling, exploring the world, writing his books. He wanted to visit every continent, every major country, find their beating hearts and transfuse them on the page. *But that would take time and money; possibly more money than he could earn with his books. He might need to find a second source of income.*

For writers like James, money was always the problem. People assumed he was well-off because they saw his name in bookshops and libraries and newspapers. They didn't know that writers ranked about 70th in the pay league, that 60% of all professional writers had second jobs, that only 20% managed to earn all their income from writing. His first ten years had been a hard struggle, but he had finally built up his earnings so that in the last two years he hadn't had to work while travelling around the country he was visiting. But he was still sleeping in his camper van most of the time, and having to be careful with money. For the moment he belonged in the 20% category. Now he wanted to travel further and longer – to South America, Asia, Africa. It would take more time, cost more money. If his book sales didn't cover that cost, then he would have to join the 60% category.

Did he *want* to marry Elaine, he asked himself. The answer was no. *Would* he marry Elaine because her money could provide him with a much easier life, allow him to travel the world in comfort and at his own pace, free him forever from the prospect of succumbing to the dreaded mortgage trap. Ever the realist, ever the pragmatist, James decided the answer was *yes*.

But he decided that he would not be the one to broach the subject of marriage or any other long-term commitment. That would have to be Elaine's call; she would have to do the proposing. He was quite happy the way things were at the moment, apart from the lack of sex. And now that he was about to plan his last trip into Europe, he knew that problem would soon be taken care of. His last European trip was to be to Portugal (he needed the sun again after the cold of Finland), then he hoped to head off to South America after that.

As was his tradition, shortly before he was about to leave on his next overseas project, he went to stay with his parents for a week. Their comfortable home in a Berkshire suburb was always an oasis of calm and harmony. He would sit in the conservatory chatting with his dad about world affairs, reminisce about the great times they had had together in the wild places, while his mother fussed over him, making sure he was well fed and had clean clothes.

With a week to go he was back at his flat, making final preparations. It was dreary, dark, end of November, and the sun of Portugal was starting to look very appealing. He was also keen to escape before the retail orgy that had replaced the traditional Christmas got underway. He found it profoundly sad to watch the good workers of Britain reduced to shuffling in their millions to the cathedrals of consumerism, there to take a plastic slide into the abyss of debt. Sad, because they had become the puppets of big business, who pulled the strings of their lives with advertising; sad, because they had allowed themselves to be so easily incited into collective hysteria. Watching them herd clone-like into the giant malls, apparently unable to resist the call of 'Silent Night' blaring from the loudspeakers, he thought it looked like a cross between an Orwellian vision of the future and The

Pied Piper of Hamlyn. George Orwell had, however, got the villain wrong. It wasn't Big Brother but big business that controlled them, and successive governments had stood by and watched them create this 'bread and circuses' society.

With two days to go before he left for Portugal, he went to say goodbye to Elaine. Over the past few weeks, she had been making pleas with him not to go, but they were timid affairs, probably being afraid of appearing domineering. She had, apparently, settled for his assurance that he would be in regular contact by phone.

In her enormous, ornamented, high-ceilinged sitting room, they drank tea from bone china, served on a silver tray, from a silver teapot brought in by Mrs Harris, her daily help. Elaine liked to play the grandee. She seemed slightly preoccupied as they discussed his travel plans. Suddenly, in a nervously swift movement, her hand darted to the bottom shelf of the coffee table and came out holding a large brown envelope. She handed it to James. 'A going away present,' she smiled hesitantly.

'Not another one,' James sighed, as he took it from her. 'When are you going to stop?' He was unable to hide his exasperation.

For a moment she looked hurt, and he felt sorry for his outburst. 'I'm just trying to help,' she said flatly, as he started to open the envelope.

He took out what appeared to be two photocopies. The first was a letter from solicitors Thomson and Smyth to Elaine. 'We have carried out your instructions…' etc, 'and enclose a copy of the revised deeds to 'Celtic-Snore'…' etc, etc. James lifted his head and looked at Elaine. "Celtic-Snore'…what's this…?'

'Read the other page,' Elaine said quietly, as though teaching a child.

James glanced down again. It was a copy of a title deed for a property known as 'Celtic-Snore' in the village of Sannox on the island of Arran. The property was owned by Mrs Elaine Sampson and Mr James Ogle. His head shot up, and his mouth fell open, and though his head was spinning with questions, the first thing that came out of his mouth was, 'Celtic-Snore?'

'My husband's brilliant idea,' Elaine explained, with a hint of contempt in her voice. 'It's an anagram of Electronics. He said Electronics paid for the house, it was in Scotland, and it was where he did his relaxing, so...' (she held her palms out) '...the name is on a plaque near the front door, but I've encouraged the ivy to grow over it.'

'I see...well no...I couldn't could I...' James strangled his joke. 'Sorry...I'm not thinking straight.' He took a deep breath and looked, incredulously, at Elaine. 'Am I to understand that you have made me joint owner of...' (he couldn't bring himself to say the name) '...your house at Sannox?'

'Our house, James,' Elaine said with panache, as she leaned over and squeezed his hand. 'I want to help you...make life a bit easier for you...'

'But this is too much,' James blurted, fighting to control his anger. Suddenly, his life was being decided for him, without his consent, without his input. He had always made his own decisions, always valued his independence, never wanted to get tied down like his parents.

And yet, here was a once-in-a-lifetime chance at financial security. The house at Sannox was worth a lot of money, and it was probably just the start of her generous plans. It was absolutely clear now that she was hell-bent on having him. In that moment he saw what he must do. He saw that if he didn't do it, it would mean endless half-meant conversations, time and energy-draining toing and froing, tedious ploys to put off the inevitable. He decided to put up a token resistance, then submit to the inevitable. 'I can't accept such a...such a...large gift,' he stammered.

'Why?' Elaine spoke deliberately. 'Because it is from a woman and you don't want to feel like a kept man. Men are always blinded by their pride, yet it is women who are supposed to be illogical. The gift is made, James. You cannot refuse it. If you want to be the man of the house you know what to do.'

She had been ahead of him all the time. She had probably known exactly what was going on in his head. It was not fair – the female of the species were born with an inherent advantage in matters of relationships – the male floundered in their wake. She had manoeuvred him into a corner, and apart from leaving the stage, there was only one way out. 'Why don't we change another name on that deed,' he said quizzically. 'Why don't we change Mrs Elaine Sampson to Mrs Elaine Ogle.' He smiled at her and raised his eyebrows to acknowledge her victory. He almost raised both of his hands as well.

'Thank you, James,' Elaine purred. 'I accept your proposal.'

They were married two months later in a London registry office, James having flown back from Portugal, taking a week's break from his tour. Elaine had made all the arrangements in his absence, and, of course, paid for a substantial reception in a posh London hotel, which is also where they spent their honeymoon.

Disastrous honeymoons are fairly commonplace and this was no exception. James's worst fears were almost, but not quite, realised. Elaine, looking stunning in her expensive silk negligee, was not frigid, but she was mechanical. She made love in a predetermined sequence, as though she had learned it off by heart from one of those magazines she was always reading. It was like making love by numbers. And when it was finished, that was it, job done, on to the next task at hand. If they had been at home, James was sure she would have jumped up immediately and started dusting or hoovering. He himself felt he should go out to mow the lawn or empty the bins. Instead they went out to the West End shows that Elaine had pre-booked – musicals, and variety shows. They were just bearable.

At the end of the honeymoon, James flew back to Portugal, glad to break loose again, glad to leave the misery of an English winter, to return to the warm sun and the warm senhoritas. Mostly, he was glad that Elaine was tied to England because of Jonathan.

That soon changed when, during one of their weekly phone conversations, she proudly announced, 'I've managed to get Jonathan into an exclusive private school as a boarder.' This was a crime punishable by death as far as James was concerned. To send a six-year-old out to fend on his own was inhuman. He wanted to protest vehemently, but what was the point, he had no authority in the matter. 'What are you going to do without Jonathan to look after?' was all he said. 'How about coming out and doing a bit of touring with me.' He felt he had to make the offer, but dreaded an affirmative reply.

'No thanks,' she replied emphatically. 'I have no desire to drive along bumpy roads in a foreign country, eating foreign food, sleeping god knows where. I'll stick to my own bed thanks. Anyway, I've got my eye on a shop in London. It's a well-known fashion shop and it is up for sale. I think I am going to buy it and get involved in running it on a daily basis. You know I've always been interested in fashion.'

'Sounds like a good idea,' James said calmly, hiding his relief.

A few weeks later Elaine confirmed that she had bought the shop in London, and also a two-bedroom apartment close to it, so that she wouldn't have to commute. She also pointed out that it would be very handy for James when he had sessions with his agent and publisher. She had bought the apartment in joint names.

And so this unlikely marriage got underway, the pattern for the next few years already set – James on tour abroad, Elaine busy with her London shop, meeting for a few weeks at 'Hidden Gem' and 'Celtic-Snore', using the apartment when attending literary and fashion events in London, occasionally popping over to the villa in Majorca. It was an interesting, eventful and privileged life, but essentially loveless.

Chapter 3

When I woke up this morning the room was already lit in a warm glow, the low morning sun beaming in its cheerful welcome. Outside, I heard a magpie warbling its gentle song, as sweet as a Schubert lullaby. It is the most evocative sound in Australia, the accompaniment to your daily life. Somebody once said it was 'like an angel gargling in a crystal vase' – a somewhat over the top metaphor, but you get the picture.

Every town in Australia has its share of magpies, unobtrusively hopping about the parks and gardens, wearing their formal dinner suits, chortling absentmindedly to themselves like happy field workers. It is like having well-dressed cheerleaders in every town. When you wake up in the morning their song seems to say, 'Good morning, the sun is shining again, it's a beautiful day again, we are still here, we are still happy, all is well.'

Am I living in a Disney film, I sometimes wonder? Have the Australian government hired Disney to come up with the happiest awakening possible? When I draw the curtains back I half expect to see Bambi on the lawn or Mary Poppins flying past.

What I do see, apart from the magpie on the lawn, is the forest and the parrots and the bright blue sky and the sparkling sea and the early-morning surfers and the early-morning boats and the paper boy and the postie and the distant sense of a small town waking, and you would need big troubles not to feel pleased to be here.

Thus starts a typical day in the beautiful town of Narooma. How can I convey to you how special this place is when words alone have obvious limitations? That is why, in the past, I have tended not to go in for lengthy descriptions, but like the skilled artist, tell the story with a precise sketch.

In this case I am going to make an exception. I am going to attempt to describe Narooma in detail. Humour me – it is pure selfishness. I want to record it for my dotage, when I may no longer be physically able to walk around it or, perish the thought, if I am no longer living in it.

In order to describe Narooma I think it is relevant to start with some general New South Wales geography.

When Captain James Cook first sailed up this stretch of coastline in 1770, all he would see, day after day, would be an endless succession of beautiful beaches backed sometimes by dunes, sometimes by low craggy cliffs, separated by occasional rocky headlands. He would see regular incursions of the sea into bays and lakes and lagoons. Immediately behind all this he would see nothing but dense, tall, green forest stretching as far as he could see in all directions, and disappearing into a distant haze of blue as it reached inland and climbed up and over what we now know as the Great Dividing Range – the mountain range that runs up most of eastern Australia. It would look like an impenetrable, unpopulated wilderness.

Make that same journey today and you will see that the scene has hardly altered. Take a boat out and look back and you can see almost exactly what Cook saw all those years ago. Come back in and pull your boat up onto any of dozens of empty beaches and you can feel exactly how those great explorers of yesterday must have felt. It is a strange, rare, and wonderful feeling to travel in time like this.

Little seems to have changed because the few towns and settlements that exist on this coast are, for the most part, set back from the beaches, hidden in the trees. Where possible, even when making clearings for settlements the pioneers left as many trees standing as possible to provide shade for themselves and the teams of bullocks and horses that did the clearing work. Now these trees provide welcome shade to cars standing in the wide streets.

And such is the hilly unevenness of this forested land that much of it was deemed too rugged to clear for farming, this being done on the cleared plains beyond the Great Dividing Range. The result is that once you leave the confines of your town or village you are in the same vast forest that Cook saw, much of which has now been designated as National Parks.

Perhaps it is this, and the great travelling distances of Australia, that explains the existence of such a strong sense of community within the country; the presence of such overwhelming nature making people gather together around the modern equivalent of the old camp fire – the social club.

Within this unspoiled land lies the jewel that is Narooma. To describe it in detail let us first take a boat out to Montague Island which lies about 4 miles offshore. Here we hire an imaginary helicopter, and fly low over the sea, back towards Narooma.

As we take off, our first impressions are those of Cook's – a wall of forest in all directions. Then we start to pick out a light line of beaches and a few dotted clearings. Now, as we close in we see beaches and headlands running north and south to our eyes' extremes; the beaches are a beautiful light-fawn colour, almost cream, and they cause the clear blue water to turn a sparkling turquoise as the ocean shallows towards them. Now, to the north of Narooma, we begin to see spatterings of houses amongst the forest on steep hillsides overlooking the beaches; to the south a larger green clearing on top of low cliffs, which turns out to be the superb golf course; to the south of that, yet another beautiful beach. It is only as we fly in over the entrance to the Wagonga Inlet that we start to see the town on our left, widely spread, as are all Australian towns, over a large hill shaped like an upturned bowl, the houses randomly spread over the top and on all slopes, running down to various conclusions – to forest, to small wharfs, to small boatyards, to the golf course, to the sports ground, to the swimming pool, to beaches, and to a large flat area that borders the magnificent waters of the Wagonga Inlet, where a few motels and caravan sites play host to lucky holiday-makers.

Wherever you stand on this upturned bowl of a hill, even in the heart of town, you can see water, either the blue ocean or the turquoise inlet. It is upliftingly beautiful in all directions. And for such a small town it is amazingly varied and visually interesting. Take a walk around it and within a few hundred metres you find so many different environments, vistas, atmospheres that you feel as though you have walked a few hundred miles.

The main road that winds its way through the town comes from the north via a steel cantilever bridge that spans the narrowest part of the Wagonga Inlet. It was built in 1931 and finally did away with having to take the tortuous unsurfaced road the pioneers hacked out of the forest, which took you right around the inlet, a distance of some 8 miles. The road passes along the flat area of Narooma, with shops on one side and a large holiday park on the other, bordering the inlet. It climbs up onto the main hill and winds its way through the town, with a few shops on both sides, then disappears again on the south side into the endless forest. Like most Australian roads it is very wide, capable of having cars parked on both sides, yet still has room for four cars to pass safely. Even the side roads and suburban streets are like this, meaning that there are no driving or parking problems. You can still do that thing long forgotten in Britain, namely pull up outside a shop, do some shopping, leave your car there and come back hours later for it. There are no parking charges anywhere in Narooma or in most small Australian towns. The wide roads reflect the space needed by the pioneers to turn a team of four to six bullocks pulling a cartload of timber.

The wide roads are one of Australia's greatest plusses, making daily life so much easier than that in Britain. The other great plus is the type and size of housing. Narooma is typical, having only one small estate of identical bungalows for retirees. All the other houses are individually designed and built to the client's specification, the norm being for an individual to buy a plot of land and instruct their chosen architect and builder. Almost all houses are detached, with plenty of land, and with an endless variety of design and materials of construction. Scattered among these newer houses you find 100-year-old clapboard and fibre houses and hotels with tin roofs. The result is a welcome lack of uniformity, and a great variety of colour, size, height, width, age, all leading to a very eye-pleasing collection of homes that enhance their wonderful surroundings. And with the plot sizes being so large it means there is always a garage, or plenty of room to park your car/s on your property, leaving the streets clear of parked cars. The contrast between the wide, empty streets of Narooma and the narrow, car-plagued streets of Britain is total. One so-called new housing estate situated in the forest on the outskirts of town consists of individual plots of five acres, where you cannot see your neighbour and would need a car to visit some of them. You can buy the land and build a very large five-bedroom house on this site, which overlooks the Wagonga Inlet, and it would be cheaper than a three-bedroom suburban semi in London.

My description of Narooma needs to pay special attention to the Wagonga Inlet. This magical stretch of water starts life when the Pacific Ocean changes into a fast-flowing river as the tide pushes it between the man-made rock walls that guide it inland. The 'river' flows between the walls, then leaves them behind as it sweeps around a series of bends, all the while overflowing sideways creating shallow water across large areas of exposed sand flats. These sand flats are home to a countless variety of estuary worms and crustaceans, including hundreds of thousands of blue soldier crabs, which march across the sand like wind-up toys when the tide is out. This is where shoals of bottom-feeding fish come in from the ocean and feed on the bounty, and where the fishermen have already dug up their bait and are waiting for them.

One kilometre later, the 'river' spreads out and becomes the main lake – the Wagonga Inlet, a mixture of deep water and more sand flats only covered at high tide. From the main lake the water continues probing inland via a number of long narrow stretches, like fingers from a hand. Here the water settles in deep darkness, surrounded by forest teaming with birdlife – egrets, sea eagles, and 190 other species (a quarter of Australia's total). Paddle a canoe up one of these fingers and though you are only a kilometre from town you feel you could be paddling up the Amazon. These deep waters are the permanent home to 50 species of fish including record-breaking dusky flathead and the elusive mulloway which grow to 60 pounds and are usually caught by dedicated night fishers.

It is in the 'river' section of the inlet that the phenomenal 'wow' producing turquoise colour is seen as, aided by the blue sky and a bright sun, the pristine water passes over the light sandy bottom.

It is also in the 'river' section, as it flows alongside forested banks, that the people of Narooma have built a magnificent boardwalk, which allows you to complete a walk from the town centre to two of the beaches. It is a substantial structure, about 1 kilometre long, 3 metres wide and superbly built from local hardwood, all safely fenced, and bolted together with stainless steel bolts. No galvanised bolts here, rusting in a year, looking ugly for 30 years, needing annual maintenance; this is a proper Aussie job, a job to be proud of. Along its length, they have built a few fishing platforms jutting out over the water, complete with rod holders, bait preparation tables, lights, seats and tapped water. During holiday time, Mum, Dad and the kids sit here all day, happily throwing a line in.

The boardwalk stands about one to 2 metres above the water, depending on the tide, and it provides a unique opportunity to get close to the sea creatures as they swim in and out of the inlet, and to those that live there permanently.

I have walked along this boardwalk every day since arriving in Narooma and every day has been a delight. I have stood for hours, leaning on the rail, gazing down at a large variety of fish – snapper, flathead, trevally, flounder, whiting, puffer fish, garfish, bream, sweep, leatherjacket, salmon, blackfish, sharks, moray eels, octopus, squid, mullet and so on. Occasionally some of the big boys pay a visit – a pod of dolphins following the shoals in, or inquisitive seals taking a break from their home on Montague Island.

By far the greatest sight is the stingrays. These graceful creatures glide around the inlet visiting the cleaning tables, which are spread all around the inlet for the convenience of the fishers. These long wooden tables, complete with tapped water, stand at the edge of the inlet and allow the fishers to gut and clean their catch and leave the cleaning up to the gathering pelicans, cormorants, gulls, various fish, and the imposing stingrays. The stingrays come in so close they are often in no more than 20 centimetres of water, with the tips of their wings protruding from it. You can bend down and touch them. They vary in size from one to 2 metres across their wings. Most of the time they remind you of graceful underwater butterflies, but occasionally, when a large black back passes silently beneath you, it looks quite sinister, like a stealth bomber seeking its target. Their perpetual circling around the inlet brings them alongside the boardwalk as they follow it to the next table. And because they are usually swimming at the same pace a human walks, you find yourself walking along the boardwalk with a stingray swimming alongside you, not more than 3 metres away. For half a kilometre you can walk with a stingray for company, as if taking your dog for a walk. And over time, it starts to feel like having pets; you start looking out for them, and waiting for them to come by, you become attached to them.

Walking with the stingrays is always a magical experience and you feel very privileged, and you wonder if there is anywhere else in the world where you can you do this.

I will leave my description of Narooma there for the moment. I could go on about many other outstanding features it possesses, but no doubt these will surface as this tome progresses. Suffice to say that an attempt is underway to record the qualities of a very special place.

James straightened his back while he scrolled back through the latest pages. He spotted a lack of flow here and there and knew he would put it right tomorrow. He also anticipated that his editor would suggest that he shorten it, that he should not spend so much time describing one place. The editor would probably be right, but James didn't care. He wanted to keep it all in for personal reasons. They would have a discussion about it and James would insist it all stayed.

He switched off the computer and automatically turned to look out of the window. Kooky sat on the deck rail, looking lobotomized as usual. James smiled at it absentmindedly, his mind not yet fully off what he had just written.

It came to him that over the past few months his love of this place had become visceral. Every single day brought a feeling of wellbeing glowing through him. Even routine trips to the shops or the bank or the library were looked forward to as he knew he would be encountering beautiful trees and flowers and birds and fish and animals and smiling people, and all the way the sun would keep him company, keep him pleasantly warm, allow him to travel in shorts, to feel light and free.

He was certain he had found the place he wanted to spend the rest of his days in, a place that already felt like home. He was determined to make it his home, if not immediately then as soon as visas allowed. He had applied for a renewal of his long-stay visa which had a month to run, and he was confident of getting it. After that he knew he could apply for a retirement/investment visa providing he had at least half a million pounds. Which is where Elaine came in, or rather needed to go out.

He was working on the assumption that she had made a will, but left nothing to him. Why would she? Their relationship had hit the rocks years ago. Though it was never going to be a meeting of souls, the marriage had been tolerable for the first ten years. This was because they were both absorbed in their work – James on his travels, Elaine with her new shop, which she had developed into one of the most exclusive in London. But gradually, as they both started to slow down, and spend more time together, their differences began to irritate, then annoy, then become infuriating.

A stage was reached where they both knew they should split up. But each waited for the other to raise the subject. Neither found themselves able to do it. James was loathe to give up the luxury and security that Elaine's money provided, while Elaine didn't want to lose her escort into the 'Arts', where James provided her with intellectual credibility among her rich fashion clients.

Slowly, without discussion, as if by osmosis, they both accepted the reality of the situation and started to live their lives accordingly. Their relationship gradually became more like a business partnership than a marriage. Most disagreements were dealt with in a calm, professional manner without the hindrance of emotional outbursts, but occasionally there would be a cold, calculated battle of attrition, sustained and fuelled by their subconscious anger at their weak selves. In every sense, theirs had become the classic marriage of convenience.

James was now exploring the more exotic corners of the globe. Parts of Africa, Asia, Australia and the Americas were all 'Ogled', during which James continued to find solace in female arms of many different colours. He suspected that, in his absence, Elaine did not seek the company of the opposite sex, though, of course, he could not be sure. He suspected that she was quite content to boss her band of employees at the shop, play hostess to important clients, and most importantly, play the belated mother to her darling Jonathan, probably the only male she was interested in.

She doted on Jonathan, now a 25-year-old civil servant in some obscure government department, seemingly incapable of talking in plain English as a result. His was a world of mission statements and platforms and stakeholders, and instigating pro-active initiatives to obviate negative outcome scenarios. Somehow the gibberish seemed to suit him. He was still small and chubby, and had been educated to saturation point, but the poor, amiable chap had not been up to the social rigours of private education and had come out withdrawn and timid.

James had no doubt that all of Elaine's estate would be left to Jonathan, and he didn't begrudge the poor bastard a penny. James had his eye on his joint ownership of 'Celtic-Snore' at Sannox on the Isle of Arran, and the apartment in London. Between them they would fetch close to a million pounds. Half of that would be enough to meet the retirement/investment visa's criteria, and have plenty left over to buy a new set of golf clubs and a new set of fishing rods, and other such essentials. All he had to do was get rid of Elaine and then persuade Jonathan to sell the properties; that would be easy, Jonathan had no interest in them, and would probably want a clean break. But he needed to act quickly, while Elaine was in Australia.

She had come over on a three-month holiday visa to check up on him. His phone calls had been vague, a master class in obfuscation. And, she discovered, they had been coming from the same telephone number for months. Warning bells had rung. She suspected he was in danger of becoming permanently entangled with his latest conquest. She had seen the emails and fan letters he received from around the world. Some had been very bad attempts at hiding amorous recollections of 'meetings', and invitations to 'call again if in the area'.

Although she accepted that he 'wandered' while he was abroad, she always wanted him to return to her. She might have lost him emotionally, but she had no intention of losing him physically. She had invested too much time and money in him for somebody else to claim the benefit. He was *hers! Her partner! Her escort! Nobody else's!*

On her arrival, she had almost been disappointed to find that he had fallen in love with a place rather than a woman. She could not understand this. She was one of the many who seemed to go through life with blinkers on, not see or be interested in the wonders of nature, the variance of cultures. She lived in her own little world no matter where she was, like the millions who flock abroad on their annual holidays, there to do exactly what they do at home, uninquisitive about the history, geography, or nature of their new surroundings.

After getting over the shock of her sudden arrival, James had made one attempt to infect her with his enthusiasm for the area and Narooma in particular. He had taken her on a guided tour, pointing out its wonders. It had been futile, of course. She even doubted if he was telling the truth. 'How could anybody fall in love with a place, for God's sake.' She believed there must be a woman involved somewhere, and she decided not to leave until he was working as normal or accompanying her back to Britain.

Happily, her nagging had coincided with his recent decision to get down to work after his long period of outdoor indulgence. Apparently placated, she said she would 'hang around until her visa ran out'. She said she was staying 'to motivate him, and to get a tan'. James knew otherwise.

After a few weeks, he could see that she was champing at the bit, wanting to get away from 'this town with no shops, no theatres, no fashion sense'; most of the things that James rejoiced in. He loved the laid-back scruffiness of the people, the total lack of interest in clothes as a fashion statement or status symbol. The standard dress of short-sleeved shirt, and shorts, often stained by old engine or fish oil, combined with any shape of hat that would protect your head, and minimal footwear – sometimes none at all – meant that you didn't know if you were dealing with a tramp or a millionaire. And that was just the women. The most popular shop in Narooma was 'Vinnies' (St Vincent de Paul) charity clothes shop. The people of Narooma boasted of the bargains they got there, which left them with money to spend on essential things such as beer and fishing gear.

The only aspect of life in Narooma that Elaine found tolerable was sunbathing, after a quick dip in the ocean. She had learned to swim late in life, at her villa pool in Majorca, with a personal coach of course. But she was not very good at it, her only stroke being a weak breaststroke, which she performed like a tense, drowning frog, her head and tight-lipped mouth as far out of the water as she could manage.

As far as she was concerned swimming had one purpose, which was to provide an overall cooling layer while she lay in the sun trying to perfect her tan. There was nothing like a golden tan to enhance the latest Paris creation. However, an uneven tan was a fate worse that death, so she had taken to looking for places where she could sunbathe naked. This led her to wander off along the coast in search of empty beaches, away from those in Narooma's immediate area, although these were never crowded. She didn't have far to go to find them, and there were many to choose from, although access was not always possible because of the scarcity of roads.

She would disappear for hours in her hired car, and James would never question where she had been. It was her consistent return that bothered him. He was always hopeful that a snake or a shark or a stonefish might have saved him a job, a job that he must complete before her visa ran out.

He felt that he had to act now, in Australia, while the inspiration was with him, the cause in front of him. If he left it until they were back in England, the inspiration might dissipate. He might lose his nerve. More importantly, he felt he had a better chance of getting away with it in Australia, where they were hardly known, where accidents were always happening to unsuspecting tourists, and particularly in a small town where a small police force would surely not be as thorough as a big force in Britain, should it come to an investigation.

Over the course of the past few weeks, after forcing his mind to think of numerous methods of disposal, drawing a line at Poe's pit and the pendulum routine, which had flashed into his mind after one of her whingeing bouts, he had settled on the decision that Elaine's death had to look like an accident. But he still had not a clue how to bring it about.

48

Chapter 4

Another Narooma midday arrived, all brightness and warmth, and tinkling with the song of the bellbirds. James had finished his morning's work, a few hundred words about the fascinating history of the area; a history which was still alive and kicking and meaningful to the people. The people absorbed it avidly and knew it intimately. Their heroes were the pioneers, the amazingly tough generations who had hacked a life out of the wilderness, and the thousands of young men who went to fight for the old country in two world wars and suffered a terrible loss. These heroes had become a counter balance to the difficult part of the country's history, that which dealt with the treatment of convicts and the aborigines.

James had referred to the aborigines by the name they knew themselves by – Kooris – aborigine being a generic term for all original occupiers of land. Within the hundreds of tribes of the Koori race, each with their own language, James had found that a forest dwelling tribe called the Yuin had been the main tribe on the New South Wales south coast. They were a 'people of grand physical proportions' who lived mostly on fish (caught with spears or in boats made of bark), oysters, swans, ducks, nuts, beached whales, seabird's eggs. Once a year they would trek inland to the mountains where they would harvest the annual gathering of millions of bogong moths, a prized food. (When in the American state of Montana, James had visited the Yellowstone National Park and heard about grizzly bears doing exactly the same thing.)

James found it very sad that 95% of the Yuin had died of European diseases such as flu, smallpox and venereal disease, probably introduced in the early days when whalers and sealers plied the coast. Some had been shot in skirmishes with the Gubbas – the white invaders. In 1879, local records showed that only two dozen survivors still lived in the Narooma area. The good news was that their descendants still lived in the Narooma area, and while most had been assimilated into the white man's world, one group had established a small settlement in the forest some miles south of Narooma, where they tried to keep alive the old traditions and live by Yuin tribal laws.

As a student of history, James knew that the terrible persecution of the Kooris by the Gubbas was, unfortunately, just another example of man's continuous inhumanity to man. It had been brought home to him when attending a party earlier in his tour of New South Wales. He had been kindly invited to the party during a casual meeting in a small hotel in a small inland country town. It took place in the large garden of the person whose birthday it was. In that warm, friendly, relaxed gathering of solid citizens, with glasses of wine and beer aplenty, and children skipping about, a man of about 65 calmly related to him, with some boastfulness in his voice, that there were no abos in that area because his forbears had made sure they got rid of them all, women and children included. He explained that after all the abo men had been shot or ran off, the white men's wives, apparently showing pity to the abo women and children, invited them to come and share their food. This they did. The food had been poisoned. 'You had to get rid of them all, mate,' he said. 'Otherwise they would have kept on breeding.'

James's faith in humanity had been somewhat restored when he later watched the prime minister of Australia offer an apology to all Kooris for past crimes inflicted on them. This took place in a long and at times moving ceremony in the new parliament house in Canberra, a place whose huge multi-coloured marble reception lobby was, in

James's opinion, a monument to tasteless ostentation, reminiscent of old Hollywood, or even Bollywood musical film sets. On entering, one expected to be greeted by Olivia Newton John and John Travolta dancing down the columned staircases, or perhaps a piano playing, bespangled Elton John grinning enormously.

Beyond the reception lobby however, the building changed completely and became an impressive piece of modern architecture of fine proportions, suitably sober and reserved. This was Australia's third house of parliament built in 1988 when the population was 16 million. The first had been built in 1901 when the population was four million.

It struck James that all who govern, whether dictators or democrats, give top priority to building themselves palaces to symbolize and demonstrate their power over the people. Their second priority is always to the funding of armies and weapons, irrespective of the state of their economies.

After such a concentrated, and at times depressing, writing session, James wanted fresh air and physical distraction. And he knew of no better way of achieving this than to go fishing. It was one of the few things left that allowed man to fulfil his basic urge to hunt and kill and provide, and, he felt, it should be on all school curricula, to take today's children out of their feather-bedded artificial world into the tough, fascinating world of nature and reality.

Fishing could be looked on as a subject of endless variety that took a lifetime of study as you learned about an infinite number of species, habits, locations, baits, rods, sinkers, lines, reels, hooks, tides, rivers, boats, currents, safety, lakes, knots, flies, methods, gutting, filleting, storing, cooking and so on. Or as a pastime as simple as throwing a hand line off a pier and hoping for the best. It all happened outdoors, usually in beautiful surroundings, was totally distracting and the thrill of a good catch could not be beaten.

A large percentage of Narooma's population owned a sea-going motorised boat. They usually kept them on their drives or lawns, mounted on a trailer, which they towed down to the many launch points around the inlet. Mostly, they went out to fish off Montague Island where they caught strong fighting kingfish or tuna or morwong. Some went to the continental shelf 10 miles offshore, hoping to hook a specimen marlin; others stayed in Wagonga Inlet and fished for flathead and whiting as they cruised its placid waters.

While, to James and other European visitors, the waters around Narooma seemed to offer an abundance of fish, the old locals lamented the good old days when the area 'roared' with them. They were referring to the fact that so many millions of salmon used to come into the inlet, the roar made by the disturbed water used to wake children from their sleep. Herded into the inlet by dolphins and the occasional shark, it was reported that they filled it to such an extent you could walk across the inlet on their backs. That you can't see such an amazing sight today can be blamed, initially, on an American.

In 1936 the American author Zane Grey came to the area and caught tonnes of fish including a 90-pound yellow fin tuna. Grey, being aware of California's large tuna canning industry, saw the commercial possibilities of a tuna canning industry in Australia and urged them to get started before the Japanese did.

In 1937 Australia's first commercial cannery was built on the banks of the Wagonga Inlet. With tuna only appearing for eight months of the year, it also started to process the millions of salmon that 'seemingly served themselves as a sacrifice to the cannery'.

Soon a new larger cannery had to be built and by 1940 it was producing three million cans of salmon a year. To catch the salmon in the inlet they used a huge 700-metre-long net pulled between two boats, and slowly pulled the salmon into specially-built holding pens. The biggest single haul on record was 9,000 baskets holding 120 pounds of fish each. James calculated that to be about 550 tonnes or 180,000 fish.

Over the next 20 years the cannery was Narooma's biggest employer, but as the fish stocks declined so did the output. Kraft bought the company in 1960, but then sold it to Heinz in 1972. They closed the plant in 1974 and the plant and wharf were completely dismantled and bulldozed to make way for residential development.

This marked the end of Narooma's short industrial era, with its other two industries – the timber mill and boat building yard – also gone. Only the oyster farms still remain.

With little to indicate that these industries once existed, Narooma has settled back to become a retirement and holiday town, its beauty tempting the urban dwellers of Sydney and Melbourne to spend their last days in a natural paradise.

James found these small-town histories fascinating because they were so recent and imaginable, unlike the long, distant histories of Europe. He liked the way streets and parks had been named after forbears who had served the community; not necessarily in grand positions, but postmen and the like.

As far as he was concerned the area's fish stocks were still exceptional, and they should get better when the recently announced marine conservation park came into being.

With the tide almost at its high point he decided to go fishing for whiting off his local beach, just 200 metres down the hill. As he collected his fishing gear together, he thought back to the week he had arrived in Narooma, when he knew nothing about the place or about local fishing practices.

He had only been in Narooma one day when he knew he wanted to experience more of it, make it a base for his planned itinerary, moving south along the coast and inland to the Snowy Mountains. He had sought the help of an estate agent to find him a house to rent on a short-term basis. The estate agent had been amiable and helpful and had driven him to various properties over a period of two days. While driving around, James had asked him where the best fishing took place. Without hesitation the estate agent had said 'the beach' and explained that there were many species that came in close. James then asked him which was the best bait to use on the beach, and the estate agent said 'beach worms'. James found this strange because, having had a stroll along one of the beaches, he hadn't seen any worm casts in the sand, such as those made by lug worms or rag worms in Britain. He pointed this out to the estate agent. 'There's nothing to see,' said the estate agent, 'they don't make casts.'

'So, how do you find them,' James had asked.

There was a slight hesitation before the estate agent explained that you had to find a long porous sock, such as the wife's nylons, put a rotten piece of fish or meat in it, and drag it along the beach where the waves break on the sand. If there is a worm present it will come up to the surface attracted by the smell, but all you will see will be the tiniest diversion of water as the wave runs back into the sea. Once you have spotted this diversion, marking the worm's presence, then you have to fix your main piece of rotten fish/meat in the water by means of a stake to keep attracting the worm to the surface, then take a separate small piece of rotten fish or meat in your fingers, stand in the water, bend down and offer it to the head of the worm when it comes up again, and grab it with either your fingers or a special pair of pliers, and pull up and out slowly but firmly. 'You have to be very quick, it is not easy.'

'Nice try,' James had said. 'This is what you tell every tourist, isn't it, particularly those with a pommy accent. I bet all you locals go down to the beach every day and have a good laugh at all the tourists walking along dragging a piece of rotten fish in their wife's tights. It's a good one, I must admit.'

'I'm not kidding, mate. You'll see,' the estate agent had said.

And he hadn't been kidding. A few days later James had spotted somebody on the beach doing exactly what the estate agent had described. He watched and learned, and a couple of days later, armed with a string bag that had contained oranges, containing a piece of fish he'd left outside for two days, a wooden stake, a special pair of pliers bought at the tackle shop, and a small plastic box for keeping the worms in, which you attached to a belt around your waist, he arrived on the beach to do battle.

An hour later he had left the beach with half a worm, soaking wet from the sudden wave surges, an aching back and thigh muscles from crouching, but having thoroughly enjoyed playing in the warm water, and eager to learn how to do it successfully.

Two months later he had become an expert with a 75% strike rate. By trial and error he had found that the secret lay in the type of fish bait you held in your fingers. The worm only showed about 4 millimetres of its head when it came up to grab the fish bait, then it bit a tiny piece off and was back down in a fraction of a second. By using a tough flesh, like squid, a piece of which couldn't be removed easily, James found that the worm hung on to it for a fraction longer, giving him just enough time to snap the pliers around its head. Even then, he missed some; you had to be lightning fast. He was to learn that many keen local fishermen had never been able to catch beach worms, their reflexes not being quick enough. He put his sharp reflexes down to his life-long playing of the fastest game in the world – table tennis.

Going to the beach to spend an hour in the warm water catching worms had become the highlight of many a day after that, sometimes more fulfilling than the actual fishing because he always came away with something to show for his efforts.

Among the many different ways he was advised to store the worms he found the best was to store them in separate layers in a box full of cool sand. They usually lived for three days that way.

The worms varied in size from 15 to 30 centimetres long and had tough heads fringed with wriggling tentacles, and a small dark mouth – not a pretty sight. James looked them up on his computer and found Australonuphis Teres to be widespread along eastern Australia, with some specimens in Queensland growing to 2 metres long and as thick as a man's little finger.

Occasionally, he couldn't find worms on the local beaches and he had to drive to other beaches to find a supply. This brought him in contact with some superb new locations, both for worming and fishing, and the joy of those days of exploration was like that of a child on an endless summer holiday.

He was just about to leave, to walk down to the beach, when he heard Elaine's car pull in at the front of the house. He hung back to tell her where he was going. She came into the living room, carrying her bag full of swimming gear, looking fidgety and distracted, head down. She didn't acknowledge his presence and remained silent.

'You alright?' James enquired.

'Had a bit of a shock, that's all.' She flopped onto an easy chair and lay her head back and let her arms dangle loosely. She took a deep breath and blew it out.

'What happened?'

'A black man frightened the life out of me.'

James said nothing, waiting for her to continue.

'I was down at Wallaga beach…you know…where Wallaga Lake goes into the sea. There's never anybody down there. I was lying in the sand dunes, sunbathing as usual. My eyes were closed. I was probably half asleep… I heard a noise and felt flicks of sand hitting my arms and legs. I screamed and sat up so quick I jerked my neck. There was a big black man dancing about just a couple of yards away. He looked wild…long black hair…and he was grinning and pointing at me as he danced…and he was naked and his thing was sticking up.'

'His thing?'

'You know…'

Elaine's primness had always been a great source of amusement to James and he liked to play on it. 'No, I don't know. Did he have a spear? Is that what you mean?'

'No…his thing…his penis.' She spat it out as though she had mud in her mouth.

'Pleased to see you, eh!' James said lightly.

'It wasn't funny.'

'I take it you were naked.'

'Yes.'

'Proves you can still pull 'em, girl.'

'Are you going to take this seriously or…'

'Only if you tell me he did more than dance and look at you. Did he?'

'No…I carried on screaming…and he picked up his clothes and ran off.'

'Is it true then,' James teased. 'You know, what they say about black men.'

'I never looked…I mean I don't know what you're talking about… oh! you are worse than the policeman.'

'What policeman?'

'I called at the police station on the way back through town, and tried to report it to them, but there was just this young constable behind the desk. He wrote it all down, but he didn't seem to take it seriously either. He mumbled something about half his luck when I told him I had been lying naked, and said he was off to buy a new pair of binos… You bloody men…'

It was very rare that Elaine swore, and it told James that she was genuinely shaken. He also suddenly realised that he had been given an unexpected opportunity. The police now had a record of Elaine sunbathing naked on a remote beach, so they would not be surprised to find her in that situation again, albeit dead. And a Koori running around exposing himself might eventually prove to be a useful diversion or suspect. But the main opportunity was for him to be seen as the caring husband as, outraged, he confronted the policeman about his unacceptable treatment of his dear wife.

'I'm sorry, Elaine,' James said seriously. 'I didn't realise you were so upset. Let me get you a cup of tea, then I'll go down to the police station and sort that young copper out.'

'There's no need for that,' Elaine said hurriedly. 'I'll be alright in a minute. Anyway, were you not about to go fishing. I can see all your gear stashed outside?

'This is more important,' James lied, and turned toward the kitchen.

Half an hour later, James approached the police station in the town centre. He had walked past it frequently on his way to the post office. It stood next door to the court house, one of Narooma's oldest buildings. This was a perfect example of a well-maintained clapboard building, painted white and with a tin roof. It sat on a grassy slope overlooking the inlet and the beaches, and was dominated by two large palm trees on either side. On trial days, rather than hide inside as you might expect, most of those due to appear in court chose to lounge about outside on the grass, taking advantage of the views, having a smoke, sleeping, chatting – all in full view of passers by. The atmosphere was so relaxed it reminded James more of a school trip waiting to go into a museum than a place where punishment was about to be handed out. The only concession to formality was that most people were wearing clean shirts and shorts, with an occasional person wearing clean trousers. James reckoned that those wearing trousers must either be the biggest villains or had committed the worst offence. A tie, and you had a killer on your hands, he guessed.

Rehearsing his aggrieved and caring husband routine, James climbed the steps to the police station and went inside. His opening gambit went unsaid, shocked into silence by the sight of the young man standing behind the reception desk, dressed in an immaculately pressed short-sleeved blue shirt. Not only was he the size of a door, he was probably the most handsome young man James had ever seen. The shining black hair, sparkling brown eyes, strong nose, olive skin, spoke of Greek or Italian blood. He looked obscenely fit and healthy. He must have been 6 feet 6 tall, and perfectly proportioned – no fat, no obvious sign of excessive muscle, yet not thin. It was as though he had been given a bigger skeleton than the rest of us and the right amount of flesh had grown on it. He should definitely be in Hollywood, James thought.

The flashing smile he greeted James with came from his eyes as well as his mouth. This was no smile learned on a customer care training course. This was the smile of a genuine country boy. 'Come to give yerself up hev ya?' he bellowed, leaning forward on the counter.

'Er…no…not quite,' James said, unable to think of a witty reply. 'Are you Constable Ricci?'

'Onmyowth.'

James wasn't sure what he had said or how many words he had spoken. He tried again. 'You are Constable Ricci?'

'Nicky, mite…everybody calls me Nicky. Can you believe me bladdy mather calling me Nicholas when me bladdy surname's Ricci. Nicky bladdy Ricci. What koind of a nime is that? Still lav her though…best bladdy mather in the world she is.' He picked up a pen, and placed a pad of writing paper on the desk. 'Now, anybody asks for me boy nime I start to mike nowts. Your nime is?'

'Ogle…James Ogle…'

'Good to meet ya, Jim.' A large hand shot across the desk and crushed his hesitant fingers. He studied James's face closely. 'Any relition?'

'Pardon?'

'Ya know.. Brett Owgle the golfer…bladdy good plier…never quoit made it big though…still he's a bladdy good commentita now…him an that Wine Gridy…best bladdy commentitas in the world now…

better then that pom Peter Ellis…Ellis used to be good, but he's got a bit whingey in his owld age…toim he pecked it in an give the young fellas a chence.'

Being a golfer, James was familiar with Brett Ogle and Wayne Grady and the pom – Peter Allis. But he didn't know what to say. He didn't agree that the two Australians were the best commentators in the world, but he didn't want to get diverted into a lengthy discussion about golf commentators, a discussion he felt sure young Nicky would have gladly spent hours in.

'Ply yerself?' Nicky hadn't waited for a reply.

'Er…yes…'

'Whats ya hendicep?'

'Fourteen.'

'Not bed for a middle-aged pom. Two meself. Hit the bladdy ball moils, but patt loik a priest.'

'A priest?'

'Ya know…caant get it in the howl mite.'

By now James had almost forgotten what he came in for.

'On holidy Jim?'

Beaten to it again. 'No…well sort of a working holiday you might put it. I'm a travel writer and I'm using Narooma as a base at the moment…'

'Best bladdy town in the world mite…born'n bred here…never want to leave it…a wroiter eh! Did yer hear about that other pommy wroiter in New Zealand…what's is nime…Nicholas…another bladdy Nicholas…Nicholas Shikespeare?'

'No,' was all James could manage.

'Bladdy fanny this…he was fishin' on a beach down there and got talking to a kiwi fisherman…he introduced himself…kiwi fishermen says Shikespeare eh! – any relition? Nicholas says no he hesn't been able to trice his femily beck to the Bard. Kiwi says I was talking about the people who mike the fushing teckle.'

James laughed. Nicky had been trying to imitate the New Zealand accent. Most Aussies would tell you that New Zealanders had 'fanny eccents'. He was also laughing at the good story, being well aware of Shakespeare Ltd, the fishing tackle manufacturers.

'That's a good 'un, I'll try and remember that one,' he said genuinely, thinking he might be able to use it at some future book do. 'And I agree about Narooma, Nicky. It is a wonderful place.'

'Good on yer, Jim.'

James had to take a moment to gather his thoughts again, remember what he was doing there. 'I've actually come to make a complaint…'

'Picked the roit plice, Jim.' Nicky held his pen ready to write.

'It's about my wife…'

'Always is, mite…noin out of ten through that doors about the woif…what she dan…blown all yer money on the powkies…drenk it all at the bowlo…'

'**No!**' James found himself raising his voice to force the interruption. 'You may remember her. She was in here yesterday. She made a complaint about a Koori disturbing her while she sunbathed. Apparently he was dancing about naked…'

'Course…bladdy hell…Mrs Owgle…thought I'd heard that nime recently…sorry mite…noice lookin' woman, Mrs Owgle…half yer lack…'

'Well, be that as it may I'm here to find out what happened yesterday.' For some inexplicable reason James found himself talking like a Dickensian lawyer. 'Can you explain why my wife was dissatisfied with your performance?' As soon as he'd said it he realised his mistake. He saw a mischievous grin appear on Nicky's mouth. Hurriedly, he went on, trying not to burst out laughing. 'She was not happy about the way you dealt with her. She thought you were flippant and disinterested and didn't take her seriously. And as her husband I'm here to see what you have to say for yourself, and if I don't get any satisfaction then I will want to see your superior.'

'No superiors here, Jim…we don't hev superiors in Austrilia. I've got a boss…Saargent Spalding…but yer wisting yer toim talking to him…he's a wenker…'

Normally, James would have exploded by now. But Nicky Ricci had such an open, honest face that James believed every word he said, and he didn't want to get him into trouble.

'So…Nicky…tell me what happened yesterday. Why did you not take my wife seriously?' James now felt quite proud of his courtroom technique. His demeanour had taken on a gravitas he didn't know he had. Maybe he should take up acting.

Unbelievably, Nicky wasn't listening to him. His head was turned sideways, his ears straining to listen to a murmur coming through the doorway of the office immediately behind him. Suddenly the murmur became much louder and James thought it might be applause, probably coming from a radio. 'Scuse me,' Nicky said and rushed into the office. James heard him shout 'Good on ya, mite'. There was a few seconds' silence, then he reappeared, slowly, his body coming out before his head, so that he could catch every possible moment of whatever was going on in there. Finally, reluctantly, the whole tower block of him stood back in front of James. 'Sorry, mite…Pontin just got another century…best bladdy betsmen in the world Pontin, mite…sorry, what were yer saying?'

By now, James was past caring, and thoroughly enjoying the antics of this amiable giant. 'I was asking why you hadn't taken my wife seriously yesterday,' he said benignly.

'Oy did tike her seriously. Oy rout everything down and it's on our foils now, and we'll be pying a visit to young Divid next toim we're down there…'

'David…David who?'

'No second nime, mite…just Divid…he's one of the Kooris lives down Wallaga way… Everybody knows im…poor bastard's as stupid as an American president… You'd call him the village idiot beck in

62

pommy lend…they troy to keep an oy on him but samtoimes he gets off on his own and samtoimes that means we get called out to tike him beck.'

James got the picture, but deliberately continued in an aggrieved tone. 'He wasn't just naked, you know. He had an erection!'

'It's a bladdy beaut an all,' Nicky laughed, 'everybody in towns seen it. All the men are jealous and all the women think it's a bladdy wiste.'

'Does it not concern you?'

'Na…he has no oydea what its for…probably thinks it's a fishing rod or samthing. I troid to tell yer woif she had nathing to worry about and I think I moit hev mide a jowk or two and she obviously hasn't loiked them. Tell her oim sorry mite, and we will be callin' to see him…even though the poor bastard caan't help himself we hev to keep an oy on him…caan't tike any chances these dyes…we'd get done for neglectin' our duty.'

'Okay, Nicky,' James said in a markedly conciliatory tone. 'That seems fair enough. Seems to have been a bit of a misunderstanding. I'll tell her you are sorry. But just for the record, I would like our little chat recorded on your files if you don't mind.'

'No worries, mite. Consider it dan.'

'And tell me, Nicky, just between you and me,' James leaned across the desk as if he had something to whisper. Nicky leaned to meet him. 'Do you think David's erection might be the best bloody erection in the whole world?'

A great roar of laughter shook the room. 'Not a bladdy chence, mite…yer lookin' at the chemp roit in frant of yer,' and the laughter continued as James waved a goodbye hand.

Half an hour later, after a beautiful walk in the sun alongside the inlet, over the bridge and up and over the forested hill, alive with bell and whip birds, James was back in the house reporting to Elaine. He told her he had given Constable Ricci a hard time and that the matter would be investigated, but explained that the Koori man, David, was not normal. 'He has the body of a man, but the brain of a three-year-old,' he said.

'Sounds normal to me,' Elaine retorted quickly.

'Wow!' James exclaimed, genuinely surprised by a rare display of wit from Elaine. 'That was funny.'

'No need for sarcasm,' Elaine replied stiffly, and walked out of the room.

James had meant the compliment, but as often happened in their conversations, wires had got crossed. He went back to thinking about more serious matters. The purpose of the afternoon's work had been achieved. The police now had on record that Elaine went sunbathing on her own on remote beaches, and that she had a caring husband who looked after her interests. This was all very well, but it did throw up the quandary that he was now restricted to disposing of her on a beach.

Forcing himself to be positive, he concluded that the restriction was a good thing. He could now throw all his creative energy into this one area of disposal rather than the hundreds that had been whirling around and fogging his mind over the past few weeks.

He reminded himself that the clock was ticking; the sands of time were running out. And now he was, literally, looking to the sands for inspiration.

Chapter 5

James was in a hurry. He had spent longer than anticipated on his morning's work and now he was dashing to catch what was left of the high tide. He hoped that the worms he had been going to use yesterday were still alive. He usually fished for one hour before high tide and up to two hours after. He had learned from the locals that the best way to find a good spot on the beach was to stand on one of the headlands and read the water. Unlike beaches in Britain, which tend to be flat and wide, the beaches on Australia's east coast are relatively steep and narrow. When the might of the Pacific Ocean hits them, massive quantities of sand can be moved at every change of tide. Sometimes they can be made steeper as sand is lifted from the seabed and deposited. Sometimes a different wave action sucks the sand off the beach and flattens it for a time, often leaving a cliff face of sand close to the dunes. The same massive action is also taking place underwater, leaving high spots and channels and holes and gutters and 'rips', a place where the water that has come in gathers to go out in a river-like rush, creating a deep channel back out to sea, a feature that has caused the demise of many unwary swimmers.

The only way to get a good view of all these underwater variations is to stand on a headland and look for a change in the colour and texture of the sea, something possible only in waters of pristine clarity. A light turquoise, turbulent area indicates shallow water, and a dark-blue, smooth area indicates deeper water. For some reason the fish like to approach the beach via a deep channel rather than cross shallow sand bars, then once they are close to the beach where the pounding waves dig up their food, they spread out along the deep gutters, again avoiding the shallow areas. By spotting these deep channels and gutters from the headland, before going down onto the beach, you are increasing your chances of success.

However, today, James did not have time for spotting, so he decided to go to a beach where spotting was not necessary, where there was a permanent channel. Cemetry Beach was in fact his favourite beach. It lay on the southern edge of town, beyond the houses. To get to it you had to drive through the forest skirting the golf course, and park in the communal cemetery, the dead of Narooma having been awarded a prime position on a cliff top with a wonderful view of the ocean.

From here, James carried his fishing gear into the forest and then down a cliff face. This involved a steep scramble, at times holding onto tree branches as he lowered himself down. It was because of this difficult accessibility that Cemetry Beach usually played host to none but keen fishers.

Arriving on this beach was, to James, like stepping back into childhood. It had a mysterious, magical quality, as though someone had brought to life the exaggerated paintings found in a children's adventure book. If a tall, old sailing schooner had been anchored out at sea and Long John Silver had rowed ashore in front of him, he would not have been surprised.

There were interesting features everywhere. Scrub-covered sandstone cliffs backed along most of its length, except at the far south end where they gave way to a couple of low-lying fields that sloped down to the beach. There were rocks everywhere, out in the surf; black pillow lava, the remnants of an ancient underwater volcano. They killed the waves as they came in. Jutting out of the sandstone cliff face and all along the beach were huge, fantastically shaped rocks. They contained large deposits of iron ore, which had obviously rusted, making them look like the remains of wrecked ships buried in the sand. At the south end of the beach was the coup de theatre – two towering rock stacks, standing like nature's gothic skyscrapers where the beach meets the sea, only accessible when the tide is out, perches for sea eagles. When an eagle took flight from the top of a stack, James imagined it to be a huge bat flapping down from the wicked witch's castle to terrify the village children.

Just back from the stacks, across the beach, over the shallow sand dunes and into the field, lay an old timber beach house complete with shutters, a dilapidated picket fence and a gate opening directly onto the beach. It was one of the most idyllic locations James had ever seen, and he often wondered how the owner had obtained permission to clear the forest and build the house. He assumed there must be private access to it via a path or dirt road through the forest behind it. Never having seen an occupant, his imagination ran riot. Home of a sleeping beauty waiting to be kissed awake, or of a mermaid who turned into a girl when she opened the gate. This end of the beach seemed to encourage fairy tales rather than boy's adventures.

It was just to the side of one of the stacks that James came to fish. The stack, and the rest of the rocks in the surf held back most of the ocean's action, and here there was a gap of about 20 metres between the stack and the other rocks which allowed the ocean to glide in to the beach without disturbing large volumes of sand. This created a permanent channel and brought the fish into a relatively small catching area. James had only had one blank day in this location; his best catch in one session had been nine whiting.

As he forced his rod holder into the sand, an expectant thrill surged through him. No matter how many times he went fishing, it never became routine, the thrill at the start of the hunt was always there. In the ocean you never knew what the day would bring. He took off his backpack, emptied its contents, and arranged its tubular steel frame so that the pack turned into a seat; not that there was much time for sitting when beach fishing. He assembled his 10-foot lightweight rod, 4-pound line, 2-ounce lead sinker and small, long shank, barbless hook.

He picked up the box of three-day-old worms, hoping they were still alive. Only two were moving. He fed one onto the hook, then wiped his hands on a pungent rag. He kicked off his flip-flops, hitched up his fishing shorts, that had five pockets and still showed the white salt lines from his last worming session in the waves, and walked into the water holding his rod high in the casting position, careful to avoid catching his wide-brimmed hat, held in place by an under-chin drawstring.

With the swell now flicking the bottom of his shorts, he leaned backwards, steadied himself, and in a smooth, long arc brought the rod over his head and released the line at the optimum point. The lead sinker soared into the sky and plunged into the sea about 70 metres in front of him. He walked back through the water to the beach, and turned the reel until the line was tight. What pleasure. A good cast was like a well-struck five iron – so satisfying.

Now he stood at the edge of the water and waited, all the time keeping the line tight as the sea moved the sinker along its bed, exactly as it was supposed to do, the choice of line weight and sinker shape and weight being critical in achieving this. The current was taking him on a gentle stroll along the beach as he followed the sinker's progress under the water, all the while his right forefinger in touch with the line to feel the slightest movement.

He started to relax, enjoy his surroundings. He lifted his head and squinted to see if the sea eagle was on top of the stack. Not at home at the moment. A slight tremor on the line; he tensed. One more and he would strike. A big tremor on the line. He brought the rod up towards himself in a firm, smooth movement. Too sudden a strike and you could pull the hook out of its mouth or damage it. Leave it any longer and the fish would swallow the bait and mean certain death as recovery of the hook took place. Ideally, you hooked cleanly in the side of the mouth, and removed the barbless hook very easily, giving you the opportunity to return the fish to the sea should it be undersize or an inedible species.

It was a whiting. He knew this without seeing it. The hard, quick tugs on the line as he wound it in signalled its powerful little body twisting and turning. A great little fighter, and delicious to eat, which is why James targeted them. With a final low sweep of the rod, parallel to the beach, James pulled the twitching body from the ocean. He picked it up with a cloth to aid a gentle grip, and quickly and carefully removed the hook. It was a bit on the small side. He decided to put it back. Before he did, he took a moment, as always, to wonder at its glistening beauty. Then he walked into the water, bent down and placed the whiting in the water, and watched it zip away at great speed. Sometimes he found himself wishing them well – out loud!

Before he baited up again, he gazed along the beach, then out to sea, and up again to the stacks. One of his euphoric spells swept over him. Every visit to the beach heightened his awareness, made him acutely sensitive to the moment NOW! He observed and remembered all that surrounded him in exquisite detail; he was alive in all possible ways; he felt the essence of life; his skin tingled.

He was aware of his amazing good fortune to be in this beautiful place, to be fishing, to be doing what he wanted to do. What tiny percentage of the world's population would ever get the opportunity to feel as happy as he did now.

He was very circumspect about using the word 'happy'. He thought it was one of the most overused and misused words in the English language, mainly because of its incessant link to the begetting of a marriage partner in all fiction since Adam and Eve. 'It looked as though happiness was not to be hers' implied she had failed to get married. 'They got married and lived happily ever after' started it all. What a joke! Statistically, you could write 50% off straight away, and who knows what percentage of happiness was left in the remaining 50% who stayed together.

The comedian, George Burns, probably had it right when he said 'happiness is having a large close-knit family…in another city'.

True happiness, James thought, did not rely on others. It lay within oneself. It had a child-like quality, a simple delight in simple things, like being glad to be alive in a certain place at a certain time. Happiness, he felt, was often wrongly associated with humour, jokes, laughing. The British were noted for all of these things, but it did not mean they were happy. On the contrary, most British humour was based on self-deprecation, of themselves and of their country. This signifies latent unhappiness. *Humour sprouts from bitter soil* aptly described the British experience.

In James's case, as he stood with the soft, warm sand between his toes, and watched the clear water of the mighty ocean curtsey at his feet, and listened to the music of its roll and hiss, and heard the birds, the far-off gulls, and gloried in the peace and emptiness of the vast blue sky, and felt the sun's warmth embrace his skin, he had no doubt that he was happy in the true sense of the word. Was it possible to love a place as much as or more than another human? Why not? Who said there were any rules, any marks out of ten.

As he turned to pick up his box of worms he noticed, for the first time, a figure sitting barely 50 metres away, among the shallow dunes, just outside the gate to the beach house. The head was bent down and hidden by a wide-brimmed hat, the clothes were the same colour as the sand, covered the whole body and were difficult to define. He wasn't sure whether it was a man or a woman, but he could see that he or she was painting or sketching; there was a board or canvas mounted on an easel and other bits of paraphernalia sitting on the sand.

It reminded James of his own youthful attempts at being an artist. Like many others with a creative urge, he had been good at drawing and painting at school, and had studied fine art at university. He had learned a lot and understood a lot, but when he painted all he produced was a good likeness of what he saw. Good enough to please friends and family and the untrained eye, but not good enough to make a living at it. He had no flair. He was too careful, too organised. When he tried to loosen up he usually finished with an unconvincing mess. Fortunately, he had recognised his shortcomings early enough and abandoned the art, leaving him more time to concentrate on his English studies. Here, his organisational ability came to the fore when compiling papers, essays, thesis. He did, however, continue to carry with him wherever he went a pad of watercolour paper, a tin of paints, and some brushes and pencils, and whenever he came across a scene he wanted to capture forever, he would spend a couple of hours producing a watercolour image of it. He found that this was the best way to remember a place, far better than photographs. Already, his latest pad contained a number of images of Narooma, including one of the beach he was now standing on, the stacks being the main point of interest. He hoped, of course, that he would never have to look through this pad in order to remember Narooma, but until he was certain that he was staying, he would continue to record its beauty.

He emptied his box of worms on the sand and found only one with slight movement. He put it on the hook but didn't hold out much hope of it catching anything. Sure enough, after five minutes in the water, he retrieved it and found only a hollow bit of skin. His fishing was over for the day. With three-day-old worms it was not surprising. There was always tomorrow. He tidied up his gear, threw the worms in the water, washed his hands, and sat on his seat to dry his toes and put his flip-flops back on.

Before he left the beach he decided to take a look at what the artist was doing. In order not to disturb him or her he walked in an exaggerated arc so that he finally approached the artist from behind. As he drew closer he could see shoulder-length hair (a woman he presumed) and some kind of walkman earphones peeking out from under the hat. This explained why she didn't hear him as he moved to stand only 2 metres behind her.

She was painting the stacks and the surrounding beach and sea, and she was good. She used quick, confident strokes, using mixed colours of a much stronger hue and tone than he would have chosen. Already he could see personality and dynamism in the picture, compared to his own accurate but bland, photo-like efforts. He stood watching for about five minutes, enthralled. Then she started to wash her brushes out and he became concerned that she would turn and get a shock. He took out the small writing pad and pen that he always carried in his back pocket to make notes as he went about his travel writing business. He tore off one sheet and on it, in large capitals he wrote VIVALDI?, guessing that she had been listening to the Italian composer's fast, colourful, music; music that had inspired her to use such vibrant colours and quick strokes.

Carefully, so as not to frighten her, he made another arc so that he now approached her face-on. With a few metres to go, her head came up and she saw him. She did not react. Gingerly, he handed her his sheet of paper. She stared at it for some time, obviously not sure of its meaning. Then, apparently, the penny dropped and she raised a finger of acknowledgement and handed the paper back.

She took off her hat, removed her headphones, and looked up at him. Something inside him stopped working for a moment. Then it kicked back in and allowed him to smile and breathe again. She wasn't beautiful in the conventional sense, but here was the beauty of intelligence, looking out of sad brown eyes.

She had dark-brown hair, smooth, unblemished skin, and delicate features. He guessed she was in her forties, but she had that indefinable quality that allows you to see that a young woman still loiters within. Her expression was one of serene melancholy, as though she had suffered great trauma and was now resigned to the fact that the pain would last a lifetime. There was no returning smile, only an acknowledgement of his presence, an acceptance of his interruption, a readiness to hear him out; all conveyed within a single enigmatic look. She blinked her eyes slowly as she studied him. But she said nothing.

'I like your painting,' James blurted out, suddenly feeling like a schoolboy in front of the headmistress.

'Do you. Thank you.' Her voice was as slow as her eyes.

'Watercolour…' James hesitated, '…is a very difficult medium.'

'Very difficult, I agree.' A soft-edged voice, maybe an American accent.

'You…'

'And you think I was listening to Vivaldi?'

James was glad of the interruption. 'Just a guess. You were using strong colours and fast strokes…'

'How do you know?' Her voice had quickened slightly.

'I was standing behind you, watching. Sorry, I hope you don't mind.'

'You're English aren't you?'

'My accent tells you,' James offered.

'That, and only the English start a sentence with the word 'sorry',' she observed.

'You're very perceptive.'

'And so are you, Mr…?'

'Ogle…James Ogle.'

'I was not listening to Vivaldi, but you were on the right lines. I was listening to Rossini. James Ogle…your name sounds vaguely… should I know your name?'

'Perhaps. If you read travel books.'

Some of the sadness went out of her eyes. 'Yes,' she said more spiritedly. 'I know them, they are in the airports. There were two on Australia – the west…and Queensland. I read them.'

James felt exultant, as though he had been knighted. He was reasonably well known in Britain, but recognition abroad was a rare thing, and coming from this particular woman seemed to heighten its significance. She had not, however, made any comment on their quality. Again, like the child in front of the headmistress, he looked for approval. 'Were they as good to you as your painting is to me?' he asked simply.

'Ah! Fishing for compliments instead of fish,' she observed knowingly. 'We are so insecure, are we not. We put our heart and soul into creating something out of nothing, but we do not accept our own judgement of it. We need somebody else, even if they know nothing about what we do, to tell us that it is worthwhile. It is the curse of all artists, Mr Ogle.'

James was delighted that she considered him an artist. He had always thought of himself as a craftsman. And clearly she was now confirming that she was a serious artist. Perhaps her name would be familiar to him. 'You are absolutely right, Mrs…?' He had noticed a wedding ring.

'Mrs Capaldi…Claire Capaldi.'

Her name meant nothing to him. 'And because you are right, I would still like to hear what you thought about my books…that is, if you can remember them.'

She dropped her right arm and started to fiddle with the pencils that stood in an old jar on the sand, as though she needed some time to think of a suitable reply.

Finally, she said, 'I remember that they were very entertaining and informative…I enjoyed reading them.'

Her words sounded too carefully chosen, her whole attitude guarded, tense. 'Thank you,' James said, not knowing whether she had been truthful or diplomatic. The insecurity never ended. But he was loving the conversation, and he asked, 'Do you mind if I bring my chair over and we talk about your painting?'

She was very slow to reply. James could sense her hesitancy. He was about to say that it didn't matter when she said, 'Alright.'

He ran across the sand like a 20-year-old, grabbed his chair, and walked quickly back to her side, arriving like a breathless 50-year-old. He shuffled the chair into the sand right next to her so that he could get a good view of the painting. 'Can we dispense with the Misters and Mrs?' he asked. 'We are in an informal country. Please call me James.' He held out his hand.

Again there was some hesitancy, but slowly she offered her small, pale hand into his large, sun-tanned hand. He hoped that the rinse of his hands in the ocean had veiled the smell of the fish and the dead worms. 'You are right, James. Please call me Claire.' Was that a hint of a smile he saw?

'So, Claire, my turn. You are an American are you not? Let me guess – California.' He spoke in an upbeat, light-hearted tone, trying to hustle her into informality.

She lifted her eyes to him in surprise. 'Precisely…how…'

'I'm good with accents, and only Americans are so incredibly serious about everything.' He was gambling on her having a sense of humour, otherwise it was the end of another beautiful friendship.

'Touché,' she smiled, and the tension seemed to go out of her body. She shuffled into a new position in her chair and she looked more relaxed. 'By the way, I had been listening to Vivaldi for most of the time. I only went on to Rossini shortly before you came along. How could you possibly know that?'

At last, James thought, *the barriers are down.* 'Well, obviously I didn't *know,* but I just work on the principle that we humans are a fairly predictable lot, we seem to carry a lot of the same computer programmes in our brains. When I used to paint I always listened to music as well, and the music definitely affected the outcome; it has that power. I remember I promised myself that one day I would produce a series of abstract paintings by playing the music of the great composers and slapping paint on as the music inspired me. I envisaged Beethoven in strong, bold, shapes of solid colours, making a uniform whole, signifying his near perfection of composition…' James lost his place for a moment.

'And what happened?' Claire now sounded eager. 'Why did you stop painting?'

'Two things. One, I reckoned if I had that idea, then, based on my same programming philosophy, it was probable that thousands of other artists had the same idea. And, two, I made a list of all the great composers I knew and it came to 87. I just couldn't see myself coming up with 87 completely different abstracts, and who the hell would buy them anyway. And I stopped painting because I realised I didn't have any creative flair, and your painting proves that yet again. If you saw my painting of this scene you would see what I mean.'

'I thought you said you had stopped.'

'I do the occasional watercolour sketch when I want to remember a special place. They are just mementoes for myself, instead of photographs.'

'This place is *very* special isn't it,' she said, turning to look along the beach, towards the town. She spoke with something approaching reverence in her voice.

'I am hoping to stay here forever,' James found himself announcing, surprising himself at telling a stranger his plans. 'Is this your first time here, or are you a regular?'

'I have been coming here for about ten years now. My husband has been coming longer than me…about 15 years. Are you giving up your travel writing then, if you are planning to stay here forever?'

'Is that your beach house?' James asked, indicating the house behind them.

'Yes.'

'I'm hoping to semi-retire when this current book on New South Wales is finished. I might do New Zealand one day, but I'm in no hurry. I will definitely be slowing right down. I haven't seen you down here before, and I've been here quite often over the past few months.'

'We have just arrived. We come over for a few months every year. I love it here. I never want to go back. Everything is so natural here, the lifestyle is how it should be – simple, relaxed, not forever striving like in the U.S. And, of course, the climate is perfect.

'So why don't you stay…don't tell me, your work, your husband's work. But a few months off every year? I suppose you can still produce while you are over here. Is your husband an artist as well?'

She half laughed, obviously finding the suggestion amusing. 'No, no, let me explain. The situation is nothing like you have imagined. For a start, I no longer paint professionally. Like you, I do it for myself. But I still paint all the time, it is my sanity.' James was about to interrupt to ask what she meant, but she hurried on. 'And Robert, my husband, does not need to work in any routine way. He owns things. He has other people working for him.' She said it in a cold, matter-of-fact way, almost with contempt.

A sudden wind came in off the ocean, whipping the painting off the easel. Automatically, James flung himself sideways, like a goalkeeper, and caught it in mid-air before it touched the sand.

'God! That was quick,' Claire gasped.

'Table tennis,' James explained as he picked himself up. 'Keeps your reactions fast.'

A door banged behind them making them turn their heads towards the beach house.

'I must get a catch for that door,' Claire said.

The door banged again. The wind was persisting. Claire started to collect her painting materials together. 'I'd better get this stuff inside.'

'I'll give you a hand,' James offered, folding the easel, and then her chair. He carried them and her painting as he followed her on the short walk off the dunes, through the field gate, up the path, through the picket fence gate, up two wooden steps, across a narrow deck, and through the mesh screen door into the beach house.

It was dark inside, the windows being small. His eyes needed time to adjust after the brightness of the beach.

'Just dump them where you can,' Claire shouted from the far end of the room, where she was laying her stuff on an old kitchen worktop. James propped his three items carefully against a bare timber wall, and looked around, his eyes gradually becoming accustomed to the new environment. It was one large, open-plan room containing a small kitchen area, a lounge area with two old cream-coloured sofas overwhelmed by numerous multi-coloured cushions, and a driftwood coffee table, and a dining area consisting of a driftwood table and two driftwood benches. He assumed there was a bedroom and toilet through the back. It was absolutely basic; no frills or modern comforts whatsoever. No sign of a television, or a phone or any other of today's electronic 'essentials'. Its only acknowledgement of the modern world came in the form of a refrigerator and electric kettle in the kitchen area. It reminded him of the basic cottage he rented on the Isle of Arran when he was younger, though this was much bigger.

James could not imagine that this was their permanent home for a few months, but he did not dare ask in case of offence. She was a very arty lady after all.

Claire met him in the centre of the room and said thank you. She then stood, eyes down, and remained silent. She was taller and slimmer than he had imagined, and in her sand-coloured long-sleeve blouse and long skirt, looked like a delicate flower that would bend in the slightest breeze. He felt an urge to put his arm around her to stop her blowing away, to protect her from the harsh winds of life that had saddened her eyes.

Clearly, there was going to be no invitation to a seat or a cup of tea or a drink of any kind. He could sense that she was not comfortable with him being inside her house, and wanted rid of him. They hadn't spoken about her painting yet, but the moment had gone. He would visit Cemetry Beach again, to seek another opportunity. Somehow, it seemed important.

James backed towards the door. 'Well…I'll be going. It was nice meeting you, Claire.'

'Yes…you too…' Her words came out small and cut off, as though she was releasing a small amount of air out of a balloon that was at bursting point.

As he turned to open the door, a thought came to him. He considered it as he opened the door and stepped out onto the deck, back into the golden light, the comforting sound of the sea's caress, and the wind that had now settled to a friendly breeze. A pair of pelicans was using it to show off their skills as they glided above the stacks. James saw them as pterodactyls setting off on the witch's wicked business.

'Will you be going to the Four Seasons Festival tomorrow?' he asked as he turned to face her. He was referring to the classical music festival held in the town of Bermagui, a few miles down the coast. He had picked up a promotional leaflet at the library.

She stood in the doorway and looked past him, as though seeking answers from the ocean. Finally, she said, 'Yes. Robert and I will be there. We are patrons of the festival. I will be very busy, so if I see you and appear to ignore you please don't be offended.'

'I can take a hint,' James said as evenly as he could, realising now that what he had thought was her natural reticence, had been nothing more than an attempt to hide her displeasure at his presence without appearing impolite. 'But whether you like it or not, I'm going to wink at you from a distance, so there!' And he turned quickly and walked off.

Back home, he consulted the promotional leaflet for the festival. It was a remarkably ambitious project for a town of only 2,000 people, which had apparently been going for many years, and which attracted top performers from around the world as well as from Australia. It had a large organising committee, and patrons included knights and ladies and even an ex-prime minister. And there among them was

Robert and Claire Capaldi. They were obviously people of some standing, and therefore, probably, some wealth. He switched on his computer and searched for Robert Capaldi.

James now had at his disposal several websites recommended to him by his old colleague, the business editor on the London paper. He had become tired of James using him as his search engine, and handed over some of his sources.

An hour later, James sat staring at the screen with his mouth open. It had been like that for most of the journey through the various sites. Robert Capaldi owned 253 companies and was one of the richest businessmen in America, thought to be worth three billion dollars. He made Elaine's late husband look like a market stall holder.

He was 61 years old, obviously older than his wife, and like a lot of entrepreneurs had not done well academically, leaving school at 16 with no qualifications. He had been born in Brooklyn, New York to Italian parents, and christened Roberto, changing his name to Robert at the age of 21. He was the eldest of two brothers and one sister. After school, he had started work at his father's brewery in New York, his father insisting that he start at the bottom cleaning out the vats after each fermentation. He was 19 when his father was murdered (this was getting interesting), and he took over as owner from then on.

At this point James had switched his search to Robert's father, Ernesto Capaldi. His jaw had dropped even further. One site had him categorised under simple headings: Occupation – gangster, racketeer, bootlegger. He had arrived in America in 1915 from Sicily along with three brothers. They had immediately recruited a gang of mobsters and set up protection rackets. When Prohibition became law in 1920 they got involved in bootlegging, gambling and prostitution. When Al Capone left New York for Chicago in 1921 to set up his empire there, the Capaldi brothers took over his patch and ran the illegal liquor racket, which was more profitable than gambling or prostitution, until Prohibition ended in 1933. After that the brothers split up and Ernesto concentrated on the business he knew best – liquor. He bought a small brewery in Brooklyn and became a legitimate businessman, eventually making his beer a national brand. He was killed in a drive-by shooting outside his home in 1969. The murderer was never discovered, but was assumed to be somebody carrying a grudge from back in his old gangster days.

Still catching his breath, James returned to Robert Capaldi. He owned companies in virtually every market, from drink to food to transport to insurance to casinos to airlines to energy to telephones to television to newspapers to movies, and so on. In recent years he had spent time in Washington advising two presidents on economic and business affairs. He was patron of a number of well-known charities, and known to give large monetary donations to all of them. He played a prominent part in the success of the San Diego Yacht Club when they won the prestigious America's Cup in 1988 and 1992. He was well known in Hollywood and often seen at parties thrown by the big movie and TV stars.

His first marriage to millionairess Helena Beckstein lasted 12 years and ended in divorce in 1987. He married artist Claire Martin in 1995. Their main residence was in the San Diego area of California. They were believed to own other properties around the world, including Switzerland, Bermuda and Australia.

Robert Capaldi's hobbies were listed as sailing, game fishing, and golf. He owned a 23-metre ocean-going yacht called 'The Man'. He was a member of the San Diego Sailing Club and La Quinta Golf Club. His handicap was two, and he made regular appearances in prominent Pro-Am tournaments alongside tour professionals such as Tiger Woods.

James leaned back from his computer and found he had been holding his breath. He let it out in a long exhalation. His thoughts were scattered. Father a gangster, probably Mafia, billionaire, presidential advisor, America's Cup winner, and married to a delicate flower like

Claire. What an unlikely outcome, an unlikely couple. You never know who you are going to meet on a beach.

No wonder she was wary. She was probably used to having some kind of minder or bodyguard with her. She must spend most of her life in the public eye, have endless calls on her time, entertaining, attending charity events, sporting events etc. etc. She had probably been in the White House, met presidents. She probably had maids and butlers. She was probably enjoying the first time alone in months, feeling anonymous and secure in friendly little Narooma, when up I pop and confront her. She would not be used to that, she would be wary and possibly frightened.

Now he was looking forward to seeing her again at the music festival. He wanted to see if the personality she displayed on the beach changed when she was in the public eye. Did she change and become the life and soul of the party? He also wanted to see this important husband of hers. They shared the same hobbies – fishing and golf – though James was feeling decidedly second best when comparing his 30-centimetre whiting with Robert's 3-metre marlin, and a handicap of 14 compared to a handicap of two. Did he look like an American businessman or a gangster, or were they one and the same thing? His imagination was taking over again. He really didn't have time for all this. He must apply himself to Elaine's demise on a beach. *Now come on*!

Chapter 6

Although the town of Bermagui is only half the size of Narooma and much less accessible, being a few miles off the main highway, it is probably better known than Narooma throughout Australia. This is because American author Zane Gray based himself here in 1936, and subsequently let the world know that the big game fishing in this area is outstanding. Large marlin, tuna and sailfish have been attracting game fishers ever since. They come from around the world, and include many wealthy Americans who arrive in the summer when the warm northerly currents bring the big fish close to shore. It is this closeness to shore that is the main attraction. Back in American waters, in the San Diego deeps off California, you have to travel over 100 miles out to sea, and stay overnight on board large boats if you want to catch the big ones. The area around Bermagui and Narooma is where the continental shelf of Australia is at its narrowest. Just 15 kilometres offshore, the shelf ends and the vast deeps begin. In a small, fast boat you can be out fishing for marlin within an hour, spend all day fishing, and return to shore in the evening after a day to remember.

Now, its small, picturesque harbour plays host to a flotilla of boats specially designed to cater for wealthy big game hunters. They are for hire complete with an experienced skipper and crew who know the waters. They are equipped with flybridge helm stations and usually a single 'fighting chair' where the strapped-in fisher can do battle with a leaping marlin, the butt of his powerful fishing rod sitting in a gimballed mount.

Bermagui has two other claims to fame. It is one of the most scenically beautiful places in Australia, and it plays host to the Four Seasons Festival of classical music.

It sits on a spur of land sticking out into the ocean, most of the town sitting on a gently sloping hill facing north, thus bathing it in sunshine for most of the day. Stand on any of its rocky headlands or quiet beaches and look out to sea, and you also take in all the forests, mountains and beaches that appear to the west, running up the coast for mile after mile. It is a view of unspoilt natural beauty. It reminded James of the coastal grandeur of northwest Scotland, the exceptions being the species of trees and the constant blessing of the omniscient sun.

James would have been happy to live in Bermagui had it also had an inlet like Wagonga, and had its golf course been a match for Narooma's. He had heard about a mining executive who had fallen in love with Bermagui and decided to commute to work from there. His office was in Perth on the west coast of Australia, over 3,000 miles away. Apparently, every Monday morning his wife drove him to a small airport about an hour from Bermagui, where he got an hour-long flight to Melbourne. From there he had a five-hour flight to Perth, and a taxi to his office. It was the equivalent of commuting from London to Cairo. He spent the week in Perth, then repeated the journey in reverse every Friday, leaving him free to enjoy his beloved Bermagui every weekend.

The Four Seasons Festival had started in 1991 and grown to become a three-day event. On the first day, James found himself sitting in a small community hall listening to four composers, including an American minimalist, discuss their composition processes with ABC radio's top arts presenter. He was in the habit of listening to her daily interview programme and it was a delightful surprise to see her attending such a small-town event. Among the composers was Peter Sculthorpe, Australia's most esteemed composer who held the title of 'Living National Treasure'; the other lesser title available being 'Legend'. Australia certainly knew how to praise its achievers. James did not see Claire Capaldi among the audience.

Later that afternoon the first concert took place out of doors on the grassy slopes overlooking one of Bermagui's beaches. There was no admittance charge and ambling holiday-makers could stop and listen as they pleased. For James the highlight was a didgeridoo solo, so evocative of all Australia.

The following day he attended a full day of concerts given in an outdoor amphitheatre created in a forest clearance by cutting steps in the hillside. With a cushion and bottle of water, and a snack, a pleasant day was had listening to musicians from Turkey, India, America and Australia, and a soprano from Paris. The music covered the centuries from Bach to Arvo Part and was accompanied by birds, frogs and the occasional welcome breeze. In the evening he took part in what was called the 'Feast in the Forest' during which the audience sat around tables under the spotted gum trees and enjoyed a convivial feast of local oysters, prawns and wines.

Only now did Claire and Robert Capaldi make their entrance. And what an entrance! James, like the vast majority of the audience, had arrived wearing typical outdoor casual clothes – slacks, open-neck shirt, sandals. Claire Capaldi was wearing a full-length kingfisher-blue evening dress with high neck and full-length sleeves. A single string of pearls adorned her neck and her hair had been styled. James hardly recognised her. He did a second take when he saw the man standing next to her. But he should not have been surprised. In his experience, more often than not, people did fit into their stereotypical image. He was looking at an American gangster.

Robert Capaldi obviously craved attention. His near-white suit with black shirt and yellow tie stood out a mile, as did his oiled-flat, suspiciously black hair, his deep tan and his bleached-white, perfectly uniform teeth. He was about the same height as Claire, slim and dapper.

Together, they glided around the tables, stopping to say hello, share a joke, his teeth flashing like an Ethiopian monkey's. From a distance, Claire Capaldi had looked serene, floating through the crowds with a regal air, a smile here, a nod there. But now, as she passed close to him, and gave not the slightest hint of recognition, why did he see a timid young woman hiding behind a mature smiling mask? And where was the smile in her eyes? To James, those dead brown pools looked fatalistic. She was carrying out her bidden duty, he decided. He also decided that worse things happened at sea, and that it was none of his business, and he polished off his wine before taking his leave.

Back home, he found Elaine sprawled on the sofa watching yet another studio-based television show in which a hyperactive compere whipped the audience into a screaming frenzy about the prospects of four check-out girls, a window cleaner, a failed jockey, and an overweight nail consultant becoming the latest pop sensations. Their mere appearance on this programme automatically bestowed upon each of them celebrity status, and they would be invited to appear on 200 celebrity-based programmes within the next month. The analysis and opinions of the four celebrity judges was listened to with more awe and attention than that given to Churchill's war speeches. He left her to it and went into his office to do some revising of his previous day's work. Today's enjoyment of the music festival had given him the subject for tomorrow's start on a new chapter. He had decided to give the festival's third and final day a miss, forget about the Capaldis, and get on with some work.

The next morning he was up early, and after a quick breakfast out on the deck, accompanied by Kooky and the lorikeets (no doubt already the name of a budding pop group), he went inside, switched on his computer, and after a short study of the ocean through the window to see if any whales were about, sat down to work.

The word 'culture' is as often misused as the word 'criticise'. Its typical misuse is carried in the statement 'Australia is a country without culture'. What the speaker means to say is that it is a country without sophisticated, refined or intellectual tastes in manners and the arts. All countries have a culture, being their distinctive customs, products, outlook, way of life, whether they are sophisticated or not.

In my travels around Australia I have found the above sentence to be more than just grammatically untrue. Its intended meaning is also untrue. In my previous Australian books covering Western Australia, the Northern Territory and Queensland I did not cover the subject of culture. Perhaps this is because they are such under-populated areas where the senses are occupied and overwhelmed by space and nature; perhaps, in retrospect, it was just an oversight.

Now that I am in New South Wales, the most populous state, and having here experienced some of the best 'cultural' moments of my life, I think I should say a few words to dispel this widely held myth about Australia.

Starting with the mass media, I would say that here Australia does lag behind Britain in certain areas. This is almost entirely due to the fact that the ABC cannot, like most other public service broadcasters, compete with the BBC. This in turn is due to the fact that there is no licence fee in Australia, funding being taken from direct taxation. Having said that, ABC's output on radio and television is of a very high standard, and contains many programmes bought from the BBC. Where Australia outperforms British television is in the existence of a special channel for foreign-speaking immigrants. SBS channel shows news and programmes from around the world in many different languages, the highlights for me being the many foreign films available and an entire Saturday afternoon given over to the arts, where I have seen more operas and concerts in six months than in a lifetime of watching British television. Sunday afternoon is given over entirely to football from around the world. The remaining commercial channels are, alas, equally as crass as those in Britain, containing mostly American imports and reality shows. These have the clever effect of creating their own audience, because if you weren't brain dead before you switched on, you would be afterwards

In the area of specialist artistic endeavour Australia excels. In the commercial field of the cinema they have a host of big-name Hollywood stars. In opera they have the biggest permanent company in the world – Opera Australia – who spend eight months at the Sydney Opera House and four at the Melbourne Arts Centre, typically giving 230 performances a year, attended by 300,000 people. Branches of this company called Oz Opera travel all around Australia giving performances in small towns and schools. Altogether, the company employs 1,300 people, including their own opera and ballet orchestra.

Each major city in Australia has its own symphony orchestra, making a total of eight. In addition there is a national youth orchestra, and a number of chamber orchestras, the ACO being world-renowned. The best concert I have ever attended was given by the Australia Youth Orchestra in Canberra's Llewellyn Hall, on the campus of Australian National University. A massive orchestra played Mahler's Sixth Symphony with outstanding enthusiasm and passion, all enhanced by perfect acoustics in this specially designed hall for musical students. The whole experience was enhanced by being able to stay overnight in the university's own inexpensive hotel, just a short walk from the hall.

I attended another memorable performance given by the Sydney Symphony Orchestra in the Sydney Opera House. Here again, the total experience was enhanced by the wonderful environment. Milling around outside the Opera House before the concert, the crowds were dressed informally and formally, tourists and locals. I sat at an outside restaurant table, with a wonderful view of the harbour and bridge, and watched the parade while eating a fine meal. It cost five pounds. Mutzorski's Pictures at an Exhibition was the thrilling centrepiece.

Even more memorable, for multiple reasons, was a concert given by the Sydney Symphony Orchestra in the outback town of Broken Hill, in western New South Wales. Famous for being the site of the world's largest ever lode (deposit) of zinc, lead and silver, and the starting point of the world's largest mining company BHP, it is a town of 10,000 inhabitants, surrounded by spoil heaps, in the middle of nowhere. The townsfolk are proud of their mining history and have built a high-class restaurant on top of one of the spoil heaps, from where you get a good view of the town as you eat and drink in comfortable surroundings. It has also become the home of many artists, attracted by the stunning light, and the vibrant colour of the red desert, and the contrasting green foliage of the silver-barked trees. Here, the clear, dry air makes distant objects appear much closer and gives them a three-dimensional clarity. The town has 20 art galleries.

While the symphony orchestra planned to fly out to Broken Hill, to give its first ever performance there, in the newly built community hall, I set off to drive 48 hours before them. From the coast, over the Great Dividing Range, across the sheep and wine country, over-nighting at Mildura on the mighty Murray River, capital of the fruit growing region. The following day, the drive is on an arrow-straight road for four hours, the trees and shrubs slowing getting smaller, the land emptier, the soil redder. Eventually, with a view stretching into infinity in all directions, you get the feeling that you are driving on the surface of a strange planet; you can see, or believe you can see, the curve of the earth. On your journey you have seen eight cars, 12 emus, and nine camels.

After two days' driving, and having moved through a time zone, you arrive in Broken Hill, still in the state of New South Wales. As I explained in my previous books, it is impossible to describe great land distances to those who have not experienced them; they can only be experienced.

The whole town wanted to come to the concert; the hall was packed. I sat behind stocky, thick-necked miners and their doughty wives as the orchestra played a Mozart symphony and then Dvorak's New World Symphony, a piece equally descriptive of these wide open spaces as those of its American subject. For me it was a moment of heartfelt poignancy. The music of the great composers brings them alive to me. When I hear it I can hear their quill pens scratching the paper in a cold, candlelit room in old Europe. If only they knew that their scratchings would still be listened to hundreds of years later. They could never have imagined that they would be listened to by miners in a far-away country inhabited by people who made simple music with a hollowed-out tree branch. To describe these great composers as immortal had never seemed so apposite as at this concert.

The next day, after staying in a town centre hotel where I expected James Stewart or John Wayne to amble in, I drove 20 miles out of town to see the ghost town of Silverton. Once the home of 3,000 pioneer miners, its few remaining buildings now provide artists with a combined home/gallery, and the one remaining pub stands alone among the red dust. It all looks like a western film set. If you are old enough to remember those classic John Ford westerns filmed in Mexico you'll get the idea. It is no wonder that this place has been used for many Australian films and television shows, including A Town Like Alice, Mad Max, Priscilla Queen of the Desert, Razorback, Hostage, Flying Doctor etc. etc. The car used in Mad Max still stands outside the pub, which has photographs of all the film crews and casts adorning the walls of the bar.

I found myself walking slowly and deliberately down the centre of this 'wild west' town, doing my best Clint Eastwood impression; my jaw set, my eyes narrowed, a black cheroot hanging from the corner of my mouth. I could hear the click of stirrups, the pounding of hooves, the tinkling of the saloon piano, the raised voices, the laughter and then – silence – as coming towards me was Ned Kelly, his head encased in steel, a gun already in his hand. Automatically, my hand went to my gun belt, and with the fastest draw ever witnessed in the outback, I placed a bullet in the outlaw's heart.

Silverton takes you to another time, it expands your mind, and it must be on your itinerary.

On the return journey, taking a different route once past Mildura, I arrived in the fascinating old town of Echuca sitting beside the Murray River. Australia is not a country for boasting. It quietly gets on and does remarkable things and the rest of the world never hears of them. Here is a case in point. Think wide brown rivers a thousand miles long, think paddle steamers plying up and down them from the coast to deep inland, opening the country up, and if you are as informed as me you think of the Mississippi and the deep south of the United States.

Think again. Here, along the Murray River is the largest paddle steamer fleet in the world. Deep in the heart of the bush, Echuca became an inland port, a place where giant bales of wool were shipped down to Melbourne's international docks, and supplies brought back. Its incredible 19th century timber docks still stand and play host to the paddle steamers now used for tourist trips. The docks stand about 20 metres high with three docking platform levels, reflecting the differing heights of the river as drought gives way to flood. The river itself contains a fish blandly called the Murray Cod. It can be 6 feet long and weigh over 200 pounds.

Echuca, and the whole paddle steamer history of this area, was a total surprise to me, and once again set my romantic imagination away. I took a ride on a tourist paddle steamer, marvelled at its ancient engine, then went inside the salon and became Brett Maverick playing poker for big stakes while Laura Lee watched on, fluttering her fan in time with her eyelashes. Clearly I have seen too many westerns in my youth.

Returning to the theme of culture let me finally talk about literature and painting. The quality of Australian literature can best be described by simply listing the names of ten prize-winning authors – Patrick White, Neville Shute, Peter Carey, Thomas Keneally, Clive James, Miles Franklin, Margaret Drabble, Helen Garner, David Malouf, Tim Winton. Need I say more.

Art galleries abound in all the big cities, with much of their content coming from the outback. The outstanding light and scenery that attracted artists to Broken Hill have done the same for all outback towns, and you will find galleries in the most unlikely places. And now, much of the artwork is by Koori artists. Aborigine painting has caught the imagination of the world and is eagerly sought by dealers in London and New York as well as Sydney and Melbourne. We are attracted by what at first appears to be simple, brightly coloured abstracts. Yet we sense there is more to them than that. Somehow, the care and honesty with which they are painted speaks to our ancient selves. In fact, most of the paintings are deeply meaningful to the artist. They depict key rituals, territory marking, recording of history, story telling and relationships.

So there we have it – old Europe bringing its music to new ears, and old Australia bringing its painting to new eyes. Art is alive and well in Australia and bounding across its vast spaces like a mob of kangaroos.

That was enough for today, James decided as he stretched and turned to the window. Everything was out there as usual, except the whales. And down on the beach he could see old Eric fishing for whiting; a man from whom he had learned a lot. He was greatly tempted to go down and join him, but he had some serious murder plotting to do, and besides, he had no worms.

Chapter 7

Max Edwards is a very special man. He is a descendant of one of the few Yuins who survived the arrival of the whites a few generations ago.

As the gubbas with their diseases and aggression advanced, clearing the Yuin from their land as casually as kangaroos, so the tribe succumbed and dwindled until only 600 remained of the estimated 11,000 who called the Eurobodalla region home before 1788. Groups started to scatter and in the Narooma area two dozen survivors gathered on Merriman Island on Wallaga Lake, a few miles south of Narooma. Here, their sacred totem Umbarra (the black duck) lived. They set up their last camp and watched as the whites replaced them, and brought 'civilisation' to the area.

If you take into account the hundreds of thousands of aborigines who died by disease or battle or extermination throughout Australia, and add in the millions of aboriginal people of North and South America, Africa and Asia who died when white men left Europe and declared themselves masters of the world, you realise just how special Max Edwards is. He is the blue whale of humanity; our last chance at redemption.

The trouble is, nobody has yet told Max how special he is. He certainly doesn't feel special. Throughout his 40 years of life he has felt mostly confusion. In his early years, even his name puzzled him. How could a Yuin man have a white man's name? Later, he learned that in the past it was common for a white employer to give his own surname to any Kooris he employed, and these names had carried on through the generations. His Christian name, Maximillian, had been given to him by his German mother.

He had been educated by white people; good white people who taught him about their Christian religion and their ten commandments. Why then, did their Christian forbears break all the commandments, treat his people worse than animals, massacre them, steal their land, enslave them? How did the white authorities hide it all from the rest of the world for so long, so that the killing only ended in 1930, and the stealing of half-caste children in 1970? Why did these Christian white people not acknowledge any wrongdoing until the 1990s?

He wasn't sure whether education was a blessing or a curse. On the one hand it opened up the world to you. On the other it let you see how insignificant you were in it. Education was unsettling, he thought. It created a war between instinct and intellect. It frequently took you out of your natural comfort zone and put you in places that did not feel right.

Half white himself, and though educated by whites, Max did not understand or like many of the ways of the whites. He preferred the ways of his father, Josu, a respected Yuin elder who fought against the drift of his people towards the white man's ways, and clung tenaciously to the old ways of his people. In their camp in the forest opposite the island of Merriman, in spite of his increasing frailty, Josu was boss. Max was proud of him, and never tired of hearing his stories of the old ways.

Josu had been reliving the old ways when he met Max's mother. As a young man he had been determined to experience the feast known in the past as 'Urri Arra'. This was a time in summer when all the tribes of southeast Australia trekked into the Snowy Mountains to feast on the millions of Bogong moths that hibernated in mountain caves and crevices, escaping the heat of the lowlands. The moths fattened themselves up in preparation for hibernation and when roasted and eaten whole provided excellent, easily gathered, food.

Josu had led a small group of Yuin on the five-day walk from the coast to the mountains. They had found a cave full of moths on one of the mountains, at about 5,000 feet, and gathered a large quantity, built a fire, roasted them, and ate them. They had thanked the spirits, danced some of the old dances, sang the old songs, and wept because they were the only ones there.

The next day, Josu told the others to go back to camp, while he continued into the mountains on his own. He wanted to talk to the spirits from the highest place, a place the whites had called Mount Kosciusko after a Polish explorer. They said it was over 7,000 feet high and had the world's freshest air.

He had reached the top, and sat on its bare rock summit. His eyes had wandered over the endless forest in all directions, and the black storm clouds above. Then he had closed his eyes and spoken to the spirits. They answered immediately by sprinkling him with a cold white dust. He sat shivering with fright and cold; he had never seen snow before. It was the end of summer on the coast but here in the Snowy Mountains the winter snows sometimes started early, encouraged by the mass of the nearby Victorian Alps. In a short time all the land was covered in white, and he couldn't see the way he had come. The blizzard blew into his eyes and blinded him as he started to walk off the mountaintop.

Hours later, the blizzard still blowing, the snow lying ankle deep, he felt as though he had been walking in circles because he knew he had not been going downwards. Suddenly, shocked, he found himself standing outside a small stone house. With a frozen hand he knocked on the door. There was no reply. He tried the door. It opened, and he stepped inside.

The bare stone walls were also on the inside, and there was a wooden table and two wooden benches. The floor was made of bare boards, and there was a blackened fireplace and some logs and sticks stacked in a corner. In an old cupboard he found two blankets and some tins of cooked meat and beans, a tin opener, some cups and plates and cutlery. Then he noticed a plaque on the wall. It read:

Seaman's Hut
This refuge hut was built with money donated
by the parents of Laurie Seaman, an American
skier who perished here in a snow blizzard in 1928
It is built to his memory and to help others
who may find themselves in trouble

Josu thanked the spirits for guiding him to this place, wrapped himself in the two blankets, and lay down on the table. Slowly he drifted into sleep.

Suddenly there was a noise, the crash of a door, the rush of cold air, stumbling footsteps. He sat up quickly and found himself looking at a figure covered in snow, stamping its feet, slumping onto a bench, breathing heavily. A hood went back and he saw the long blond hair of a young white woman. She looked at him nervously.

Lotte Schroder turned out to be the 20-year-old daughter of one of the many German families who had settled as farmers in the valleys of the high country. An adventurous girl, she had been out on a routine horse ride across the high passes, when her horse had stumbled and broken its leg, and then the unexpected snow had started. She had been familiar with Seaman's Hut and had headed for it when she realised the blizzard conditions were worsening.

The blizzard continued for three more days. In that time Josu and Lotte got to know each other, ate all the food, and ate the snow in place of water. Without matches and paper they had been unable to light the logs. (Josu told Max he had felt ashamed that, as a Koori, he had been unable to light a fire in the old traditional way, and was determined to learn when he got back to the coast.) In the severe cold, particularly at night, they had attempted to keep warm by lying with their bodies together, with the blankets wrapped around them. On the third night, their young hormones had taken control and they had mated while clinging to each other for warmth.

On the fourth morning they woke up to find the snow had stopped. At Lotte's suggestion they stayed in the hut rather than try to walk out in the deep snow. She was confident that her parents would have organised a search party and would make the hut a top priority. Her confidence was rewarded when her father and four other men arrived in the afternoon, bringing extra clothes and food.

Back down in the valley, they had hurried Lotte back to her farm, and sent Josu on his way with a pack of food.

A few months later, Lotte had turned up at Merriman Island looking for Josu. She had been disowned by her parents when they found that she was pregnant and that the father was a Koori.

Lotte gave birth to Max on Merriman Island and stayed with Josu for the next five years. She had been a loving mother and Max had had a happy first few years. Then one day she was gone. Later, his father told him that she had gone to Germany because she could no longer live in a Koori camp and she had no parental home to go back to. But most of all she had gone to give her son the chance to live a full Koori life rather than be torn between two cultures.

Since then, every year, on his birthday she had sent him a letter with a photograph of herself, and a little money. He always wrote back, but she asked him not to send photographs. This year there had been no letter.

Max had inherited the strong physique of his father and the classic German features of his beautiful mother. Both Koori and white women considered him to be marakoopa (handsome). He had married his childhood sweetheart, but two years later lost her in a boating accident. He had been alone ever since.

Now, he kept himself busy with a number of part-time jobs. In the summer, when the tourists come to catch the marlin, he crewed on some of the Bermagui boats. Occasionally he drove the Bermagui catch to the Sydney fish markets. He did general maintenance work around the harbours, and casual labour for a local builder. He offloaded and stacked supplies of food at a local supermarket, and took his turn to look after David. And he did a shift at the Yuin Visitor Centre, where his people demonstrated some of the old ways to tourists and schools, and sold their paintings and artefacts.

Max had been bright enough to go on to university, but he had chosen not to. He liked physical work. It gave him satisfaction. He felt that he had earned his money. He was sure that a desk-bound job would not suit him. He had had enough education. Common sense and a good instinct got you through most of life, he reckoned. And now his instinct told him that something fishy was happening on a certain boat in Bermagui harbour.

Chapter 8

James was in a spin. His head was aching, his brain shutting down. Another long plotting session had come to nothing. He would never get rid of her at this rate. *Why am I doing this? Will it be worth the effort, the terrible risk? Is life with Elaine so unbearable?* No, of course not, it had many consolations. But it wasn't about Elaine, it was about this place. He had become bewitched by Narooma. He had to live the rest of his days here. And the only way to do that was to get rid of Elaine. It was cold-blooded selfishness on a grand scale.

He realised that the older he got the more selfish he became. Was this necessarily a bad thing? He thought not. Being selfish clarified situations, let others know where they stood. It got rid of all that latent resentment and dissatisfaction that always attended people trying to negate their own wills in favour of others.

The world was full of unselfish do-gooders who usually did more harm than good. They were often guilty of hiding reality, providing false promises and hope.

Perhaps the increase of selfishness with age was a function of nature; your brain telling you that you only have a few active years left, so make the most of them. *Look after number one,* it whispers; *you don't get a second chance.*

Anyway, that is what his brain was telling him, and he intended to follow its advice. But right now, he desperately needed worms.

Two hours later, he had walked the length of Carters Beach and Bar Beach, dragging his rotting fish in the dying waves, and found not a single worm. It was always a pot-luck thing. Had they moved themselves or had the heaving sands deposited them elsewhere? He returned to his car and drove round to Surf Beach, the town's most central beach, where access from the town centre was easy and the Surf Club had its headquarters. By now the tide was getting a bit too high for worming, but he had to give it a try. He started at the north end of the beach, under the cliff face, the whack of a golf ball telling him that somebody had just teed off on the 18th tee on the cliff top.

Off he went at a slow pace, dragging his net full of old fish through the shallow water, his bare feet enjoying their freedom, the tickling of the warm water, the scouring by salt and sand. His feet had never felt so good, so alive. In the past they had never felt anything; they had just existed in their cocoon of cotton and leather, tucked away out of sight, out of mind, only coming to notice when released from their odious prison, warm and sweaty and aching. Here, in this wondrous place, his feet had become significant, almost a star attraction. All around the house, inside and out, he walked barefoot. Now, he experienced the world through his feet as well as through his eyes. The pleasure of sun-warmed, textured carpet, the cool bathroom tiles, the smooth timber deck, the hot concrete pavement, the scrunch of the lawn's grass, the blast from the outside hose when washing sand off his feet.

Halfway along the beach, still wormless, he stopped, lifted his head and took in the scene through his sunglasses. It was the last week of school summer holidays and the majority of families had gone home. There were only a few people scattered about, lying on towels, ignoring the warnings about sunbathing, sitting on beach chairs under umbrellas, reading. A couple of athletic, sun-bronzed youths played football. A few kids screeched in the waves, their parents keeping an eye on them as they flung their young bodies at the mighty Pacific.

The kids stopped playing in the waves when they saw James walk past them. Some looked puzzled and intrigued by his strange activity.

One or two followed him and asked him what he was doing. He loved explaining the mysteries of worming to the unknowing; it made him feel as though he belonged, that he was imparting information that only a true local would know. The boys looked interested, the girls squeamish, curling up their noses and looking down at the smooth sand, now horribly aware that strange worms could be lurking just beneath their feet.

He was approaching the rocks that marked the southern end of Surf Beach, still wormless, but totally absorbed in the search, head down, eyes darting, when…

'James?' A woman's voice close behind him.

Surprised, he turned quickly. Claire Capaldi stood, holding a book. She was completely covered as usual – wide-brimmed red sun-hat, sunglasses, pale green slacks and long-sleeved blouse. It was difficult to read her expression, her face being in shadow, but he thought she might be smiling slightly. Glancing at the book, he couldn't see the title, but could see that it was written by Annie Proulx, one of his favourite authors. 'Bit heavy for beach reading,' he said flatly, nodding towards the book, not bothering to divest himself of the bag of smelly fish in his left hand or the pliers and small piece of squid in his right. She did not deserve any niceties.

'I'm afraid I take my pleasures seriously.' There was an apologetic tone in her reply. 'I am not entertained by 'entertainment'.' She made inverted commas with her fingers.

'Same here.' James found himself agreeing, somewhat reluctantly. 'Annie is a remarkable writer, takes you right into her world.'

'Have you read her short stories?'

'All of them…wonderful.'

And so they were off again, this time talking about books rather than paintings. Without anyone suggesting it, they walked to where Claire had been sitting under her umbrella. Claire sat down on her chair and James sat on the sand in the shade of the umbrella; he had left the worming gear a few paces away.

After ten minutes of Annie Proulx they started on the books of Martin Amis. Claire seemed more relaxed than at their previous meeting and voiced her opinions and enthusiasms with gusto. There was very little that they did not agree upon, and James found it a joy to share his love of literature with someone on the same wavelength. They had just started on the works of J.M. Coetzee when Claire leaned down into a large leather shopping bag and produced a flask. 'Would you like a cold drink?' she offered. 'Pineapple juice.'

'Please.'

As she poured the two drinks, one into a plastic cup, the other into the flask cup, she paused and seemed hesitant, as though thinking about what to say next. 'I owe you an apology,' she said finally.

'I reckon you do,' James replied lightly, having already forgiven her in his mind, but keen to hear what she had to say.

'I very rarely do apologies,' she explained seriously. 'Because apologies require explanations and in my case they take some believing. You should feel flattered that I am about to tell you things that few people know. I will leave you to draw your own conclusions as to why I am telling you, a comparative stranger, these things.'

James was intrigued and worried in equal measure. He had met quite a few neurotic women in his time, many keen to unburden themselves to him about their troubles, real or imagined. He prayed that Claire was not another one. 'Fire away,' he said as lightly as he could.

Claire took two deep breaths, as though readying herself to dive in the deep end. Then she paused and stared, obviously thinking it over again. Then she breathed deeply again. This was clearly a big step for her. Suddenly, a demeanour of certainty came over her, and James sensed that she was about to unburden herself. But she didn't speak. Slowly, she undid the buttons on the wrists of her long-sleeve blouse and rolled them up. She glanced all around to see if anybody was in their vicinity before she held her arms up for James's inspection.

They were thin and pale, and looked as though she had been daubing them with her watercolour paints.

James was shocked; this was not what he had been expecting. Gathering himself, he offered out the palm of his right hand and took Claire's left arm and rested it on it. He bent his head to examine the contusions. The colours – yellow, orange, brown, green, blue, purple – overlapped in starburst patterns. They were of differing hues, some light and fading, some bright and strong, indicating old bruises fading and new ones recently inflicted. He lifted his head and looked, sympathetically, and questioningly, into her eyes.

The sympathy clearly conveyed itself to Claire and undid her. Her intelligent eyes started to mist over. 'My husband is a violent man…' She struggled to control herself.

She does not want to do this, James sensed. She was regretting telling him. She was on the verge of tears, fighting to control them. She did not want to burden him with her problems. He wanted to reach out and protect her, hold her safe, say words of comfort. Instead he said, 'Go on, I'm listening.'

Claire sighed, and lifted her eyes to the horizon, somehow indicating that she was addressing the world and not him in particular. 'Please don't think I am looking for sympathy or that you or anyone else can do anything about it. You can't, they can't. I am simply telling you the facts because I think you deserve to know…need to know.'

James read this as indicating that she considered him a special case; it was most unlikely that she went around telling all and sundry about her husband's violence.

'How long?' James asked.

'From the beginning.'

'Why did you marry him…you don't seem…?'

'I married him because I was a struggling artist, and he bought lots of my paintings, and then pursued me with charm, money, adventure. He offered me the opportunity to have my own gallery, and never to have to worry about money again. I did a terrible thing. I married for money, and now I am reaping the reward. It is what I deserve…'

'Nobody deserves this,' James interrupted angrily, indicating her bruises. He turned his head to see if his raised voice had inadvertently attracted attention. A small boy digging in the sand lifted his head and stared at them, but was soon distracted again.

He turned back and lowered his voice. 'If anyone needed proof that fact is stranger than fiction then this is it.'

Claire's misted eyes returned from the horizon and looked at him enquiringly. 'I don't understand.'

James shuffled himself closer to her and gently took her left hand in both of his hands. 'We have the same story to tell,' he said plainly, looking into her eyes. 'Writing is as insecure as painting. Twenty years ago I also married for money, and I also have paid for it, but mentally, not physically.'

'Your marriage is bad?'

'Disastrous.'

Claire placed her free hand on top of his and smiled wanly. 'We have sold our souls, James, and we are being punished for doing so. We should not complain.'

James was encouraged by the 'we'. He may have sold his soul to Elaine but, in Claire, it was just possible that he may have found his soul mate. 'Of course we should complain,' he insisted. 'I complain all the time, but I'm trapped; my wife won't let me go. And you…you should be going to the police…'

'We are artists, James,' Claire interrupted. 'We are supposed to represent the best of humanity, point the way to truth and enlightenment, not to selfishness and gain. People look up to us. We have let them down as well as ourselves. We have broken the rules.'

'Utter nonsense,' James exploded. 'Society might value us but it doesn't pay us enough. Is it any wonder we seek security where we can find it. Anyway, I'm not sure I class myself as an artist in the grand way you mean. I see myself as a skilled craftsman…albeit an underpaid skilled craftsman. It seems to me that you have suffered abuse for so long that you have invented a reason…an explanation for your suffering…one that makes it bearable to you. You have transferred the blame from your husband to yourself because of your feeling of guilt, because you married him for his money…'

'Please don't go on. You are right…of course you are right. But you are not helping me, you are taking away my only prop. If I don't believe I contributed to my situation, then I simply become the helpless victim of a tyrant. To me, that is unthinkable; it reduces me to a useless whimpering nobody.'

James struggled to understand her logic, but it would not be the first time he had struggled to understand female logic. Right now, it was not worth pursuing.

'Can you not…' James started.

'Don't…please don't, James. I should never have told you. I'm sorry. You want to ask me a hundred questions, help me sort this thing out. Nothing can be done, I'm telling you. My husband is totally ruthless. If anybody gets in his way they usually disappear.'

'Disappear?' You don't mean he has them…?'

'I have no proof of course, but two people have tried to help me in the past – an artist friend and an uncle, the only family I had left. They both disappeared.

'God!' James breathed.

'And before you go thinking that I am off my head or like telling tall stories, I will tell you something about my husband that I wished I had known before I married him. He is the son of a former Mafia boss…'

'Ernesto Capaldi,' James interjected.

'You know?'

'I found him on the web.'

'Why were you looking?'

'Normal human inquisitiveness. I meet an attractive, intriguing, dare I say mystifying, woman on a beach. I want to know more about her and the people near to her. I looked up your husband, and he led me to his father Ernesto. Quite a family. eh!'

Claire swivelled her head to look in the direction of the car park outside the surf club headquarters. James recalled that she had done this twice before. 'Well, now you know that I am neither intriguing or mystifying…I'm just plain scared.'

'Are you scared right now? Is somebody watching you from the car park? Is it your minder?' Adrenaline was making James think and talk quickly.

'You really are perceptive, aren't you,' Claire observed. Yes, I have a minder, but I am not scared at the moment. I am just looking out for his car. He's new and he is a small-time gambler. I give him 100 dollars to disappear for two hours. He goes to play on those poker machines. That is why I was nervous when I met you the first time. The two hours were almost up and I didn't want him to see you. The same applies today.'

'What would happen if he saw me,' James asked, not sure that he wanted the answer.

'He would report it to Robert. Robert would question me. I would give an innocent explanation. Robert would accept it once, possibly twice, but a third sighting of the same person and you are in trouble. I think he has people followed and investigated and if he suspects they might cause him trouble, disappeared. What this new minder doesn't realise is that if Robert finds out he is letting me out of his sight for one minute he will also probably disappear.

'How can you put up with all this…live with such a man?' James queried.

Claire sighed deeply, indicating her displeasure at being asked such an obvious question. 'Do you not think I have tried to escape? I have lost count of the times I have tried. He always catches me or finds me. Do you not think I have contemplated suicide? I used to... frequently. But then I reckoned if I did commit suicide he had won in some way. So here I am, resigned to my fate, trying to take something positive out of each day...trying to enjoy my painting and reading and a little bit of freedom when my minder goes gambling...'

Without thinking, James blurted out, 'Have you ever thought of killing him?' He found himself astonished that he had asked such a question.

'Good heavens, no!' Claire gasped, and withdrew her hands from his. 'What a barbaric thought.'

'Sorry...sorry,' James spluttered. 'I don't know what made me... I'm not used to this...' Nervously, he grabbed a handful of sand and let it run through his fingers, and looked around the beach for something to help him change the subject or distract Claire. Nothing came to his aid, or to his mind. The silence that ensued was occasionally broken by the screams of children and screeches of sea gulls and he was grateful for their interruption. Was Claire's mind as numb as his at this moment?

Eventually, she swivelled her head again towards the car park. 'I think you had better go,' she said without feeling.

James wasn't sure whether she wanted rid of him because of his barbaric question, or whether she was concerned about the minder coming back. 'Can I see you again?' he pleaded like an impulsive youth; the experience of age momentarily silenced by...something eternal?

Claire raised her eyes in surprise. 'Do you really want to? After what I have told you? There is nothing in it for either...'

'I want to,' James insisted, fully aware that his emotions, and his insatiable inquisitiveness, were ruling his brain. He just couldn't walk away.

'Thank you,' Claire said sincerely. 'There is nothing I would like better than to see you again.' Her eyes were starting to mist again.

'Where?' James's urgency almost sounded like a demand.

Claire contemplated for a moment, then, 'Come to the beach house in the afternoons,' she said slowly, thoughtfully. 'If I have company, I'll hang a red towel on the picket fence…red for danger. If there is no red towel, then I am alone. If I am on the beach and my minder is in the beach house I will wear this red hat. If you see anything red you must stay away from me. I don't want to be responsible for your disappearance.'

'Understood.' James paused, then continued. 'I'm finding it hard to believe this is real you know. I was an avid film-goer in my youth and now I feel like I'm living in one of those B movie melodramas.'

'This is no film, James. This is the real thing and you must never forget it.'

'I will try to come every afternoon,' he said quietly, and took hold of her hand again. Hands have their own language, and theirs started an intimate conversation.

'How does he make those marks?' James asked suddenly, sympathetically. 'Don't tell me if you don't want to.'

'He nips,' Claire said dismissively. 'Isn't it pathetic. One of the richest, most powerful men in America and he nips like a spiteful schoolgirl. It is surprisingly painful.'

'Just your arms?'

'Yes. He boasts about it. Bruised arms can be explained away by any number of reasons, he says. And he's right.'

'I'm so sorry,' James said humbly, lowering his head. 'It makes me ashamed of my gender.'

'Don't be. Just keep your promise…come to the beach house.'

It was time to go. James bent his head and kissed the back of her hand. Then he stood up and smiled down at her. She smiled back. He went to pick up his worming gear, and then he walked off the beach without looking back.

Chapter 9

Over the next seven afternoons, James drove to Cemetry Beach and carried his fishing gear along it until he reached the vicinity of the beach house. He set up his gear ostensibly to do a routine fishing session, then glanced in the direction of the beach house.

Only once was he unable to spend time with Claire. Her minder was clearly not bored with putting her money in the poker machines.

They sat and talked, sometimes in the beach house, sometimes on the beach. The restriction on their time together made them hurry their conversation, cut corners, get straight to the heart of things. They wanted to know all about each other, how they had both ended up in their similar, fraught, situations, and what the future might hold in store.

James learned that Claire always came over to Australia in advance of her husband. He always flew into Auckland, New Zealand where he kept one of his ocean-going yachts. From there, together with three crew (bodyguards), he sailed across to Bermagui. By the time he arrived she had to have their large homestead, on 50 acres, overlooking the beach at Beauty Point, stocked with food and drink, suitably staffed, and ready to party. He always invited sailing, fishing and drinking friends, local politicians and hangers-on to celebrate his first night in Australia.

After that, Claire and Robert went their separate ways for most of their time in Australia. When not out sailing, Robert spent most of his time big game fishing, hiring one of the special skippered and crewed boats out of Bermagui. Any time he had left over was usually spent with the same people, drinking in the town's main hotel. Often, the drinking party would end up back on his yacht, and he would spend all night there. Claire said he fancied himself as the new Ernest Hemingway, even though physically and intellectually he was dwarfed by the famous writer. She described him as driven, always busy, always on the phone; but never reflective – on himself, his life, his effect on others. 'At the end he will have lived an exciting, hectic, pleasure-filled life,' she said. 'But he will have learned absolutely nothing of value. He is an empty vessel.'

Claire was more relaxed than normal because, she explained, even though her minder was still around, Robert had sailed down to Melbourne for a few days. He did this every year to visit his many relatives, Melbourne now being the home of a large Italian population. Later in the month he would sail up to Sydney for the same reason.

In the meantime, Claire enjoyed being on her own, walking the beaches, painting, reading; all the simple things she couldn't do back in California without the paparazzi following her, looking for photographs to fill their pathetic celebrity magazines. This was ostensibly the reason Robert insisted that she had a minder, though it became clear later that her minder had other duties as well.

For his part, James gave Claire his life story as honestly as he could. He even admitted that he had not been faithful while travelling the world. He told her his marriage was a disaster not through anyone's fault, but simply because they had absolutely nothing in common, shared no interests. He told her he would probably have gone on forever in the marriage, finding consolation in the comfort and security that money brings, had he not discovered Narooma. Now he was desperate to live there forever, and Elaine wanted none of it. He was still in the process of struggling with this dilemma. He did not explain how he intended to solve it.

Displaying a passion James had not seen before, Claire exclaimed that she also had fallen in love with Narooma. She would happily give up all her money and status, and of course her abominable marriage, to set up home in a place as basic as the beach house, there to live the simple, artistic life.

As their intense meetings progressed, James began to realise that he was as hooked as a struggling whiting. All his senses and his experience told him to get up and go, that he had enough problems without adding to them, that rescuing damsels in distress and happy endings only happened in Hollywood movies. Yet he could not leave her. For the first time in his life he wondered if he was experiencing that feeling that most people call love. He didn't particularly like the feeling. He could not make sense of it, and that bothered him. He liked to *know* what was going on, what was happening to him. He liked to live by logic and reason, and this feeling encouraged him to ignore both. He was no longer in control, he was being swept up by something indefinable and very powerful, and he seemed unable to fight it.

On the sixth afternoon, as they sat on the beach holding hands, talking, watching the sea eagles against the blue sky, he felt certain that he had found his soul mate, that Claire and he and Narooma were a perfect combination, that they were worth risking everything for. But logic told him that he was falling into the trap of all dreamers. *Be content, you fool,* it said. *Don't go looking for the unattainable. Your expectations are doomed to failure. You are all animals blindly following your instincts. Be content with what you've got – comfort, security. You are not dead. Be content with that!*

But one more glance at Claire and logic lost the battle once more, and something indefinable told him that he should start thinking of becoming a double murderer.

Chapter 10

The Yuin Visitor Centre is a short drive off the highway between Narooma and Bermagui. The dry clay road forms a yellow slash through the tall forest. It is pitted with potholes and deep gutters caused by storm washouts. Tourists without four-wheel drives sometimes struggle, but their slow progress can enhance their chances of seeing goannas, wallabies and parrots. On arrival in the forest clearing, they are greeted by three large log cabins, home to a museum, an activity area, and a souvenir shop/tea room.

Max Edwards and two others are on duty today. Between them they will offer to give demonstrations of ochre painting, boomerang and spear throwing, didgeridoo playing, building huts and canoes out of tree bark, explain typical Yuin artefacts, take people on four-wheel drive tours to sacred sites such as Gulaga (Mount Dromedary), take people on boat cruises on Wallaga Lake to see the sacred sites and middens on Merriman Island, explain the meaning of photographs and heritage displays in the museum, sell boomerangs, clothing, paintings and other crafts, and tea/coffee and snacks in the souvenir shop/tea room.

Today, they have no pre-bookings from coach parties, schools, or special interest groups, so they are experiencing another very quiet day. There are days when they receive no visitors at all, and Max is always prepared for such an eventuality. He takes the opportunity to carry out routine maintenance tasks, service and clean the dust-spattered four-wheel drive, overhaul and clean the boat, or drive into Bermagui to replenish the tea-room stocks. Occasionally, he will sit down in the clearing and create a painting or grab his rods and go fishing.

In all these activities he usually has the close company of David. Max is David's favourite. David follows him around like a devoted dog, babbling his nonsense, getting in his way, but Max never loses his temper.

For the past half hour, while Max has been doing running repairs to some of the wooden chairs and benches in the tea room, David has been shouting 'fish...karmai...fish...karmai...fish...karmai...', confusing his limited English with his limited Koori. He always does this when he is bored, when there are no visitors. When there are visitors, he usually joins in with them and quietly watches all the activities as though he has never seen them before.

He wants Max to take him fishing; fishing with the giant worms, the 'karmai'. Finding the karmai is one of his most favourite things.

Max sits on the chair he has just finished repairing. He shuffles about a bit. It wobbles slightly, but it'll do. He stretches his arms and yawns; he is also getting bored; perhaps not bored, but stir crazy. He has been indoors too long, he wants the breeze on his face. Fishing with karmai starts to appeal. It's a couple of months since he went fishing with karmai. He wanders over to the museum, finds his old mate, Len, sitting half asleep in an armchair, a shaft of sunlight highlighting the grey hairs in his head, and asks him if it is alright if he goes fishing with David, will Len lock up at closing time?

'Go for your life,' says Len. 'Bring me a couple of walamai (snapper).'

Max steps out of the museum and shouts for David, thinking he is still in the tea room. A shrill laugh immediately behind him makes him jump, and tells him David has followed him, as usual. Max turns and smiles at him, and says, 'Come on mate, we are going fishing.'

David jumps in the air, and claps his hands, and grins enormously, and they both run to Max's battered old ute, parked in the shade under a spotted gum tree, jump in and drive away. Max has a couple of rods, already rigged, lying in the back of the ute. He has rods everywhere; beach rods, lake rods, boat rods, spinning rods, all collected over many years and placed strategically so that he can always get hold of one wherever his day takes him. He likes to keep his freezer full of the fish he has caught, not have to buy any at the supermarket, doesn't know where they have come from, how old they are.

The beach where the karmai lived was 20 minutes' drive south of Bermagui. As far as Max was aware only the Yuin knew about it. At this point, the coast was very rugged. From the sea all that could be seen was a continuous barrier of large rocks sticking up out of the water, and steep cliffs behind them. However, between the two, at the foot of the cliffs, lay a shallow stretch of sand about 400 metres long. It was apparently inaccessible from land or sea, but Max's father had taken him there as a boy, telling him that his father had taken him when he was a boy.

From the coastal highway, which twisted and turned through the hilly, forested land, about half a mile inland from the cliffs, it was impossible to imagine that there was an accessible beach in the vicinity. But at some time in the past the Yuin had discovered a narrow gorge that cut through the rocks that formed the cliffs. It was very difficult to find but once found surprisingly easy to negotiate. The beach turned out to be unsuitable for fishing because of all the rocks in the water, but it did have two unusual phenomena.

David had grinned throughout the whole journey, his two missing front teeth a permanent reminder that his irregular behaviour could occasionally alarm people and attract aggression. Max had a strong sense of protectiveness towards him, and worried when he wandered off on his own. He was always relieved when it was the young policeman, Nicky, who brought him back. Unlike some of the older policemen who frightened David and sometimes threatened to lock him away for good, Nicky was friendly and able to keep David relaxed. As a result, Max and Nicky had struck up a casual friendship, stopping for a chat whenever they met.

David was still grinning when Max turned off the highway, drove across the clay shoulder, and parked his ute under the trees. Max jumped out, picked up the rods from the back of the ute, waited for a car to pass out of sight, then headed into the forest, patting his shirt's top pocket to make sure he still had his small insulated plastic box containing pieces of squid. He had previously picked this up from the tea room freezer, confident that Len would let him go fishing. David followed two paces behind, still grinning, eyes excited, his arms dancing in the air like drunken snakes.

Chapter 11

Over the last few days, after his morning writing sessions, his two-hour afternoon visits with Claire, and time spent trying to plot a murder or two, James had been continuing his daily search for the elusive beachworms. Things were getting serious. All those nearby beaches he relied on as reserves when Narooma's beaches went wormless, were proving to be equally devoid of Australonuphis Teres.

He mentioned the fact to one or two of the local fishermen he regularly bumped into. A man he knew only as Don, surnames being used only when unavoidable, such as when filling in government forms or asked for by other authorities, told him that he had known it happen only twice in his 30 years of fishing around Narooma. Standing on the boardwalk, bare-headed in the afternoon sun, his hair shaved short, his skin a deep shining mahogany, holding so many rods he looked like a prisoner behind bars, he came up with a theory.

It is the unwritten law of all fishermen that when an unusual natural phenomenon occurs they must always profess to know why it has occurred, thus showing off their exceptional knowledge of the workings of the natural world, or at the very least come up with a plausible theory, which is the next best way of demonstrating this knowledge.

Don reckoned their disappearance was probably caused by the recent very dry spell. 'Drought on land, drought in the sea,' he said importantly. James had heard this expression before, when other fishermen were explaining the scarcity of fish at a particular time. 'Nothing coming down the rivers to feed them,' they said. This had a ring of reason to it, but why should drought also affect the beachworms? 'Sand gets too dry,' explained Don. 'They go deeper and further out under the water. You can't get at 'em.' This sounded like complete nonsense to James, as the worms lived where the waves broke, a place always wet. But he did not question Don, a man he respected, who had given him many tips about how and where to fish, unlike some of the others who kept their secrets to themselves. Don was the best fisherman he had ever met, and the most devoted. Perhaps one explained the other. Or, perhaps he needed the fish more than most; he was disabled and didn't work. Whatever the reason, he never seemed to fail to catch, whether on the beach or in the inlet or on a boat. For his holidays he always travelled two hours down the coast to the pretty town of Merimbula – to go fishing.

For a while, James had resorted to using an alternative bait to beachworms. This was the nipper (salt water yabbie), a shrimp-like crustacean possessing one crab-like claw, which buried itself in the estuary sand, leaving a telltale hole. To harvest them quickly a clever person had designed a tubular steel vacuum pump, which when placed over the hole and plunged, sucked up a 30-centimetre tube of sand, which hopefully contained the nipper. After a while all the bending and pumping could be quite tiring if you were not fit, and James much preferred the gentler art of worming in the waves.

He found himself pumping nippers one late afternoon alongside a bent, scruffily dressed old man, obviously in his eighties. As he watched the old man's slow, stiff progress, although tired himself, James felt he should offer to help. He had assumed the old pensioner was on a week's holiday and hoping to catch a couple of small fish in the inlet. James's offer was graciously turned down, the old man explaining that he was just putting in an hour's inlet fishing that night while waiting for his mate from Melbourne who was arriving tomorrow. They had met in Narooma for the past 50 years to go fishing. The old man had towed his boat down from Sydney that day, and tomorrow they would both be going out beyond the continental shelf to catch marlin. James had been embarrassed. He felt very much the inferior, pale, weak pom, his own beach fishing efforts now seeming quite pathetic compared to what the old man did. This old man was obviously seriously strong, experienced, and wealthy enough to own a big, deep-water marlin boat. Here were lessons you learn quickly in Australia – you can never tell by appearances, and senior people carry on living adventurous lives.

Apart from the hard work involved in pumping nippers, James found that they were not a good bait when beach fishing, though deadly in the inlet, the fish seemingly able to spot a bait that was not in its natural environment. So today he was back in search of beachworms, which meant he was travelling much further down the coast to find new beaches. He drove past all of Bermagui's beaches, the local paper having announced the same lack of worms in its fishing reports, and was heading for the beaches around the small town of Tathra. He was unaware of any other beaches between Bermagui and Tathra, the land being hilly, rugged and cliff-lined, and even if there was any, it was apparent that they were not accessible by road or forest track.

He drove up yet another forest-lined hill, around another forest-lined bend, dropped down into another forest-lined valley, turned another bend and was about to disappear around another when he spotted some activity to his left. A Yuin man was lifting fishing rods out of the back of a ute that was tucked in under the trees, about 20 metres off the highway. That was all he saw before he had to drive around the next bend. He was puzzled. Where could this man be going fishing? As far as he knew, this bit of coast was nothing but dense forest and high cliffs. Was he actually going fishing? Maybe he was just getting rid of some old rods? If he was going fishing, this was an opportunity too good to miss. A local Yuin man must know the best places to fish; maybe he could follow him and find out. For the moment, the beachworms were forgotten as he turned his car and returned to park beside the ute.

Quickly out of the car, he searched the immediate vicinity for a pathway into the forest. He couldn't find one, so he plunged into the forest and walked as fast as he could. The forest was not as dense as he had imagined, and with the ground being generally flat he made good progress. He was, however, aware of the noise he made as his feet crushed the dry leaves and bark that littered the ground.

After about ten minutes of forward progress, and having seen no sign of a path or the Yuin man, he was beginning to doubt the wisdom of his actions. Now deep in the forest, he was finding it difficult to be sure in which direction he was travelling. He had heard of people becoming disorientated and walking round in circles in these conditions. A few clouds assembled overhead and turned the already dim light into a sombre haze. The forest took on an eerie aspect, not helped by the flutter of birds, rustles in the undergrowth, and the far-off laughter of a kookaburra.

He decided to turn round; it wasn't worth risking getting lost or worse just for the possibility of a good fishing spot. As he turned, he heard a distant but distinct human sound; high-pitched laughter, almost a cackle. He turned again and headed towards the sound. As he moved forward, the sound getting louder, he realised that it was a human attempting to imitate the kookaburra and making a very bad job of it.

Suddenly, he saw movement ahead. There were two of them, not one. The man carrying the rods was leading, moving in a steady, relaxed way. The man following, dressed in a bright red shirt and blue jeans, moved in a jerky, exaggerated fashion, his head rolling, his long, wild hair bouncing up and down, his arms twitching. James saw that it was him who was putting his head back and trying to laugh like a kookaburra.

James followed them, occasionally stopping or stepping behind a tree to avoid discovery. Soon he found that the forest had ended and he was following them into a very narrow gorge, between high, vertical walls of naked rock. The gorge twisted and turned and in places was only as wide as a man. This enabled James to follow without being seen. A dank, musky smell of moist vegetation filled the air, the sun unable to penetrate the deep, overhanging walls.

The gorge was little more than a hundred metres long, James estimated, as he saw the light ahead that announced its end. Cautiously, he stepped out into the bright light of the afternoon sun, the clouds having moved on. Although he had been hoping to find a place to fish by following the Yuin man, he had expected it to be a rock platform or something similar. He was very surprised to find himself on a narrow beach.

He found cover behind a large rock and surveyed the scene. The two Yuin men were halfway along the beach to his right, the one in the red shirt doing a dervish-like dance in the sand as he followed the first man. Out in the waves, all along the beach, there was a massive presence of rocks of all shapes and sizes. This was no place to fish. The beach itself was also littered with large rocks, and was backed by steep cliffs, the gorge having cut a way through them.

Using the large rocks for cover, James edged his way along the beach, following the Yuin men. Three-quarters of the way along, they stopped. The beach was wider here, half of it being wet and compressed flat by the constant comings and goings of the tide. At the water's edge the outgoing tide had exposed a continuous wall of smooth rock running parallel with the beach, about 50 metres long and 2 metres high. It was so uniform and rounded it looked like a giant whale lying half buried in the sand. The first man lay his rods against a large rock in the middle of the beach and walked back towards the cliff face. The red-shirted man followed him and they disappeared behind yet more large rocks. They emerged carrying two large, old-style surfboards, and hauled them across the dry sand, and then the flat wet sand, to within a few metres of the whale-like rock. *Surely they are not going surfing*, thought James.

Then they did a strange thing. They walked up and down and around and about, stamping their feet, as though testing the strength of the sand. The red-shirted man did this with great gusto and at times seemed to be carrying out a war dance compared to his more sober partner. Eventually, they came together at a certain point and looked down and apparently agreed on something.

Taking hold of their surfboards they bent down and pushed them away from themselves, sliding them across the wet sand to within 2 metres of the whale-like rock, the boards being about a metre apart and at right angles to the rock. Then very quickly, they scurried, almost crab-like, across the wet sand and knelt on the boards. They were facing each other, about a metre apart.

James was fascinated. He found himself watching with his mouth open. He swallowed and felt the dryness in his throat. Without taking his eyes off them, he took a tube of mint sweets from his shorts pocket and popped one in his mouth.

At the same time, the first man took something small out of his top shirt pocket and started to move it across the surface of the wet sand. Opposite him, Red Shirt was watching intently, like a stooped heron about to spear a minnow. To James, they looked as if they were worming. But they hadn't dragged anything along the beach to find out where the worms were. It was as if they knew precisely where the worms were and were busy with the second stage of worming, the presentation of a small piece of fish or squid.

Sure enough, after only a minute there was a flurry of activity. The first man seemed to plunge his fingers into the wet sand, presumably to grab the worm without using pliers, and Red Shirt began to dig at the sand feverishly with his hands, throwing clumps of it all over the place, including over his partner's clothes and face. Then Red Shirt was plunging deeper into the sand, and now both of them were digging deeper and faster. Soon the first man started to rise from his knees, and as he did so, James could see that he was pulling up with both hands an enormous worm. Now Red Shirt was rising from his knees, carrying the tail end of the worm. Together, holding on to the worm, they scampered back across the wet sand as though it was hot coals. They lay the worm down gently on the dry sand. Then, by means of the long ropes attached to the surfboards, they pulled them back onto the dry sand. Red Shirt was obviously excited, dancing around the worm and making guttural noises. Suddenly, he bent down and picked it up and held it vertically. It stretched from the sand to his nose.

James had read about the existence of giant beach worms, but thought they were all up in Queensland. Now he knew better. But he was still puzzled by two things – why did the men stamp their feet, and why did they use the surfboards?

They were on the move again, wrapping the worm in a large rag produced from inside the red shirt and carrying the surfboards back to their hiding place behind the rocks under the cliff face. Returning to pick up the rods, they then moved away from James towards the southern edge of the beach, and he watched them clamber up and over the rocks at the end of the beach and disappear around a corner. Perhaps that was where the good fishing spot was.

James decided to follow them, but not until he had checked out the area where they had been worming. As he approached the area, even though all the sand was wet and firm, he noticed a slight variation in its colour. Within a few metres of the whale-like rock, all along its length, the sand was slightly darker, as though the rock was casting a shadow over it. But the sun was in the wrong place.

James approached the rock, taking off his flip-flops, leaving them in the dry sand. He walked across the firm wet sand until he reached the change of colour. He stopped and then took a step forward. At first nothing seemed different, but as he stood still, slowly his feet started to sink. Within a minute he was up to his ankles and feeling a strong suction effect. With a lot of effort, he pulled one foot out and took one more step forward towards the rock. This foot also sank and he found himself panicking as both feet were sinking fast. It was time for the escape technique he had learned after previous adventures with quicksand. He lowered himself so that he was lying on his back. He threw his arms backwards and grabbed at the sand. At the same time he pulled up with his legs. After much grabbing and pulling he finally managed to free himself and scramble towards safety.

Back on dry sand, gasping like a beached whale, he now knew why the Yuin men tested the sand and used the surfboards. He had come across quicksand twice before: once in a Brazilian river estuary, and another time in a swamp area of Kenya's rift valley. He had been tempted to try them as well, with similar panicky results. He never learned.

What he had learned, however, through his travel research, was that quicksand was not a deadly killer per se, as portrayed in Hollywood movies, or pulp fiction. It did not swallow you up. Rarely did you sink beyond waist level. However, many deaths did arise simply from being trapped and unable to move, therefore becoming victim to hypothermia or thirst or starvation or drowning or animal attack and the like. A dark thought interrupted his reverie. It dropped in suddenly, as if through a letterbox, the sudden clatter of its arrival shocking his mind. *Was this the place where he could get rid of Elaine?*

The thought knocked him sideways, made his legs tremble, his racing heart race faster. Shakily, he lowered himself to sit on the sand. Questions and scenarios started to feed into his brain. How to get her here? How to make it look like an accident? How to ensure she was found dead, so he could claim early ownership of the properties. How to get away from the scene himself, when her car would have to be left at the scene? How to avoid detection? There was so much to consider.

Some answers started to suggest themselves, but before he could contemplate any serious plotting he realised he needed some factual statistics – the depth of the quicksand and the height of high tide.

Breathing heavily, he raised himself from the sand and walked back towards the cliff face. He found the surfboards tied to a rock, undid one rope, and continued to look around the beach. As he had hoped, there was some driftwood, mostly broken tree branches. He found a relatively straight branch, about 2 metres long, and dragged it and the surfboard down to the edge of the quicksand.

He slid the board onto the quicksand and stepped across onto it. Moving to the farthest end of the board, he took the branch and pushed it down into the sand. With medium pressure, he found it sank quite smoothly and steadily, like pushing through a deep mix of fresh concrete. But with approximately 1 metre of branch still to go, he encountered resistance. He pushed hard but managed only a few extra centimetres of penetration.

One metre of quicksand would suck you in up to your hips, James reckoned. That was definitely enough to trap you permanently. Still standing on the board, James raised his eyes to look at the whale-like rock a few metres away. The high tide mark, clearly indicated by the change of colour and the clinging shells and weeds, was more than half way up the rock, about 1.5 metres above the sand. The high tide would certainly cover the head of anyone trapped in the quicksand.

So, the technicalities were in place. It was feasible. Elaine could be found trapped and drowned. It could be made to look accidental. With the adrenaline pumping and his mind now racing, James knew it was time to go home and do some serious thinking. This might be the best chance he would ever get.

Before leaving the beach, he returned the surfboard, tied it up and threw away the tree branch. Then he walked along the water's edge looking for good places to swim. He would need something to attract Elaine to this place. He was in luck. Because of the multitude of rocks everywhere, the waves were calmed. Many clear, calm, shallow pools formed among the rocks, perfectly adequate for Elaine's little breast strokes.

Finally, he could not resist walking to the rocks at end of the beach to see where the Yuin men had gone. He climbed up and onto the rocks and carefully manoeuvred his way across their mainly smooth surfaces. It wasn't long before he came to the place where they had disappeared around a corner, a tall vertical rock marking the spot. Keeping hold of the rock with his right hand, he slowly edged around it.

The Yuin men were standing about 50 metres away. James ducked back, momentarily startled. Then he slowly poked his head out for a second look.

He was looking at a horseshoe bay, backed by the same cliffs, but without a beach. Instead, a ring of platform rocks ran around the foot of the cliffs, and the open sea, unhindered by any rocks in the waves, came right in to the foot of the platform, and its colour told James that it was deep. It was an ideal place for rock fishing, and he had heard of big fish coming into such places along the coast.

The Yuin men were standing sideways on to him, both holding rods angled towards the sky. Only now, seeing them standing like that, their rods appearing to be attached to their bodies like long, thin phalluses, did it occur to James that Red Shirt might be the man who had frightened Elaine. What was his name? It began with a D. Daniel…Dennis…David…yes…David.

Black thoughts dropped through his letterbox again; this time in a flurry like Christmas cards. *Elaine is found dead on a beach frequented by the man who the police know exposed himself to her; who is already well known to the police for his strange behaviour. If the police have any doubts that Elaine's death was an accident, and they then found something connecting David (Red Shirt) to this beach, they would believe they had a murder suspect. Footprints possibly – Red Shirt wore nothing on his feet.*

James didn't want David or any other innocent person to be convicted of his crime, but if the police suspected foul play rather than an accident, then it would help his cause considerably if they spent most of their time pursuing the wrong person.

James was amazed at how diabolical his thought process had become and at how quickly a supposedly civilised human can revert into savagery. He wondered if he had suddenly become evil or was he simply contemplating what any other dissatisfied male would do given the opportunity. Was he the exception or the rule? He decided he was the exception. Many men might contemplate murdering their wives, but very few would carry it out. Yet he still did not feel evil. Perhaps that only came after the deed. Could he live with that? If it meant getting Narooma, and possibly Claire, yes he could!

It was time to go. Just before he dodged back behind the tall rock he saw the first man's rod bend like a bow. He had a big fish. Beside him, Red shirt jumped up and down with excitement. James's heart did the same. He turned and made his way back along the rocks and down onto the beach. As he walked along, it suddenly occurred to him that, because of its hidden nature, he could possibly be the first white man to have walked on this beach. He felt like an explorer, like a member of Captain Cook's crew. Now he was wearing tight breeches, a loose shirt and a black hat. He had a scar on his face and a patch over his right eye, and he was carrying a pistol. Those must have been extraordinarily exciting days. He decided to name the beach on behalf of the Queen. He thought for a moment. Captain Cook had been famous for stating the obvious, naming places strictly in accordance with their appearance or after a particular event that had occurred there; thus Mount Dromedary for a mountain with two peaks and Cape Tribulation where his ship ran aground on a reef. 'I name thee Quicksand Beach, and I claim thee on behalf of Her Majesty the Queen,' James said out loud and found himself automatically looking around to see if anyone had heard him. He had only the birds and the sun and the gently lapping sea for company.

And then he regretted it. Although he had just been play-acting, it reminded him of the arrogance of his forebears who had sailed around the world claiming and naming other people's lands. 'I rename this beach Big Worm,' he said out loud again, 'and I claim thee for no one.' No beach should be owned, James thought. They should be everybody's no-man's land.

Smiling to himself, he left the beach and moved into the gorge. It had been a worthwhile day. He had killed two birds with one stone. He had found a great source of worms and a great place to fish. And possibly, a great place to dispose of another bird.

Chapter 12

Max was loading his catch into the chest freezer when his father walked in. He had the lid propped open with a stick because the retaining spring had failed. Its squeaking hinges and rusting edges told of its age, but it had been a bargain at five dollars in a garage sale nine years ago. The whole kitchen smelled of fish and stale cooking oil.

Josu used a walking stick now, a straight chunk of gum tree picked up years ago and intricately carved by him to look like a red-bellied black snake. He leaned on it as he waited patiently for Max to finish. He looked old and frail beyond his years, the result of a hard life trying to earn a living within the white fellas' world. His once powerful body had lost muscle and his silver hair hung down to touch rounded shoulders. He had many ailments but refused to be examined by a white doctor, preferring to mix his own medicines from the local plants, as shown by his grandmother. He had also refused to take any help from their social welfare system when money ran out, and at times he had gone hungry. Max thought his stubbornness was foolish, but he still admired it, as did all the clan. He was still the most respected elder in the camp, the one they turned to for advice, the one who knew all the old customary laws, the one who had final say in disputes. He relied on Max to see that his wishes and judgements were carried out, and as a result Max also had good standing within the community.

Max finished stacking the fish, which he had gutted, filleted and cleaned while still on the rocks. 'Good catch?' Josu enquired.

'Not bad,' Max replied, while turning to wash his hands at the sink. 'A couple of snapper, one for Len, three salmon and two gummy sharks.'

With his door always open, Max knew that his father, and anybody else who needed them, would come and help themselves to the fish. They were not *his* fish. He did not own them. There was no word in the Koori language for *owning*.

Josu shuffled across the lino-covered floor and took a seat at the plastic kitchen table, laying his stick on it, pushing the salt cellar out of the way. Max turned towards him and stood leaning back on the sink, sleeves rolled up, brown arms folded.

'We have problem,' Josu said plainly. 'Sam again.'

'What now?' Max sighed, knowing his father was referring to a 16-year-old who was making a bad name for himself.

'The police want him for stealing grog.'

'Where from?'

'Remember he got that job at Bermi crewing on big boat to Melbourne. He says they didn't pay their promise, so he went back at night and took some grog. Might be true might not, never know with that fella.' Josu paused and stared into space; he looked tired. 'Anyway,' he sighed, 'somebody must have pointed him because police come looking for him. He hid in the bush when they come. I asked the police for proof and they clammed up so they haven't. I want you to take Sam to the Moonya in the morning. Tell him stay there till the American boat goes. Without proof the police will stop when the boat is gone.'

Max was tired of helping Sam out of trouble, but loathe to let him fall into the hands of the police. He shared his father's opinion about white fella's law. It did not make sense to them to let strangers argue a dispute and then let other strangers decide on the outcome, and the punishment, if any. Their outcomes could be decided on technicalities rather than facts, victims had no satisfaction, and punishment by lock-up in prison was abhorrent. In Koori law, the accused and the victim put their own case before the elders, and if found guilty the accused's punishment was decided by the victim, with guidance from the elders on suitable punishments. If either the accused or the victim were unable to be present, then members of their families substituted for them, giving out and receiving the punishments. The main purpose of Koori law was to satisfy the victim. It was all based on the simple principle of 'payback'. The victim had to be suitably paid back for the crime committed against them. It was all done in the open, the victim had satisfaction, and all saw that justice had been done. Some of the punishments, like spearing the thigh, were thought of as barbaric by the whites, and banned by white law, but most Kooris preferred this to being caged in prison.

Since the whites came, the elders had had to create new punishments for the crime of stealing. Because there was no such thing as *ownership* in traditional Koori culture, there had never been a crime called *stealing* and no Koori word existed for it. If Sam had stolen from the American boat, then he would be punished by the elders. They would rely on Max to get the truth from Sam.

Sam looked very surly when Max picked him up early next morning. He wore his usual white sleeveless vest that showed off his muscles. Short, powerful, and aggressive, he had been a handful ever since his father went walkabout when he was four. Yet, behind the aggressive bravado, Max sensed, lay a basic goodness and a genuine artist. It was Sam who provided most of the paintings that went on sale in the visitor centre. His paintings reflected his personality. Max had watched him apply the paint in a careless, almost violent manner, yet finish with a meaningful picture full of vibrancy and flare. What Sam needed was discipline and direction.

A slight moistness filled the air as the rising sun evaporated pockets of dew. Scattered swarms of tiny insects hovered in the lutescent glow. Sam had that 'chip on the shoulder' slouch adopted by young men faced with an authority they dare not challenge. He threw his bags of clothes, bedding, painting materials and other possessions in the back of the ute, already well stocked by Max with food, and climbed slowly into the passenger seat. Neither of them spoke.

The Moonya (safe house) lay deep in the bush behind the Yuin's sacred mountain, Gulaga. It was a half-hour drive on bush trails, followed by an hour's walk into intractable bush. Josu and other elders had built the large wooden cabin many years ago, and as far as they knew nobody had discovered it since. They had built it hidden in the trees next to a clearing where they could perform their traditional ceremonies in absolute privacy. It had always been known as the Corroboree Jaanga (ceremony hut) until a few run-ins with white law had made them also use it as a Moonya (safe house). It stored all their ceremonial artefacts including clap sticks, head-dresses, didgeridoos, body paints etc, and was equipped with six basic bunk beds, a table, a couple of chairs and a tap which delivered water from a nearby creek. While many of the singing, dancing and chanting ceremonies, such as those asking for a good supply of rain and food, lasted only a few hours, the ceremonies initiating adolescents into adulthood could last for days, as the rules and philosophies of the tribe and the young person's obligations to the tribe were explained, followed by trials of fortitude. Hence the need for somewhere to sleep overnight.

Because of his white education and subsequent self-education, Max now no longer believed in the meaning of these ceremonies, or the overall spiritualism of his people, but he knew that their belief was constant, an everyday way of life, unlike the whites who mostly tuned in once a week on Sundays. And his people believed in the sacredness of things they could see and touch – the land, the rocks, the creeks, the animals, unlike whites who believed in one big spirit they couldn't even see. He also preferred the Koori's belief that time is circular, not linear, that each generation is strongly connected to the past and reliving the same past activities. And were not the stories (fairy stories to him) passed down about the creation of the land a good way to look at the land, to preserve it rather than to exploit it.

One of the Yuin stories told of their sacred mountain, Gulaga, being a mother mountain who had two sons, Najanuga and Barranguba. Barranguba, being the oldest, was allowed to move furthest away from his mother when he grew up, so he went out to sea to watch the fish and the whales. He is now called Montague Island by the whites. The other son, being younger and smaller, was only allowed to move a short distance away and is now a secondary peak close to Gulaga. They call him 'Mummy's Little Boy'. Contrast that to the whites, who dug holes in the side of Gulaga (Mount Dromedary) to find gold, and slaughtered the seals and built a lighthouse on Barranguba.

The whites may have advanced in technology, thought Max, but their religious beliefs were just as irrational as the Koori's and had proved to be more harmful.

Arriving at the Moonya, both sweating and tired after carrying their heavy loads through the forest, they quenched their thirsts from the tap and lay on the wooden bunks to regain their strength. Max then helped Sam to settle in, and they both stacked the food supplies, mostly tinned, in a shaded corner. Sam went back to lie on the bunk. He had barely spoken since they left camp.

'Outside,' Max ordered.

Obediently, though slowly, Sam lifted himself from the bunk and slouched out of the cabin. Max followed. 'Sit,' he ordered.

Sam walked into the small sunlit clearing and sat on the grass, bark and leaf-covered ground. Max followed and sat down facing him, their knees almost touching. He stared for a long time at Sam, saying nothing. Around them, the bush was silent. Two flies landed on Max's forehead, one on his nose. He ignored them. Sam's head went down. 'Look at me,' Max ordered. 'You will tell me the truth.'

Everybody in the clan knew how it was with Max. Those big wide-spaced brown eyes bore into your spirit, and you thought he already knew the truth without asking for it. Very few lied to Max. He was straight. Tell him the truth and he looked out for you. Tell him a lie and he disowned you. He was a bad enemy.

'Did you take grog from the American boat?'

'Yes.'

'Did they pay their promise?'

'Yes.'

'Why did you take it?'

'I like it. They are rich…they have plenty…they just leave it lying around.'

'What did you take?'

'Whisky, beer.'

'Where is it now?'

'All gone…me and mates drink it. One beer left.'

'How do the police know you took it? Were you seen or recognised?'

'No, I wasn't seen by anybody. I went at night…it was dark. I think one of my mates pointed me. We got drunk…we had a scrap. I hurt him…he said he would get payback.'

'Which mate?'

'I don't say.'

Max knew there was no point in pushing him to disclose the name. Logic didn't work in these circumstances. 'You will be punished by the elders when you come back to camp,' Max said sternly.

Sam nodded his head in acceptance.

Max rose to his feet. 'But you have told the truth. Stay here. Don't go wandering. Do some good paintings for the visitor centre. I will be back with more food in a few days.'

He walked back into the cabin, took a long drink of water from the tap, and picked up the large backpack in which he had brought the bulk of the food. He was about to leave when Sam, who had followed him in, said, 'Here.' He handed Max a can of beer.

Chapter 13

Elaine was out on the deck, sitting at the dining table, looking like a seal out of water – all wet hair and smooth skin, sunglasses spoiling the analogy. She must have just finished her shower after an afternoon swim – her wet towel hung over the deck handrail. There was no sign of any parrots, but she couldn't silence the bellbirds in the nearby forest. She was reading a fashion magazine, a cigarette wasting in her left hand.

James deliberately slammed the sliding mesh door to announce his arrival on the deck. He walked the few paces and stood in front of her, holding a large bunch of brilliant orange and yellow flowers (Asiatic lilies, the florist had told him). Elaine's left hand reached out and tapped her cigarette's ash into a glass ashtray on the table. She didn't look up.

James coughed.

Elaine's head didn't move, but her eyes peered over the top of her glasses. 'Who died?' she said flatly, and lowered her eyes again.

'They're for you,' James said earnestly, and placed them gently on the table in front of her.

'What do you want?' Her head stayed down.

'Nothing.'

'Has the sun finally frazzled your brain?' She turned a page and carried on reading.

'No…it's just a little something…'

'Why?'

'I don't know…just an impulse. Us humans are complicated creatures you know. We are not predictable, which is what makes us more interesting than the animals. The lion will always pounce on the wildebeest. We humans are not as reliable. Sometimes we will let the wildebeest walk by, and sometimes we will even hope it has a nice day.'

'Philosophical crap!'

'No thank you, I had one this morning.'

Elaine lifted her head and placed her magazine on the table in front of her. 'You think you are funny, don't you?'

'Occasionally.'

Her attention focussed on the flowers. 'They're very nice. Where did you get them? Pinched them from somebody's garden, no doubt.'

'That florist in mid-town…outside display…saw them when driving past…thought you might like them…screeched to a halt…bought them…they are all yours legally…I rest my case.' James started to back away. 'And now I am going to rest my legs…done a lot of walking today. He moved away towards the door, leaving Elaine with a frown on her face, but her right hand on the flowers. Phase One was complete.

His plan was to spend the next few days softening Elaine up so that when he suggested they spent some time together on Big Worm Beach it did not come as a shock to her, and she might respond favourably. But he knew he would have to be subtle about it, not make it obvious that he was building up to something. It would not be easy; he was aware that women in general, and Elaine in particular, had a built-in bullshit detector.

The following day, James paid little attention to Elaine as he went about his daily business of writing in the morning and going out in the afternoon. But when their paths did cross he was just that bit more pleasant and accommodating. He noticed that she had put the flowers in a vase and enhanced the display by adding some greenery from the garden. That evening, he casually mentioned that he had to go to Canberra the next day to pick up a spare part for a broken fishing reel. Did she want to go with him and have a look round the shops? As he expected, Elaine jumped at the chance.

During the three-hour drive to Canberra, James was on his best behaviour, and when they met up for lunch he made sure it was in one of the best restaurants in town. In the afternoon, while Elaine trudged around the shops, he tried his swing on one of Canberra's best golf courses. In the evening, on the return journey, he took her to a favourite fish restaurant overlooking the bay in Batemans Bay, where they watched the comings and goings of people, birds and boats, as they ate a delicious Lobster Mornay. Elaine arrived home tired but replete, and after he had carried in her bags of shopping, she thanked him for a lovely day and shuffled off to bed. So far so good.

James found that his plan fortunately coincided with the annual horse races at the small town of Moruya, 40 kilometres north of Narooma. It lay in the flood plain of a broad river, and its flatness provided one of the few places along the coast where a race track could be built. It also played host to a small airport, linking the area to Sydney and Melbourne with scheduled flights.

In the weekly newspaper, 'The Narooma News', James had seen photographs of last year's races and noticed the significant emphasis placed on the 'Ladies Fashion Parade'. This was obviously how small-town Australia played at being Ascot. He showed the photographs of the parade to Elaine and suggested she might want to enter or at least go to see the parade. After some obligatory scoffing at most of the fashions on display in the photographs, Elaine eventually decided that 'it might be worth taking a look'.

On the day itself, Elaine turned up wearing one of her best London outfits, looked stunning, and walked away with first prize – a magnum of champagne. It had been the first time she had had the opportunity to dress up since coming to Narooma, and she clearly loved it.

Having never been to the races before, James found the day quite interesting, and although he lost a few dollars on his bets, was more than happy with the day's outcome as far as 'Plan Elaine' was concerned.

And so his plan progressed. Each day or alternate day, James found some way of spending time with Elaine and making that time enjoyable for her. He congratulated himself that he was doing it surreptitiously and that she did not suspect an ulterior motive.

Until the night they returned from a trip to Narooma's quaint old cinema, where James had sat through a tedious American romantic comedy, so obvious and cliché-ridden that he entertained himself by mouthing the script before the actors. However, Elaine had enjoyed it and that was all that mattered.

They had settled down for a nightcap in the lounge, James doing the honours, when Elaine said, 'What's this all about, James?'

'Have I put too much soda in?' James enquired innocently, knowing she was on to him, hurriedly trying to think of Plan B.

Elaine sighed. 'Stop prevaricating. God! You are so obvious at times, you know quite well I am not talking about the drink.'

James bought a few more seconds by gulping his drink and pretending to cough. He took his time putting his glass on the coffee table in front of him and taking out his handkerchief. He coughed a bit more, dabbed his lips with the handkerchief and put it back in his pocket.

'Strong stuff,' he said, clearing his throat and settling back into a comfortable position in his armchair, arms resting on the arms, concentrating on looking relaxed and innocent. 'Now, what were you saying?'

Elaine stared coldly at him. 'Why have you suddenly become Prince Charming again?'

'Again?'

'You used to be charming when we first met.'

James looked thoughtful. 'Mm…yes…I suppose I was.'

'So?'

'So, I couldn't keep it up. One eventually responds to the serves one receives. You started to serve me faults and I hit them back.'

Elaine looked incredulous. 'So it's *my* fault you became a cheating bastard?'

'Glad you admit it.'

'You're impossible to talk to,' Elaine seethed, flinging herself back into her chair and looking away from him, signifying that the conversation was over.

James's plan was disintegrating before his eyes. He needed to get back on track. 'Listen, Elaine…I'm sorry…I….'

'You've got another woman, haven't you?' Elaine was glaring at him.

James shook his head slowly and smiled tolerantly, giving himself half a second. He spoke sympathetically, 'Now who has been affected by the sun? I'm denying it of course, but supposing I had, why would that change my behaviour to you; it hasn't in the past.'

Elaine looked flustered. 'I don't know. Maybe you now need to assuage your guilt.'

James continued with his sympathetic tone, 'Assuage eh! Nice word. You been swotting again?'

Elaine didn't reply. She folded her arms and let out a deep sigh.

James went on the attack – the best form of defence. 'Can you really imagine me taking up with any of the local women? You've seen them. George Best said that most of them looked like Bulgarian shot-putters.'

'We're talking about you, not George Best,' Elaine fumed. 'I didn't see many Bulgarian shot-putters at that fashion parade the other day. You never took your eyes off that young woman in yellow. In fact, you must be one of the few people who has a surname that describes your main activity.'

'Oh no I'm not!' James said in an exaggerated pantomime voice. 'What about Oscar Wilde. Apparently, he was livid most of the time. And Melvyn Bragg. He's not shy in coming forward. And I personally know a gay man called Bent…'

'Alright, alright, can you stick to the…'

'And that young woman in yellow. I reckon her surname was Nicholas, which is why I was looking.'

Elaine looked to the heavens and sighed again. 'Can you ever be serious?'

'Yes, when I've got a fast downhill putt.' James regretted it as soon as he said it. 'Sorry…sorry, I can't help it. We're like a comedy duo. You keep feeding me and I do the punch line.'

There was no comeback from Elaine, and James had run out of steam. A silence settled between them. James rose from his chair and picked up both glasses. 'One for the road?' he asked cheerfully.

'No…I think I'll go to bed.'

James sat back down and put on his genuine voice. 'Before you go, let me put you out of your misery. You are quite right, as always. I have been making an effort to please you. But, believe it or not, my motive has been honourable. Your visa expires in three weeks' time. I thought I would try to make those weeks pleasant for both of us. I'm tired of the usual slanging match, and I assumed you must be as well. There is no other woman. There is just a wish for peace between us before you go back.'

Elaine had been staring at the floor. She lifted her head. 'I thought you were coming back with me.'

'Yes, I was planning on coming back with you, but I now think I need a bit more time. Another month should see the job finished. I want to go down to the Victorian border. There's a coastal town called Eden, which apparently has an interesting history in the whaling industry. I'd like to investigate that, and then go up into the Snowy Mountains to find out about the famous hydroelectric scheme, and the skiing. More snow up there than Switzerland, they say. It shouldn't take more than a month, then I'll be home.'

Elaine looked unsure. 'What about this place? You said you wanted to stay here.'

James shrugged his shoulders. '*C'est la vie.* We can't always get what we want. Maybe I can pop over for a couple of weeks' holiday in the future, if I come down to ogle New Zealand.'

'Now that sounds much more sensible,' Elaine said with an air of satisfaction. 'I could never understand you getting so attached to a place. It's so…immature.'

James felt the tide turning in his favour. He wondered whether to seize the moment and invite her to spend tomorrow afternoon with him at Big Worm Beach. He decided otherwise; he wasn't totally confident in the timing. He had to get the timing exactly right. *Softly softly catchee monkey.*

Elaine was still talking. 'Look, James, I'll accept your explanation for now. You are probably lying, but you might be telling the truth. At this stage I have no way of knowing. What I do know is the last few days have been so nice. No arguments, no snide remarks. We've been getting along just fine. If only you could be like this all the time we wouldn't have a problem.'

James clenched his teeth in order to control himself. *How do you respond to such an illogical thought process?* 'Good,' he nodded, feigning surrender. 'I'll continue to be on my best behaviour, and we'll see how things pan out, eh?' He rose quickly from his chair and started to leave the room.

Elaine was caught by surprise. 'Right…right…goodnight…'

During the past few days of 'good behaviour' James had been seeing less of Claire. Her husband had returned from his trips to Melbourne and Sydney and she was often unable to come to the beach house. Faithfully, James had turned up there at every opportunity, but when there was no red towel to be seen and the door was locked, he knew she had been unable to get away.

The few meetings they had had brought them closer, and confirmed his belief that they were indeed soul mates. When there was no answer to his knock on the door he felt like a stood-up lovesick teenager.

With free afternoons ahead of him, normally his thoughts would then have turned to fishing, but the worms were still missing from the local beaches, and he had decided not to go after the worms on Big Worm Beach as he did not want to risk having his car seen in the vicinity. James had, therefore, spent most afternoons on Narooma's wonderful golf course.

Unlike most courses, which tend to be on the edge of or well out of town, Narooma's course was prominently central to the town, right on the sea front. Apparently an early settler had bought this prime piece of land overlooking the ocean and ran sheep on it. The town had grown inland from it, leaving a perfect setting for later generations to build a golf course with an outstanding location.

The clubhouse, a magnificently modern two-storey edifice of floor-to-ceiling glass, which allowed panoramic views out to sea and along the coast, had also become central to the town's social life. It had hundreds of members who never played golf, but came to use its extensive bars, games rooms and restaurants. It even had a 300-seater theatre upstairs, where entertainment of all types took place, and from where a balcony jutted out, equipped with a powerful telescope with which to watch the passing whales.

As with everything else in the glorious town, James never tired of it. From the undulating fairways on the first nine holes, perched on the cliff top, the views were magnificent. You could see beaches and headlands stretching north and south, some of the colourful town, glimpses of the inlet and wharf, Montague Island, whales, fishing boats, dolphins, seals, birds, all against a background of azure sea and sky.

The second nine had been cut from virgin forest, the roller-coaster fairways weaving their way around a salt-water lake inhabited by numerous multi-coloured waders. Parrots and kookaburras kept you company as you ambled along. The majestically tall trees lining the fairways gave each hole a cathedral-like atmosphere. The greens were superb – smooth, fast and true, and the overall challenge was hard but fair. And best of all, the sun rarely let you down. It seemed to be constantly on tap, always at the right temperature, as if you could pre-order it with your golf buggy. All this for one fifth of the cost of an English course.

The hole that set the pulses racing was the par three third. Both the tee and the green, some 140 metres away, were perched on the cliff edge. Between them, nature had taken a massive bite out of the cliff, leaving a complete void between the two. Countless badly hit balls had plummeted into the void, there to rest on the sea bottom until rescued by diving schoolboys intent on making pocket money. The tendency to lift your head too soon to see where the ball had gone was a common cause of failure. But occasionally, when you struck your iron shot perfectly and watched the ball soar over the deadly void and land on the green, it brought great satisfaction.

One particular day, James had been standing on the third tee considering which iron to play. A southerly breeze had got up making the hole play longer, and lowering the temperature slightly. He still found it difficult to get used to cold weather coming from the south, to north-facing houses being the most desirable, and to December and January being the hottest months. At times he felt that Australia was upside down as well as 'down under'.

He needed to keep the ball low against the breeze. He had decided on a punched five iron, and was taking it out of his bag when he heard a loud voice calling, 'Jim, hang on there, mite.' James looked up and saw a large figure, pulling a trolley full of golf clubs, bearing down on him from the direction of the clubhouse. He was wearing the usual outfit of shorts, shirt, peaked cap and sunglasses and was therefore difficult to identify from a distance.

He walked up to James, held out a very large hand, and said, 'Good to see ya, mite, moind if I join ya.' Constable Nicky Ricci grinned the grin of a man not expecting to be turned down.

James shook his hand carefully and said, 'Not at all, Nicky…good to see you too… glad of the company. I didn't recognise you without your uniform on…day off is it?'

'Yes, mite. Chores this morning…practice this arvo…big comp on this weekend…club championship.' He pulled an iron out of his bag. 'Off ya go, mite…age before beauty.'

James did as he was bid, placing his ball on the tee and taking his stance. 'Great hole this,' he observed casually, as he shuffled into position and set himself to strike the ball.

'Best bladdy howl in the world, mite,' came the inevitable reply, and James had to step away from the ball.

'You've missed your vocation, Nicky,' he laughed. 'You should be working for the Australian Tourist Board.'

Nicky smiled broadly, but made no comment. Obviously, his mind was now set on the golf. James settled again, feeling quite nervous with a two-handicapper watching him. Two final look-ups at the hole, and he started his swing, concentrating on keeping his arms and body slightly more forward than usual, to keep the ball low. It was a good strong hit, but his arms had come slightly across his body, and the resultant slice was taking some distance off the ball. He held his breath as he watched it just clear the void and land in the grass to the right of the green. He was quite satisfied – no disaster.

'Good one, mite,' Nicky said generously, as he stepped forward to take his turn. He didn't use a tee; he just dropped his ball on the ground and took up a tall, relaxed-looking stance. James couldn't believe he was using a nine iron. A short, smooth, effortless swing and a huge piece of turf sailed into the air along with his ball which soared to a great height across the void, then fell vertically to the green like a large hailstone.

James always watched good golfers with a mixture of pleasure and envy. Like most people he found the game difficult, and it was a pleasure to see someone make it look easy, to see a beautifully struck shot soar into the distance. But then came the envy and frustration. How did they do it? How did they create such power from such easy swings? It was one of life's great mysteries. 'Great shot, Nicky,' he said genuinely.

They set off for the green, walking around the edge of the cliff where nature had taken its bite. They both glanced down at the turquoise sea, surging and washing against the rocks. A pair of seals lounged on the rocks. One of them raised its tail and started to flap it against the rock, making a clapping sound. 'Must've seen my shot,' quipped Nicky.

'That's your seal of approval,' James replied drily.

Nicky laughed, and bellowed, 'Aw! Nice one, Jim…I'll catch me mites with that one.'

At the green, James chipped on and two-putted, while Nicky two-putted for his par three.

On the next par-four hole, James watched in awe as Nicky took out a huge driver and swung it with the same easy grace. The CRACK! as the club connected with the ball was like a rifle shot, and James half expected the ball to break into a thousand fragments. Instead it flew away low like a bullet, making a WHOOSH as it displaced the air; then it started to climb into the sky like a jet taking off, and finally it curved downwards, disappearing from sight.

'You shouldn't be allowed out,' James joked. 'What chance have normal mortals got?'

'Didn't quoit catch it roight,' Nicky said seriously, bending to remove his tee peg.

With some trepidation, James took his turn, and produced, for him, quite a good drive. They walked down the fairway together, and found his ball about 200 yards from the tee. He skied his second shot with a four wood, and was still a few yards behind Nicky's drive, which lay only 50 yards from the green. A poor chip, and James finished with a six. A good chip, and Nicky finished with a birdie three.

And that was how the afternoon continued. James continuously out-driven by about 100 metres, and finding his game unravel as he made the mistake of trying to keep up with Nicky. His swing got faster and shorter and the only thing soaring was his scores. However, with Nicky for company it was impossible not to enjoy the round. Between shots they exchanged golfing stories, police stories, pommy jokes, and fishing yarns. Nicky also kept up an endless flow of questions about James's travel writing, culminating in him asking James if he could let him have a signed copy of his book on France, to give to his mother, who had always wanted to visit that country, being passionate about food and drink. James said he would be delighted, and would get his agent to post him a copy over. Immediately, James saw this as a great stroke of luck. Not only did it keep him well in with the local police, it also gave him the opportunity to provide himself with an alibi when the fateful day came around.

While the luck was running his way, he decided to push it a bit further. As they left the 18th green and headed for the clubhouse, James said casually, 'You remember that young Koori, David, who upset my wife.'

Nicky turned his head. 'Yeah?'

'I think I saw him in town the other day. There was a young fellow in a red shirt flinging his arms about. He was with an older man… tall…well built.'

'That'd be Divid alroight. Always wears a red shirt. Some of his mites call him 'Matchstick' 'cos of it. Down't know how many red shirts he's got but they alwise look clean. Other fella was probably Max, his best mite…good blowk.'

James nodded. 'Right…I thought it might be him. Poor lad obviously has problems.' Then he added quickly, 'Can I buy you a beer, Nicky,' to emphasise the casualness of his enquiry. He hoped his apparent sympathy for David had been noted.

'Ta mite,' Nicky said. 'I could murder a beer.'

'And don't tell me, Nicky,' James began, putting his hand on Nicky's shoulder, 'the beer in the clubhouse is…' – he invited Nicky to join him and together they chorused, 'the best bladdy beer in the world,' and they entered the clubhouse laughing.

Another few days of 'good behaviour' passed without incident. James had his eye on the tide tables. He had to get the timing of the tides right, as well as the timing of when to ask Elaine to join him on Worm Beach. He needed the two extremes – a very low low-tide followed by a very high high-tide. This would ensure that the quicksand was exposed at low tide, and that there was sufficient water at high tide to cover a trapped human. Such tides came around every month as the levels varied slightly each day, and James reckoned that he could do the deed on any of four days, when the tides were within his measurement targets.

Things had been going smoothly since their little fracas after the trip to the pictures. They had both settled into a 'be kind to each other' routine. James felt that the time was now right. And tomorrow was the first of the four-day tide window. It was time for action. Suddenly, he realised the weirdest thing – that he was experiencing the proverb 'time and tide waits for no man'. Was this realisation prophetic? Had he been given a sign? *Don't be ridiculous – get on with it!*

He had struggled with his concentration during his morning's work, and now he sat opposite Elaine at the outside table, having just finished lunch. He was psyching himself up to ask Elaine to go to Big Worm Beach with him. She was making small talk about things in the garden which she had been taking care of in recent weeks; the care amounting to little more than regular watering of crops and flowers; the lawns being left to the care of a local contractor.

He was finding it very difficult to say the words that would set in motion the events that could lead to the death of his wife. This murder business was not as easy as it sounded. It took guts, and not the type that was hiding his belt from him. He didn't know yet whether he had enough of the other type.

Time and again he started his run-up. The words came to the tip of his tongue, arrived at the delivery point, then decided not to fling themselves down the pitch. He thought of bringing on his spinner. If he could find a bit of rough just outside her usual thought patterns maybe a well delivered googly would do the trick.

He was still dithering like an English cricket captain, running out of balls, his self-esteem being hit for six, when a miracle happened. Elaine hit her own wicket. He had only been half-listening to her; heard her say something about it being nice to be able to pick a fresh lemon from the garden to slice into her gin and tonic. Now she was on about the tomatoes being huge and ripe and the lettuce needed using and she had some very nice ham from the butcher and how would he like it if she was to make up a salad tomorrow and they went to the beach together for a swim and a picnic. *Women! Bless them! They have the answer to everything. Even their own demise.*

'Sounds good to me,' James said, as coolly as he could in the circumstances, trying to convey an air of pleasant routine. 'Funny thing is, I meant to suggest something similar myself, but I forgot all about it. You remember I was having trouble finding beachworms... well last week I drove down past Bermagui looking for some, and I came across this beach that had some, and I noticed that it also had some really good swimming spots...you know...nice calm, shallow water. There's a lot of big rocks about 50 yards out in the sea and they kill all the waves. It looked really inviting. I meant to tell you about it, but I forgot. Starting my senior moments early, eh!'

'Would I be able to sunbathe naked?' Elaine asked, while gathering some of their lunch crockery together.

'Yes, it's quite isolated,' James replied casually, thrilled that she had not raised any objections. 'Actually it's a bit off the beaten track… about 15 minutes' walk…you'd be okay with that wouldn't you?'

'So how did you find it?' Elaine questioned suddenly.

James thought quickly, and went with the truth. 'I saw a couple of Koori blokes with fishing rods, and I followed them.'

'How enterprising!' Elaine exclaimed.

'Which reminds me,' James hurried, keen to get back in the driving seat, 'there is also a terrific spot for fishing at the far end of the beach. That's where the Kooris went. You wouldn't mind if I took a rod along and tried it, would you? We could take both cars. I know you don't like all the tackle and smell of fish in mine, and if it's as good as it looks I might want to stay back and carry on fishing while you'll probably want to get home sooner for your shower.' James found himself holding his breath waiting for her reply.

'Seems sensible,' Elaine said routinely, as she rose to her feet and started carrying crockery into the house. 'Shall we go after lunch… you'll be working in the morning, won't you. How about 1.15…after a light lunch. By the time we get down past Bermagui it'll be about two when we get there. Is that okay?'

The timing was perfect. Low tide was at 1.45pm. 'It's a date,' James said enthusiastically. *Easy!*

Chapter 14

The big day arrived – sunny as usual. James had slept well, and as he showered and dressed he was surprised at how calm he felt. He had been expecting doubts, nervous tension, even trembling. Maybe he *was* a natural, had a talent for murder as well as writing and table tennis. Perhaps living with Elaine had sent him over the edge, turned him into a cold-blooded killer. Or, maybe all humanity was able to adapt to killing without too much fuss; history certainly suggested so.

Breakfast on the deck with Elaine passed without incident. The constituents of the picnic occupied most of their conversation. Should they take boiled eggs or cheese to go with the ham; should it be chutney or salad cream? Out of habit, James even found himself telling Elaine that Australians referred to a cool box as an Esky. As if she needed to know anything ever again.

After breakfast, his work went well. His concentration was untroubled; the words flowed. He wrote nearly 2,000 words under the chapter heading 'Landscape Variety', in which he pointed out that New South Wales was the state with the greatest variety of landscape in Australia. Between its sub-tropical north and temperate south, lay pristine beaches, rain forests, lakes, the Blue Mountains, the desert outback, grassland plateaus, national parks, the snow-capped Snowy Mountains, and the Great Dividing Range. He highlighted examples of each, and recommended one or two 'must include in your itinerary' places to visit.

Lunch also passed uneventfully, though he found himself cold and unemotional as he listened to Elaine express her enthusiasm for their forthcoming day out together. She was looking forward to seeing 'this new beach'.

He even had a ten-minute snooze after lunch, and was only woken by a squabbling pair of lorikeets crashing into the bedroom window. He sat up in time to see them shake their heads, touch gloves, and fly off to continue their fight elsewhere.

It was only as he was loading his fishing gear into his car that he noticed his hands were shaking. This seemed to be going on without any conscious input from him – he still felt calm. He didn't have time to analyse this phenomenon in detail. In a split second of introspection he thought it might be caused by a subconscious mental programme which only kicks in when extraordinary situations have sent the conscious mental programme into a state of denial. Not bad for a layman, he thought as he placed his two-piece 12-foot rod and fishing tackle in the car, and switched his concentration back to the task in hand. The backpack containing his tackle also now contained his small digital camera.

His main concern when planning the event had been how to ensure that Elaine entered the quicksand area, which covered only a small percentage of the beach. He came up with numerous ideas, surprising himself at his own ingenuity, but after mentally running through the various scenarios, eventually recognised that none could be guaranteed to work. In the end he decided on a simple Plan A backed up by a less simple Plan B.

His second main concern had been the possibility of him or his vehicle being seen near the scene of the crime. The car itself wasn't a major problem as it was a popular model and colour. Dozens of similar cars could be seen in the area. But he had to allow for the possibility that the ground could be wet, and thus leave tyre imprints in the clayey ground where he had to park, off the highway. He would take a garden rake, he decided. Simple but effective.

The car number plate had exercised his mind considerably. Eventually, he decided he could risk the rare possibility of it being recognised on the way south to Bermagui, since he could make up many excuses for being in that area before the event. But he intended to make the number plate unreadable on the way back, since he knew the timing of death could be accurately assessed by pathologists, and he wanted there to be no possibility of connecting him to that area both before and closely after the event.

For his own disguise on the way back from the event, he had bought a wig of long fair hair with matching beard, from an on-line company. These, together with a large plastic container of water, a rag and sponge were placed in a black zipped bag in the boot of his car. In the glove compartment, he placed the copy of his book 'Ogling France' which had recently arrived from his agent. On the passenger seat lay a new brown 'cowboy' hat, with a very wide brim, and a new pair of white-framed sunglasses, which he intended to wear while driving to the event, and which he hoped would afford him a modicum of disguise. He also ensured that he was carrying his credit card to buy petrol, and enough cash to buy chocolates.

Now, as he helped Elaine load the Esky into her car, noting that she was wearing the new lightweight straw hat which she had bought on her recent shopping trip to Canberra, and was totally inadequate for dense forests and salty beaches, he hoped that neighbour Valdis would be out in her garden or sitting on her deck, and notice that they left separately, as they did on most occasions.

They got into their cars simultaneously, having agreed that James would lead the way. James pressed his remote control device and the garage door started to rise. He gave a brief thumbs up to Elaine, then reversed out of the garage, down the short drive and onto the road. He saw that Valdis was indeed sitting on her deck. He waved to her, and was pleased to see her wave back. At the same time he saw Elaine emerge from the garage, and close the door with her remote. He roared quickly away, trying to give the impression to Valdis, and anyone else watching, that he was not waiting for Elaine; that they were not going somewhere together. He had previously agreed with Elaine that they would not travel in convoy as they both knew the road to Bermagui, and they preferred to travel at different speeds. They were to meet at Cuttagee Beach, just south of Bermagui, which they both knew, and James would lead from there to Big Worm Beach.

Once out of sight of the neighbours, James donned his new sunglasses, and then his new cowboy hat, pulling the peak low over his eyes.

The journey through town and then on the tree-lined highway was uneventful. He kept a watchful eye for police cars and saw none, and also for cars similar to his. Here he was in luck, counting six of identical model and colour. Soon, after turning off the highway on to the Bermagui road, he passed the sign advertising the Yuin Visitor Centre. He sincerely hoped his plan would not lead to the involvement of David or any of his mates. He wanted it to go perfectly; for the authorities to quickly acknowledge that Elaine's death was an accident; for his subterfuge, alibis and disguises to prove unnecessary.

As he passed through Bermagui, posters announcing the Canberra Fishing Club's annual competition caught his eye, together with a large marquee and smaller tents close to the marlin weigh-in station. He made a mental note to pay a visit later, and watch the big fish come in.

His mind was still calm, though his hands were still shaking as, shortly afterwards, he took the coast-hugging road south. Soon, he was pulling up alongside a deserted Cuttagee Beach. He removed his new cowboy hat, and new sunglasses, and hid them on the car floor under a cloth. He got out of the car and put on his usual peaked golf/fishing cap, and sunglasses, and waited for Elaine. Only two cars came by before she arrived. On each occasion he dipped down behind his car, out of sight.

Three minutes later, she arrived, pulling up behind his car. In those three minutes James had leaned back on the warm car bonnet and stared out to sea. His mind was blank. All that registered was the two different blues of the sky and the sea and a sense of their infinity. He closed his eyes and let his head fall back to feel the sun. Its gentle warmth caressed his face, penetrated his pores, made him glow inside, made him feel alive. He felt like purring. This was what today was mostly about – the climate. Its importance could not be over-estimated, he felt. It was the background canvas on which we all paint our lives. It was easy to paint a bright life on a bright background. But how hard it was to bring brightness to a grey background. Didn't most people want an easy life? Didn't most people instinctively adore the sun and head for it at every opportunity? Given the choice, wouldn't most people prefer to live in a climate like this? He had made that choice. He was not being unreasonable.

The sound of the car pulling up broke his reverie. He lowered his head and turned towards it. He couldn't see Elaine because of the sun's glint on the windscreen, but assumed she could see him, gave her a brief wave, and got back in his car.

They set off in convoy and James settled down to concentrate on finding the place to leave the highway. With most of the route being tree-lined it was difficult to distinguish a particular place. He had memorised the place he was looking for as being between two bends about 100 metres apart; the first being a severe left-hander in a flat valley stretch, and the second being a slow right-hander climbing steeply out of the valley.

At last the left-hander appeared. He hugged the bend, straightened up, indicated left, and checked his mirror to see if Elaine was behind him as he pulled off the highway. She was, and followed him as he bumped across the wide clay shoulder. He need not have worried about tyre marks; it hadn't rained for a long time, and the yellow clay was rock-hard. He drove as far under the overhanging tree branches as possible, jumped out quickly, and guided Elaine into a position which shielded his car from view from the highway. The ground under the trees crackled as he walked on a layer of tinder-dry bark and leaves, shed over many dry seasons. No tyre or footprints would be left here.

James carried his fishing gear and the picnic Esky, leaving Elaine with only a light cotton bag containing her towel and creams, as they set off through the forest. He made no attempt to warn her of the damage overhanging branches could do to her flimsy hat, and expected to hear cries of anguish behind him. But they never came. He turned and saw her a long way behind, bending and dodging under and around the branches. Clearly, she was taking great care with her new acquisition.

He waited for her at the entrance to the gorge. She looked a little flustered but didn't complain. They passed slowly and silently through the shaded gorge, and finally emerged into the dazzling brightness of the beach.

Elaine stopped and looked around. 'Well, it is certainly remote, I'll give you that,' she said in her 'I'm not impressed' voice.

James knew she would have hated that walk through the forest, but, in the spirit of their newfound conviviality, was making an effort not to berate him. This was the best she could do. He turned right and said, 'Follow me.'

Halfway along the beach, about 30 metres short of the whale-like rock, which he noticed was fully exposed by the low tide, he stopped. 'This is a good spot for swimming,' he said, indicating a calm stretch of water created by the protecting rocks.

Elaine glanced at the water, then, in apparent agreement, lowered her bag to the sand and bent down to undo her laces.

'I'll leave you to it then,' James said lightly. 'I'm just going on past that big rock on the edge of the water. Looks a bit like a beached whale doesn't it? I'll fish from there. I'll take the Esky. If you fancy a drink before picnic time, give me a wave and I'll have it ready for you. See you later.' And without waiting for a reply, he set off quickly.

Plan A was simply to hope that, after her swim and sunbathe, she would walk to his position for a drink, and in doing so, walk close to the rock and into the quicksand. He needed her to move well before picnic time, to give him sufficient time to arrange his alibis.

He gave the quicksand area a wide berth as he walked past it, and set up his fishing gear about ten paces beyond it, very close to the water. It was, he knew, a useless spot for fishing, with rocks showing above and below water. But he was not there to catch fish; he was hunting for a bigger prize.

He went through the motions of baiting up and casting out, and reckoned that, from her position about 80 metres away, Elaine would not be able to see that he had no bait on his hook. He placed his rod in its holder and sat down on his backpack chair, and waited for events to unfold.

Time, of course, passed slowly. Looking along the beach, he saw Elaine take her posh hat and dress off and put her swim-hat and goggles on. She already had her favourite yellow swimming costume on. He watched her walk down to the water's edge and make a conventional entry, edging forward very slowly, giving her warm body time to get used to the relatively cold water. With the water up to her waist, she finally lunged forward and started her version of the breaststroke. While she swam, James left his seat and pretended to be doing 'fishy' things just in case she looked along.

Ten minutes later she came out and walked back to where she had left her clothes. James saw her shake out her big towel and lay it on the sand. Then she looked around the beach in all directions, obviously checking to see if they were still alone. James waved to her, but she didn't respond. She stripped off her goggles, swim-hat and costume, put on her sunglasses and lay down on the towel, naked.

James had long ago given up nagging her about the dangers of sunbathing. Like millions of others, she ignored all the televised government sponsored warnings against sunbathing and smoking, but still expected free treatment from the health service if one of the cancers struck. The insanity of their decisions led James to the conclusion that half the population were either mad or had a latent death wish. Both conditions seemed to arrive, gift wrapped, in the package marked 'puberty'.

Thankfully, he knew she was down to five minutes each side. Topping up, she called it. Grilling instead of frying, he called it.

Sure enough, after precisely five minutes he saw her turn over. He gathered bits and pieces of fishing gear and put them back into his backpack, ready for a quick getaway. He took in deep breaths to stop himself tensing, occasionally finding himself breathing in time with the breaking wavelets; even sounding like them. A pair of oystercatchers suddenly appeared on the sand in front of him. They started running in and out of the water, piping their frantic call, like toddlers screaming with fearful delight. For a moment he was back in the Hebrides.

She was sitting up. She was standing up. She was drying herself with her towel. She was rubbing cream into her skin. She was smoothing her hair with her hands. She was putting her underwear on. She was putting her dress on. She was putting her new hat on; replacing her sunglasses. She was sitting back down, pulling something out of her cotton bag. She appeared to be reading. It was a magazine. Damn! This was not good. He hadn't reckoned on her bringing her daily dose of trivia to the beach. She could absorb herself in magazines for ages. Now she was lighting a cigarette; she was getting settled. This was getting worse. He needed a quick result; time was not on his side.

James went to the Esky and lifted out a flask containing tea, and a bottle containing orange juice. He turned to face Elaine, and shouted and whistled to attract her attention. He lifted the flask and bottle above his head, offering her a drink. She lifted her head, studied him for a moment, then waved her right hand like a windscreen wiper, indicating that she did not want a drink. Her head went back down to her magazine. James turned his back to her and shouted a four-letter word at the sky. The oystercatchers flew off. Plan A had failed.

James bent down, rummaged around in his backpack, and lifted his camera out. Plan B was to persuade Elaine to pose for a photograph in front of the whale-like rock, thus leading her into the quicksand.

He started to walk slowly towards Elaine, intent on looking unhurried. He paused occasionally to get down on one knee and take a photograph of their surroundings. It took him about four minutes to get alongside Elaine. 'How was your swim?' he asked casually.

Elaine looked up, her face in the shadow of her hat, her eyes unreadable behind her sunglasses. 'Fine…nice and warm. How's the fishing?'

'Hopeless,' James said quietly. 'I think I'll be moving further along when I get back. Just thought I'd spend a few minutes taking some photographs.' He indicated his camera. 'Sure you don't want a drink?'

'I'm fine thanks. I'll get one later.' Elaine's eyes returned to her magazine.

James knelt down with his back to her and pointed his camera out to sea. Then, still on his knee, he turned to face her, pointed the camera at her and took a shot.

'Don't, James,' Elaine demanded, making the universal complaint. 'I'm not ready…my hair's a mess…I'm not dressed properly.'

James played his part, making light of her complaints. 'Don't be silly. You always look good. Your hair is absolutely fine. Anyway, you can't see much of it under that new hat. Goes well with that dress…your new hat.'

'That's why I bought it,' Elaine interjected, with a slight edge in her voice.

'Tell you what,' James enthused in a raised voice. 'If you stood up I could get a picture of the full outfit...you know...the way it's supposed to look. Take your time...do something with your hair if you have to. It'll make a nice memento for us to take home... remind us of Australia...the beaches. Most of all it will remind us of a nice day out together.' *That last bit was a hell of a gamble. I hope her bullshit detector is switched off.*

Elaine was getting up. Had the bullshit worked for once? Probably not. She probably saw it as an opportunity to show off to her fashion cronies and staff in London. She had taken her hat off and was combing her hair with a plastic tool that looked like a balding porcupine. After a few deft finger flicks through her hair, the hat went back on, and she started arranging the hang of her dress; pulling and flicking and smoothing.

'Are you keeping your sunglasses on?' James squeaked, his voice not functioning properly. He hoped it was caused by the heat and tension, and not the result of playing the role of a Mayfair photographer.

'Of course,' Elaine said dismissively, but without rancour, as she put the finishing touches to her preparation. Finally she lifted her head. 'Now, where do you want me?'

James cleared his throat. 'You'll need to stand with your back to the sea,' he indicated. 'Otherwise, your face will be in shadow.'

They both shuffled into their positions, a few metres apart, instinctively moving away from the towel area so that it didn't appear in shot. James stood up for the first shot. He looked through the viewfinder. 'Can you lift your head slightly...still a bit of shadow there.'

Elaine obliged.

'That's fine...good...hold it...' He pressed the button. Quickly, he knelt down. 'I'll take one from lower down. It will make you look taller and give a better outline against the sea and sky.'

Again, he pressed the button. Then he got slowly to his feet, fiddling with the camera. He was looking at the results. 'Mmm…not bad,' he said hesitantly. 'You look great…but it's all a bit bland…it could do with something else in the background. Come and have a look.'

Elaine made a small sigh as though it was all too much trouble, but then she plodded through the soft sand to stand beside him. James angled the small screen so that she could see. 'There's no background, is there,' he suggested. 'The sea and sky seem to disappear…they're very faint. It must be the sun…too much light.'

Elaine bent closer, touching his arm as she studied the photographs. 'They seem alright to me…'

'Look,' James interrupted, pointing his hand along the beach. 'Why don't you go and stand in front of that big rock along there, the one that looks like a whale. That'll give us a much better background. The colour of the rock will make a good contrast with your dress.'

Elaine turned and looked along the beach. She sighed again. 'Oh!…I can't be bothered. I just want to sit and relax. They'll be fine. We're not entering a photographic competition are we? Why don't you get back to your fishing, and I'll come along when I'm ready.' She started to move back towards her towel.

Plan B had also failed. Instinctively, James's head went back to shout another four-letter word at the sky, but he managed to stop it escaping by clenching his teeth.

His best-laid plans had done a Robbie Burns. And worse still, he suddenly realised, their failure had created an unforseen problem. If Elaine sat there for another two hours before coming along to join him for the picnic, he would have to make sure that she *didn't* walk into the quicksand, because he would not have sufficient time left to arrange his alibis, and they were absolutely critical. Without an alibi, the whole thing was too risky. What a shambles! He didn't seem to be cut out for this murder business at all. He certainly wasn't a natural. He wondered if there was a 'How to Murder' course he could go on; there were courses for everything these days.

He kicked at the sand in frustration, and watched it swirl away from him. The afternoon breeze had started. As usual, it came in quickly to start with and would calm down later. Today it was coming from the northwest. Its initial burst was enough to lift Elaine's new hat from her head just as she reached her towel. She gave a yelp before she gave chase along the beach. Her running was as un-athletic as her swimming, there being no knee lift; her legs travelling as far sideways as forwards. The hat was winning. James might have been slightly amused had he not had more serious things on his mind. Unless he could, somehow, get her into that quicksand within the next half hour, he would have to abandon the idea. He would then have to come up with a completely new idea or give this one a second attempt, persuade her to come back to this beach.

Elaine stopped briefly, about 20 metres away, and shouted at him to come and help. Dutifully, he set off walking after her. Only now, as he watched her start running again, did he notice that her hat was busily rolling and bouncing towards the quicksand area. It couldn't, could it? She couldn't, could she?

He slowed his walking pace and watched the drama enfold in front of him. The hat, now under the influence of his will as well as the wind, rolled unswervingly towards the quicksand area and finally entered it, slowing down on the damp surface. It came to rest, briefly, against the whale-like rock, then continued rolling along the rock face, in short, slow bursts, slowed down by the friction with the rock. Eventually, it was brought to a halt by a small outcrop of rock, covered in sun-bleached barnacles, looking, coincidentally, like the callus growths on the right whale.

Elaine doggedly kept up her pursuit, and was running as she entered the quicksand area. What a woman! Who needed carefully thought out plans? He needn't have bothered. This was a do it yourself job. She had instigated the picnic. Now she was doing the dirty work for him. He felt like a magician whose glamorous assistant had taken over the show and dismissed him from the stage.

Because she was running, Elaine was a few paces into the quicksand area before any sinking effect took place. Even then, she was able to carry on walking slowly, dragging her feet out of the soft sand, until she reached the hat. Only when she stopped to pick up the hat, examine it, and brush sand off it, actions that took about six seconds standing in one place, did the full surface tension of the sand start to give way.

Her feet were covered when James arrived on the scene, standing on firm sand about 10 metres away. 'Changed your mind eh?' he joked, lifting the camera in front of him. 'Now that we've got you here, pop your hat back on and we'll take the picture.' Knowing how quicksand behaves, he wanted her to stand in the same place as long as possible.

'My feet are sinking,' Elaine pointed out calmly, as she gave the hat one last inspection, then carefully placed it on her head. Obviously, she was not yet alarmed by her situation.

'Just a bit of soft sand,' James said reassuringly. 'You'll be okay. Right…lift your head again…smile…that's it…look to the right a bit…a bit more…that's good…hold it…whoops I missed the button… hang on a minute…hold it again…good…that's it…done.' He looked up to see that she was now up to her ankles. Unless she knew about the 'lie on your back' escape technique, her fate was sealed.

Elaine was trying to pull her right leg out. In doing so, she leaned to the left, putting more weight on her left leg, sending it deeper. Therein lay the problem. With a great effort she managed to free her right leg, but because of her sinking left leg could only replace the right leg on the sand a short distance in front of her. Here it quickly went down as she transferred her weight to it in an effort to pull up her left leg. All this movement added to the destruction of the surface tension in the sand and it became progressively more liquefied and thus less supportive. 'James,' she cried, as she realised what was happening, 'I'm getting stuck. I can't get my legs out.' A waver had crept into her voice.

Before doing anything else, James let his eyes wander over the entire beach, and up and along the cliff top. He needed to ensure there was nobody about. Had there been, he would have carried out a rescue.

Satisfied that he had the place to himself, he made no attempt to rescue her, but in order to delay the screaming panic that was bound to follow, he said, 'I'll go and get my fishing rod. Grab it, and I'll pull you out.' He started to run away.

'James…James…don't leave me…'

'I have to get the rod,' he shouted over his shoulder as he ran on. 'Stay calm. 'I'll be back soon.'

Thirty seconds of running brought him to his fishing spot. Now he took his time. He lifted the rod from its holder and started to wind the line in. Suddenly it stopped. He was snagged on a rock. It was not unexpected in such a rock-strewn area, but he had hoped to avoid it; he didn't want to leave any trace of his presence, not even a bit of fishing tackle. Try as he might, he couldn't free it, and reluctantly he took his knife and cut the line. He took his time completing the wind-in, dismantled the reel and packed it away, split the rod into two 6-foot lengths, piled the rest of the tackle into his backpack, put it on his back, and with his split rod in one hand and the Esky in the other, he walked slowly back towards Elaine.

By this time, she had started to shout his name in ever-increasing volume and panic. He hoped there was no one in the vicinity to hear her. He would need to get away quickly now, both to arrange his alibis, and not to be found in the area should someone happen along, though that chance was rare in such an 'off the beaten track' place.

As he approached her, he could see that she had sunk up to her knees, her dress starting to splay out on the quicksand. She was gesticulating wildly, and shouting. 'Hurry up…hurry up…you… what the hell are you playing at…I'm still sinking…hurry up, for God's sake…what are you doing…where are you going…'

James had not stopped. He carried on walking past her, along the beach, ignoring her shouts of disbelief, her pleas, her curses, her screams, her silence. He had to stay hard, cold. If he had stopped for one moment, he knew he would have rescued her. It took a great effort of will to keep walking. Where such strong, cold-blooded single-mindedness came from he didn't know.

He reached the place where she had left her towel and the cotton bag containing her wet costume, creams and other sundries. He, temporarily, laid down his rod and the Esky and gathered up Elaine's items, including the magazine, which had been blown a few paces away by the breeze. Spotting a series of large rocks about 30 metres along the beach to his left, he carried Elaine's items to them, and placed them behind the largest rock, laying out the towel and generally presenting the items as they had originally lain. He didn't want them to be found by chance, and possibly taken away. He wanted them to be found by the police, who would have already found her car near the highway. He was taking this 'belt and braces' approach in case anything happened to Elaine's body. His expectation was that she would be found trapped in the quicksand, drowned by the incoming tide. But the power of the ocean was an awesome thing. He couldn't rule out its buoyancy and strong wave action possibly lifting or pushing her out of the sand, and washing her out to sea. Without her body, and without strong evidence that she had been on that beach, and probably met with an accident, then James would have to wait many years before her death would be officially declared by a coroner, and her estate put in the hands of her solicitor. He would not be able to get his hands on the two properties he wanted to sell.

Satisfied that the rock would also look like a typical shelter for a woman who liked to sunbathe naked, he returned to pick up his rod and Esky, and without looking in Elaine's direction, he turned and made his way to the gorge.

Back at his car, after storing his gear, he took out the sponge and the bottle of water and he walked a few paces. He cleared the dead bark and leaves from a small area of ground, revealing the hard yellow clay beneath. He poured some water on the clay and worked it in with his sponge until the clay softened and the sponge was covered in a wet, yellow coating. He took the sponge to the car and smeared the yellow coating all over the number plates, making them unreadable. This would not attract much attention as cars from the bush were frequently seen in town in this condition. He intended to pick up a lot more matching dirt and dust later.

In the car, he put on his wig and beard, and new white-framed sunglasses. He started the car and edged slowly out, past Elaine's car, and with nobody in sight on the highway, he drove onto it. He glanced back to see if he could see Elaine's car from the highway. It was just visible in the shadow of the trees. Searching eyes would find it. Perfect. He put his foot down and headed back towards Bermagui.

North of Bermagui, he turned off the highway onto the old road that the pioneers had built in 1882, the one that had to find a way around the Wagonga Inlet, before the 1931 bridge spanned it. This would enable him to emerge north of Narooma without having to drive through it, another touch of 'belt and braces'.

The road was rarely used now, except for the occasional tourist and a few bush property owners, and it remained unsealed. He drove as fast as the road would allow; its convoluted twists and turns as it cut its way through the forest and around the outcrops and over the hills and streams making him marvel at the ingenuity and strength of the pioneers. Slowly, as planned, his car became immersed in a layer of dust and dirt, which gave extra credence to the unreadable number plates.

Twenty minutes later, he emerged back onto the main highway at a point between Narooma and the village of Bodalla, a few miles north of Narooma. He was in a hurry. It was Friday afternoon and most businesses closed early. Australians insisted on their long weekends; they were sacrosanct. The weekend was for the family. No work, no overtime, no mail deliveries.

He cruised slowly through Bodalla, noting that the garage was still open, its rusting metal placard announcing PETROL, ICE, FISH TACKLE, HOT PIES. When north of the village he pulled into a lay-by and removed his wig, beard and sunglasses, replacing them with his usual hat and sunglasses. He got out of the car, and with the clean rag he had packed, cleaned the number plates so that they were now readable. Then he drove back into the village, and pulled up at the garage. It was a sprawling old clapboard building with a tin roof supported by numerous rough-sawn wooden posts; the whole structure sagging slightly, starting to look part of the natural surroundings, not man made. He filled up with petrol, at the same time checking that his fishing rod could be seen through the car window. A flock of Galahs was flitting and squabbling in the surrounding trees. A school bus pulled up nearby and disgorged a motley collection of children, looking less than uniform in their uniforms. They shouted and ran and scattered, full of Friday-night glee.

Inside the garage shop he took out his credit card and offered it to the wiry, slightly stooping, middle-aged man who had emerged from the back. He was wearing dirty brown overalls and was wiping his hands on a rag that the pioneers must have used. He had that look that told you he was good with his hands, happy in overalls, didn't own a suit, never went on holiday. He was probably proprietor, mechanic and shop assistant, all in one.

'Okay paying with this?' James showed him his credit card.

'No worries, mite,' the man said, taking it carefully by its edges, and starting to process it.

'Could you let me have a proper receipt for that?' James asked routinely. 'Need it for expenses.' He actually needed it as proof he had been north of Narooma and travelling south at that time on that day.

'No worries.' The man turned to write out the receipt.

James said, conversationally, 'I'll be in the doghouse with the wife when I get home. I promised her some whiting for tea. Fished all afternoon at Tuross…not a thing.' James felt safe nominating the coastal village a few miles further north. He was unknown there, and he could claim to have been alone on any of its vast surrounding beaches and waterways, a good 70 kilometres north of the scene of the crime.

The man turned and gave James his receipt. 'What bait were you using?' he asked, apparently interested.

'Pippies,' James lied. 'Couldn't find any worms.'

'Next time, try these,' the man said, taking a small plastic packet from a shelf and handing it to James. There was some sort of imitation crustacean inside. 'Soft plastics…everybody swears by them these days…never fail,' the man insisted.

James knew about soft plastics, that they were no match for live beach worms, and that the man was trying to make a sale. But he was delighted to be involved in a conversation that the garage man might be able to recall should he be asked by the police. Time for some more 'belt and braces'. 'Yes…okay… I'll take them and give them a try,' he enthused. 'And could you let me have that big box of chocolates.' He pointed it out on a shelf. 'Better take something back for the wife, eh!…keep the peace.' He grinned, and laughed weakly. His hand went to his pocket. 'I'll pay for those with cash.' He hoped this thoughtfulness would be remembered.

Fifteen minutes later he was driving into Narooma, coming from the north, across the bridge. In spite of the things he had done that day and the things he still needed to do, he was, as always, distracted by the scenery. He couldn't help slowing down to admire it. Such beauty demanded it.

On both sides of the bridge, Wagonga's turquoise water stretched away and merged into verdant forest. To the west, Gulaga Mountain sat like a mother hen, wrapping its protective wings around the town. To the east, the river, the boardwalk, the promise of surf and sand. Everywhere – the sun. A daily joy. The reason for today. He was still concentrating on this justification when he continued driving down the main street, parked in mid-town outside the fishing tackle shop, and walked into the police station.

A trim young woman, who looked as though she should still be at school, sat at the reception desk. At least, James assumed she was sitting, she looked so diminutive compared to Nicky. A dazzling white smile and a warm, enthusiastic 'Hi' greeted him, making him feel like her boyfriend come to take her to the pictures.

James swallowed and cleared his dry throat. 'Hello. Is constable Ricci in today, I have something to give to him.' He held up a parcel containing his book 'Ogling France'. He had signed it and gift-wrapped it in a flowery paper he thought would appeal to Nicky's mother. What better alibi than to appear relaxed in a police station on the day of the crime, to pass on an expected present to your friend, the policeman.

The policewoman looked at the parcel. 'He's not in today, back on Monday,' she said, not taking her eyes off the parcel. A slightly nervous smile twitched across her lips. James took the opportunity. 'Don't worry,' he declared. 'It's not a bomb. I'm not a terrorist.' He produced his biggest grin.

'No!…No!…It's not that,' she blurted, still smiling. 'I know you're not a terrorist…well…I don't know…but… It's the wrapping…it's so feminine. Are you sure it's for Nicky?'

James decided to use the situation to his advantage. The more they joked together the better his alibi. 'Don't tell me I've blown his cover,' he said seriously. 'I assumed he came out years ago. Nobody hides their preferences these days.'

'You're having me on,' the policewoman laughed, a touch of uncertainty lingering in her voice.

'Yes, I am,' James grinned. 'Sorry…couldn't resist.' He offered the parcel to her. 'It's for his mother. A birthday present. It's a book…'

'Oh! Are you the writer fella,' she interrupted, taking the book from him. 'He mentioned meeting you, said you were a good laugh.'

'That's me,' James beamed. 'Laugh a minute Ogle.'

'Is that your name, Ogle? Are you any relation…'

'Don't you start,' James pleaded.

'Pardon?'

'Sorry…it's a long story. Ask Nicky when you see him. Look, I'll have to go…things to do before the shops shut. It's been nice meeting you. Tell Nicky I've signed it, and I'll see him around, probably on the golf course. Thanks very much.' He turned to make his way out. Better not to overdo the familiarity; better to appear pleasant, but routinely busy.

'I'll see that he gets it on Monday,' she smiled. 'Nice meeting you too.'

It couldn't have gone better, James decided, as he stepped out into the sunshine and breathed the proverbial sigh of relief. *Mission accomplished.* He felt the tension of the day start to leave his body.

He walked a few paces then stopped at the kerbside, waiting to cross the road to his car parked outside the fishing tackle shop. He was concentrating on the passing cars when a familiar voice came from behind him. 'Let you out have they?'

He turned to find Dennis, one of his table tennis oppos, passing by, grinning under the shade of his ever-present pork-pie hat. 'Just took the cuffs off,' James got in quickly, as he watched Dennis walk on.

Dennis half turned and raised his voice. 'See you tonight, mate.'

James forgave himself for forgetting that Friday night was table tennis night in the golf club. Usually, it was one of the highlights of his week, and only a traumatic day like today could have made him forget. Now that he was aware again, he was delighted. Not only would it take his mind off the day's events, it would also provide yet another innocent input to his 'day of normal routine', and an excuse for leaving it late to phone the police about Elaine's non return. His run of luck was continuing. Before crossing the road, he walked along to the newsagent and did something he had never done before. He bought a lotto ticket.

The golf club's free minibus dropped him outside his house at 10.35pm. Normally, he got home about nine o'clock, not bothering to stay on for a drink, but tonight he had stayed longer in order to delay his phone call.

It had been a good night as usual. All the table tennis regulars had been there – Dennis, Kaye, Narelle, Jim, Ken and a couple of holidaymakers – Gary and Enid from Sydney. Having played the game at a high level in his younger days, James had been pleasantly surprised to find that the small town of Narooma was home to two state veteran champions and one national veterans champion. Their games together could be fast and furious, and were always played in a competitive but friendly manner, and provided great fun and exercise. The location on the top floor of the golf club provided superb views over the golf course, the ocean, up the coast, and out to Montague Island.

While admiring the view, in between games, James had been joined by Gary who, like many, came to Narooma for the fishing. He told James that he was desperate to move to Narooma now that he was retired, but Enid wouldn't because she wanted to be near the family in Sydney. He spoke with real bitterness in his voice, and had the defeated look of the tamed male. It was a very familiar story. James had almost suggested his solution to Gary, but thought better of it; Gary didn't look the murdering type, he seemed to have lost his spirit. The encounter had boosted James's morale. He was strong. He had asserted himself. He had bent the bars and escaped.

As he had expected, playing table tennis had taken his mind off the events of the day, but now that he was back home, pacing the floor, wondering when precisely to phone the police, he was waiting for some reaction to kick in. He felt he should be thinking great philosophical thoughts about the meaning of life and death, about life with Elaine in particular; at the very least having some positive thoughts about her – an epitaph. But what was the point? The deed was done. Nothing he said, felt or thought could make a jot of difference. Life went on. Elaine was dead. Long live his plan. He wasn't being cold or evil, he was being true to his own fatalistic understanding of the fragile split second of life we all occupy on this planet. Would anything on earth significantly change if Elaine had lived another split second. Of course not. He didn't believe in the butterfly effect. There was no great universal effect from this deed – just a small early vacancy.

It was 10.40pm. Elaine had been in the quicksand for approximately eight hours. High tide had come in about two hours ago. Elaine must be drowned.

He was surprised at how calmly he thought of these things. There was still no reaction kicking in. He didn't feel much at all. A lot of his reading down the years had been books on psychology and philosophy, finding human behaviour and the human condition endlessly fascinating. Now he wondered if he might be experiencing Freud's 'constancy principle' which suggests that the mind is always seeking to return to minimal stimulation and will rid itself of emotion if its equilibrium is threatened.

Dissociation was another possibility; his defence systems so busy reorganising themselves that it left no room for other emotions. Perhaps remorse or some other reaction would kick in later.

He picked up the phone at 10.45pm.

'Narooma police, Constable Molly Jones speaking.'

James recognised the voice of the young woman he had spoken to earlier. He took a second to enjoy the fact that she had such a nice traditional name. Molly probably marked the end of another

Australian name era. The Marys and Dorothys had given way to the Charlenes and Kylies, and now anybody younger than Molly seemed to have been given names taken from science fiction comic books. To gaze upon the angelic face of a curly-haired five-year-old girl, while her mother introduced her as Zanti, and her little brother as Guk, still took some getting used to.

'Ah! Hello,' James stuttered. 'It's James Ogle here. You remember I brought a book in earlier…'

'Yes, James,' came an eager voice, as always using the Christian name.

'Sorry to bother you at this time of night, Molly, but I'm really concerned about my wife. She hasn't come home yet. She went for a swim after lunch and I haven't seen her since.'

'Do you know where she went swimming?' Molly's voice had become businesslike.

'No, I don't. She never tells me. She likes to explore and find quiet places where she can sunbathe with no clothes on. I'm always nagging her about it, telling her it's not a safe thing to do, but she won't listen, she's very…stubb…' He let his voice break for effect.

'But you haven't been in the house all day, have you?' Molly pointed out. 'While you were out, she could have come home and gone out again. It's still not that late, is it?'

'I'd thought of that myself, Molly, but I've searched the house and there's no sign of her swimming costume or towel, or the dress and hat she went out in. I can't remember what she had on her feet. I know it's not very late yet, and I suppose there is a chance she has gone out somewhere, or gone somewhere straight from her swim, but it is not like her to do so. She is only here on holiday and hasn't got any friends to visit that I know of. And she doesn't go to the pubs or restaurants on her own. I'm really worried.'

'Try not to worry, James,' Molly ordered, putting her training into use, trying to sound mature and in control. 'These situations usually have a simple explanation. Look, I'll take down a few details, and I'll pass them on to the next shift. There's not much we can do in the dark. If she doesn't return by eight o'clock in the morning, give us a ring. Sergeant Spalding will be on duty then. Is that okay?'

'Yes, that's okay, Molly. There isn't much you can do now, is there. What details do you want?'

'At the moment, I'll just take down what time your wife went out, and what time you have spent in and out of the house since then. I can get all the other details later if...' Her voice trailed away as she realised what she was implying. 'Right,' she hurried on. 'You say your wife went out after lunch?'

'That's right, we both went out at the same time, about half past one. I went up to fish at Tuross. I did see Elaine turn left onto the highway, heading south. She was obviously going into town or south of it. I was at Tuross all afternoon, and came back into Narooma about...oh! whenever it was I came into your office...that was my first stop in Narooma...what was that...about 4.30?

'Yes, approximately.'

'Then I went to the supermarket for a few things, and then back home about five. I was expecting to find Elaine in the house then, but she wasn't. I made myself some tea, and then I went out to the golf club about 6.45. I go there every Friday night to a table tennis club. I was there all night playing table tennis, and got home about quarter of an hour ago. I've been searching the house for her things ever since.'

There was a short pause, presumably while Molly completed her notes, then, 'Okay, James, I've got all that and I'll pass it on.' Molly was trying to maintain an upbeat tone. 'You won't forget to phone us if she turns up, will you?'

'Let's hope I'm doing that in the very near future,' James replied in a suitably sincere tone. 'And thanks for your help, Molly.'

Molly signed off with the ubiquitous 'No worries'.

James put the phone down and walked out onto the deck. The air was still warm. Millions of stars momentarily took him out of his own miniature world. The bellbirds were silent, but the cicadas had taken over. Had he thought of everything? Or were his worries just about to begin?

Chapter 15

Sergeant Spalding was not what James had expected. Nicky must have been referring to his personality rather than his competence when he had described him so colourfully. Compared to Nicky he was dour and drab, a man whose age and waist measurement were in the late forties, whose jowly face bore the hangdog look of those experienced in dealing with the worst of humanity. (James knew that even a beautiful, harmonious place like Narooma was not free of crime. The local paper told of some drug use among the young, illegal taking of fish and gastropods, and the occasional burglary and drunken behaviour.) But the sergeant was also thorough and courteous. He was one of the old school. He actually called him Mr Ogle.

After James had phoned him at eight o'clock the good sergeant had immediately driven to James's house and had searched the house and double-checked his statement to Molly. By nine o'clock he was sitting out on the deck sharing a coffee, filling in written details while asking James a multitude of questions, against a background of tinkling bellbirds. The parrots had flown off when they realised they were not going to be fed, but Kooky remained, sharing their table, staring at nothing, unaware of the drama that humans create for themselves.

James had slept surprisingly well, needing an alarm to arouse him early enough to wash down his car. He had paid particular attention to the tyres in case they had picked up something that could be traced to where it had stood, beside Elaine's car. After that he had rubbed his eyes until they looked puffy and sore, and he hadn't shaved. He had also trampled on his clothes to crease them, then put them back on, hoping to indicate that he had sat or lay about in them all night.

He was aware, however, that his unkempt appearance might not register any significance with a man who had never seen him before, and who was used to the heedless appearance of the laid-back people of Narooma. In a weary voice he told the sergeant he hadn't been able to sleep or eat any breakfast, though a bowl and plate in the dishwasher told another story.

The sergeant asked him for a recent photograph of Elaine. James managed to find the newspaper cutting showing Elaine winning the fashion parade at Moruya races. He suggested that the sergeant might get the original from the Narooma News office. This also reminded him to delete the photographs he had taken on Big Worm Beach.

When the sergeant asked him if there could be any reason for Elaine not to have returned home, such as a domestic argument or family problem, James had been prepared. He openly admitted that theirs was not a close relationship, citing their long time spent apart because of his work as the main reason. This admittance would make him appear honest, and, anyway, they could find this out simply by questioning friends and relatives in the U.K. should they need to. If he pretended they were close and they found to the contrary, then that would throw suspicion on him. But he counter balanced his admittance by stating that they had been on very good terms recently, that there had been no arguments, and that he was unaware of any family problems, all of whom were in the U.K. anyway.

The sergeant completed his notes then told James he would be instigating an immediate search. Between them they agreed it was very unlikely that Elaine would have travelled far just for a swim and sunbathe, though her requirement to be naked might extend the area. They agreed that a search for her car between Bateman's Bay to the north and Tathra to the south should cover the likely area, and that the emphasis should be on the south since James had seen her car setting off in that direction. He didn't know the number of her car, but was able to give the make and model and hire company name.

Sergeant Spalding explained that he would be calling on assistance from police stations along the coast and, should the car be found near a beach, he had the ability to call on the assistance of coastal patrol vessels, shark-spotting planes and commercial fish-spotting planes. He would of course consult with James before doing this, and keep him informed at all times.

James thanked him profusely and told him that he would also go out searching, he couldn't bear to sit doing nothing. He was starting to enjoy this acting business.

The sergeant suggested that James would be wiser to stay at home near the phone, but it was up to him. He checked his notes to see if he had recorded James's mobile number, then he shook hands and departed. He hadn't said 'no worries'.

The only searching James did after the sergeant left was for the soap he had dropped on the shower floor. After a leisurely shower and a fresh coffee he ambled into his office, intent on doing some work. But after staring at the computer screen for a few minutes he realised that he couldn't concentrate. He suddenly felt heavy and lethargic, in mind as well as body, as though he had done the Times crossword while running a marathon. The stress of yesterday's events was finally taking its toll.

He switched off the computer and returned to his bed. He lay on his back, arms and legs spreadeagled, did some deep breathing to expel the tension, then closed his eyes and let nature take its course.

Two hours later the bedside telephone woke him up. A salesman started his spiel about how much money James could save if he switched phone companies. James cut him off mid-sentence. He sat on the edge of the bed and blinked his eyes and shook his head; he felt a bit better.

A light lunch out on the deck, with Kooky for company, and he felt ready for some sort of moderate activity. He wanted to go to Cemetry Beach to see if Claire was there, but that was out of the question for numerous reasons. Instead he decided to play safe. He had told the sergeant he would be going searching, so that is what he would pretend to do.

He drove his car south to Handkerchief Beach and spent an hour or so walking its length, close to the dunes where someone might choose to sunbathe. Then he drove south again to Mystery Bay and repeated the exercise. As always he enjoyed the walking and was glad to find that his mind gradually went into that trance-like state that all long-distance walkers recognise.

At the end of the afternoon, physically tired, he returned home, surprised that he had received no calls on his mobile all afternoon. There were no messages on the answer machine either. Clearly, Sergeant Spalding's searchers had found nothing. He found this worrying. Why had they not spotted Elaine's car? He was sure it would be seen by experienced searchers looking for a car. He decided to phone in, ask how the search was going, play the anxious husband again.

'Narooma police, Constable Molly…'

'Hello Molly, it's James Ogle here. I take it you know about my meeting with Sergeant Spalding this morning. He said he was going to start a search for my wife. I presume you have nothing to report yet.'

'No, sorry James, I'm afraid we haven't. Her tone was more apologetic than necessary, he thought. 'We've had quite a lot of officers on the northern search, but unfortunately there was a serious crash on the Princes Highway down near Bega, so most of their officers were engaged with that. Hopefully, tomorrow they will be able to release some to help with the southern search. We will let you know as soon as we find…'

'Thanks Molly, I know you will…I'm sure you are doing your best…I just needed to know the phone was working okay…just had to do something…you know.' *Russell Crowe eat your heart out.*

'I understand, James,' she said with touching sincerity.

She would have made a good Nicole Kidman.

'I was out all afternoon myself,' James offered dolefully. 'Looked all around Handkerchief Beach and Mystery Bay…nothing of course. I'm going to have an early night and start again in the morning…just thought I'd give you a ring…goodnight Molly.' He hung up quickly, before she could reply. He wanted to leave her with an impression of someone consumed with anxiety and perhaps slightly confused as a result. He had said 'goodnight' deliberately, as if he was on his way to bed. It was just late afternoon.

At least he had an explanation for the non-discovery of Elaine's car. The police in the south had been busy with other things. Hopefully, they would find it and Elaine tomorrow; the sooner the better.

He poured himself a gin and tonic and took it out onto the deck. He was greeted by the sun, brightening his world and his spirits, though the height of the hill behind his house meant that the sun would soon disappear. Already shadows were spreading into the forest canopy. But it would be an hour or so before they crept down to the beach, and so he was able to sit and watch a handful of surfers make the most of another beautiful evening. The encroaching shadows made the beach and sea look brighter than usual, as though lit by floodlights.

When he found himself sitting in shadow, feeling a drop in temperature, James retreated to the house. Here he rustled up a microwave meal from some leftovers in the fridge, accompanied by a glass of chardonnay.

After dinner he put out some food for the birds and did one or two other inescapable domestic chores. Finally he moved to the lounge, where he stared vacantly through the window in the direction of the ocean. He was at a loose end. Although he was physically tired, it was far too early for bed. Suddenly, his mind clicked back into gear again and he found himself reliving yesterday's traumatic events. Elaine's despairing cries started to replay over and over.

He needed distraction. Work was out of the question; it was too much effort. And reading, for once, seemed to be too much trouble. It was Saturday night, television's night of light dross, perhaps that might fit the bill. He would give it a try.

He armed himself with a bottle of whisky and a glass, sat in his favourite armchair, and pressed the remote. It had been years since he had subjected himself to so-called 'light entertainment', since he had found at a fairly early age that he was not entertained by it. He was entertained (using the word in one of its many proper senses – i.e. 'the action of occupying a person's attention agreeably') mostly by learning something he didn't already know, through the medium of books, radio or television. What he saw as television's 'forced trivial entertainment', immediately recognisable by bright colours, screaming studio audiences and shouting hosts, left him cold. He could, however, spend an agreeable half hour watching good comedy, whether of the situation or stand-up type. Good comedians and comedy writers should be awarded more recognition, he felt, since they contributed greatly to the well being of people. Half an hour with Rowan Atkinson and you could cancel your appointment with the psychiatrist. Did not the old hierarchies recognise this by appointing court jesters? The Royals still appointed a poet laureate; why not bring back the court jester, this time voted for by the people, and ceremonially crowned on a new public holiday given over to the celebration of laughter.

The comedy fare on James's television was notable by its absence. Saturday night did not appear to be comedy night. However, by switching through the channels at frequent intervals he did manage to find a few things that held his attention for a while, and therefore served their purpose. In fact, he found himself having to admit that, compared to the stuff that went out on day-time television, during which watching somebody put up a shelf or dice some carrots was a highlight, Saturday night was an improvement. As he switched, so he poured, and by the end of the night he was suitably drunk.

Hazily, he made his way to the bedroom and soon he had himself tucked in, waiting for his brain to bring down the shutters. Half an hour later his eyes were still closed but his head was spinning; he wasn't sure whether it was caused by the alcohol or stress or both. His brain wouldn't let him rest. It seemed intent on asking the same questions over and over again, questions he had already asked himself a hundred times. Perhaps, now that the deed was actually done, now that the questions were no longer hypothetical, it was wondering if the answers might be different. How had he become a killer? Were his actions evil or unnatural? Were we civilised creatures who occasionally experienced atavism, or were we wild animals who had invented civilisation to try to stop our destructive impulses? Both seemed to be true. Had not conflict and tribal war been seen as the norm until recently? Had not the few invented laws to stop the many killing each other? But, equally, had not the many been led to killing by the few? The constant was the killing – the survival of the fittest, the basic law of nature. Civilisation and the rule of law had brought long periods of peace in recent times. But this had been *between* peoples, not *within* them. Their basic animal instincts could not be changed by mere rules. Suppressed yes, changed no. Along with taxes, suppression was the main tool of civilisation. Was there much sign of vital life in the average city street? Were not most people dull-eyed and disinterested, the look seen in a caged animal? Did they not *really* want to take a knife to their boss, mate immediately with those they found attractive?

All he had done was free himself from suppression for a while, give vent to his atavistic self. What he had done was natural, not evil.

He had temporarily stepped out of his civilised straightjacket. Now he would tie it back on again and attempt to fool those who enforced the rules of civilisation.

His brain churned like a washing machine, questions and thoughts tumbling around in a whirlpool of alcohol.

Chapter 16

A noise in the far distance? Is it in his dream? Getting louder. Insistent. A phone. It's a telephone! His arm went sideways and found it as he propped himself up on his elbow and glanced at his watch. Twenty past ten. 'James Ogle,' he croaked into the mouthpiece.

'Sergeant Spalding here, Mr Ogle.' His voice sounded pensive. 'How are you this morning?'

'Not too bad,' James lied, while he eased himself into a sitting position on the edge of the bed and wished himself alert.

'I've got some news for you,' the sergeant said quietly. He paused for a while, letting his tone take effect. Clearly he used this tactic to prepare people for bad news. 'A patrol from Bega station have just rang in to say they believe they have found Mrs Ogle's car...'

'Where?' James shouted urgently, his actor's hat back on.

'Just off the coast road between Bermagui and Tathra...'

'You mean in a lay-by?'

'No, off the shoulder, under some trees.'

'What on earth was she doing...are you sure it's her car?' James was getting into the swing of things, wakening up quickly, but he was dying for a coffee.

'Yes we're certain. We checked with the hire company. But just for the record we would like you to come down and confirm it, if you feel up to it. Have you got a spare set of keys?'

'Er...no,' James stuttered. 'I mean yes I'll come down, but I haven't got a spare set of keys.'

'No worries, we'll get a set from the hire company, or we'll find another way in if we have to. Can you come to Narooma station and then follow me down there. And in the meantime can you start to think of any reason why she would be in that neck of the woods. There doesn't appear to be a beach along that stretch of road so it doesn't look as though she went swimming.'

'Right, I'll be along as soon as I can, Sergeant, but frankly I've just got out of bed…didn't get to sleep until late…so…'

'Take your time, Mr Ogle. Have some breakfast. I'm going to start calling in a full-scale search party from all the coastal stations, so I have plenty to do. Just come when you are ready.'

What a thoughtful chap, James thought, starting to feel slightly guilty at putting such a good man to so much trouble. 'Thanks, Sergeant, I'll be along as soon as I can,' he repeated with sincerity.

Once again, in order to appear desperately anxious, he didn't wash or shave or comb his hair, and he put on the same crumpled clothes. He gulped down a mug of strong coffee, grabbed a banana and was on his way in ten minutes. He arrived breathlessly at the police station, a sliver of banana strategically hanging from the side of his mouth.

A young constable he hadn't met before was at reception. He took one look at James and shouted over his shoulder, 'Mr Ogle's here, Sarge.'

Sergeant Spalding appeared in the doorway behind the reception desk, still talking to someone in that office. 'And see if Nowra can spare anybody…let me know.' He turned towards James. 'Thanks for coming down, Mr Ogle…shall we go.'

James followed him out, both pausing to put on their sunglasses as they stepped onto the street. James crossed the road, got into his car and waited while the sergeant turned his car around and roared away.

Sergeant Spalding was obviously used to driving fast, and James had to pay more attention than usual to keep up. However, his speed didn't stop him from enjoying Mahler's majestic third symphony as they flashed between tall trees, swept along deep, grass-filled valleys, crossed rumbling timber bridges spanning lakes adorned with birds, slowed through Bermagui, and hugged the beach-blessed coast road, matching the roar of the Pacific with their engines. The symphony's inimitable final movement, which seemed to encompass *everything known to man,* was coming to its incredible celebratory finale when they slowed down for the sharp left-hander. James switched off his C.D., and prepared to play his role.

Five police cars were parked under the trees, close to Elaine's. Only one policeman was visible. James followed the sergeant and parked beside him. Here was another stroke of luck. If, in the unlikely event that the police came to suspect him, and it led to a thorough inspection of his car, any speck of material found on the tyres, that might have incriminated him by linking him to this place, could no longer do so.

He jumped out of his car, slamming the door behind him, and ran across the tile-hard ground to Elaine's car, apparently hyperactive with anxiety. The commotion started the tree cicada's engines, and sheltering flies joined in. The warm air buzzed and hummed. He walked around the car quickly, fussily, peering through its windows, knowingly trying the locked doors.

Sergeant Spalding arrived at his side. 'It is her car, isn't it?' he said quietly.

'Yes...yes,' James stammered. 'I just don't understand it...what on earth is it doing here.' He shook his head for emphasis.

'You can't think of a single reason why Mrs Ogle's car should be in this vicinity?' the sergeant asked formally.

'No,' James said definitively. 'She said she was going swimming as usual. I haven't seen a beach for the last three miles. We're inland a bit here, aren't we?'

'We're about 1 kilometre from the coast here.'

'And are there any beaches on this stretch?' James asked innocently. 'Is there any access to them from here?'

Sergeant Spalding waved at some flies that were pestering his right ear, catching his sunglasses with the tips of his fingers. He shuffled them back into position, then eased his hat back slightly. 'The locals reckon there are one or two small beaches at the foot of cliffs… they've seen them from helicopters…but as far as they know there is no normal access to them. There are no roads or trails or footpaths. Nobody comes here to go swimming or anything else. Why would they when there are so many miles of accessible empty beaches all around?'

James shook his head again. 'It just doesn't make sense, does it?'

'I don't like asking this, Mr Ogle,' the sergeant said hesitantly. 'But do you think she might have been meeting somebody? You did say your relationship wasn't very close. Perhaps she has been telling you she is going swimming and then…'

'I don't think so,' James said in a slow and studied manner, bringing his hand to his cheek, apparently letting the suggestion run through his mind. 'I think I would have known. But let's face it, Sergeant, I'm passed the age of being certain about anything, as I'm sure you are.'

James was keen to get him off this tack. He wanted him and his searchers to find the beach as soon as possible. 'I wonder if there *is* a way from here to one of those beaches you mentioned. Perhaps she saw somebody else with swimming gear stop here and head into the bush,' he suggested. 'Perhaps she followed them. Where are your men searching?'

The sergeant seemed taken aback at being questioned himself. 'Yes, we have thought of that possibility, Mr Ogle,' he said coldly. 'I have eight men in there spread out over half a k, all moving from the highway towards the coast. Two more are coming from Nowra this afternoon.'

James decided to push harder, emphasise his concern. 'No disrespect, Sergeant, but shouldn't we be having a detective inspector involved by now.'

As expected, the sergeant was not amused. 'This isn't London, Mr Ogle,' he squeezed through gritted teeth. 'This is small-town Australia. I am following our laid-down procedures. We are in a period of risk assessment now. When we come up with more definite...'

'I've got to help,' James interrupted dramatically, making a sudden move towards the bush. Behind the drama he was calculating how he might be able to lead them to the gorge without being suspected of prior knowledge.

'No...come back, Mr Ogle,' the sergeant shouted. 'You can't go in there...come back.'

James trudged back, looking irritated. 'What's the problem?'

'I know you want to help,' the sergeant started gently. 'It's only natural. But, unfortunately, as far as we are concerned, until we know better, we have to treat this area as a possible crime scene. Anything found in this area, any evidence, has to be found by the police, otherwise it would be inadmissible. Do you understand? If, for example, you had murdered your wife in there, you might want to return to pick up something you had left behind, or drop something to implicate somebody else. You are free to search anywhere else, but not here at the moment.'

'Yes, I see,' James said as calmly as he could. 'Obviously I hadn't thought of that...I was just keen to...' He had been shocked to hear the sergeant talking along those lines, even as an example, and he guessed it was one of the sergeant's tricks to stimulate a reaction. There had been no need to personalise the example like he did. He must not underestimate this experienced sergeant.

The sergeant was speaking quietly to him. 'Now, let's just do what you came down to do. Let's just make absolutely certain this is your wife's car. Constable, over here.' As the constable approached, the sergeant explained. 'We haven't been able to get a key from the hire company yet, so the constable is going to open the car without one. Is that okay with you?'

'Yes,' James agreed wearily, glad to get back on safe ground. He took his glasses off and rubbed between his eyes as though tired and stressed. Automatically, he slapped at something that had landed on his bare knee.

The constable moved to the driver's door and did something James couldn't see. He opened the door, leaned in and James heard all the door catches click open.

'After you,' the sergeant invited.

James leaned in the passenger side and opened the glove compartment. He took out a full packet of Elaine's brand of cigarettes, and some documents relating to the hire of the car in Elaine's name. He handed them to the sergeant. Then he moved to the boot, where he found Elaine's light waterproof jacket, which she always carried in case of showers. He held it up. 'All Elaine's,' he said plainly, and let his head drop in what he thought was a suitably dejected pose.

'Right...thankyou, Mr Ogle,' the sergeant said quietly. 'Now, is there anything in the car that belongs to you or that you want to take away with you?'

James shook his head slowly, while continuing to stare at the ground.

'Try not to get too despondent,' the sergeant said comfortingly. 'I've seen a few situations like this, and they never turned out as bad as they looked at the start. She'll turn up somewhere. There'll be a simple explanation eventually. I would suggest you go home and do some more thinking, and if you come up with anything that could possibly explain her absence, however trivial, let me know. And, if you feel you must go out searching yourself, please take your mobile, and please let me know where you have searched, and of course, if you have found anything. I will be having this car examined by forensics here, and then towed away for further examination. I'll inform the car hire company and ask them to suspend their hire charges while it is in our custody. If you need access to it for any reason, you will have to go through me.'

James nodded without lifting his head. 'Yes…thankyou, Sergeant,' he said resignedly. 'I'm sure you are doing your best. I'll do what you say…' And he trudged off, head down, hoping he wasn't overdoing the scolded sheepdog look.

On his return to Narooma he drove down to the Cemetry headland, walked to the cliff edge, and using his binoculars tried to spot Claire on Cemetry Beach. The beach was empty and there didn't appear to be anything coloured hanging on the picket fence outside the beach house, though he couldn't be absolutely certain at such a distance. It was possible, therefore, that Claire was inside the beach house on her own. But even if she was, he wouldn't go down to meet her. To get away with his crime he reckoned he had to be one step ahead of the police at all times, to assume worst case scenarios. At this moment he was assuming he was being watched by the police; a very unlikely scenario at such an early stage, but he was taking no chances. If they were watching, they would assume he was searching for his wife. All he had been hoping for was nothing more than a glimpse of Claire; he really was becoming a sad lovesick case.

Returning home, he took a belated shower but didn't shave, put on some clean clothes, relaxed, poured himself a beer, and did what most Australians did at every opportunity – switched on the television to watch their national cricket team take on the latest touring side.

All going to plan so far.

Chapter 17

The following morning, having had no contact from Sergeant Spalding since he left him yesterday afternoon, James decided to spend time on his manuscript. He wanted to finish the book as soon as possible, get it out of the way so that he could start a new life in Narooma free of all previous connections, considerations and necessities. He wanted it in the publisher's hands within the next two months. This meant finishing his present stint of writing up his previous New South Wales travel notes, then visiting the town of Eden re the whale story, the Snowy Mountains re the hydroelectric story, and writing those visits up within the next few weeks. He would also have to allow for a short trip back to England to tidy up his and Elaine's business affairs and organise property caretakers.

After breakfast on the deck, shared as usual with the rising sun and his ornithological pals, he moved into his office. As he sat waiting for the computer to boot up he wondered at what point he should contact Jonathan to tell him his mother was missing. Thinking again about possible police suspicion, he decided it was too early to contact Jonathan. It could be taken as an indication that he already knew the outcome of the search. And, ordinarily, people would try not to worry relatives without definite news or a longer missing period.

His screen lit up, and after checking his emails, again containing a gentle push from his agent, he started to work. Under the heading '*A Foreign Country*' he wrote:

This is my third visit to this fascinating and unique country, and although this book is specifically about the state of New South Wales,

I think it is time to digress slightly and talk about Australia in its entirety, particularly about its 'foreignness'.

Prior to my first visit I, like thousands of other Brits, assumed that for all the known differences in size, landscape, and climate between Britain and Australia, to all intents and purposes it would essentially be Britain in the sun. After all wasn't it colonised by the British, with a political system based on Westminster. Didn't they talk the same language, play cricket, and drive on the same side of the road.

It comes as a bit of a shock, therefore, to find yourself in a country that not only looks foreign, but, as you get to know it, is just as culturally foreign as many others you have visited.

The foreign look comes not only from the sun-kissed landscape, but also from the architecture. With so much land to spare, a typical small town will have a preponderance of large, single-storey detached houses (bungalows) with overhanging roofs to keep the sun out, verandas or decks for outside living, large gardens – the back one always known as the backyard, and ample garage space for off-road parking. The town will be spreadeagled over a wide area, with lots of open spaces, sports grounds and open-air swimming pools, the suburban roads being two to three times wider than in Britain. The general appearance is more like California than Kent.

Tour the country and you will find the distances and speed limits displayed in kilometres, not miles, and you may pass through time zones. It is illegal to park 'facing the oncoming traffic', i.e. your vehicle must be parked facing the way you are travelling. You can find three different speed limits within a suburban mile.

New, modern hotels are the same as everywhere else, but old hotels, usually the largest building in town and covered in wrought-iron decoration, are known as 'pubs'. In the cities they rarely offer accommodation, while in the country their accommodation is very basic and cheap. Most tourists stay in modern motels or in cabins on caravan sites.

Stop for a beer and you will need to learn a new language. You cannot order a pint or a half. Depending on which state you are in you will need to order a stubby, a glass, a butcher, a beer, a pot, a schooner, a handle, a middie, or a 10-ounce. All are different volumes of drink. The beer itself is always of the lager type and always chilled. As a result there is little taste, but lots of strength with an average alcohol content between 4 and 5%.

There is a marked contrast between the fast-moving, modern-looking cities and the slow-moving, old-looking rural communities, where community spirit and conservative values predominate.

Very large, lavishly appointed, social clubs, with hundreds of members, dominate the entertainment and leisure scene. Massive bars, restaurants serving cheap food, wall-to-wall television sets showing sport on which you can place a bet, and an army of flashy poker machines tell of a people who are much more socially minded than in Britain, who object to paying a lot when eating out, and who love gambling.

Sport plays a major part in daily life with active participation from childhood to the grave. If you are a football fan you will be disappointed because it has a minor status in Australia, the dominant sports being that brutish wrestling match called Rugby League and their own unique game of Australian Rules, also known as 'Footy'. This is played on a pitch the size of an English county, and while it looks like fun to play, suffers from the same weaknesses as basketball in that you need to be 7-foot tall to play it, and the scores are so frequent they become routine rather than exciting, games ending with scores in the hundreds. Cricket, swimming, golf and sea angling are all very popular. However, perhaps surprisingly, statistics show that more time and money is devoted by Australians to artistic pursuits than to sporting ones.

I could write a separate book on the complexities of Australian politics and the results of those complexities, but I will try to limit myself to a few salient observations. Although the main central government – the Federal Government – formed in 1901 and situated in the purpose-built city of Canberra, follows the principles of Westminster, its powers are still quite limited. The six states have refused to give up their independent status and each, therefore, still has its own government complete with a premier and a full ministerial team. This means that in the country there are seven health ministers, seven education ministers, seven attorney-generals etc. etc., all passing their own separate laws and competing with each other and with central government. The result is typically seen in the twin towns of Albury-Wadonga, each on either side of a state border, where the hundreds of differing laws mean that residents keep crossing over to take advantage of the laws they favour.

With a further level of government at local council level, Australia seems to be overburdened with bureaucracy and in a permanent state of electioneering, with government terms lasting only three years. Voting is also complicated due to a preferential system where each candidate has to be listed in order of preference.

The extent, complexities and inefficiencies of the laws passed by so young a country has to be experienced to be believed. From notices telling you precisely how many metres you may walk your dog on a beach, excluding when there is an 'R' in the month, to a seven-volume taxation bible, the bureaucrat's work is everywhere to be found. If you are unfortunate enough to come in contact with any of their public service departments, such as immigration, taxation, health service etc., you will receive a different answer to the same question depending on the clerk behind the desk or in the call centre, and the state or country you are in. It is little wonder that only 20 million people have found their way to these shores while 200 million arrived in America. One suspects that millions gave up on the paperwork.

Having said all that, politics and bureaucracy are also a nightmare in most other countries, and in Australia they are a price worth paying for the joy of living in such a beautiful, sun-blessed country.

It is in the natural world that Australia's foreignness is truly emphasised. Seven hundred species of eucalyptus trees, kangaroos, duck-billed platypuses, crocodiles, snakes, parrots are all a far cry from oak and ash and sparrows, starlings, foxes and deer. A whole new world of...

The telephone on his desk extension was ringing. James swivelled his chair and picked it up. 'James Ogle,' he sighed with practised weariness.

'Sergeant Spalding here, Mr Ogle.' There was a notable pause before he continued – some bad news was on its way. 'I think you should prepare yourself for some bad news, Mr Ogle.' He paused again, allowing James time to respond. James didn't reply. 'We have found some women's items on a beach, and a hat in the sea. They fit the description you gave us of what your wife was wearing and carrying…'

'Where?' James gasped anxiously. 'Which beach?' They haven't found her body? It's on the same beach; they couldn't have missed it. They haven't mentioned quicksand? Where is her body? It must have washed out to sea. Damn!

'It's a beach close to where your wife's car was parked. We found access to it through a narrow break in the cliff rock…'

'How the hell could Elaine have known about that?'

'That's a question we have been asking, Mr Ogle, but before we get into a telephone discussion, we need you to come down to formally identify the items. Do you feel up to driving yourself down? If not, I'll send somebody to pick you up.'

'I'm okay,' James sighed. 'I'll manage.'

'Right, thanks Mr Ogle. I'm on the beach at the moment. I'll meet you where we parked last time, and I'll lead you from there. Any problems give me a ring on my mobile. I gave you the number.'

'Yes…I'll bring it with me…I'll be down as soon as I can.'

James put the phone down, saved his work onto his back-up C.D., switched off the computer and walked through to the kitchen. He made himself a strong coffee, and while drinking it changed into some crumpled clothes, smeared a little butter on his hair, ruffled it, and checked his unshaven look in the mirror. He would rub his eyes to make them look puffed and sore when he got close to his destination.

Things had not gone according to plan. Without a body he would have to wait to sell the properties. He had anticipated that possibility, but it still annoyed. The consolation was that without a body it would be very difficult for the police to instigate a murder enquiry. At least they had found her swimming gear and her hat; they now had cause to believe she had gone missing from that beach, and the presence of quicksands would add to the probability that she had met her death there. Surely they would eventually sign an affidavit to that effect.

James took another look at himself in the mirror. *This is it,* he said to himself. *The show is on the road. There is no turning back. Will you be able to cope?* he asked himself. *Yes,* he told himself confidently, finding himself narrowing his eyes in a Clint Eastwood expression, aided by his unshaven jaw. He tried the sardonic sneer.

What was he doing? This wasn't a movie; this was real life and death. He turned away from the mirror and rebuked himself. He must not become complacent; he must stay alert, stay ahead of the game.

Sergeant Spalding looked hot and bothered when James met him at the appointed place; he was not built for bush and beach walking. He greeted James in a perfunctory manner, and immediately led the way into the forest. On entering the gorge, James raised his voice. 'I can't believe Elaine came through here on her own. She was not that adventurous. She must have come with someone, or followed someone.'

Sergeant Spalding turned to answer him, catching his shoulder on a small, prickly shrub that had made a crack in the rock face its home. 'Fu...' he shouted, feeling his shoulder for leftover spines. He had

194

stopped walking and looked quite weary. 'You'll have to forgive me, Mr Ogle. I'm having one of those days. Everything that can go wrong is going wrong today. I won't bore you with the details.'

James felt sorry for him. Hadn't we all had such days? Then his survival instinct cut in. Was the sergeant telling the truth, or was he play-acting to put James off guard? James would assume the latter; he had come to respect the sergeant's capabilities. He would stay on guard.

'We have come to the same conclusion,' the sergeant continued at last. 'None of the local officers helping with the search had known about this access to this beach. None of them had ever been on this beach, though, as I said before, some had seen it from a helicopter. It would be extremely unlikely for your wife to have found this place on her own.' As he said this, he shifted his head and looked James straight in the eyes. It was a look that had the weight of his long experience behind it, one that said 'I always suspect the spouse', that was accusatory, intimidating, searching.

The sergeant had served him a fast one, but James, his mind operating at table-tennis speed, stepped back and took the pace off the delivery with calm control. He was careful not to blink, and assumed a look of serious thoughtfulness, indicating that the sergeant's searching look had not registered with him because he was too busy thinking of other possibilities. 'It's completely baffling isn't it, Sergeant,' he said eventually, returning the sergeant's gaze with wide-eyed innocence. 'I still have to go with the idea that she followed somebody. I can't believe that she had a pre-arranged meeting here.'

Sergeant Spalding dropped his gaze, turned and continued walking through the gorge. *Spalding – 0 Ogle – 1*, James thought as he followed dutifully.

On arrival at the beach, James glanced to his right and, shielding his eyes from the glare of the sun, noticed a policeman standing in the general vicinity of the rocks where the surfboards were located, and another close to the quicksand area. He turned left, following the sergeant, and found another constable standing beside the rocks where he had placed Elaine's things. They appeared to be lying exactly where he had put them.

James glanced questioningly at the sergeant, who nodded, and James made a hurried dive for Elaine's bag. Kneeling in the sand, with anxiety written all over his face, James took out her towel and then her yellow swimming costume. He cuddled this to his cheek for a long time, as though in fond remembrance, and then raised it to his nose. He looked up, pitifully, at Sergeant Spalding, and nodded slowly. 'They're hers,' he whispered resignedly. 'The costume is slightly damp and smells of salt water. She must have had a swim here...' He let his voice trail off for effect.

'And there are no other clothes here,' the sergeant added. 'It looks as though she had a swim, then changed back into her normal clothes. What happened after that is the mystery. If she intended coming back for them, then she has probably met with an accident preventing her from doing so, or, I'm afraid, we have to consider foul play. If she left them there deliberately, then she may have had a plan to disappear on purpose, with or without an accomplice, either for a short time or a long time. There are many alternatives to consider, Mr Ogle, and I will be raising our risk assessment category to medium to high, and this means that a detective inspector will be called in as supervising officer, though I will probably remain as your main point of contact. We will be making enquiries at all the doctors and hospitals in the area in case she has been admitted recently, and then move on to financial institutions to see if she has withdrawn money, and then possibly get the media involved. After that, we will start contacting her relatives in the U.K. to see if she has contacted them recently, and to see if they have any idea why she might choose to disappear. You might want to prepare them for our call. Have you any questions?'

James looked suitably shocked and dazed. He shook his head slowly. 'No...no...that all seems...alright...'

'Right!' the sergeant said abruptly, turning to the constable standing close by. 'Bag up these items and get them to forensics a.s.a.p. See if they can come up with a time when they were last immersed in sea water. An educated guess would be better than nothing. Now, let's get off this beach quickly.'

He started to march away, James struggling to keep up. When they reached the entry point to the gorge, Sergeant Spalding waved to the other two policemen, indicating that they should follow him off the beach. He didn't wait for them, but forged ahead, urgency in his stride.

James was puzzled and not a little worried. Spalding had made no mention of the quicksand or the surfboards, yet clearly he was aware of them. And why was he calling his men away, and why was there so few of them? Surely they would have increased their search numbers after finding Elaine's clothes?

When they arrived back at their cars James decided to probe a little, hopefully without raising suspicion. 'I hope you don't mind me asking, Sergeant,' he started meekly, 'but why are you bringing your men off the beach? Should you not be intensifying your search now that you have found Elaine's clothes?' He avoided eye contact with the sergeant, and awaited his blunt reply.

Sergeant Spalding, now red in the face from his exertions through the forest, leaned back on the bonnet of his car, crossed his arms, let out a deep breath, and hesitated before he said, 'That's a reasonable supposition, Mr Ogle, but in this instance there are other factors we have to consider.'

'Such as?' James queried gently, surprised at the sergeant's calm reply.

'I am not at liberty to say, Mr Ogle. Police procedures must be...'

James leapt in, 'Please don't talk to me about procedures, Sergeant. My wife has disappeared. Have I not the right to ask that everything is being done to find her? Have I not the right to ask you what steps you are taking to do that, to query what seems to me to be, if anything, a lack of police procedure? I ask again, why are you withdrawing your men?' Not bad at all – attack the best form of defence.

Sergeant Spalding uncrossed his arms and stood up straight. It was clear from his body language that he did not like his authority questioned. Again, James waited for the blast. Again, he was surprised. 'Look,' the sergeant said evenly, obviously restraining himself, 'I can understand your concern. Believe me I have seen a number of these situations; I know how stressful they are. All I can say is that we found things on the beach that didn't belong to your wife. We need to know who they belong to. We have left them there and intend to watch the area to see if their owner returns.'

'What things?' James shouted, almost hysterically. 'You don't mean weapons…'

Sergeant Spalding took a step forward and raised his hands in a 'calm down' manner. 'No…no, we didn't find weapons…nothing like that. They are everyday objects, but we need to find their owner for obvious reasons. 'To eliminate them from our enquiries' is the usual expression.'

James let out a sigh. 'God, this is awful. Why can't you just tell me what you found instead of letting my imagination run away.'

'I have already told you too much, Mr Ogle,' the sergeant insisted. 'You must not forget that until Mrs Ogle is found this is classed as a crime scene and all information gleaned here must be kept confidential.'

James felt that he had pushed as far as he dare. He assumed the sergeant's men had found the surfboards. It was sensible to stake out the place to see if the owner returned. If they did eventually trace them to David, that would lead them on a long and fruitless chase, he hoped. But he couldn't discount the faint possibility that they had also found the line, hook and sinker he had left in the sea. Surely, however, it would be impossible to prove that they belonged to him.

The sergeant had not mentioned finding the quicksand, but no doubt that was just more information he was duty bound to keep quiet about. Once the stakeout was over, James expected the authorities would infest the beach and the surrounding area with DANGER warning signs, thus spoiling more of the natural landscape. James felt regret that he would be responsible for this and for spoiling the Yuin men's fishing spot.

He moved to his car and started to open the door. 'I'll leave you to it, Sergeant,' he said apologetically. 'I'm sorry if I…I don't doubt your competence…I just needed to know…'

'That's alright, Mr Ogle,' Sergeant Spalding smiled. 'All in a day's work, as they say.'

James got into his car and wound down the windows to let the hot air out. He was about to wind them up when the sergeant stepped forward and leaned down to speak to him, one hand resting on the warm car roof, unknowingly ending the life of a small spider that had lowered itself on the finest of threads from the tree above.

'They tell me you are a bit of a beach fisherman, Mr Ogle,' he said friendlily, a slight smile pushing back his hanging jowls, a bead of sweat about to drop from his aquiline nose.

Immediately, James was on guard. 'A bit would accurately describe my fishing prowess, Sergeant,' he replied cordially, waiting for the thrust after the feint.

'I've just taken it up,' the sergeant smiled. 'Coming up for retirement soon…need a hobby that keeps me out the wife's way. I'm not catching much though. When would you say was the best time to go beach fishing, morning or evening?'

Not the thrust I was expecting, James thought, assuming the sergeant was going to question him about the tackle they had found in the sea. 'Well, I just follow the general consensus, which is that you follow the tides, not the time of day. Most beach fishermen, myself included, fish about one hour before high tide, and one or two hours after.'

The smile left Sergeant Spalding's face. 'On the afternoon of your wife's disappearance, your statement says you were at Tuross, fishing all afternoon. On that afternoon the tide was low. Why would you be fishing at low tide on that particular day, Mr Ogle, when you normally fish at high tide?'

Here was the thrust. James smiled knowingly, and spoke calmly. 'I'm impressed, Sergeant. You are very thorough. But it is not necessary to play tricks on me to find out the answer to your questions. Simply ask me directly and I will tell you anything you want to know. You seem intent on trying to catch me out for some reason. I assume it is because you see me as possibly being involved in my wife's disappearance. I know you are only doing your job, but I can assure you, you are wasting your time with me.

'I suppose it does look a bit strange fishing at low tide, but the fact is that a couple of weeks ago I came across an article in a fishing magazine which was all about giving fishing at low tide a go. The gist of it was that when the high tide recedes, some fish species, including the whiting that I fish for, don't go out with the tide, but stay behind in the deep gutters left by the wave action. They lie there in concentrated numbers, waiting for the high tide to return, making them an easy target. If you are lucky enough to find one of these gutters, the fishing can be excellent, it said. I thought I'd give it a go. I did not know my wife was going to go missing on that day, did I? That is merely coincidental.'

'And was the fishing excellent, Mr Ogle? The garage proprietor at Bodalla where you stopped for petrol said that you had caught nothing.'

'My, you have been busy, Sergeant. And so soon.'

'We need to strike while the trail is hot, Mr Ogle.'

'I am surprised the garage man remembers me…anyway, he is quite right, I caught absolutely nothing. I obviously wasn't lucky enough to come across one of those gutters. The article said it was always an outside chance, which is why, I suppose, most people keep on fishing at high tide.'

'And what was the name of this magazine?' Sergeant Spalding was not backing off.

'You don't give up, do you, Sergeant,' James said patronisingly. He had prepared for this question coming up, and had the magazine in his desk at home ready to back him up. But for now he thought it best to appear vague about it. If not, it might reveal that he had an alibi already prepared. 'Oh, I can't remember,' he said dismissively. 'There's lots of 'em, and they all sound pretty much the same.'

'Can you remember who wrote the article?' the sergeant persisted.

James put his head back and closed his eyes, as though in thought. 'Now, I think I might be able to remember that,' he said studiously. 'I've seen him on television fishing programmes. It's a Greek-sounding name…Rob…that's it…Rob…Paxanos, or something like that.'

Sergeant Spalding was starting to look a bit deflated. Clearly, he also knew about one of fishing's well-known television presenters, Rob Paxevanos. 'Have you still got the magazine, Mr Ogle?' he asked in a more subdued tone.

'I'm sure I'll have it somewhere,' James replied brightly, staring up at the sergeant, who had started to straighten up and back away. 'I rarely throw out fishing magazines. I'm always referring back to them. There is so much to learn, isn't there, Sergeant.'

Sergeant Spalding turned away quickly and gestured to one of the constables to join him. James guessed that his expression was thunderous as he addressed the constable. 'I want you to escort Mr Ogle back to his house and take possession of a fishing magazine that Mr Ogle will give you. Keep it in a safe place until I get back.'

The constable acknowledged the order with a brief 'Sarge' and moved towards his car. Sergeant Spalding turned back to face James.

'I'll be in touch, Mr Ogle,' he said flatly, and walked away before James could reply.

James closed his windows and started his engine, thought of revving up and leaving the sergeant in a cloud of dust, then controlled himself. A man consumed with worry wouldn't do such a thing. He moved away slowly and quietly, the constable's car following too closely, like an animal sniffing his exhaust.

As he got underway and settled into the journey, James realised that the 'thorough' sergeant had not asked him the obvious question – 'Can you prove that you were on the beach at Tuross all that afternoon'. Perhaps he was saving it for later when it became apparent that Elaine was not going to show up, when suspected foul play was the official line, and when a detective inspector was calling the shots. It seemed to James that the sergeant had already overstepped his remit. Surely it was his job to search, not to question. And to be doing it so early, even before a body had been found, was surely not normal procedure. It was as if he was trying to prove himself or impress his colleagues. Maybe that was why Nicky Ricci had spoken so disdainfully about him, maybe he always overstepped the mark into other people's territory, thus making himself unpopular. No doubt there was some kind of political machination behind it, all organisations suffered from them. Whatever the cause, James decided to raise the question of Sergeant Spalding's early and persistent questioning of him with the new detective inspector; again defending himself by attacking.

Back home, James invited the constable in, offered him a cold drink, and invited him to follow him as he walked around the house pretending to search for the magazine. After an appropriate interval he went into his office and 'found' the magazine in his desk drawer, making suitable exclamations. He presented it to the constable, resisting the temptation to make a witty comment about Sergeant Spalding learning from it, and watched as the constable left with his prize.

While in the office, he switched on the computer and re-read the chapter he had written that morning. Entitled 'A Foreign Country', it now seemed to him to be bitty, somewhat disjointed and generally of poor quality. Clearly he had not been functioning properly when he wrote it. It would need a complete overhaul. He would tackle it in the morning; there was cricket to watch and beer to drink for the rest of this eventful day.

Chapter 18

'Jonathan.' Hello, it's James. How are you?'

'Ah! James, hello. I'm fine, just fine. I was just settling down to watch the local derby. Arsenal are playing Chelsea tonight – up the Gunners.'

He sounded as though he had been drinking, though not excessively. Jonathan did nothing excessively. James was phoning him just after breakfast, using the kitchen extension. In London it would be approaching 8pm.

Like most men they didn't contact each other very often, but when they did they were usually pleased to hear from each other. It was a typical masculine relationship without need of the constant contact and reassurance that women sought. They had nothing in common except Elaine – wife and mother – but they saw no reason to introduce their differences into their infrequent get-togethers. Their relationship was played on neutral ground and both were content with a draw.

James hesitated before he spoke again. How do you tell a doting, sophomoric son that his mother is missing? 'You might want to switch the T.V. off,' he began quietly. 'I'm afraid I have some worrying news.'

Jonathan did not reply, presumably waiting for James to continue. James had been dreading this part of the plan, but now that Spalding had said the police would be contacting relatives he could delay no longer. 'It's your mother, Jonathan. She has gone missing. Three days ago she went out for her usual swim but didn't come back. I assumed there would be some innocent explanation but informed the police just in case. Now they have found her swimming gear on a remote beach, but there is still no sign of her.'

'God!' Jonathan breathed down the line, then waited for James to continue.

James went on to tell him the full story from the perspective of an anxious husband, reassuring Jonathan that the local police were doing everything possible, and that there was no need for him to come out to Narooma, it would serve no purpose. With his actor's mask firmly in place he went on to ask Jonathan if he could think of any reason why his mother might *choose* to disappear. Jonathan reassured him that he was 'not aware of any situation in my mother's life that would lead to that conclusion'. Clearly, his bureau-speak had now overflowed into his everyday conversation.

James eventually came to the main point of his call. 'I'm sorry to bring this up at this time, Jonathan, but I think it would serve us both well if we thought ahead. If, God forbid, something has happened to your mother there are many practical considerations to be taken into account. As you know I've been away from England for almost a year now, so I'm not up to speed with your mother's business and property affairs, and we haven't discussed them since she came out here…'

'Don't worry, James,' Jonathan intervened. 'Before she left she gave me a full scenario on all her portfolios and asked me to oversee operations while she was absent. I interface weekly with her shop manager and regularly monitor her property managers. I believe I have developed sustainable relationships with all of them and am now playing a key strategic role. My considered view is that her mission statements are being fulfilled and all incoming revenue opportunities are being maximised. My overall analysis is that her various portfolios are all operating successfully, although she might want to consider developing more sophisticated evaluation frameworks. I had a long phone interface with her last week and she seemed happy with everything I reported to her.'

James had been cringing while listening. To hear the beautiful English language used in this way was anathema to him. This jargon was the refuge of fools trying to hide their inadequacies. Which was precisely why Jonathan used it so much. He had never been able to cope with stressful situations – walking away from them rather than tackling them – or alternatively, hiding behind jargon and bluff rather than admit he couldn't cope. To use such a plethora of jargon in this instance indicated to James that he was in big strife. 'Come on, Jonathan,' James said reassuringly. 'You can be honest with me. You don't have to impress me – I'm not your mother. You have nothing to prove to me. Come on, tell me, what is the true situation?'

A sigh of resignation came down the phone, then Jonathan's voice followed, speaking quickly as though hurrying to unburden himself. 'Well to tell you the truth I've been having trouble with a couple of the property agents, and Mother's shop accountant. They all know Mother is away, and they don't seem to be willing to share information with me. I didn't mention it to Mother because I didn't want to spoil her holiday.'

'Do you think there are any specific problems?' James asked, hoping that the answer would be no.

'Well...I don't know, James...*that* is the problem. They could be hiding things from me, from Mother, or they could be just asserting their egos against their boss's son. I just don't know.'

'Hmm,' James mused. 'While the cat's away, eh!' He had always had a soft spot for Jonathan. Ever since he had stood aside and said nothing while the poor little rotund bugger had been packed away to that dreadful private school, and then watched his painful progress through it without interfering on his behalf, he had felt guilty, and with the guilt came sympathy, and, occasionally, the need to make up for his omissions. 'Look, Jonathan, don't you worry. You just concentrate on your own job. I'll get over as soon as I can. It shouldn't be long now; this book is nearly finished. I'll throw my weight about a bit…get them back in line.' He actually wanted to get over there as soon as possible to talk to his solicitor about the length of time he needed to wait before selling his share of the two jointly-owned properties, and to say hello/farewell to his parents, agent, publisher and a few friends, and generally tidy up his affairs before returning to Narooma to semi-retire.

'Thanks, James, but I should be able to manage,' Jonathan replied. 'I'm quite used to performing in a multi-tasking environment.'

James's knuckles tightened on the phone. If he heard another word of jargon coming through it he would have to smash it. Either Jonathan was now incapable of talking any other way or he had had more alcohol than James imagined. *Probably needs it, poor bastard.*

James decided to finish the conversation. Not only was the jargon driving him mad, but his feelings of guilt, and sympathy for Jonathan, were starting to come to the surface. He couldn't afford to let emotion take over, he had to stay detached and in control. 'Jonathan,' he said in a sympathetic tone, 'I'm really sorry to bring you such worrying news. Let us hope our fears are unfounded, that there is an innocent explanation, and your mother turns up with it very shortly. I will, of course, keep you up to date on a daily basis. Don't hesitate to phone or text or email whenever you need to. We have to support each other through this. Alright, Jonathan…?' An emotional wobble had crept into his voice and he stopped speaking. This time he wasn't acting.

Jonathan seemed to reciprocate. 'Yes…alright James…thanks for…' The phone went dead.

James stared questioningly at it, then replaced it on its wall-mounted cradle. He had not been surprised by his own vulnerability to emotion – he was not an insensitive monster – and, obviously, Jonathan had been affected as well. The phone rang, shocking him. His heart was thumping when he picked it up. Recovering quickly, he prepared himself for Spalding's baritone voice, but was relieved to hear the pleasant tenor of Nicky Ricci speaking in a quiet, almost reverential tone, 'G'day Jim…just thought I'd give ya a ring…see how ya cowpin…sorry to hear about ya missus, mite. Me and Molly's howldin the fort whoil Spaldin' and his mob are out lookin' for her. Ya mast be worried sick, mite. Anythin' I can do, you let me know, mite…'

James sighed. He was sorry that good people like Nicky had become involved, but he had to continue with his charade. 'Thanks for ringing, Nicky,' he said dejectedly. 'I appreciate it. I am worried sick, but I have to hope that she'll turn up eventually…I have to keep hoping…' He did his usual fade-out for effect.

'She will, mite, she will,' Nicky insisted. 'She's probably gone to… Oh! Jees, sorry mite…I was gowin to mike a jowk there…oim not very good at this koind of thing.'

'Don't apologise, Nicky. I'm really pleased you rang; it was very thoughtful of you. And if I do think of anything you can help me with I will get in touch. And please thank Molly and all the rest of your staff for their help; it is really appreciated. And, of course, Sergeant Spalding, he really is working so hard.' If there had been a station dog James would have thanked that as well – he was on a roll.

'Okay, mite…thanks…now you tike care.' And he was gone. Another typically abrupt ending to a short male conversation.

James replaced the phone and started to move from the kitchen to his office. As he did, still thinking about the conversation with Jonathan and a myriad of other matters, he realised he was not capable of concentrating on reshaping and improving the work he had done yesterday. He changed direction and made his way out onto the deck.

Kooky was perched on the handrail and cocked his head to one side as James sat down at the table and stared out to sea. A parrot would have looked inquisitive; Kooky still managed to look vacant.

James let the familiar sunlit scene wash over him, hoping it would have the usual soporific effect. Up to a point it did. His outer edges started to relax as the sun warmed his bare arms, and his ears took in the gentle hiss of the distant waves and the nearby tinkle of the forest bellbirds. But his inner core would not relax. It stayed tense, knotted, reflecting the busyness of his brain.

As he ran his overall plan, recent events, and future needs through his mind's computer, like a sequence of photographic slide shows, one picture suddenly popped out of the crowd. Claire! He needed to see her sooner than he had planned. It would be risky but he could not avoid it now that Spalding had said they would use the media to help find Elaine. If Claire saw an item about Elaine's disappearance in the local paper or on local television she might blunder into coming to see him. This might raise suspicion of an affair, and thus a motive, to any watching police. Even if she didn't come to see him, he still needed to tell her before she found out in the media. If he didn't, Claire would wonder why, and become suspicious herself.

Twenty minutes later he was walking along Cemetry Beach. As far as he could tell he had not been followed. There had been no strange cars in the vicinity of his house, and a convoluted detour through the town revealed no following car. Still, he was taking no chances, and as he walked along the beach he pretended to be searching among the shallow dunes which formed at the foot of the cliffs.

Previous high tides had left a few sun-bleached timbers, bird and fish skeletons, and the occasional detritus of careless humans, but the vast majority of the fine, cream-coloured sand was pristine. It gathered between his bare toes as his feet sank into its warm luxury, and slowly built up between his feet and his sandals. Occasionally he stopped to flick the sand free, pausing momentarily to take in the beauty of the place before returning to his stride.

As he approached Claire's beach house he could see a red towel hanging on the fence. A small pulse of adrenaline shot through him. She was there, but so was her minder.

When he arrived in front of the beach house he moved down to the water's edge, took off his sandals, and walked into the water, calf-deep. Head down, he ambled backwards and forwards as though he was a tourist taking a paddle, hopefully giving Claire time to notice him, careful not to lift his head to look at the beach house.

A few minutes later he thought he heard the sound of a car driving away at the back of the beach house, though he could not be sure because of the sound of the waves. He found himself holding his breath and hoping. Time dragged very slowly, and he was about to raise his head when Claire's voice came across the sand. 'James,' she shouted, 'James.'

He lifted his head and saw her waving as she walked quickly towards him. In his hurry to meet her he rushed through the water, soaking the bottom of his shorts.

Stepping onto the beach, he just had time to pick up his sandals before she crashed into him, wrapping her arms around him in a fierce embrace, her cheek hard against his chest. This was the first time he had seen Claire openly display emotion and it took him by surprise. And it could not have happened at a worse time. If the police were watching him they would be in no doubt that they were witnessing a close relationship. Already part of his brain was thinking of a plausible story to tell them if questioned. *A friend who had suffered a recent bereavement...* He wanted to break free from her immediately and seek shelter from prying eyes, but such was the intensity of her embrace he could not bring himself to do so. Instead he dropped his sandals and wrapped both his arms gently around her and said, 'Well hello, it's nice to see you too.'

For a while they just stood holding each other, the feathered edge of the breaking waves occasionally reaching their bare feet, caressing them, tickling them. James's cheek was also being tickled, a warm breeze from the north lifting Claire's hair into his face. He didn't move. They were the only people on the beach – felt like the only people in the world.

'Are you alright?' James whispered protectively, wondering if her unusual display was a reaction to recent subjection to her husband's violence.

'I'm fine…now,' Claire whispered back, still holding him. 'I'm just glad to see you. I was beginning to think you had given up on me. You must have been busy?'

If only you knew.

James hugged her tighter, thrilled that she had missed him so much, not sure how she really felt about him until now. Ever alert, he said, 'I take it you got rid of Arnold?' (He had a habit of appointing nicknames to people whose character or appearance easily suggested them. Thus, her squat, heavily muscled minder had become 'Arnold' as in Schwarzenegger.)

Claire nodded as she released herself from his arms, but still held onto his hand. 'Yes, I've sent the big boy out to play. Shall we go and sit on the deck and have a cup of tea and play mummies and daddies.' Her slow Californian accent gave frisson to the suggestion. She started to drag him towards the beach house.

'My! Somebody is in a good mood today,' James exclaimed, as he allowed himself to be pulled along. Then he remembered his sandals and broke off temporarily to go back and retrieve them. Her light mood now made the purpose of his visit even more burdensome. Better to get it over with quickly, he decided.

As he caught up with her again, taking her hand, they looked at each other and said together, 'I've got some news.' James spoke with a frown, Claire with a smile.

'You first,' James conceded, attempting a smile. 'Yours is obviously good news.' They continued walking towards the beach house.

Claire hesitated, realising that James had bad news to announce, then said, 'It looks as if I am going to be here longer than expected. Robert has been contacted by his lawyers in the States. They have been telling him to stay away for a while. Apparently a well-known

Democrat politician has been questioning some of Robert's business activities and getting a lot of publicity. Robert won't be worried. He pays his lawyers a fortune to deal with these matters. He believes money can buy you anything. The lawyers are confident they can handle the situation, but have advised him to stay away until they have it under control, just in case. They say it could take weeks or even months. So here stands one happy lady. More time with you, more time in Narooma.'

She turned to him, smiling. But it didn't last long as she saw that James's initial smile had faded quickly. 'I don't think I want to hear your news,' she said hesitantly. 'I've never seen you look so serious.'

They arrived at the beach house, turned left onto the deck and sat on a weathered wooden bench, their backs leaning against the wall of the beach house, facing the sea. James felt relatively safe from distant binoculars here, the overhanging roof hiding them from everything but a boat at sea. He was distracted for a moment as he watched a sea eagle swoop down to land on one of the fairytale rock towers. Sensing reticence, Claire squeezed his hand to encourage him to speak.

'Elaine is missing,' he said quietly, his eyes still on the eagle.

'What?' Claire queried. It wasn't clear whether she was expressing astonishment or simply hadn't heard him; the plangorous sound of the waves could sometimes mask conversation.

He turned to her and spoke loudly. 'Elaine has disappeared.'

There was a sudden flash of excitement in Claire's eyes, an automatic, immutable reaction to his words. It died as quickly as it appeared, signalling her mind taking over from her emotions. It was replaced by a look of grave concern, apparently acknowledging the tragedy of the situation. 'Disappeared? When…are you…?'

'Four days ago,' James intervened helpfully, knowing it was a difficult announcement to respond to. 'The police are involved. They have found her swimming gear on a remote beach south of Bermagui, but so far there is no sign of Elaine.' He let his head drop as a sign of concern, but knew he couldn't overplay his anxious husband role with Claire because she was aware of his disregard for Elaine.

'Why didn't you tell me before now?' Claire pleaded. 'Maybe I could have helped…given you some support. Poor James, you must be so worried. I know you didn't get along, but after all those years together…' She didn't need to conclude.

'I couldn't phone you, could I,' James pointed out. 'We agreed never to use the phone. A long silence followed, then James said quietly, 'I don't think you realise the implications of Elaine's disappearance. I shouldn't be here now. I am putting you at risk. We are both at risk.'

Claire looked puzzled. 'I'm sorry, James, this is happening too fast. I can't think. I can't see what you are getting at?'

'It's me that should be apologising,' James said quickly. 'I might have got us both into trouble by coming here. Believe it or not, until Elaine turns up or is found, I am under suspicion. The police are treating the beach where they found her swimming gear as a crime scene, and I am not allowed to go there. It is normal police procedure, they tell me. So you see, if they see me having a meeting, a *clandestine* meeting with another woman, an attractive woman, while my wife is missing, they could easily put two and two together and come up with five. If Elaine does not turn up alive, then this meeting could be seen in a very bad light for both of us. Apart from anything else it could become public knowledge and your husband would get to know.'

'Heaven forbid,' Claire breathed, obviously mostly concerned about her husband knowing. 'So why have you come now?' she asked sharply. 'Why take the risk now?' The implications were clearly dawning on her.

'Because the police told me that they are going to use the media to help find Elaine. If you had seen the information in the media and I hadn't told you first, you would be wondering why. But, more importantly, until Elaine's disappearance is solved one way or another,

I had to let you know that it is not safe to see each other. I had to risk seeing you to tell you it is too risky to see you. I know it sounds crazy but there it is. We are dealing with the plodding hand of inflexible law procedures. If you don't bend before them they can crush you. Many an innocent person has fought that battle and lost.' He sighed and gazed out to sea.

He had been careful to include the word 'innocent'. He had even started to convince himself that he was. Elaine had brought about her own downfall by chasing her silly hat into the quicksand. He had not laid a finger on her.

Claire put her hand on top of his. 'This is awful,' she whispered sympathetically. James assumed she was referring to the fact that they couldn't see each other for a while, but he was mistaken. 'Four days is a long time to be missing,' she went on. 'I know when these things happen in the States the police start to get very worried after 48 hours. But hey! You know how things are in some parts of the States. I expect it is different here… Sorry James…I'm just babbling…I don't really know what to say to comfort you…'

'I know,' James said. 'I understand. None of us know what to say to the terminally ill or at funerals – this is almost the same. I just hope we have an answer sooner rather than later. I can't imagine what it would be like never to know.' He shuffled in his seat and put his arm around Claire's shoulders. 'Anyway, let's not get prematurely morbid.'

Claire snuggled closer. 'What do we do now?' she asked miserably. 'Here I was all happy to be seeing more of you and now this.' At last she was thinking of herself. James noticed that she had not asked a single question about the detailed circumstances of Elaine's disappearance. She did not ask questions, she offered support. She was very special.

James was about to answer her question when he noticed that the breeze had displaced her hair, leaving her delicate neck exposed.

He could easily fall in love with that neck, that fragile column of life, the soft, smooth curve where it disappeared under the shoulder of her dress. He had a thing about necks. He had even fallen in love with giraffe's necks in Africa – how graceful they were. He wanted to kiss Claire's neck, feel its softness, taste its saltiness, perhaps smell a hint of fading perfume. But he didn't. That way lay frustration. She took her marriage vows seriously, and though her iniquitous husband did not deserve it, she would not be unfaithful to him.

'I'm afraid we have no choice, Claire. We must keep our distance until this thing comes to a conclusion,' he said dejectedly.

'This thing?'

'Sorry, I didn't mean to sound so insensitive. I'm tired, I haven't been sleeping.' Lying had now become easy to James.

'You started a sentence with 'sorry' again,' Claire joked, trying to recover from her perceived mistake. 'It's me that's insensitive. Here you are, tired out with worry and I am picking you up on semantics. I am so sorry, dear.'

This was the first time Claire had used an endearment. James felt as if he had received a gold medal at the Olympics. Such power in a single word.

'You called me 'dear',' he smiled. 'You are turning into a loose woman.'

'Shall I not do it again, then?'

'You must never stop. I am addicted already.'

Claire turned her head and looked away from him, out to sea. She sat like that for a long time, her back an implacable barrier between them. Was she putting the brakes on, reminding him that they had no future together, or was she blushing, or weeping, or confused, or unhappy, or happy, or… James was desperate to know.

She raised in him a deep yearning. He was as sure as anyone can be that they were meant for each other. Even to be thinking in such clichéd terms confirmed that something significant was happening between them. The pragmatic, cynical shield that had served him well over most of his adult life was continuing to weaken each time he met her. It was as if her warm femininity was softening it, like a horseshoe in the blacksmith's flames. He felt himself changing in her presence, becoming exposed, heating up, becoming malleable, losing his tensile strength. He knew he was inexorably succumbing to the oldest flame in the world.

With a teenager's romanticism, he saw them sitting together on this beach for the rest of their days; sharing their love of nature, music, art, literature and all that Narooma had to offer. How to accomplish this was too difficult to contemplate at this juncture, but he knew he would be putting all of his mental energy into its achievement once his release from Elaine was complete.

He had already fantasised about the possibilities. He would become the hero and challenge her violent husband to a fight to the death, or once he had money from the sale of the properties, hire a professional killer, a hit man. The latter seemed to carry more chance of success. He had seen a lot of gangster films as well as westerns, and he saw himself sitting on a high stool at a hotel bar sliding an envelope containing 50,000 dollars along to a man looking suspiciously like Lee Marvin. Next he saw the papers announcing the death by shooting of well-known billionaire businessman Robert Capaldi…

'Tell me, James,' Claire said without turning. 'You have travelled the world for 30 years. You must have seen many special places. Why does this place feel so extra special? I can't quite put my finger on it. I have seen equally beautiful places, I even live in one, yet there is some quality here that is different. Can *you* explain it?'

James was surprised to be directed back into routine conversation. He had been half expecting to be drawn into a deep and meaningful discussion about their relationship. Perhaps this was Claire's way of avoiding talking about such things, about the unachievable.

He thought for a while, then said, 'It's very difficult to analyse such a subjective thing, but I'll give it a try. Perhaps the quality we find appealing here is unpretentiousness, everyday ordinariness. Perhaps it is also what is *not* here that appeals. Narooma is a beautiful, small Australian town in an extraordinary setting. Its beauty has not fallen foul of the developers. It has not become the playground of the rich, the place to be seen. It is unspoiled. The people who live here love it, and want to keep it that way. The way they feel fills the air we breathe. Perhaps it is the quality of their lives that we can feel. Add to that, wonderful wildlife, and a perfect climate, and it becomes an unbeatable package. How's that?'

'I guess that about covers it,' Claire said, turning to look at him affectionately. 'You have explained it well and I concur with your analysis. In other words – I just love the damned place.'

James laughed. 'Me too.'

There was a pressing silence as they both looked out to sea, holding hands, happy to be sharing their love of Narooma, sad to be denying their love of each other.

'What will you do if Elaine doesn't return?'

Although Claire had asked the question quietly, James could sense the urgency behind it. He replied in an equally quiet tone. 'I will have to return to the U.K. to sort out our affairs. I was going to tell you that I need to go soon anyway. Elaine's son has not been coping with her business while she has been here, and I need to see my publisher and agent, this current book is coming to an end…'

'I'd forgotten about her son…poor boy. Is he coming over?'

'No, I've told him there is no point at the moment, there is nothing he can do. He can't cope with difficult situations. He is better off staying at home, and I think he realises that, he is not pushing to come over.'

'I see,' Claire sighed. Then she asked quietly, 'What will you do about Narooma?' There was almost a tremor in her voice.

'Nothing can change that,' James said firmly. I will return and continue to live here…and I'll wait for your return every summer.'

'No you won't!' Claire said emphatically. 'Everybody makes promises like that. They're called holiday promises. You will meet someone else while I am away, and you will be embarrassed when I come back next summer. And you will avoid Cemetry Beach. Don't worry, I will not be expecting anything else. You will be free and I will still be married.'

'Leave him.'

'He will kill me.'

'We will go to Dzhibkhalantu.'

'Where's that?'

'Outer Mongolia. You can't find places you can't spell, I've learned that on my travels.'

'There is no hiding place from Robert Capaldi, believe me. Anyway, it will be too cold.'

'I will keep you warm.'

'We are being silly.'

'I love you.'

'James…'

But James could stand no more, and leapt to his feet, and ran from the beach house and along the beach towards the town, and for the first time saw no beauty anywhere because of the tears in his eyes.

218

Chapter 19

He had a hangover the next morning. It wasn't caused by drink, though he had ended the night with a few, but by the lack of it, by dehydration, lack of food, and exhaustion.

After leaving Claire at the beach house, he had jumped into his car and headed north – it could have been anywhere. He found himself at Dalmeny Beach, left his car and started to walk along the beach towards Potato Point.

The tide was in, leaving only soft sand to walk on. The afternoon was hot with a slight breeze coming off the water. He had enjoyed worming and fishing on this beach before, but thoughts of this, or of the antics of dolphins surfing the waves a few metres away, did not enter his mind.

His mind was no longer thinking, but feeling. A procession of guilt, sympathy, frustration, concern took their turn at marching past. Each emotion tried to dominate, shouldering their competitors out of the way. His mind became a bear-garden as they fought for his attention. Eventually they fell upon each other and became a single entangled intrication, like a tight knot that could not be undone.

He trudged on, head down, breathing hard. Gradually the physical effort took over and told his mind to take a break. His mind went blank as the rhythm of the walk lulled it into submission, just as it did when he walked the mountains of Scotland in his younger days. Perhaps, unconsciously, his body had known that this is what he needed.

He arrived at a cliff face where a few perched houses marked the hamlet of Potato Point and the end of the beach. He sat on a rock close to the water's edge to cool off his feet. The unexpected shock of the water told him how hot he had become. He dipped his arms in the water, glancing at his watch. He was surprised to find that it was late afternoon. Then he remembered that the beach was 11 kilometres long and the going had been slow in the soft sand. Now he realised that his mouth and throat were bone dry and he was feeling very tired.

He shuffled up the beach and through the dunes that formed in a gap in the cliffs, until he reached an outlying house. There, knowing there was no shop in the hamlet, he begged a drink of water and some block-out lotion from a middle-aged woman he found asleep under an apple tree. She also gave him a plastic bottle full of water to take away with him, and offered him some apples, which he gracefully refused. He could not bring himself to ask her for a lift back to Dalmeny, and it clearly had not entered the woman's head that he might be without transport. So he took his leave and set off back along the beach.

Three hours later, exhausted, and with little memory of the walk, he arrived back at Dalmeny. The sky was darkening as the sun set inland, and he started to shiver as his warm skin registered the temperature change. Hardly able to bend, he climbed into his car and made his way home. Here, having topped up with more water, he took three cans of beer into the bathroom and spent the rest of the night soaking in a bath full of tepid water. He climbed into bed just after midnight, not having eaten since breakfast.

His hangover was soon dispersed with more water, then tea, and his hunger with a conveyor belt of buttered toast, the crumbs of which were eagerly pounced upon by the usual entourage of birds he shared the deck with. Kooky watched the feeding frenzy from his perch on the handrail with an expression of dazed perplexity. 'I know how you feel mate,' James found himself saying to the kookaburra, recalling the events of yesterday.

Kooky stared back blankly, like a new baby. And just like a new baby it was impossible not to talk to it. 'I said the 'L' word yesterday, Kooky,' James admitted, as though to his best friend. 'Yes, ME! And I think *you* are stupid!'

It was not that he hadn't said the 'L' word before; he had said it often over the years. 'Of course I love you, Kaari', as he farewelled Helsinki, promising to return. 'Angelita, how can you doubt that I love you', as his Spanish trip came to an end. Similar spurious outpourings had been delivered to Gabriela in Brazil, Brigitte in France and Astrid in Austria. Others had not required such enunciations.

'Trouble is, Kooky, this time I meant it.'

Now he started to wonder how Claire had taken it. She was American after all, and wasn't it the Americans who had started the trivialisation and devaluation of everything by excess and exaggeration. The special had been turned into the everyday. In their language, the ordinary had become 'awesome' and 'I love you', once a rare, considered and serious confession expressing the deepest of feelings was now simply an ending to every phone conversation. It had become just another way of saying goodbye. How the great poets would turn in their graves. They had considered love to be so precious as to be almost indescribable. Their poems about love rarely carry the actual word, its meaning is to be found hidden in their other words, like a precious stone in the ground. Yet, this very absence, this very rarity, makes your heart pound.

Claire might have taken it the American way. Had he not jumped up and ran off immediately after saying it. Now, on reflection, because he did love her in the true meaning of the word, he began to hope that she *had* taken it as 'goodbye'. He should not have burdened her with his outburst. She had enough to deal with at home, and was obviously trying desperately to keep their relationship on a 'friends only' basis.

James found it interesting that his mind was engaged in such thoughts while the grave matter of Elaine's disappearance stayed in the background. He assumed it was the escape mechanism at work again.

He swallowed the last of the tea, and started to rise from the table. He moaned as yesterday's long walk took its toll on his aching muscles, making him feel like an arthritic gorilla as he slowly straightened up. 'Thanks for listening, Kooky,' he grimaced as he took his leave.

After taking the breakfast dishes into the kitchen, he made his way to the office to check his emails. On his side desk, the telephone answering machine light was flashing. He cursed himself for forgetting to check it last night. 'You have two messages,' it announced. The first was timed at 6pm and came from Sergeant Spalding. He started by saying that he had tried to contact James earlier, both on his home phone and on his mobile, but without success, and he had also left this same message on James's mobile phone. Once again, James cursed himself. He had forgotten to take his mobile with him yesterday. He really needed to get a tighter grip on things; he was getting sloppy.

Spalding went on to report that further land searches and new sea patrols by air as well as boat had revealed nothing. Tomorrow they would be continuing their searches and also starting to involve the local media, including press, television and radio. He asked James to contact him in the morning to agree details of this before he went ahead. Finally, he informed James that a Detective Inspector Goodfellow had been assigned to the case and would no doubt want to talk to him soon. This brought James back to full adrenaline-primed attention. He needed to go through all his scenarios again, rehearse his reactions, rehearse his answers, become word perfect.

He was still thinking about this when he pressed for the second message. 'James, it's Mum...' Immediately, James knew something was wrong. Her tone said it all. She was usually so upbeat. And she rarely called him; he always called them, saved them the cost.

He listened with a sinking heart as he heard her wavering voice tell him that his Dad had collapsed while out walking, and was now in hospital, and the prognosis was not good. She gave him the hospital telephone number and the ward number, and left it at that.

She never made any demands on him. She didn't ask that he drop everything and rush home. She had always left him to make his own decisions, always been deferential because he had made a name for himself, because he was always busy with his important writing. She didn't accept it when he had told her, repeatedly, that it wasn't important, that it was just a way of making a living. She did not seem to comprehend that she and Dad were still the most important people in his life.

He slumped into his chair, his throat constricting, his eyes misting, his adrenaline dissipating. Things were piling up on him. His plans were becoming hijacked by events. Everything seemed to be happening out there, involving him, but mostly outside his control. Elaine's body had not been found; he had fallen in love with a violent billionaire's wife; he had a new detective inspector to face; he had his wife's businesses to sort out; he had to finish writing a book; he was planning his retirement; and now his father was on his deathbed. A wry smile crept across his face – he was living in a television soap opera.

However, he had no doubt what he had to do next.

'Narooma Travel, Mandy speaking, how can I help you.'

'I need an urgent flight to London, today, tomorrow at the latest. It doesn't matter what it costs. And, of course, I'll need a local flight from Moruya to Sydney.'

'Single or return?'

'Return.'

'Are you alright for passport and visa and insurance?'

'I have a British passport. Can you get me some insurance?'

'No problem. Can I have your name, address, phone number, and age please.'

Next, just in case they were able to get him a flight today, he raced around the house, checking security, emptying household bins, checking fridges and freezers. He changed into travelling clothes, feeling stifled in long trousers and socks after so long in shorts and bare feet. He started to pack a small suitcase, collecting all necessary documents, not forgetting a C.D. copy of his incomplete book.

He had left the answer machine on, not wanting to be disturbed by Spalding or Goodfellow. Now it rang, and he listened to Spalding questioning his whereabouts and why had he not contacted him to discuss the media information. If he did not hear from him within the next hour, he was going to go ahead without his approval. A similar message had been left on his mobile.

The phone rang again. It was Mandy from Narooma Travel. James grabbed it. '…we have found you a business-class flight with Qantas Airlines, leaving Sydney tonight at 2020, arriving Heathrow tomorrow at 1205. There is also a connecting Moruya/Sydney flight leaving Moruya at three o'clock this afternoon. Total price including insurance will be $7857. Do you want me to book them?'

'Yes please, Mandy. You've been a great help.' And he gave her his credit card number.

Next, he booked a taxi to pick him up at 2.15pm to take him to Moruya Airport. It was done. He had about two hours to spare before the taxi came.

He rang his parents' house. There was no reply; his mother was probably at the hospital. He told her answering machine the details of his flight. He did not ring the hospital, didn't want to interrupt, didn't believe you should until someone was getting better and happy to chat.

He emailed his agent, telling her he was on his way to London, explained the circumstances, would contact her when he had time.

He rang Dennis, told his answering machine he would not be at table tennis for a week or two, explained the reason.

He finished off his packing, remembering to include a pullover and waterproof for his arrival at Heathrow. He would pick up more warm clothes from his flat in London. He shivered at the thought of England in winter. He had arrived in winter many times before, and he always hated it – the greyness, the drabness, the stark, bare trees, the damp cold, the huddled, fast-walking people.

Briefly, he thought of quickly driving to Cemetry Beach to see if Claire was at the beach house, but decided he didn't have time. Now he was regretting that they had agreed never to phone, hadn't exchanged their phone numbers. He hoped she would not think his extended absence was deliberate, that his dramatic exit from their last meeting had been the final one, his expression of love his way of saying goodbye forever. He had to get back as soon as he could, run to reassure her. He hoped she would still be there.

With half an hour to go before the taxi arrived, he made himself a sandwich and a cup of coffee and took them out to the deck table. Kooky was not on the handrail, he was in the bush with his mate. There were no parrots in the garden. There were no surfers on the beach. Suddenly, James felt lonely and vulnerable. He thought of Mum without Dad and his eyes misted.

With a few minutes left, he took his suitcase outside, locked up the house, and walked up the hill where he had seen Valdis working in her garden. He asked her to keep an eye on the house while he was away, told her she could help herself to everything in the fridges and freezers, handed her the keys, asked her to fill the bird bath if she had time, gave her all his relevant telephone numbers, said he hoped to be back within two weeks. The taxi arrived while they were talking.

As James climbed in, he realised he should have phoned the company he had rented the house from; no doubt there would be some insurance implications. *Too bad*, he thought as the taxi pulled away. *Can't think of everything.*

On the way to Moruya airport the taxi driver stopped twice. First for some petrol in the village of Bodalla, then apologising for his forgetfulness, for some cigarettes at a garage on the outskirts of Moruya. As he pulled out of the garage, he said to James, 'Bloke behind's got the same memory as me…followed me into both garages.' James turned quickly and just caught sight of a blue saloon, parked on the forecourt, before they drove out of vision. It had looked like a Ford Falcon, quite old, a very common car. *Surely not the police. Must be a coincidence.*

At the airport terminal, a building not much bigger than the average bungalow, the taxi driver waited, engine running, while James offloaded his suitcase. In his mirror he noticed the same blue car pull up in the shade of a tree. On reflection, he didn't think it was worth another mention.

The one-hour flight to Sydney took place in a propeller-driven, Havana cigar-sized plane that flew at relatively low altitude. From his window, James was again reminded of the emptiness of the continent. Here, even though he was in Australia's most populated state, and flying along the coastline where everybody wanted to live, there was only an occasional sign of human occupation. When the plane arrived over Sydney he was shocked as always to see such a massive urban sprawl in the midst of such wildness. But the shock again turned to wonder as the plane banked in and gave him a bird's eye view of one of the most magnificent harbours in the world.

After the short bus transfer from the domestic to the international terminal, he still had three hours to wait. It was getting close to five o'clock and he owed Sergeant Spalding an explanation. He found a quiet seat and made the call on his mobile.

'You are where!' Spalding shouted. 'Did you say Sydney Airport… what the hell…'

James went on to explain about his father.

'How do I know you are telling the truth?' Spalding spluttered.

'Thanks for your sympathy, Sergeant,' James replied coldly.

'Of course, I'm sorry if it's true,' Spalding insisted, 'but I have a job to do, and in these circumstances that takes priority.'

'What circumstances?' James led him on.

'Do I have to remind you that your wife is still missing, and until her disappearance is explained, you should not be leaving the country.'

'I understand that, Sergeant,' James said calmly. 'But my priorities are not as easy to determine as yours. My wife is missing; my father is dying. Which priority would you choose, Sergeant? Do you think I want to leave the country? Do you think I don't want to help you find my wife? Do you think I want to fly 12,000 miles to watch my father die? I am sorry I haven't had time to get back to you about the media information, I have had other things on my mind.' He paused briefly, then continued, 'If you take down these telephone numbers, you will be able to contact me while I'm in England.' He read out a prepared list of all his contact numbers. 'If you do not believe me,' he went on, 'I suggest you ring the first number. It is my mother's number. However, I would prefer it if you didn't, she is 84 years old and visiting my father in hospital most of the day. She could do without hearing an Australian policeman asking if her husband is ill, or if she is lying on behalf of her son. Anyway, Sergeant, you are going to have to trust me, I am about to board the plane. I hope to be back within two weeks, and…oh…I have left my house keys with the woman in the house above mine, Valdis is her name. I would be most grateful if you could look in on her to see if she has any problems.' James heard Spalding start up again, 'I am still not…' He clicked the phone shut. He hoped he had not gone too far.

Three hours later he found himself again looking down on the harbour as an engineering miracle thrust him and his fellow passengers into the sky.

Chapter 20

He found himself sitting beside a gentile pair of 70-year-olds who introduced themselves as Harry and Janice. Everything about their appearance spoke of good health and well being, the exception being their eyes. They had a sad story to tell. Travelling business class was their 'final fling'. They were returning to what they foresaw as a 'life of misery' in England, after spending 'seven glorious years' in Australia. For inexplicable reasons, it seemed to James, both governments had conspired against them. Australia wouldn't allow them permanent status even though they had brought and spent their pensions and life savings in the country, creating jobs without taking one themselves. Worse still, Britain had not paid them any annual increase in their state pension since the day they left, this being the unbelievable standard practice for retirees in Commonwealth countries, but for no others.

The result was, fearful of ever-increasing private health insurance costs, which non-permanent Australian residents had to pay, coupled with a static pension income from Britain, they had decided, very reluctantly, to return to England simply to obtain their state pension increases.

How both governments, particularly the British, could treat pensioners in such a way was beyond their comprehension.

James offered them no comfort by observing that most politicians were self-seeking, and concerned themselves only with issues that would get them elected. He pointed out that the problems of a few thousand expatriate pensioners, a problem unknown to the general population of either country, one that did not affect them and would therefore not be an election issue, would not be a priority for the politicians.

Like James, they had lived by the sea in a large detached house. Like James, they had fished, golfed, bowled or played tennis throughout the year. They were glowing with health. For the first time in their lives they had had a new car. Now they looked forward to life in a rented flat in Ramsgate, where most of their family lived. There would be no fishing – none left; no golf – too expensive; no swimming in the sea – too cold; perhaps a few weeks of bowls in the summer, and a second-hand car. Their only consolation was renewed access to the N.H.S., a service they would almost certainly need as the climate and its consequences took their toll.

There was genuine sadness in Harry's eyes when he said, 'Our only hope now is a lottery win.'

James imagined himself in their position. He had been living the same wonderful lifestyle. Here he was on a plane to England. The thought of not being able to return to Narooma was almost unbearable. His vow to become financially self-sufficient had just become reinforced. Unlike Harry and Janice, he must not become a victim of the perverse and inexplicable decisions of politicians.

His vow was further reinforced when, half an hour later, he picked out the Qantas in-flight magazine from his seat pocket and started to read an article entitled 'The Happiest Place On Earth'. In it, a British scientific study (by New Economics Foundation) had concluded that Australia was the third happiest country in the world. Costa Rica was first, and remarkably, the rest of the top ten were all South American countries – 143 countries containing 99% of the world's population had been studied. Life expectancy, population interviews, and environmental factors had been the main factors in the study. Britain came 74th and the U.S.A. 114th. These scientifically produced facts and figures simply confirmed what James had unscientifically observed in his 30 years of globetrotting – a sunny climate and a natural environment produced happy people, providing there was no stark poverty.

He slept for large chunks of the journey, his mind demanding a break from the tensions of the last few days. So he felt refreshed, though travel scruffy, when the captain announced that they were approaching Heathrow. The captain went on with his usual approach banter including the fact that the ground temperature was eight degrees. A mass groan of displeasure swept through the plane. 'And it's mid-day. No wonder they're always whingeing,' an Aussie wag shouted as the moaning died away.

If there is anything more depressing than a city in winter in a cold climate then James has not come across it. Even its few redeeming features – its avenues of trees, its parks, have lost their charm, the trees turning into stark, spindly giants, the type that frighten children in fairy stories, while the parks look drab, dun and abandoned. Under a low, grey sky, the dirty pavements, smeared with deposits from a million begrimed vehicles, choked with their fumes, play host to rushing, swaddled people looking harassed and dejected.

In his hired car, James drove from Heathrow to his Kensington flat. He always carried a key for it, never knowing, over the years, when he might be landing back in London. It had become his routine first stop, a place to change clothes, generally freshen up. Today he hoped to have this done by mid-afternoon, then to drive on and arrive at his parents' Berkshire home by early evening.

As he drove past the harassed throngs, he noticed that the population exchange showed no sign of slowing down. In many areas of the city only the architecture and the temperature told him that he was in London, not Lagos. Over his lifetime he had watched hordes of Brits doing a 'Harry and Janice', taking their money and flying off in search of the sun. Millions had gone to live in the Mediterranean countries, others to South Africa, Florida, and Australia. Their places had been taken mostly by people without money, from poor countries. As he watched those dark skins shivering in the London cold he thought they or their forefathers must have been very desperate indeed.

He had seen the same displacement in cities around the world, making them a hodgepodge of cultures, no longer a true representative of their country; a situation, he suspected, that pleased nobody. Only outside the cities did you find the genuine heartbeat of a country. Already he was impatient to leave London behind.

It was about 2.30 when he parked his car in the basement car park, his and Elaine's allocated spaces kept free at all times, at staggering cost. The slow, jerking drive, the crowds, the greyness, the cold had taken their toll and he was feeling worn and irritable when he carried his suitcase into the lift and pressed the number 2.

It was only a few paces from the lift across the wide, carpeted corridor to his flat. He yawned as he placed the key in the lock, and hoped Elaine had left some coffee in the kitchen. He stepped into the flat hallway, and heard her voice. His heart stopped. He held his breath. He listened intently. Her voice came from the lounge at the far end of the hallway. He couldn't make out what she was saying, but there was no doubting it was Elaine's voice. As he quietly lowered his suitcase to the floor her voice stopped, but there followed immediately a burst of laughter. A woman and a man were laughing and giggling. Next came a male grunt followed by a playful female scream. She sounded as if she was being chased around the sofa. Then it went quiet.

James took a step forward, senses alert, breathing quickly, heart pounding. He tiptoed past one bedroom, then the bathroom. He paused before continuing, waiting, listening, worrying. How could Elaine have escaped the quicksand? How could she have flown home? Had she gone back to the Narooma house and taken her passport while he was out? What was he going to say to her? How could he face her? What the hell was she doing with another man in their flat? He tiptoed past the next bedroom and approached the silent lounge.

The door was ajar. Gently, he pushed it open with the tips of his fingers and stepped quietly into the lounge.

It is very instructive as well as disconcerting to come across humans copulating. When one of the humans is your dead wife and the act is taking place on your lounge floor in mid-afternoon one is entitled to be lost for words. When, eventually, they came to James's shocked mind, the words were bizarre, ridiculous, and uncomfortable. It was also comical to watch the intellectual superstars of all the earth's species totally and earnestly engaged in the favourite activity of a mindless rabbit. The lesson learned is that intellectual rigour is no match for animal instinct.

Totally absorbed in their coupling, they had not seen or heard James come in. From where he stood all he could see was the naked back, very white bottom, and un-muscled legs of a brown-haired plump man. All he could see of the woman was the bottom half of two suntanned, spreadeagled legs.

For what seemed an eternity James stood watching, undecided about what to do or say. He thought of clapping his hands together to give them a shock. He even thought of politely turning around and leaving the room until they had finished. Then he started to psyche himself up. He was an Englishman was he not, and this was his castle, and some unknown man had entered his castle, and was entering his wife, in the afternoon, on his best Persian rug. Suitably stirred into anger he took a pace forward and said firmly, 'Good afternoon.'

The number of flying limbs probably exceeded the number of shrieks and expletives, but James couldn't be sure. For a man of his girth the plump man moved surprisingly quickly, rolling and pushing himself to his feet with alacrity, revealing himself to be a red-faced Jonathan, using both hands to hide his embarrassment. The young woman beneath him, to whom James would be eternally grateful for not being Elaine, was apoplectic with fear and panic. Her inability to move gave James time to study her attributes at his leisure. She was the antithesis of Jonathan;

opposites had definitely attracted here. Tall, spare, small-breasted, short fair hair, nice pointed face, she looked like a Polish high jumper.

James's lingering gaze finally seemed to activate her, and she scrambled to her feet, a look of horror on her face. Now she was desperately trying to cover up those parts of her anatomy she had been flaunting with abandon only 30 seconds ago, and which James had already studied. She was having trouble trying to cover three items with only two hands, creating a draft as her arms switched up and down like a pair of malfunctioning windscreen wipers. Finally, her agony was over when she managed to work out that one horizontal arm could cover two breasts leaving the other hand free to hide her fair little beard, leaving James to conclude that she probably worked in the same government department as Jonathan.

Now she was turning and squinting and peering, obviously looking for the pair of glasses that sat on top of a set of clothes that had been very neatly folded and placed carefully on the sofa. Jonathan's clothes lay alongside hers, also neatly folded and placed with care. Now James was sure they came from the same department. He suspected their 'irresistible passion' had been preceded by a planning meeting in which a risk assessment form had been filled in, forward strategies and scenarios had been considered, and watches had been synchronised to ensure the accomplishment of their 'mission statements' at the same time.

James turned to Jonathan, who was still standing as though in a football player's wall, just outside the penalty area, waiting for the free kick to be taken. 'Late lunch?' James quipped.

'We're on flexi-time,' Jonathan replied seriously.

James controlled himself and said, 'That's a new name for it.'

'Oh really?' Jonathan enquired, clearing his throat. 'I've never heard it called anything else?'

James saw a chasm of misunderstanding opening up between them; no doubt it would be amusing, but he didn't have time to indulge himself today. He decided to have pity on them, to leave the room and let them get dressed. Then he remembered he had a question to ask, though by now he thought he knew the answer. 'I heard Elaine's voice?'

'That would be the answer machine,' Jonathan explained. 'We always leave it on. We get a laugh listening to mother trying to talk in a posh voice. She tries to copy her posh clients...'

'You are laughing at your mother while she is missing?' James accused convincingly.

'No!' Jonathan protested strongly. 'I'm worried sick about her, but...well...the answer machine thing has been a long-running joke...and I listen to it because I want to hear her voice. We laugh with fondness, not ridicule.'

'So this is a regular thing, then?' James snapped, pretending to be annoyed.

Jonathan looked nonplussed. 'Er...yes...I suppose so...just the last few weeks. Sorry!'

James turned and started to walk away. 'I'm going to make some coffee. Would anybody like some?'

Two 'yes pleases' followed him to the door.

'We'll have a chat after you get dressed,' he flung over his shoulder as he left the room.

Once in the kitchen he let out a great sigh. *No Elaine...what a relief! Fancy falling for the old answer machine paradox.*

He found a good supply of coffee, sugar and fresh milk, obviously brought in recently by Jonathan and ?, made three cups of coffee, and put them on a tray with sugar and milk and spoons. He went into the hall and removed his suitcase into his bedroom, sorted out some clean clothes, and used the en-suite bathroom to freshen up before returning to the kitchen. Assuming they would have had time to use the main bathroom and now be dressed, he carried the tray from the kitchen into the lounge.

They were standing side by side, almost at attention, their contrasting shapes outlined by the afternoon light coming from the window behind them. An odd couple indeed. James put the tray on the coffee table in front of the sofa.

'We are *very* sorry,' Jonathan said in a tone so sincere that James was sure they would have leapt out of the window if he had decided that was to be their punishment.

'Never mind that,' James said dismissively. 'Are you not going to introduce your girlfriend?'

Jonathan swivelled an indicative arm. 'This is Malenka,' he said almost sheepishly. 'She came over from Poland about six months ago. We work together.'

Malenka stepped forward, smiled nervously, and held out her hand. She looked even taller with her clothes and shoes on, and her glasses made her look quite bookish. James shook her hand, and asked, 'Have you ever represented your country in the high jump?'

'Er...no,' she half smiled, giggled nervously, and took a step backwards.

'Well you should have done,' James insisted. 'You are perfectly equipped to do so.'

She exchanged a puzzled glance with Jonathan, both clearly wondering if he had lost his mind.

'How come you are so suntanned?' he went on with his interrogation.

Malenka dropped her eyes guiltily, and said, 'It is not real. It is from a bottle.'

'Take note, Jonathan,' James said loudly as he turned in his direction. 'This is what you are up against. Deceit, camouflage, subterfuge. What colour will she be next week? Will she have pink hair and white skin? Will she have two tonne of shining metal piercing her white skin? Will she have had something lifted or dropped or expanded or removed? In fact, how can you be sure this *is* Malenka? This could be Maurice from Accounts who had the operation.'

As he spoke, James saw their expressions change from deep concern to smiles as they slowly realised that he was in badinage mode. 'We really are sorry,' Jonathan confirmed while still smiling.

'Please stop apologising,' James said. 'Forget it. Relax. After all, where would we be without men and women enjoying their *lunch breaks*. We wouldn't be anywhere would we. We wouldn't exist.' There was a pause, which James thought might turn out to be a pregnant one in the circumstances, while they considered his words. But they did not reply. They were, apparently, still working on it when James said, 'Let's sit down, our coffee is getting cold.'

Once seated, James went on, 'Now I am going to apologise. I am sorry for disturbing you. Had I not thought Elaine was involved I would have tiptoed away and left you to it. Frankly I can't think of a better use of an empty flat on a dreary winter's day. But why the floor for goodness sake? There are two comfortable beds to choose from. I expect you to make good use of them in the future.'

Before Jonathan could intervene with his obvious questions, James continued, 'I'm aiming to be in the country for only two weeks maximum. I have to get back to Australia as soon as possible, for obvious reasons. I'm going to my parents' house tonight and I'll probably be up there all week. Next week, I will probably need this flat at some time. I have meetings with my agent and others, and you and I, Jonathan, need to make plans about the future and your mother's businesses, based on the worst-case scenario eventuating. (He was trying to speak in a language Jonathan would understand.) I will phone you and arrange a time to suit. So if you could give your lunch breaks a miss next week, I'd be grateful. After that, the scene is all yours, folks. As far as I'm concerned you can touch base here as often as you like.'

Jonathan and Malenka turned to each other and beamed like Christian believers. They were not to know that James was planning to sell the flat at the earliest opportunity, and that, having observed that Jonathan's brain had been relocated for the time being between his legs, he would try to take advantage when sorting out Elaine's business and property affairs.

The next half hour was spent in amiable though earnest conversation, mostly about the circumstances of Elaine's disappearance and James's father's illness. Then the lovebirds checked their watches and agreed that flexi-time limits were approaching critical mode, and they took their leave with much flapping of grateful wings.

James finished his domestics, then phoned his mother. She was about to leave for the hospital and asked James to meet her there. She did not think that Dad was going to last much longer.

Chapter 21

They sat at either side of the bed, his mother holding his hand, James leaning in, touching his arm. The morphine was doing its job, his dad's eyes were closed. His mother looked tired, a resigned blankness in her kind eyes. She had been sitting like this for days.

'Most of the time he is asleep,' she explained to James when he arrived. 'But sometimes he wakes up and he is very alert and lucid. He will be pleased to see you, say his goodbye.'

James looked down at the white-haired, wrinkled head on the pillow. Here was the man who had looked after him as a child, played with him, taught him, advised him, become his best friend, his constant back-stop. Here was an eternal bond, beyond time, beyond knowledge. And now he was leaving him and James felt like a child again, and he wanted to shout and scream 'Don't go, Daddy, don't go'. He loved him so much he daren't think Hollywood thoughts, dramatic heart-tugging epitaphs. If he did he would collapse with grief. Instead, like everybody, he just sat and stared and watched him fade away, and thought that which was bearable.

After a long, mostly silent vigil, James left the ward, sought out a vending machine and brought back two cups of tea. He found his mother smiling as he handed her the cup. She nodded her head and eyes in the direction of the bed. James followed her direction. Dad was awake and propped up on an extra pillow. 'James,' he smiled, 'James,' and held out his feeble hand. His eyes were excited, energised.

James sat down and took his hand in the same movement. 'Hello Dad,' was all he could manage.

'Do me a favour, James,' his dad started hurriedly. 'Take me to Arran. Put my ashes in your golf bag and give me one last round at Blackwaterfoot. Then scatter me off the black rocks in Whiting Bay where we used to fish.' He was speaking quickly, as if he had been rehearsing this speech and needed to blurt it all out while he still could. 'Happiest days of our lives, James, happiest days. Who knows, one day I might wash up on one of your Australian beaches. Watch out for me, won't you.'

James felt his eyes filling.

'Don't be sad, James. I've been so lucky. I had good parents and a wonderful wife and you, a wonderful son…and a pretty long innings. Nothing to be sad about there, is there?' And then, speech apparently over, he closed his eyes and shrank back into the pillow, and he slept for one more hour before he was pronounced dead.

He had died with a slight smile on his face. Or was it a grimace of pain? James didn't know. What he did know was that from now on he would feel as though something solid, like an arm, had been wrenched from his body.

Two days after the funeral, James, accompanied by his mother and an ash-filled urn, arrived in Brodick on the Isle of Arran. He had, of course, been unable to refuse his father's dying wish, even though it would delay his return to Narooma, even though a round of golf in a Scottish winter was not usually to be looked forward to, or even possible. However, though he had not experienced one himself, he had heard all about Arran's mild winters; the reason, locals said, for the island being able to display a good number of palm trees and other exotic plants. It was that magical gulf stream, they said, wrapping the islands in its warm South Atlantic current.

Because of his mother's age, he had split the journey north into two days, staying overnight in a hotel on the shores of Ullswater in the Lake District, another of his dad's favourite places, and conveniently close to the M6 motorway. He had not told his mother about Elaine's disappearance, or about his wish to spend the rest of his days in Australia. These things would keep for later. He had asked her what her future plans were, and she had intimated that she would stay where she was, among people she had known for years. She reminded him that she had a sister and two brothers living close by and numerous nephews and nieces who all came to see her, and she would never be lonely or needful. This was her way, James knew, of telling him to get on with his own life and not to worry about her. He had previously checked the Australian visa situation for aged parents but found that only permanent residents could bring them in.

From Brodick they did not head north to 'Celtic-Snore', but south to a farm at Shannochie, favoured by his parents in recent years, after many years of staying at Braehead Farm in Whiting Bay and the old cottage in Blackwaterfoot where James did his early writing. They had stayed only once at 'Celtic-Snore', at James's behest, but were honest enough to say that it was too big and grand, and lacking in the atmosphere they sought, that of a typical island cottage.

It was indeed mild, the air still, the sky a light, steely grey. The coast-hugging road, passing through Lamlash and Whiting Bay was a delight as always, the palm trees doing their exotic best to warm the winter atmosphere. Within half an hour they had reached the south of the island. Here road took to the hills and looked down on fields sloping down to cliff faces, rock-strewn beaches and open sea. It was as if you had a grandstand seat on the whole world. The enormous vista of sea and sky, framed at the edges by the Scottish mainland, the Kintyre peninsula, and a distant Northern Ireland, stretched into infinity. Centre stage, out at sea, sitting like a giant pyramid on a vast, smooth sheet of glass, the extinct volcano – Ailsa Craig – claimed your awestruck eyes.

It was this spectacular view, lit by the sun until very late on long summer nights, which had finally attracted his parents to the south of the island. Here they had stayed in a cosy cottage, a converted byre, named 'Eryb' by Shannochie Farm owner, Christine McBride.

Now, she stood outside the cottage, a collie at her heels, waiting to greet them as they pulled up. His mother had phoned her, explained the circumstances, asked if they could stay for two nights only. She had kindly agreed.

Christine's greeting was warm but respectfully muted, and soon they were alone in the cottage, passing most of the evening reminiscing about their happy family holidays on the island.

A weak sun in a pale-blue sky greeted them early next morning as they made the short but spectacular drive to Blackwaterfoot. In spite of her age his mother had insisted on accompanying him around the 12-hole course, and soon they were on the first tee, the beach just beyond the left rough, out of bounds. James had brought his father's bag of clubs and had tucked the urn into one of its pockets. 'Here we go, Dad,' he said as he sent a moderate drive down the first.

Without making a conscious effort, James found himself talking to his dad at every shot, asking him which club he should take, should he chip or run, where the slope was on the green. He did not feel self-conscious or embarrassed. In between recovering her breath his mother smiled encouragingly.

After playing the famous hole called 'Crows Nest' whose green appears to be halfway up a cliff face, he stood on the tee of his dad's favourite hole. Its lofty position gave you a panoramic view of the course, the beach, the sea and Kintyre, a view of great beauty on a hot summer's day, and always memorable in any weather. It was a longish par three, the green having a drop-off to the right, lots of rough all around it, but no bunkers. After conferring with his dad, James picked out a five iron, concentrated hard and managed to hit a beauty straight at the green. Thrillingly, he saw it land just a few feet from the flag.

He was picking up his tee, thinking about how much his dad would have enjoyed the shot, when he heard his mobile ringing in one of the golf bag's pockets. He rushed to undo the zip and take it out.

The deep voice of Sergeant Spalding greeted him. They had spoken to each other almost daily since James left Australia. James had told him of his need to stay in England for his father's funeral, pretended to be checking up on Spalding's search progress, maintained his pretext of deep concern. Spalding had reported that there had been no feedback from his media announcements, but with excitement in his voice had told James of the discovery of quicksand on the beach, and his plan to obtain the latest detection-scanning machines from Sydney which would show if anything was buried within the quicksand. Two days later, James held his breath as Spalding reported that the machines had discovered the remains of two small wallabies, but nothing else. It was looking more and more likely that the sea had taken her.

Spalding's last call had been to inform him that he had been instructed to cease his enquiries, that enough local effort had been spent on the search, and that the case had now been taken out of local jurisdiction and handed over to the central N.S.W. Police Force Missing Persons Unit which coordinates all enquiries within Australia and overseas. And because Elaine was a British citizen, the British police had been informed together with the British Salvation Army Tracing Service and The Missing People Charity. The Australian Salvation Army and Red Cross Tracing Units had also been informed. He had given James the website addresses and phone numbers of all these services together with the website address of a Missing Persons Counselling Service.

James had been delighted with the news. It looked as though the case was about to become just another statistic, joining the 30,000 others who went missing each year in Australia. Why then, was Spalding phoning him again?

'Remember I told you there were some objects on that beach, and we were going to stake out the place to see if anybody turned up to claim them,' Spalding spoke quickly, excitedly.

'Yes,' James said cautiously, putting his tee in his trouser pocket.

Spalding hurried on. 'Two people turned up yesterday and we have them in custody for questioning.' He sounded very pleased with himself.

James thought he had better match Spalding's enthusiasm. 'That's brilliant, Sergeant. How did you manage that? I thought you had handed the case over?' He was not too concerned about his mother hearing such a conversation. She would assume it was something to do with his work, some research he was involved with. Anyway, she was slightly deaf and was sitting some distance away on the bench beside the tee, quietly contemplating the beautiful view. For a moment, he thought he saw her lips moving. Perhaps she was also talking to Dad.

'We have, but I asked our routine car patrols to keep their eyes open. They spotted a ute under the trees where your wife's car was found. They went into the bush and found two aborigine blokes coming out of the gorge carrying these objects.'

'What can I say?' James gushed. 'I'm really impressed. You never give up, do you. What were the objects by the way?' James had to ask, knowing Spalding was referring to the surfboards. He wondered why they would be carrying the boards through the gorge, and if the two men were David and his mate or other Yuins who also used that beach.

'Still can't tell you that.' Spalding sounded supercilious, like the boy who owned the ball.

'Have they told you anything about my wife?' James demanded anxiously, cursing himself for not asking this question sooner.

'Not yet, but we have just started questioning them. Look, I suggest you get back here as soon as possible. If these two blokes cough anything you don't want to be on the other side of the world, do you?'

Spalding was playing mind games, James thought. Clearly, he still suspected that James was responsible for his wife's disappearance, and had 'done a runner' to England, there to remain, never to return to the scene of his crime. He was using the discovery of the two men to test James again. In his mind, if James refused to come back quickly as he was suggesting, then this confirmed James's guilt. An innocent husband would want to be on hand should the men have something to reveal about his missing wife. He wasn't to know that James was desperately keen to get back to Australia at the earliest opportunity regardless of the discovery of the Yuin men.

James now saw an opportunity to take advantage of Spalding's muddled thinking, and, hopefully, to get him off his back once and for all. Once that was achieved he could take his time with all the other stuff. He needed to demonstrate to Spalding yet again that Elaine's disappearance was top of his agenda, that he was as anxious and distraught as ever.

'You are absolutely right, Sergeant,' he said condescendingly. 'I need to be there. If those two blokes have…' He paused for effect, then lowered his voice to a reverential tone. 'Tomorrow I am fulfilling my father's last wish and scattering his ashes in the sea off Scotland. After that I have inescapable duties to my mother who is with me, and other unavoidable legal responsibilities to attend to. These will take two or three days. I had intended to spend a few more days here on other personal matters, but now I will forego these and return to Narooma as soon as humanly possible. I should, therefore, be back within three to four days.'

'Oh…right…' Spalding hesitated, 'a very wise decision.' Spalding had clearly been taken aback by the reply, and had then tried to cover himself with an authoritative remark. 'Give me a ring when you get back,' he continued uncertainly, 'and I'll bring you up to date.' The phone went dead.

James wasn't sure whether Spalding had hung up or they had lost the signal. He *was* sure that Spalding would now be thinking twice about his guilt.

He walked over to his golf bag and put the phone back in the pocket. He looked about him. Here he was standing on a golf course on a Scottish island in the middle of winter, talking to his dead father, breaking off only to talk about his dead wife to a man on the other side of the planet. Even Brazilian soap operas were not this bizarre. He felt as if his life was becoming surreal. He wondered how long he was going to be able to keep all the balls in the air before one fell and exposed him.

Quickly, out of necessity, he dismissed the thought and set off in pursuit of the ball that lay on the green. He forged ahead and spent the time waiting for his mother to catch up, sizing up and practising the putt that lay ahead, a curling 9-footer. When she arrived at the green, he took his time, stroked the ball, and watched as it curled, hesitated on the lip, then toppled sideways into the hole; a birdie – always a thrill. His mother clapped her gloved hands and said, 'Well done.' She didn't enquire about his telephone conversation.

An hour later the round was over. James had enjoyed it in spite of the cold and the circumstances. It had been a journey of loving remembrance, never just a duty.

Back at the cottage he made up some lunch with supplies from Blackwaterfoot's only food shop, the owner having changed since his younger days, and then they both had an afternoon nap.

In the evening they drove to the Kildonan Hotel for dinner, and spent most of the time with more recollections of past family holidays on Arran. Later, after hurrying into the cottage out of the bitter westerly wind that buffeted the car door as James held it open for his mother, they agreed that an early night was called for.

The next morning the wind had exhausted itself and they awoke to another calm, cold, blue-sky day. After thanking Christine McBride for her hospitality, they drove up to Sannox, where James obtained the key from the caretaker and did a quick tour of 'Celtic-Snore' while his mother stayed in the car. He returned the key to the caretaker who supplied them with a cup of tea and a run-down on next summer's holiday bookings. James did not mention his future plans to sell the property, which, hopefully, would occur the following year.

Then it was back to Whiting Bay; to the black rocks, the place where, at seven years old, his father had first introduced him to the joy of fishing, where summer days were endless, where heaven existed, where young James had wanted to stay forever.

He parked the car on the grass verge, helped his mother from the car, and took the urn from the boot. Together they made their way down to the pebbly beach, which led to the black rocks. James would have liked to climb to their favourite high spot on the rocks, where a long cast used to be made, but he knew that his mother could not manage it.

There were rarely any waves on this sheltered side of the island, so he was able to guide her to the water's edge. Here they stood right alongside one of the large base rocks, touching it, inhaling its sea-weedy smell, seeing the familiar creatures that clung to it, watching the clear, gentle water lap against it.

After a while, he took hold of her arm and placed the urn in her hands. Without a word she took the lid off and immediately bent down and tipped the ashes into the water. Quickly, without a moment's glance at the dispersing ashes, she turned away and started back up the beach. James, surprised, turned and followed her and grabbed her arm to help her over the pebbles. 'Mum?'

He could feel the shaking of her body coming through her elbow; gently, like an engine ticking over. As they progressed up the beach the shaking increased, until arriving at the car she felt like a human earthquake.

He helped her into the passenger seat, then dashed round to the driver's seat. She had taken off her glasses and was leaning forward, head down, sobbing unreservedly. James was at a loss; he had never seen such emotion from his placid mother. Somehow, he felt excluded. Then he felt that he should be doing something to ease her grief. Gently, he laid the palm of his hand on her heaving back, and said, 'He said we were not to be sad, that he had been lucky…'

'Don't give me that patronising shit,' his mother shouted at the car windscreen, throwing her head back. 'Sod him…he's just a speck of fucking dust…why should I listen to a speck of fucking dust…'

'Mum!' He had never heard her swear.

'It's not just him,' she bawled. 'It's me, it's you, it's all of us… *everybody* on this beautiful planet is going to finish up like that. None of us are going to see it again, *EVER!* One day my husband is standing on those rocks looking like a Greek God, the next he's in a bloody dish. It's unbearable.'

James had his own tears now. 'It *is* unbearable, Mum,' he whispered sincerely. 'Why we all don't go screaming crazy is beyond me.'

He agreed with her, wanted to support her, give her permission to go crazy with grief, shout and swear, scream and curse, tear and smash. Momentarily, she had taken on the torment of the whole human race as well as her own, and she needed to explode. He took her in his arms and held her tightly and tried to absorb the volcanic eruptions that shook her, the lava of her anguish gushing down her ruined face.

Eventually she gave out a deep, rumbling sigh and became still. Slowly, she released herself from his arms and wiped her face with her saturated handkerchief. She squinted, looking for her glasses. James found them for her. She put them on and let her head flop back against the headrest. She was breathing deeply, eyes closed.

'Thank you, Mum,' James said quietly.

'What for?' she croaked.

'For crying for all of us.'

'I hardly ever cry,' she snivelled.

'You should do it more often. It's good for you. I cry every week.'

'Really…why?'

'For the same reasons. When I think that one day I am not going to see the sky for the next trillion years. When I think of Mozart dying so young as I listen to his music.'

'How *do* we bear it, James?' she breathed.

'Distraction,' he said. 'We distract ourselves with work and play…'

'But at night…before we sleep…I'll be alone…'

'We are all alone with our thoughts, Mum.' He was not being hard; he was being truthful; she had asked not to be patronised.

'I'm dying for a cup of tea,' she gasped. 'I'm probably dehydrated now.'

James took this as a signal that she'd had enough of profound self-exposure, and was looking to be distracted back into the refuge of mundanity. He resisted making a joke about her using the word 'dying'. 'There's a nice coffee shop in the middle of the village,' he said. 'Let's go there.'

Chapter 22

Four days later, exhausted, James lay slumped in a business-class seat, not bothering to look down on London as the plane took off. He had achieved quite a lot in that time. He had shepherded his mother through the morass of administration necessary when a partner dies. He had ensured that she was surrounded by family members, with promises of future support, though he felt sure this would have happened anyway. He had spent an evening with Jonathan going through the problems he was having with Elaine's property managers, giving him some tips on how to deal with them, promising to take up the cudgel on his return. Long telephone conversations with his agent had been fraught as he told her of his plan to retire to Australia and she tried to persuade him not to. Obviously, she was trying not to lose her share of the income his work generated. Such were her pleadings, he half promised her that he would Ogle New Zealand at some unspecified future date, and promised to deliver his current New South Wales manuscript within two months, a promise made with fingers crossed behind his back.

He had also managed to get two hours in Little Missenden's Red Lion pub with his old flatmate Simon Mathews, who had now progressed to a large detached house by the river, the fruit of writing a weekly political column in a national daily. Over the years they had kept in touch and James had watched Simon become increasingly bitter and disillusioned with the state of Britain, his columns becoming more acerbic as he got older. James always made a point of reading them on-line whenever he was abroad. They had even played a small part in his decision to retire to Australia, such was their vehement condemnation of life in Britain.

James had the advantage of his travel experiences, which had included visits to countries of unimaginable poverty, corruption, violence and injustice, and after one such visit he had promised himself that he would never again condemn the failings of his own country. However, over the years he had found it increasingly difficult to keep his promise as he witnessed or read about the political mistakes and absurdities that Simon wrote about. Even so, whenever they met, James always tried to temper Simon's rage at Britain with tales of much worse horrors abroad. Simon's usual riposte was that those countries had never ever risen from their knees, while Britain had not only risen, it had traversed the world with giant strides and set standards admired everywhere, standards that were now being allowed to dwindle and die because of a love affair with short-term money-making by men in suits, with no regard for the long-term social, moral or aesthetic consequences. He described it as enormously disappointing at best, as criminal neglect at worst.

He wrote: 'Britain's economy used to be based on the exploitation of the masses. Now it is based on the gambling of the few. For the sake of our society both systems need to be rejected.'

James had always been impressed with Simon's altruism. He hoped that he really meant it, and didn't write it just for journalistic effect.

Simon also wrote,: 'Britain is now like a shrivelled-up old colonel with blocked arteries, lying in his bed still barking out orders, unaware that his elite troops have been disbanded and are now working in call centres.'

And; 'The affluence of big business is real; that of working people an illusion based on debt. Inside small houses, pale, fat children play with their pile of electronic gadgets or watch television with their exhausted parents who both work long hours for low wages to pay for the house, car and electronic gadgets that big business (supported by the money lenders) have persuaded them to buy by propagandizing that life is not worth living without them.'

'So how does the Old Girl look to *you* after another year away,' Simon asked, always keen to get the opinion of his travelling friend.

James had been enjoying his pint of real ale, something he missed in Australia, and took another drink before answering. 'Well…I agree with virtually everything you write, but unfortunately I don't think these problems are unique to Britain. Most western countries seem to have followed this irresponsible path, and are now starting to reap the consequences. From a personal point of view what bothers me most about the Old Girl are the practical difficulties you face when trying to live your routine daily life. The housing, the roads, the towns are simply not able to cope with the modern phenomenon of mass ownership. Even the smallest towns are gridlocked, parking is an expensive nightmare, and the small houses can't contain all of today's gadgets.'

'But Australia can cope?' Simon asked plainly. There was a hint of sharpness in his voice, as though he was accusing James of desertion, having learned of his retirement plans earlier in the evening.

'Yes, Australia and America. Don't ask me what gave their pioneers the foresight to build wide roads and space their houses out, but they did. It could even have been luck or laziness, making the turning circles easier for their teams of horses and bullocks. And of course, the land was cheap and plentiful, and so the houses are much bigger than they are here. I can tell you, the effect this has on the average working person's daily life is quite significant.'

'Obviously significant enough to tempt you away from the shores of your dear old mother country,' Simon jibed.

'Well, no actually,' James contradicted. 'On their own they are not enough to tempt me away. I'm still quite fond of the Old Girl.

It's the Australian climate that tips the balance. By that I mean the coastal climate in the southern half of the continent. It's a massive attraction for me, and people like me who enjoy the outdoors, sport and wildlife. It's given me a completely new lease of life, I feel like a youngster again. Add those other things in and, frankly, there is no comparison between the quality of life in small-town Australia and small-town Britain.'

'What about big-town Australia?'

'Can't really comment…never lived in one.'

'So, is there *anything* you'll miss about the Old Girl when you settle down over there?' Simon queried.

'Absolutely,' James insisted. 'The B.B.C….the N.H.S….the variety of accents, village pubs, real ale…the highlands of the north… the Open golf championship…'

'I just can't imagine leaving London, the capital of the world, to live in barbecue-land,' Simon interjected.

'Good,' James chided. 'Leaves more space for me.'

Simon snorted, 'Well, I for one will not be joining you or any of the other mass exoduses to the sun. If it is as good as you say I would have nothing to complain about, and that's how I make my living. You do realise, don't you, that we Brits have evolved under centuries of grey skies. We have become programmed to moan about the weather and everything else we don't like. We are designed to moan. If there is nothing to moan about over there you might go mad.'

'Australia also has politicians, Simon. Need I say more?'

'Enough said. Happy moaning.'

The night had ended with a toast to friendship, the usual promises of keeping in touch, and a grinding of teeth and moistening of eyes as they embraced, then went their separate ways.

Now, as the plane levelled out high above the cold, grey blanket of England's winter sky, James stretched out and looked forward to a welcome sleep. Eyes closed, he thought of Harry and Janice and how he would feel if he had been forced to return and remain under that grey blanket. This led to the recollection of a conversation he had with a psychologist at some long-forgotten function. 'Do you know what makes humans happier than anything else?' the psychologist asked imperiously, smugly waiting to assert his knowledge.

'Sex…money…drink…setting fire to a banker's hair,' James joked, trying to deflate the smugness.

'LIGHT!' the psychologist proclaimed loudly, ignoring James's joke, and making those standing nearby spill their drinks. 'Put humans under grey clouds or in dark rooms and they tend to shrink and become miserable. Put them under a blue sky or in a light room and they thrive. We are just like plants. Have you not noticed that in England the conservatory is the most popular place in the house?'

Recalling that his chats with his Dad had always been in his parents' conservatory, James had meekly agreed, and then made an excuse to move on before he became the psychologist's involuntary sounding-board for the rest of the evening.

The loud-mouthed bastion of knowledge had been right, James thought, as he adjusted his pillow, left Harry and Janice to their unhappy fate, anticipated the sunlight of Narooma, and smiled inwardly as he drifted into sleep.

Twenty-three hours later, half of which had been spent sleeping, James was back in the Havana cigar, shielding his eyes from the morning sun, not long surfaced from its sleep in the distant, indigo depths of the Pacific Ocean. He looked down at a palette of olive-green and cerulean and turquoise and cream, as the plane followed the coastline from Sydney to Moruya. In spite of the grief he carried at the loss of his father, and the possible trouble ahead, his spirit soared. A return to this place of beauty made him feel like a child returning to his favourite seaside beach.

Flying in low over the turquoise sea just before touching down on Moruya's tiny airfield was almost worth the ticket cost alone. Stepping out, once again, into the sun, into the unspoilt arena of forest and river, he felt as if he was returning home.

Half an hour later, after renewing his acquaintance with the quiet trees and the glistening rivers and lakes, from the taxi's window, he arrived back in Narooma. Now he *knew* he had come home.

He hurried to the lounge, now stuffy with warm air, and opened the sliding patio door leading to the deck. He slid the insect screen door along and stepped outside. He was hoping to find his feathered pals all lined up to greet him, but of course, not having been supplied with food for a few weeks, they had deserted him, albeit temporarily, he hoped. The bellbirds were tinkling as usual, but all was quiet down on the beach, and little seemed to be happening out at sea – no boats, no whales. He was about to go back inside when a flutter of wings announced the arrival of Kooky on the deck railing. No doubt, it had been watching from its perch in the forest. James stepped forward and stroked the top of its head. 'G'day mate,' James said with an Australian accent. 'How've you been keeping?'

Stan Laurel looked back at him, vacantly. If he could have spoken, James imagined he would have said something like, 'Where've you been, you stupid baastard, I'm staarving.'

Before leaving England, he had phoned Valdis to tell her of his return and so when he went back inside he was able to make himself a strong, sweet, milky coffee from the supplies she had kindly bought in for him. While drinking it, he phoned the police station to let Spalding know he was back. He wanted to show how keen he was to assist with the search again, and to listen to the voice of the man who thought he had done a runner. He expected it to be subdued.

Constable Molly Jones answered, welcomed him back, heard him out, then told him that Spalding was out on other business, but she had a note that said Detective Inspector Goodfellow would like to talk to Mr Ogle on his return. Could he call in to the station as soon as possible. When James asked her if there had been any further developments in the search for Elaine, Molly said that she was not aware of any, but he would need to talk to Inspector Goodfellow about it.

Since there didn't appear to be any urgency in the situation or in Goodfellow's request for an interview, James told Molly that he would call in tomorrow afternoon at three o'clock, making the reasonable excuse that he was jet lagged and also needed to catch up on domestics. He added that he would, however, make himself available at any time if Inspector Goodfellow demanded it. Molly said it all sounded reasonable to her and, if she didn't get back to him, he should consider the appointment made.

James now decided to call his mother to tell her of his safe arrival, unpack, have an early lunch, maybe an hour's siesta, and then go down to Cemetry Beach to look for Claire. It was still risky, he felt, but perhaps not quite so risky as when Spalding was on the case. He would not be taking any chances, however, and would disguise his movements as before.

He *had* to see Claire. He had to know her reaction to his confession of love; had to know whether she had taken it as he had meant it, or simply as a way of saying goodbye, and whether she took that goodbye to be permanent or temporary. However, the romantic emotions that had carried him away a few weeks ago had now been somewhat tempered by time, distance and the trauma of his father's death. Reality had returned from its short vacation and taken up its usual place at the head of his table. It told him that Claire had probably been right. They had been sharing a holiday fantasy. She was married and would be staying so, nothing indicated otherwise.

But right now he needed to know that she was all right; explain exactly what he had meant. If she still wanted to see him, he would try to prolong their fantasy as long as possible, then step aside when it was time for her to leave. Then he would wish her well and hope to see her next summer. What happened in between was unknowable. He would be happy just to be living in Narooma, with or without a partner.

He actually slept for two hours after lunch, the jet lag taking its toll, but he still had plenty of time to take his car on a convoluted route around the town before emerging on the cliffs above Cemetery Beach. He was confident he had not been followed.

His first step onto the beach was the same as dozens of others he had taken in the past. Why did time change everything? Was he about to walk along the beach to talk to Claire, or was this a step he had already taken weeks ago when going fishing; they both felt exactly the same. Why did time decide which one it was? Why was this not the step he had taken so recently with his mother when taking his father's ashes for scattering on the Arran beach? He had always been fascinated with the phenomenon of time. He knew that in a few days or weeks he would step onto this beach again, and remember this conversation with himself and ask himself the same questions, wonder which step it was, and receive no satisfactory reply.

He forced these meanderings from his mind and set off along the beach. The afternoon breeze had strengthened to a wind, which brought powerful waves crashing and hissing and surging up the soft sand. Occasionally, he had to dance out of the way because, forgetfully, he was still wearing the good leather sandals he had travelled in. The wind had also brought some dark clouds down from the Snowy Mountains, making the beach take on the appearance of a scene from a villainous fairytale; the two stacks, now being pounded by white water, looking like the ruined castle haunts of wizards and witches. For the first time he sensed an atmosphere of foreboding on his favourite beach.

That atmosphere was added to when he found the beach-house empty. The shuttered windows and doors told their own story. This was how it had looked before Claire had arrived. She had not normally closed the shutters during her short absences. He walked around the building, trying to peer through joints and gaps. There was no sign of life within or without. Why would she leave? Their stay had been extended, she had said? James sensed that something was wrong. Not only the sky was now being visited by dark clouds.

The next morning, Narooma was wearing its brighter clothes again. Blue sky, sparkling sea, chortling magpies, tinkling bellbirds all brought their cheerfulness to James's breakfast table, sparking off a small helping of positive thoughts. Perhaps Claire had gone off with her husband on an extended trip within Australia, making sightseeing use of their extra time in the country. They could even have flown up to Asia for a month. There could be so many innocent reasons why she had put the shutters up. Then he slapped himself on the forehead. *Dummy.* If their yacht was still berthed in Bermagui harbour then they were still based in the country. He would go see after breakfast.

Bermagui was its usual charming self, bustling with late summer activity. Dozens of four-wheel drives hitched to boat trailers covered the tarmac and grassy verges all around the pretty harbour. Boats of all shapes and sizes came and went through the narrow harbour entrance, some carrying the spoils of an exciting early-morning visit to the fishing spots out near Montague Island. Already the gutting tables were busy with kingfish, tuna and the occasional marlin. Tied up around the harbour walls were a wide variety of vessels, from rusty old trawlers with their plethora of wires, cables and ropes, to sleek game-fishing boats awaiting their rich owners or hirers, to elegant sailing ships and small yachts visiting for the day.

James headed for the berth where he had previously seen the Capaldis' large ocean-going yacht 'The Man' tied up. It was not there. He walked around the entire harbour, thinking that they might have moved it after one of Robert Capaldi's sea-going trips. It was not to be seen. He resisted the temptation to ask other boat owners if they knew when and where it had gone. He did not want to attract attention to himself, particularly in relation to anything involving the Capaldis.

Now, that feeling of foreboding revisited him, and in spite of the usual bright morning around him, he felt dejected as he made his way back to his car, and then to Narooma.

Lunch was followed by another siesta, and then as the clock approached three, it was off to keep his appointment with Detective Inspector Goodfellow, whose lack of urgency to see him now convinced James that Spalding's urgent invitation to hurry back because he had two men in for questioning, was simply one more ploy to test his honesty and motivation.

Inspector Goodfellow had just finished filming a commercial for a well-known brand of razor blades. At least, that's how it looked to James as he took his seat opposite him, the desk between them empty save for an A4 lined writing pad and pen, and a file containing half an inch of documents. For three o'clock in the afternoon Goodfellow looked remarkably well groomed, his neatly clipped dark hair, smooth, shiny face, and impeccable shirt and tie making him look like a plastic replica of a 40-year-old American sales executive. After his firm handshake and a greeting which thankfully didn't include 'And how are you today, Mr Ogle', during which James got a whiff of cologne, he sat back in his chair with the confident air of someone used to being in charge and finding it easy. He did not look, feel or smell like a policeman. James became wary.

'I want to do two things,' Goodfellow said briskly, glancing at his expensive-looking watch. 'First to say how concerned and sorry we are about your wife's disappearance and your father's recent death, and second to apologise for Sergeant Spalding's investigative over-enthusiasm. I've read through the file and talked to him and he seems to have jumped the gun a bit. He's an excellent policeman but sometimes he works too hard and tries too hard. In these country areas we are pretty much fully stretched all the time, and we try to cover for each other as best we can. I'm based at the Bega station 90 k's away and have to cover investigative work there and in this area.

Had your wife's case been immediately passed to Bega, which it should have been since the beach in question is much closer to Bega than to Narooma, I would have been on the case sooner, and you would not have had to put up with Sergeant Spalding's questioning. He was acting in my best interests as usual, trying to take on some of my work before handing it over. But the trouble is he's not a trained detective, and sometimes he doesn't follow procedures...'

'There is no need to continue,' James interrupted, tired of listening to Goodfellow's subtle assassination of Spalding, who was clearly more intuitively suited to investigation that this plastic man was. 'And there is no need to apologise. I had already guessed that what you have described was the situation, and I was happy to make allowances for Sergeant Spalding. I could see that he was just trying to do a job. In fact, I was very impressed with much that he did, he is clearly a very hard-working man.' That should cross that one off his list, James thought. 'Now, what can you tell me about these two men that the sergeant brought in for questioning?' He was pushing on, trying to take the initiative.

'Ah yes...I let them go, there was nothing to hold them for.'

'Sergeant Spalding told me they were Kooris and they had been carrying some objects off the beach where Elaine went missing?'

Goodfellow sighed. 'Spalding should not have divulged those details to you. Look, before you decide to go on a personal crusade to find out who they are, I'll tell you, and also tell you that they have been investigated and that they have had nothing to do with your wife's disappearance. One of them was the man called David who your wife complained about some time ago. I do read the files. I can tell you that David wouldn't hurt a fly.'

'I remember him,' James said studiously. 'He exposed himself. He's backward, isn't he. Are you sure? What about accidentally?' He didn't want to push too far with David, who could not defend himself.

'You can never be sure, but we had nothing to hold him for anyway,' Goodfellow insisted.

'And the other man?' James queried.

'His name is Max Edwards and he's a good citizen, and I don't want you bothering either of these men. Is that understood?'

James did not like his tone, but was glad that the presumption of guilt that Spalding had pestered him with had not been displayed by Goodfellow. Indeed, he seemed to be acknowledging that James was a distraught husband, who might do something unlawful in order to find his wife. But, might he be playing good cop/bad cop in cahoots with Spalding? James was taking no chances. He decided to push again, as a distraught husband would. 'So I am expected to simply take your word that this man Edwards is a good citizen and therefore could not have harmed my wife? You will have to do better than that, Inspector.'

Again, Goodfellow sighed. He straightened himself up and leaned forward, placing his fingertips on the desk like a piano player. His watch flashed as it passed through a shaft of mote-filled sunlight playing across the desk. 'Max is a good bloke,' he said with a touch of exasperation in his voice. 'I've known him for years. He's the son of the chief elder on the Wallaga settlement. He's respected by everybody. He's well educated. He has no criminal record. He works with us. Occasionally he feeds us information when he thinks our intervention will stop his young blokes getting into trouble. It was Max who came to us with the beer can that one of his young blokes stole from Capaldi's yacht. Spalding didn't know this when he brought him in.'

'So, he helped you arrest one of his own?' James queried, assuming he was doing no more than helping the discussion along to its eventual conclusion. He tried not to show a reaction to Capaldi's name.

Goodfellow frowned deeply. 'No, he did not help us arrest one of his own. That youth is still wanted.' He continued to look puzzled.

'Then I don't understand the significance of what you are telling me,' James said plainly.

Goodfellow jerked his head back, an expression of disbelief wrinkling his plastic forehead. 'Have you been walkabout the last couple of weeks, Mr Ogle?' he asked, like a teacher interrogating a student who had got a simple question wrong.

'Not exactly,' James replied tersely, annoyed at Goodfellow's tone. 'But I have been very busy. Come to think of it, I haven't seen or heard any news since I went to the U.K. Are you telling me that I've missed something important?'

'So you haven't heard the Capaldi story?' Goodfellow's head oscillated sideways in disbelief.

'Who the hell is Capaldi?' James raised his voice, still alert to the possibility of a trap.

'Strewth,' Goodfellow gasped. 'You have been out of touch. It's been the biggest story in the world for the past two weeks...and it all started here in little Bermagui when Max Edwards brought us that beer can. Anyway, it has nothing to do with your wife's disappearance, so let's get back to that, eh?'

'...Right,' James hesitated, desperate to know the Capaldi story, but not wanting to appear more interested in something other than Elaine's disappearance. He couldn't wait to get back to his computer to check up on the last two weeks' news.

'Look,' Goodfellow started again, 'we didn't let those men go just because we knew and trusted them. I told you, we investigated them. We questioned them about their presence on that beach, and why they kept surfboards there...'

James couldn't resist interrupting; Goodfellow needed bringing down a peg or two. 'You asked them why they kept surfboards on a beach?' He raised his eyebrows exaggeratedly.

'Yes, very funny,' Goodfellow noted, then pressed on, adopting his teacher's role again, this time speaking to a backward student.

'It is *not* a surfing beach, there are rocks everywhere.' He stared into James's eyes, putting him in his place.

James felt suitably chastised. He should have remembered. Won't do it again, sir. *One nil to Goodfellow.* It wasn't all bad though; his slip had confirmed his apparent ignorance of the beach and its environs.

Goodfellow continued with the lesson. (James started to fidget, easing his shorts out of his crotch, wondered what was for pudding in the school dining room.) 'They had been using them to lie on, on a soft sand area where they caught beach worms for fishing.'

'Sergeant Spalding mentioned quicksands,' James contributed in a suitably neutral tone.

'Yes, that's the area. It was scanned. Just a few animal remains were found.'

'So why were they removing the surfboards?' James asked tiredly.

'Did I say they were removing the surfboards?' Goodfellow frowned, peering at him.

Adrenaline shot into James. He had become careless. *Think... quickly.* 'It was Sergeant Spalding, wasn't it? He told me the men were picked up while carrying objects off the beach. Now you have told me about the surfboards, I just assumed that is what they were carrying.'

Goodfellow hesitated, apparently unsure of the explanation, but eventually carried on. 'Max told us that they were worried about somebody stealing them, now that we knew about the beach. By *we,* he meant whites. He said that it had been a sacred beach for their people for thousands of years and until we came along, no whites had ever set foot on it. He had seen our footprints. He was very upset, and said his father and the rest of his people would also be upset. We had to go to their settlement to apologise to the elders. They didn't look happy. While we were there we told them we needed to carry out another search for Sam, the boy who stole the beer from the yacht, but we were actually looking for any sign of your wife. We searched all their houses, not expecting to find anything, and we didn't.'

Goodfellow paused, and James, concerned for the moment about putting his foot in it again, remained silent.

'I really don't think there is anything else we can do with respect to these two men,' Goodfellow eventually offered.

'No, now that I have a fuller picture, I must admit it doesn't appear so,' James said condescendingly, keen to end the interview.

Goodfellow started writing notes on his pad so James, anxious now to hear the school home-time bell, took the opportunity to say, 'Are we finished here? I suppose any future contact will be through that N.S.W. Missing Persons Unit that Spalding told me about?'

Goodfellow lifted his head briefly to say yes, then continued writing. Eventually he stopped scribbling and placed his pen neatly beside the writing pad. 'Sorry about that,' he half-smiled. 'Bit of a stickler for making notes, wish my constables were.'

James started to rise from his chair, but was stopped by Goodfellow's raised hand. 'Before you go, Mr Ogle…' He paused as he pulled the half-inch thick file towards him and opened it. 'Just for the record, so I can close this file, I'd like to ask a couple of questions if you don't mind.'

Ah! The famous last-minute question scene. He had obviously been watching all the television detectives, James thought. They all did it. Just as the villain was walking away, relaxed, out came the vital question disguised in an innocently enquiring tone; or sometimes it was the detective who walked away, and turned at the doorway, his question usually starting 'By the way…'.

'Fire away,' James said casually, folding his arms and settling back in his chair, all the while calling his grey matter up to the starting blocks.

'Can you prove that you were at Tuross on the afternoon of your wife's disappearance?'

About time too, James thought. He pretended to be thinking, then replied, 'Probably not…I walked well up the northern beach until I found a good gutter…I saw one other fisherman in the distance…but other than that… I can't think of anything or anybody that can help me prove I was there. My car was parked down at the sea front… maybe you could find somebody who remembers it…'

Goodfellow stared at him, intimating that he could read his mind, tell if he was lying. James returned with a wide-eyed 'why are you looking at an innocent man like that?' look, and Goodfellow gave in.

'I understand that your wife is a rich woman,' Goodfellow went on.

James wanted to point out that it was not a difficult thing to understand once you have looked at her bank accounts, but resisted the temptation and said, 'Yes.'

'Do you know if she has made a will?'

James gave a wry smile, 'Hmm, I can see where you are going with this. Yes she has made a will, and she took great pleasure in telling me that her son Jonathan is the sole beneficiary. There is no motive there, Inspector…I make a good living by my own efforts…'

'What about the motive of hate or jealousy?' Goodfellow got in quickly, leaning forward for emphasis.

'You tell me, Inspector – it is beyond my comprehension or experience.'

'Why did you buy chocolates for your wife when you weren't on good terms with her?'

'Are you serious?'

'I'd like an answer.'

'Are you married, Inspector?'

'Fifteen years.'

'Then you will know that I could give you any one of 20 reasons why a man buys his wife chocolates, be they in love or in hate, and you would accept it.'

'Granted…pick one.'

'No…I'll tell the truth. Elaine was due to go back to England. I had been making an effort to be nice to her during the last weeks so that we didn't part on bad terms. I'd been taking her to fashion shows and the pictures etc.…we had actually been having a good time together for a change. The chocolates were just another farewell sweetener…if you'll pardon the pun.'

'And what were your plans after she had gone?'

'To follow her home in two or three months' time when I've finished my current book.'

Goodfellow suddenly became animated. 'That reminds me,' he said as he reached into a desk drawer and pulled out a book. 'Would you mind signing this copy of Ogling Kenya. We bought it a few years ago, before we went on a safari holiday. We both enjoyed it… found it interesting…useful.'

'Delighted to,' James enthused, pleasantly taken aback by this change in the conversation. 'What are your Christian names?'

'Colin and Anne with an E.'

'Can I borrow your pen?' James started to lean across the desk.

Goodfellow nodded and James picked it up. It seemed to be gold plated. While he wrote, he said, 'Did you see the Masai?…interesting people!'

'Very.'

'And beautiful.'

'My word.'

James handed the book and pen back to Goodfellow. 'I've signed it 'To Colin and Anne – Jambo from James'. That was all the native language I learned while I was there.'

'Same here,' Goodfellow laughed. 'Thanks.'

There was short pause, then Goodfellow went into wrap-up mode. 'Although we are handing the case over to the M.P.U., we will be reviewing it here at regular intervals. It's a strange case, and frankly we're lost for an explanation. How she found that beach without help is a mystery; nobody in these parts knew there was access to it. She appears to have been fully dressed because only her wet swimmers were in her bag. Her car was still there. The area has been thoroughly searched. So where did she vanish to? The sea would be the obvious conclusion, but fully dressed? Maybe an accident, but we cannot rule out foul play or even abduction.

'Just for your information, if she's not found within 60 days the M.P.U. will probably ask you to supply dental and x-ray records of her to put on their database. This is so that if her body turns up in the future they can match it up and identify it. After that, once the P.O. in charge of the investigation decides that no further enquiries can be made, usually when he believes the person is dead, he'll report the matter to the coroner with a view to getting a Presumed Death Certificate issued. I'm really sorry to talk along these lines, Mr Ogle, but the situation doesn't look good. If there's anything more we can do locally, please don't hesitate to ask for me.' He stood up and walked around the desk, holding out his hand. 'Good luck,' he said as they shook hands, James having risen to meet him.

'Thank you,' James said in a subdued tone. 'And please thank all the other officers who helped in the search, particularly Sergeant Spalding.'

'No worries,' Goodfellow said, as he escorted James to the door. James was half expecting a 'Have a nice day' to follow him out, but thankfully it didn't materialise.

Once outside the station, James took a series of deep breaths and expelled his tension. It seemed to be over. The local file was as good as closed. It would become just another statistic in a distant system already swamped with cases. He would tackle them later about signing affidavits for the coroner; there had been plenty of evidence put on file to jog their memories if necessary. He had got away with it. He had done it. What a clever boy! He felt he should mark the occasion. On his way home, he pulled into the small car park behind the centre of Bar Beach, walked over the sand dunes, jogged down to the sea, checked there was nobody in earshot, and stood and shouted at the top of his voice, 'NO WORRIES.'

Chapter 23

James's celebration did not last long. Too soon it became overshadowed and then displaced by his concern for Claire. From the beach he drove home quickly, rushed to his office, and switched on his computer, anxious to read the 'Capaldi story'. They were Californians – he would check the Los Angeles Times.

Sitting waiting for the screen to light up, he realised that his pulse was racing, and he was slightly breathless. Maybe a reaction to the tension of the interview was setting in, together, perhaps, with the stress of his hectic trip to the U.K. and the death of his father. The 'Capaldi story', whatever it was, would not relieve his tension, he felt sure; good news stories do not dominate the headlines for two weeks. It had already happened, it was beyond his influence. It would be sensible to put his concern and curiosity on the back burner until tomorrow. Now he *was* alarmed – he was starting to think in Jonathan-speak.

He switched off his computer and walked slowly to the lounge. Here he poured himself a small whisky, then slumped into an armchair. Glancing out of one of the full-height windows, he noticed that the light was dimming. He knew roughly what time of day it was, but he did not know what day it was.

A calendar (not yet allocated a destination since its arrival at Christmas) on the bottom shelf of the coffee table told him that it was Friday. Friday! – table tennis night! What better way to relax the mind than through vigorous physical exercise.

After a simple pasta-based meal, he took a shower, changed and drove to the golf club. It was comforting and reassuring to get back to some sort of routine, see all the familiar faces of his table tennis oppos. They were mostly retirees, sensibly leaving Sydney, Melbourne, Canberra, and the hot inland towns, where they had made their living, to reap the rewards of life in Narooma. All appreciated its beauty, its tranquillity, its climate. Most were sports nuts, adding swimming, tennis, boating, fishing, bowls, croquet, or golf to their weekly diet of table tennis. Some did voluntary work, usually connected with the sea rescue or fire services or the youth of the town. They tolerated the pom with the fanny eccent. They were good companions.

By now they all knew about Elaine from the local media coverage instigated by Spalding. One by one they offered their condolences, asked if they could help in any way. James did not add further gloom to the proceedings by mentioning his father's death. Instead he reminded them of the old joke about the golfer on the first tee taking his hat off as a hearse drives by. 'Least I could do – it's the wife' was the punch line.

Soon the subdued atmosphere lifted and a normal night of serving, spinning, chopping, prodding, pushing, looping and smashing was enjoyed by all, particularly James who threw everything into it and finished soaked in sweat.

Back home, his third shower of the day and a strong nightcap sent him to bed totally relaxed.

Breakfast on the deck was a brief affair, Kooky and the lorikeets for once being ignored by their absent-minded provider. James carried his second cup of coffee to his office and switched on his computer.

The Los Angeles Times offered an archives section which he clicked on. But there was no need to use the Search facility. On the right of the screen under the heading 'Most Read Articles' the top five all included the name Robert Capaldi. Headlines such as *'Capaldi The Drug Baron'*, *'Billionaire's Secret Life'*, *'Capaldi Linked to Mafia'*, *'Police Arrest Robert Capaldi'*, told their own story. James clicked on the last one. He was shocked to see a large photograph of Capaldi and Claire, dressed in evening wear, holding glasses of wine, talking to a smiling president and his wife. Clearly the paper was using one of their archive photographs taken at a past function to highlight the status of the man. He started to read the article: *'Following the now famous tip-off from an Australian aborigine which led to the biggest drug bust in American history, Californian police today arrested billionaire Robert Capaldi at his San Diego home…*

James read on, eyes rarely blinking, hardly able to believe them. He devoured that article, then another, and another, then switched to the London Times and the Daily Telegraph, and found front-page coverage on them as well. They likened it to the discovery that Richard Branson was the world's biggest drug dealer. Naturally, the Australian papers were full of it. Max Edwards had given interviews but had not allowed them to take photographs of himself or his settlement. A beaming Inspector Goodfellow stood in front of a group of police officers outside Bega station. Bermagui harbour was splashed all over the pages. *Good for the fishing businesses*, James thought momentarily.

Now he could see why Goodfellow was so amazed that he had not heard the story. The gist of it was that a young Yuin boy, Sam (who was still missing), had sneaked on board Capaldi's yacht and stolen a few cans of the well known beer that Capaldi's huge American breweries exported all over the world. Sam and his mates had drunk all but one can, which he had then given to Max Edwards. On opening it, Max had found it full of heroin, neatly wrapped and packaged, obviously by a machine. Max had taken it to Constable Nicky Ricci and told him where Sam had obtained it, and that a few weeks earlier he had seen a man carrying three large fishing tackle boxes off Capaldi's yacht. The man had been dressed like a fisherman but something about him – his too-clean clothes, his fast walk, told Max that he wasn't. Nicky had passed it all on to Bega police station, and they had called in the Sydney Drug Squad.

They were in the process of organising a 24-hour watch on the yacht, when it was reported that the yacht had set sail from Bermagui harbour. The yacht was stopped by coastguard patrol vessels and the crew taken in for questioning. Capaldi was not on board. He had apparently been tipped off (by person/s still unknown) and flown out of Australia with his wife, presumably preferring to take his chances in America where he had an army of lawyers.

The Sydney Drug Squad found no heroin on the yacht, but the pilot of a shark spotter plane called up to help spot the yacht, reported having seen two men tipping boxes over the side as he swooped low over them. Tipped off by the Sydney Drug Squad, the American police had raided all of Capaldi's breweries, and had eventually found two distribution warehouses, one on the east coast, one on the west, where the drug replacement system took place. (Packs – slabs – of the famous beer were opened up, and two cans of beer on the inside of the pack were replaced by two cans of heroin. The pack was then resealed and specially marked for identification by the recipient.) With much investigation still to be undertaken, American drug authorities believe that Capaldi had probably built a huge American and world-wide drug distribution empire using his brewery, transport and shipping companies. Renewed interest was now also being taken in Democratic Senator Bradford Schutz's proposition that some of Capaldi's companies were involved in money laundering. Much speculation as to why Capaldi himself would risk carrying drugs on his yacht existed, interviews and articles with and by psychologists among others filling the inside pages and television studios.

After his arrest, Capaldi was released on bail of $10 million. Australian authorities were expected to seek his extradition.

This was clearly a running story and James's relish at following the inevitable expositions, and hopefully Capaldi's downfall, was tempered by his concern for the intense media pressure it would put on Claire, and by the impossible thought that she may have known something about it. Surely not – not Claire.

For the next two days James settled down into something approaching a normal routine, polishing up some of his work, planning his trip down to Eden, taking walks along the boardwalk to see the stingrays, all the while devouring everything the media continued to pour out about the Capaldi story. He started taking his meals on a tray on his knee in front of the television so that he didn't miss anything. He was in this position when a morning newsreader announced that Robert Capaldi had committed suicide at his home in San Diego. He had shot himself in the head. His wife, Claire, told police that he had spent the last two days in long meetings with his lawyers. At some point he had quietly left a meeting saying he was going to the toilet. A shot was heard and he was found dead in the toilet with a gun in his hand. A spokesman for the group of lawyers said that during the meetings they had advised him that a prison sentence was almost inevitable.

James almost spilt his coffee. This was better than any gangster film he had ever seen, and it was real, and he had a small part in it. He wondered if Capaldi's death might result in a much bigger part. Would it eventually be possible for him and Claire to get together? He dared to hope. Who said beach fishing for whiting wasn't exciting! That was where it had all started. Now he had a chance of landing the biggest catch of all. Eat your hearts out, you big game fishermen with your fancy boats and swivelling chairs.

Two days later, during which endless articles and interviews about Capaldi filled every page and waking hour, one of his arrested henchmen – crewman, chauffeur, and bodyguard Lorenzo Zappi (Happy to his friends) – decided to spill the beans, obviously in return for whatever the police offered him. He told them that he had hated Capaldi who had treat him, and most other people, like dirt, and he hoped he rotted in hell. Fear of his own death had kept him working for Capaldi. He said Capaldi was a vicious, ruthless man who had surrounded himself with soft, cuddly, artistic people like film stars, artists, writers, musicians, and fashion designers so that he could camouflage his own persona and present himself as a benign businessman who patronised the arts.

After then lifting the lid on an astonishing catalogue of crime including many murders, from other gangsters trying to muscle in on his drug empire, to company executives who got in the way of takeovers, Zappi then announced that it had been Capaldi who had shot his father in the drive-by shooting. Capaldi boasted that he had been brought up to succeed his father in the Mafia, but his father had gone soft. He had used his father's brewery as a means of distributing drugs, made a fortune, and bought other legitimate businesses with the money. He turned out to be good at legitimate business but always preferred the thrill of the underworld. That is why he risked carrying drugs on his yacht from New Zealand to Australia – he still wanted to taste the action. He had been doing it for years, sailing from Bermagui into Melbourne and Sydney to supply his Italian family members, as well as supplying direct from the yacht to drug dealers who came to Bermagui ostensibly to go game fishing with him. He had said Australia was so laid back it was like taking candy from a baby.

And I thought I was a bad boy, thought James. Clearly, Capaldi had become careless, and 'good citizen' Max Edwards had brought him down, inadvertently aided by a young fella called Sam who was, apparently, still on the run.

James decided he did not want to know anymore. He had heard enough of Mr Robert Capaldi. It was time to get on with his own wifeless life. Claire, obviously, would be tied up for months, possibly years, sorting out the affairs of such a man, his businesses and her own future. He would try to put her out of his mind for the time being.

It did not take Australian police corruption investigators long to find out who had tipped off Capaldi. The use of tried and tested methods relating to personal involvement, timing, and living beyond one's means lifestyle, soon led them to the conclusion that Detective Inspector Goodfellow was the bad fellow. His bank statements revealed regular payments for part-time work as a security consultant from an Australian import company. The company was part of a Capaldi-owned group.

James had not been surprised. The silly man, who had obviously been Capaldi's 'eyes and ears' in the local area, had flaunted his extra money.

The fact that both Spalding and Goodfellow were now 'off his case' made James even more relaxed about his own situation. It was definitely time to get on with things, to start a new life. He would let a suitably proper time pass before he started to deal with Elaine's affairs back in England. In Narooma, he would eventually clear out her wardrobe and take her expensive clothes to Vinnies charity shop; the ladies of Narooma would soon snap them up.

But first things first – he had made promises to his agent and publisher about finishing his current book – that must take priority. He would go down to Eden tomorrow, spend a few days, research the story of the whaling industry, come back, write it up, then go to the Snowy Mountains for the hydroelectric story. He spent that afternoon and evening doing his usual packing, informing, booking, cancelling routines, and was completely prepared for his morning departure by the time the sun lay down to sleep somewhere behind Mother Gulaga.

Chapter 24

He was off again. Doing the thing that earned him a living, hitting the road, off to see new places, find new stories. Although he had been doing it for 30 years it still brought a mix of excitement and pleasure. What was it about travel that did this? He had come to the conclusion that it was mostly to do with the escape from responsibility. If you lived a 'normal' life of nine to five you had bills to pay, lawns to mow, routines and responsibilities. On the road you left all that behind, you watched them being carried out by other people as you passed them by in your car, on a train, on a horse, on a camel. The word 'travel' and the word 'escape' had become symbiotic to James, especially when home life with Elaine had grown tiresome.

However, the perception that the travel writer is escaping to a life of glamour is a myth. There is nothing glamorous about squatting over a stinking hole in the ground, with hundreds of flies determined to land on your nether regions, cursing yourself for forgetting to pack toilet paper. Or about standing at the window of a dilapidated hotel looking down on people in rags while your stomach readies itself for its third caber toss of the evening. Or about being bored witless by motel life. Or about fending off gaunt-cheeked, dull-eyed kids trying to sell you one cigarette.

But today's trip, like many, would be a pleasure. It would be short – about 150 kilometres; it would be scenic – he had decided to take the coast-hugging road rather than the main Princes Highway; it would end in a comfortable establishment in a civilised Australian town, and he would be back home in Narooma within three to four days.

To accompany him on this scenic route, in his happy mood, he had brought mostly Mozart, and he heard the piano concerto No. 21 start up as soon as he pulled away from the house.

Soon he was on the familiar road south, and taking the familiar turn off to Bermagui to start the quiet, scenic route down the coast. He knew this would take him past the scene of Elaine's demise, but it didn't bother him. There were so few roads in the region it was inevitable that he would be using it occasionally if he was going to live in Narooma forever.

Concerto No. 21 had been replaced by Symphony No. 40 by the time he passed through Bermagui. He turned it down as he started to enjoy the company of Cuttagee Beach and others. Windows down, he liked to listen to the sounds of the sea along this quiet stretch, another vehicle a rare sight. Then it was windows closed and Mozart back on as the trees started to dominate on either side.

He drove at a pace in keeping with the winding nature of the road, but was not surprised when a car slowly gathered in behind him. Most locals drove faster than he did; the driver, hidden by the sun visor, could be a busy farmer or an impatient youth. When James came to a straight stretch he slowed down to allow the other car to pass. But it didn't. It stayed close behind. And now he noticed that it was a blue Ford Falcon. He swallowed.

He had only glimpsed the blue Falcon in the Moruya garage so he was unable to identify them as the same, but the fact that it had refused to overtake him made his pulse start to race. He switched off Mozart, gripped the wheel and concentrated his mind. Was it one of Spalding's men? Had he been followed ever since the event? If so, they were incredibly good at their job, he hadn't noticed them. Had Spalding and Goodfellow been in cahoots after all, let him think he had got away with it, then pounce when he was relaxed, when he made a mistake? Had the whole episode made him paranoid? The Falcon was a common car, the driver was taking a breather, he would pass all in good time, there was nothing to worry about. James decided to pull to a stop on the next straight stretch, sort it out once and for all.

Onwards he drove along the tree-lined, twisting road, constantly checking his mirror, the blue car always the same distance behind, as though being towed. A car whooshing past in the opposite direction made his heart jump. He breathed deeply to calm himself down. He started to adjust his mirror to see if he could catch sight of the driver. He couldn't, and when his eyes came back to the road he realised he was approaching the sharp bend beyond which lay the place, under the trees, that led to Big Worm Beach.

The bend being so sharp, he had to concentrate as he curved his car around it. As he started to come out of it he saw an old truck approaching on the other side of the road. Suddenly a ute came out from behind the truck and came towards him on his side of the road, the two vehicles side by side blocking the road – a collision was certain. Instinctively, he threw his car onto the left hard shoulder, braked, gritted his teeth, and held his breath. Earth, stones, dry leaves, small branches and wallaby droppings clattered the underside of his car as it skidded along, throwing up clouds of yellow dust. It jerked to rest abruptly, safely. Heart pounding, breath still held, knuckles white on the wheel, he saw through his windscreen, on which tiny spots of yellow dust were starting to snow, that he was just a few feet short of the trees under which he had parked his car next to Elaine's.

He switched off the ignition. He could hear his heart thumping in his ears. He had been guided here, forced here.

Looking through his mirrors and the remnants of the swirling yellow dust, he saw other vehicles moving towards him. He undid his seatbelt and heaved himself out of his car, breathing heavily. He was furious, but also frightened. Shy, retiring men did not pull a stunt like this. This was not the police!

The blue Falcon pulled up alongside. The truck and the ute passed by and took shelter under the trees. These vehicles quickly disgorged three Koori men who ran towards him brandishing tree branches as thick as an arm. 'Best to stand your ground' an experienced French explorer had told him in a Brazil hotel, when recounting a meeting with some naked, fearsomely painted, spear-thrusting Indians in the Amazon forest.

Bravely, stoically, as advised, James pulled himself to his full height and waited for them. He was somewhat reassured by the fact that they were not naked or painted, but wore shirts and jeans, and as well as branches, two were also carrying mobile phones. They slowed down as they neared him and positioned themselves around him, a few metres apart, blocking any attempt at escape. The Falcon window came down and a voice and a brown arm told him to move his car under the trees alongside the others. James climbed back in and did as he was told. The Falcon followed him into the shade of the trees.

James and the man in the Falcon got out of their cars together, and faced each other. Although he had only seen him from a distance before, James was pretty sure he was looking at Max Edwards. Up close, he was unforgettable. The best of both races had definitely come together in this handsome, strong-looking man whose large, sand-coloured eyes spoke of authority without malice. Max pulled a handkerchief from his pocket and wiped the back of his neck, at the same time walking about in a slow arc inspecting the overall position of men and vehicles. Occasionally, he glanced towards the road. He reminded James of a Bengal tiger he had been lucky to see in India. It had moved languidly, unthreateningly, almost pet-like, yet nobody doubted its power over them.

Max Edwards finished his prowl and returned to stand in front of James, who, as yet, had not let them know how furious he was. Max's tiger eyes bore into James's Berkshire eyes. James tried not to blink.

'You trespassed on one of our sacred sites, Mr Ogle. You will be punished.' Max spoke clearly and matter of factly, in a regular Australian accent.

'So did many others,' James coughed, the dust and the exertion catching his dry throat. 'Are you going to punish them all? Are you going to punish the police?'

'Only you. You were the first. You brought the others.'

The police must have told Max when they questioned him about Elaine's disappearance, James realised. Goodfellow hadn't warned him about possible punishments. Perhaps he didn't know they did such things. Perhaps there hadn't been a trespass for many years. But wait a minute; the blue car was following him *before* Max and David were taken in for questioning?

James thought quickly. The only other explanation was that Max had seen him on that first day, when he followed them to the beach. Had the Yuins been following him ever since, waiting for an opportunity like this? But the road block had been pre-arranged? How did they know he was taking the coast road today? Who had he told? What had he booked or cancelled, or arranged?

Yet, if the Moruya Falcon *was* simply a coincidence, and it hadn't been following him, then his first explanation became valid again. There were lots of questions, ifs and buts. As yet – few answers!

'But I didn't know,' James argued. 'How was I to know?'

Max responded calmly, 'Ignorance is no excuse. That's what your law says.'

James couldn't believe what he was hearing. 'You can't just force somebody off the road and then threaten them,' he blustered. 'It's against the law.'

'Not against our law, Mr Ogle.'

Max waved his arm in a herding motion, 'Now follow those two into the bush. We're going to the beach. You know where that is.'

Two of the men walked into the forest. James followed. Max and the other man followed him. For some reason James was glad they hadn't brought David.

This is ridiculous, James thought as he trudged along. It's like something out of a bad Tarzan movie. When they reached the gorge, James stopped, turned and said to Max, 'How do you expect to get away with this? I'll report you to the police.'

Max smiled wryly. 'You won't be able to…move on.'

Now James was scared. Up to now he had envisaged his punishment would be part of a strange ceremony during which he would suffer a ritual smearing of an animal's blood or something similar. He had not expected violence in any form. Now the unemotional certainty in Max's voice indicated something approaching terminal violence.

He started to shiver as they passed through the gorge, his sweat-soaked shirt turning cold in the shade. The thought of what lay ahead didn't help.

At the end of the gorge, a large, apparently temporary, Council notice had been erected: 'DANGER. Do not enter. This beach contains quicksands'.

Stepping out onto the sunlit beach was a physical relief. Immediately he felt the sun warm his shoulders, his back. He knew the shivering would soon be over. But he was wrong. As the Yuin men marched him along the beach, it persisted. It was nerves now. He was frightened.

He tried to pull himself together, told himself that the time when white men were slaughtered by natives for invading their land was long gone. Now he was regretting switching on this thought channel. His overactive imagination was taking over. Up in Queensland he had read that the last acts of cannibalism, on remote northern islands, had taken place in the 20th century. Were the Yuins out to beat that record, bring it into the 21st century, re-name it the 'human taste experience'? Was he to be boiled or stir-fried? Had he become part of a new reality television show? Did they have a celebrity chef lined up to present it? His eyes darted about, looking for large iron pots suspended above piles of driftwood, for cameras hidden behind rocks, for a hyperactive man wearing a tall, white hat. He saw none and quickly switched off the channel.

He still couldn't believe that a civilised man like Max, 'good citizen' Max, would condone or instigate violence for such a minor thing as trespass. But he knew nothing about Yuin law, Yuin customs. Maybe in their law trespass on sacred sites was the ultimate crime, the crime to beat all others, even murder. He wasn't comforting himself on this channel either.

When they reached an area close to the quicksand they stopped. The four men formed a 3-metre-diameter circle around him, then sat down on the sand, legs crossed, branches placed in front of them. James was left standing in the middle. He felt like an impala surrounded by lions. 'What now?' he asked Max.

'We wait. Sit if you want.'

James eased himself to the ground and shuffled into a comfortable position. He started to find a ridiculous amount of solace, even pleasure, in the feel of the soft, warm sand, then realised this was the feeling of the man on death row as he ate his last dollop of mashed potatoes.

Time dragged on. The men sat watching him. They didn't speak. James had a strong urge to start telling jokes…Did you hear the one about…but decided his captive audience did not look particularly receptive. 'Is the passage of time part of my punishment?' he asked flippantly, trying to mask his unease. 'I can tell you it is working very well. I am ageing before your eyes. This is much more subtle than I expected…'

'We are waiting for the elders…my father,' Max interrupted. 'They decide your punishment.'

'How do they know I'm here?'

Max held up a mobile phone.

'Ah! Thank God for the wonders of technology,' James joked. 'If you'd still been using pigeons we would be here all night.' A little light went on in Max's eyes. James was sure he was laughing inside. The three wise men remained blank. They looked sour, and heavy, as though they were constipated, or maybe they knew they were going to miss Australian X Factor. 'You know this is going to ruin your image with the police, don't you,' James carried on, his tone still jocular. 'They think you are a cross between the Pope and Mother Teresa after your uncovering of that drug dealer.'

Max didn't respond.

'Is your good reputation not important to you?' James went on, knowing he was talking rubbish, but having nothing better to do.

For some reason, Max responded this time. 'I've told you – they won't know.'

James wished he hadn't asked. For the next ten minutes his mind became absorbed with all the practicalities that would surface if they did bump him off. He realised that he couldn't do anything about them if they bumped him off, but he couldn't help thinking about them. What would they do with his car? Would his unfinished book be published, like Schubert's 8th Symphony? Who would cancel his dental appointment? Who would pay the bill if it wasn't cancelled? Who would get into the house to find the bill and his unfinished book? If he went missing as well as Elaine, could Jonathan cope? Would his Polish high jumper help him over the hurdles? Who would cancel table tennis and feed Kooky? What would happen…

Three distant figures emerged from the gorge. They started to walk towards James's beach party. They seemed to be taking a long time. They were *elders*, they were walking slowly, James finally worked out.

As they drew closer, James could see that the two outside figures were half naked, their bodies covered in daubs of white paint. They were each carrying a surfboard. James caught his breath.

The central, slightly stooping figure, who was smaller than the other two, appeared to be the chief elder. He was wearing a full-length, brilliantly decorated cassock and a conical headdress apparently made from wound hair, with birds' feathers sticking out the top, and covered in white and red painted stripes. Somehow attached to this headdress was a decorated face-mask, probably made from bark, also daubed with white paint. The only signs that a human occupied this facade was an occasional flash of eyes behind the mask cut-outs, and a glimpse of steel-grey hair at the shoulders. The chief elder was also carrying two clap sticks and a didgeridoo.

At least I have a one-man band to see me off.

Max and the three wise men stood to greet the elders. James followed suit, keen to create a good impression, then realised that good manners might not be relevant in the circumstances.

The Yuins all stepped aside as the chief elder approached James and stood within three paces of him. James felt totally belittled, helpless and exposed, like a man about to have a prostate examination. He decided to concentrate on his surroundings. If these were to be his last moments he wanted them to be spent in the appreciation of earthly beauty. His eyes moved to the waves – clear as glass, curling, folding, breaking, mullet fry helplessly displayed, the final surging hiss, warm and welcome as a woman's kiss.

The chief elder was removing his headdress. He handed it to one of the three wise men. Then he removed his mask and did likewise. Finally he removed the steel-grey wig, and said in a feminine voice, 'Hello James…long time no see.'

James's knees wobbled. He had to steady himself. 'I wondered where you got to,' he said.

Elaine dropped the two clap sticks and the didgeridoo, picked a few small feathers out of her hair and flicked it into place in her habitual way. Then she took off the cassock and stood dressed in clothes James thought were still hanging in her wardrobe at home. She looked James up and down as if she had never seen him before, as if he was some repulsive creature that had just crawled out of a swamp.

James held out his arms indicating everybody around him. 'You went to all this trouble just for me? You shouldn't have, really.'

The sneer was still on Elaine's face. 'You deserve it, James. You went to so much trouble to get me here.' She turned towards the quicksand and stared at it for a long time, as if remembering her ordeal in it.

Her face was pathetically sad when she turned back to him. 'How could you do that to me?' she asked disbelievingly.

'Beats me,' James replied.

Elaine looked incredulous. 'Is that all you've got to say?'

James sighed. 'You're asking me to explain how an ordinary human being with no history of mental instability or violence can turn into a murderer. I don't know the answer.'

'Bullshit,' Elaine spat. 'There's always an answer…a motive.'

This was a stronger, more confident Elaine. Something had changed in the last few weeks.

James hung his head. 'I was infatuated,' he mumbled.

'I knew it…I knew it,' Elaine boasted. 'There *was* a woman.'

'There was no woman,' James insisted. 'I was infatuated with Narooma…the place…I told you.'

Elaine threw her head back. 'God! That makes it worse.' She rubbed her forehead vigorously with the fingers of her left hand. 'And your cunning plan was? You must have guessed you are not in my will?' She was shouting at him now.

'The two joint properties,' James admitted.

Elaine looked puzzled. 'But my share would have passed to Jonathan?'

'I would have persuaded him to sell the properties.'

'Yes, you probably would have,' Elaine said after a short pause. 'He would be easy meat for a devious bastard like you.' She frowned. 'And you would have been happy with that amount of money?'

'It's all I need to live here.'

'You could have asked for it?'

'You wouldn't have given it.'

'You're right.'

By now James reckoned that the wide-eyed onlookers, who appeared to be at a tennis match, had forgotten all about the X Factor. 'Just out of interest,' he said, 'before you subject me to any more verbal abuse, would you like to tell me how you escaped from the quicksand, where you have been hiding for the last few weeks, and how you managed to persuade these gentlemen to help you?'

Elaine snorted. 'What's the point. It won't change anything. It doesn't matter where I was in the past. What matters now is where you are going in the immediate future.' She glanced towards the quicksand.

'Now I'm dying to know,' James observed, and paused for laughter. When none came he said, 'Come on, Elaine, you know what I'm like. Not knowing is worse than dying...'

'Another good reason not to tell you.'

'Please Elaine...I'll put a good word in for you when I get to heaven...'

'Tell him, Max, for goodness sake,' Elaine intervened. 'Anything to shut him up.'

James was intrigued at the relaxed, intimate way she had spoken to Max, as if they were old friends. Or recent lovers?

Max stepped forward and stood beside Elaine. She glanced up at him with a look that said 'my hero'. James saw Derborah Kerr looking up at Burt Lancaster in the 'From Here To Eternity' beach scene. As long as they didn't go the whole hog and re-enact the famous kiss in the waves scene, he could live with the image. The rest of the cast didn't quite fit, though one of the three wise men could have passed for Ernest Borgnine.

'I came down to the beach that night to do some balloon fishing off the rocks,' Max started. 'There was a good high tide. I saw Elaine in the water and rescued her...'

'He was marvellous,' Elaine interjected. 'I don't remember much about it, but apparently he kept diving down and digging with his bare hands. He said he was digging for about 20 minutes…then he dived down and swam between my legs and lifted me out on his shoulders…incredible.'

Now James could understand the 'my hero' look; he clearly deserved it.

'Elaine was in a bad way,' Max went on. 'She was shivering and drifting in and out of consciousness. I thought she was suffering from shock. I carried her back to my ute and took her to my home which was much closer than any hospital or doctor…'

This time it was James who interrupted. 'You carried her all that way…on your own?'

'Yes…the fireman's lift. She got heat from my body and water from her lungs.'

He is *Burt Lancaster,* James thought enviously.

'At home I wrapped Elaine up and did all the first aid things I'd learned after I lost my wife at sea…but she didn't respond well, she wouldn't wake up. I thought it best not to move her…I might have been wrong…but anyway she slept all night in a warm bed. The next morning she was a bit better but not conscious all of the time. I was going to drive her to hospital when my father pointed out that the police would be looking for her. If they found her car, he said, they would find the beach and then the surfboards. The surfboards are very old and worn; they would know they belonged to Yuins. If she was not able to tell them the true story they would get suspicious and might arrest me for kidnap. He told me to hide her until she was well enough to speak and tell the police what really happened. I didn't agree with him. I told him the police would believe me. But he doesn't trust them and he is my father and I did as he said. I took her to our safe-house…an old wooden cabin in the bush.'

'But you have a good reputation with the police,' James said. 'They would have believed you.'

'Not certain,' Max said. 'They also know that I'll do anything to keep my people out of prison. They could have thought I was covering for somebody, like I have with Sam.'

'So you know where Sam is?'

'Yes.'

'He's been looking after me for the past few weeks,' Elaine butted in, 'and very well too. We've become good pals. He's a great artist and I'm going to sell his paintings in London…create a little gallery/coffee room in my shop…it's always been too big…'

'Don't tell me you've been living in the bush in an old wooden cabin all this time?' James said disbelievingly. 'What about your shower, your daily change of clothes, your make-up, your lotions and potions…your magazines…'

'Looked in my wardrobe lately have you, James? I don't think so. While you were away in England, my friends here took me home one night and I removed half my clothes and everything else I needed, including my passport. And Max and Sam made the safe-house…it's much more than an old cabin…they made it more comfortable for me, brought stuff up from the settlement.'

'But why?' James almost shouted in disbelief. 'When you recovered, why didn't you go to the police and tell them what happened, or come home and tear into me?'

Again, Elaine looked adoringly at Max. 'This man is very wise as well as strong and kind.' *She'll be telling me he wears his underpants outside his clothes next.* 'He and his father stopped me from doing just that. I was all for rushing to the police and having you arrested for attempted murder. They pointed out to me how stupid our legal system is, how it would take months or years to come to court, how it would cost a fortune for lawyers, how a clever lawyer would probably get you off because you didn't actually touch me…basically how it would be a waste of time and money and finish with no justice or revenge for me. Then they told me about payback – their system of justice. They said that I – the victim – should choose what your punishment should be, and they would help me because I was going to help Sam. I had also been paying them to follow you so I knew when you made your trip down to Eden for the whale story…I take it that is where you were going today…you see I do listen, James.'

'What did you pay them with? The police had tabs on your accounts?'

'Not on my company accounts, James. I got my p.a. to transfer some money from the company account into the Yuin's visitor centre business account. For supply of paintings by Sam, I called the item. Told my p.a. she would be fired if she breathed a word of my whereabouts. Max withdrew that money from the visitor centre account and gave it to me and, hey presto, I was up and running. He went out and bought a mobile and a laptop for me and anything else I needed and I was soon back in touch with the world. I emailed Jonathan and told him I was alright, but lying low, and he would be out of my will if he told anybody.'

'So you have been hiding in the bush, costing the police a fortune in manhours looking for you, worrying your son, overstaying your visa, patiently waiting for me to take this drive today so that you can take your revenge at the scene of the place where your hat blew off. I take *my* hat off to you, I didn't know you had it in you.'

By this time, the audience had sat back down on the beach, in a circle, and were staring up at them, enthralled. This was better than 'Neighbours'. A few seagulls had dropped in behind them knowing that humans on beaches means food, either for themselves or to catch fish.

'Thank you, James…your second compliment since we got married.'

While James had been absorbing all this information he began to think that they were telling him too much. Should Max have told him about their safe-house; should they have mentioned the whereabouts of Sam? It could only mean one thing…

'Anyway, that's the story, James,' Elaine announced. 'I hope your curiosity has been satisfied.' She turned and addressed the three wise men. 'Now, let's get on with what we came here for. We're in luck, the tide's out.'

The three men stood up and gathered around James. 'No point in wasting things,' Elaine said. 'Give them your sandals, your watch, your sunglasses and any money you've got.'

James did as he was told.

Two of the men took hold of an arm each, the third stood by, threatening him with the tree branch. The two elders carried the surfboards down to the edge of the quicksand, and after doing some kind of sinking tests, lay the surfboards side by side on top of the quicksand, facing into it. The men dragged James down the beach until he was standing just behind the surfboards, on firm sand. He didn't struggle; he knew it would be useless against such odds. Max and Elaine looked on, apparently silent supervisors.

'Lie,' one of the elders ordered, and the two men holding his arms forced James to a sitting position on the boards. Then they grabbed his shoulders and forced him down so that he was lying on his back across the full width of both boards.

By this time, James had become fatalistic, resulting in a stream of clichés entering his head. *What will be will be. Can't say I don't deserve it. I've made my bed, now I'm lying in it.*

Now four men came to the end of the boards where James lay, and they bent down and lifted the ends of both boards simultaneously causing James to slide down as they lifted the boards higher and higher. Quite quickly and smoothly, James slid down the boards and onto the quicksand, still on his back. Instinctively, he flung both arms out wide, trying to achieve maximum surface area support. The moisture in the damp sand felt cold to his hot body as it penetrated his shirt and shorts. He felt crucified in every sense of the word.

He now knew that Elaine meant business. The men obviously knew that the quicksand wouldn't envelop a standing person, but *would* cover someone lying down. He was being buried alive.

But it was going to be a long, tortuous process. After the initial contact, which felt similar to lying on a damp medium/soft mattress, nothing seemed to be happening. He wondered why it was called *quick*sand when it was just the opposite; *slow*sand would have been more appropriate.

The weight of his spreadeagled body did not appear to be sufficient to break the surface tension of the sand. Without his sunglasses, he lay squinting up at the blue sky, watching the occasional gull pass over, hoping it didn't relieve itself. The initial cool shock of the damp sand soon passed and his body became quite comfortable in its soft, restful position.

For some inexplicable reason he started wondering how many years might pass before his skeleton was discovered, along with a few more wallabies. If it was thousands of years, might his body become the study of future genealogists struggling to understand the primitiveness of their aggressive ancestors. Would they decide that the bones of his left hand were thicker than those of his right hand because he had used it as a weapon, when in fact it came from years of gripping a Zenith Golf Company's ZT-82 titanium Driver with Hyperbolic FCT, COG precision plus Ylam 32 shafts and new EEW webs, giving more PFTS and improved MOI. To have believed this marketing drivel would have been even greater proof of his primitiveness than their theory.

These important thoughts were cast aside when he realised that one of the men had walked along the surfboards towards him, and was now prodding and poking the sand around and under his body with a long tree branch. He was trying to reduce the sand's viscosity by stirring up latent water, thus breaking the surface tension, making the quicksand more flexible. And he was slowly succeeding. Very gently, imperceptibly, James sank lower in the sand. The man worked hard. Maybe he was on a bonus as well as flexi-time, James thought ridiculously, as he felt his feet and shoulders sinking.

After a long passage of continuous prodding, James was halfway down and the man was tired. He handed over to one of the others. James wondered if their union, probably renowned for branch agitation, would approve this change in shift patterns.

However, his *sang-froid* started to leave him as – during the next poking session – carried out by a more powerful man, he felt himself sinking more quickly. A downward impetus seemed to have set in and soon he felt his legs and most of his trunk disappear beneath the sand. The weight and powerful grip of the sand felt dreadful. Instinctively, James tried to struggle against it, but to no avail. It reminded him of one of his repetitive dreams where he cannot move, where he is trapped, being held and suffocated, desperately trying to free himself – then becoming flooded with blissful relief when he wakes up to find himself entangled in harmless bedclothes.

Now his shoulders, neck and upper arms were under, only his head and hands above the surface. He kept looking sideways to see if he could see Elaine. He couldn't. Should he shout for mercy, for forgiveness? Should he shout for help in the remote hope of a stranger being in the vicinity? He thought not. The die was cast. The fat lady had sung. The horse had bolted. The Grim Reaper was on the next shift. The end was nigh. It saddened him, as a writer, to think that he could only think of clichés as he was about to quit this mortal coil.

His ears were under now. The sounds of the ocean, the gulls – gone forever. Beneath the sand – louder than expected – he could still hear the ominous, piston-like slosh of the thrusting branch. Only his mouth, nose, eyes and fingertips were still blessed by contact with air. In the blue above him he saw Claire's smiling face. Then – slowly

– the quicksand oozed in and took the blue, but not Claire. Now she was in a blind, black space within his head. She stayed there as – gasping – he thrust his lips upwards into an exaggerated open kissing position, trying to keep them clear of the encroaching ooze. Now his nostrils were starting to fill, and he started to rapidly suck and blow like a woman giving birth, as his lungs demanded precious ether.

James had always suffered from mild claustrophobia, hating closed spaces, the Underground, having to leave the guided tour of Broken Hill mines, loving the open places, the mountaintops, the deserts, the beaches. Suffocation was his worst nightmare. He found its mental torment excruciating. Elaine could not have chosen her revenge more exquisitely.

His nose was full. He sucked in one last breath through his mouth, and closed his lips as the ooze enveloped them. The noise of the thrusting branch ceased.

He thought of his mother as the pressure in his head started to build, his ears started to ring. He began to feel dizzy as oxygen became scarce and carbon dioxide plentiful. He felt himself diving down a deep, dark pit, then swimming through fog, then feeling sick as his brain went on a roller-coaster ride. Now he felt as though he was levitating, and hoped this signified a journey to a higher place.

Two angels were pulling him up from his glutinous grave. His eyes were still closed but he could sense the light. He forced his eyes open, expecting to see Saint Peter with his welcome-pack. Instead, through the mist of his dizziness, he saw two figures swaying as though part of a desert mirage. Slowly they came into focus and revealed themselves to be two hairy Yuins pulling his arms out of their sockets. He shouted in pain, but they persisted, and gradually pulled his head and shoulders clear of the quicksand.

Repositioning the surfboards, they managed to get a wide sling-like rope around his upper chest, under his arms. Returning to solid sand, they and the other five Yuins lined up and pulled on the rope.

With much grunting and cursing, from James as well as them, they succeeded in pulling him clear of the quicksand.

He lay like an abandoned seal pup – gasping – helpless – pathetic; his shorts and underpants around his ankles, his genitals exposed, the alabaster whiteness incongruous. Elaine looked down at him, triumphantly. She had shaken him to the core, humiliated him, terrified him. She felt satisfied. She liked this payback system.

James looked up at her through encrusted eyelashes. He summoned up some strength and gasped through his caked lips, 'Well, here's another nice mess you've gotten me into.'

'You don't know how lucky you are,' Elaine scowled. 'I wanted to kill you, but Max wouldn't help me to do that. He said payback has to be equal. I didn't die, so you shouldn't die. You can thank him, not me.'

'Thanks Max,' James gasped, as two of the men half-lifted him, took off the rope, and collected it together. Two others were retrieving the surfboards. Max placed James's sandals, watch, sunglasses and money in a pile on the sand close to him, then moved to stand beside Elaine. He remained silent.

'Here's what's going to happen,' Elaine said. 'I'm going to the house tonight to pick up the rest of my things, then Max is taking me back to the safe-house. As soon as I can get a flight I will be flying to London. I will email you when I'm back in 'Hidden Gem'. You can then tell the police here about my return, and that I've given you no explanation for my disappearance. Leave that to me – I'll think of something. Tell them I am offering to pay for their search time. I will have all your things packed and shipped over to you. I will get my solicitor to start divorce proceedings. I'll tell him the grounds are your adultery – should create less fuss than attempted murder. You won't contest it, of course. I will also ask him to get the two joint-properties valued, and send you a letter informing you of their value, and a further letter in which you agree to transfer your share of the two properties to me. After you sign and return it, I will send you half of the valuation of the two properties. Why? Because the sooner I make a clean break from you the better. I never want to see you again or talk to you again. I was happy to use money to get you. Now I am more than happy to use money to get rid of you. We will correspond by email and letter until our separation is complete.'

This was a new Elaine. Assured and tough, but generous. A few weeks in the bush had worked wonders. Or was it a few weeks with Max – he seemed to work wonders wherever he went. Now he was even responsible for saving James's life. Whatever or whoever had caused the change, James was grateful for it. Elaine had faced the reality of their situation and come up with sound, practical, generous solutions. *If only we'd done this years ago.* 'Thanks Elaine,' he said.

Elaine switched her eyes from his face to below his waist. 'You should cover that up – the gulls might think it's a winkle. Goodbye James.'

What a civilised way to end a marriage, James thought as he watched Elaine and her unlikely assistants walk away.

Chapter 25

A few weeks later James sat at his computer putting the finishing touches to 'Ogling New South Wales'. In spite of his ordeal at the hands of Elaine and her new friends he had pressed on to Eden to research the whale story. Thankfully, he had found his car keys still nestling safely in the Velcroed pocket of his shorts, where he habitually put them. A wash-down in the sea and a change of clothes back at his car and, though still very shaken by the episode, he had decided to continue his journey.

After a few days in Eden learning about the whaling industry, which lasted for 100 years and ended in 1930, he had returned home, finding the house now empty of all Elaine's paraphernalia. His arrival coincided with the arrival of an email from her telling him that she had arrived at 'Hidden Gem', and confirming her willingness to pay the police for their search time.

James took this information to the police station and found Sergeant Spalding in residence. Spalding put on a good act but couldn't totally hide his shock when James told him that Elaine was alive and well and in England. His faith in his copper's instinct was no doubt taking a battering. James pleaded ignorance as to where Elaine had been and suggested Spalding should contact her if he wanted the story. When Spalding became angry at the waste of police time, James told him about Elaine's offer to pay, and he calmed down.

Eventually, after a few more details were discussed, mainly about informing other authorities, James offered his hand and thanked Sergeant Spalding for all his efforts. He told him he rated him much higher than the now infamous Inspector Goodfellow. Spalding had a wry smile on his face when he shook hands. 'No worries, Mr Ogle,' his mouth said. But his eyes said, 'I still believe you were up to something.'

Two days later, after refreshing stocks and clothes, James drove up to the Snowy Mountains – two hours inland from the coast.

Here, in late summer, he found a big drop in temperature, people wearing warm clothes, shops selling skis and snow-chains, villages that looked like they had been transplanted from the Austrian Alps. The aesthetic was very European, the area having become the home of many European mainland immigrants, bringing their expertise in winter sports to the snow playgrounds of Australia.

In between research for his book James had taken the opportunity to walk in the mountains again, and found that above the tree line, at 5,000 feet, the land took on the appearance of all high places. He could have been walking in Scotland or the Lake District as he scrambled over heather and bogs and streams and rocks and small, dirty patches of last winter's snow. It took a close encounter with an unperturbed echidna to remind him that he was still in Australia.

His research into the hydroelectric scheme took him about a week as he travelled over the mountains, through the forests, and by the lakes that the massive enterprise covered. It was truly a remarkable feat of engineering on a colossal scale and he hoped he could do it justice with words and photographs.

Now he was doing just that, sitting at his computer, finishing off another day's work. Another couple of days and he should be in a position to transfer it to his agent. He would breathe a sigh of relief and she would email her enthusiastic thanks.

And that would be that. No more travelling. No more writing. Although – never say never. Who knew what the future might bring? He may have to start writing again to earn enough money to stay in

Australia. The conditions of the Investment/Retirement Visa 405 for which he had applied were incredibly difficult to meet initially, and then to maintain. In effect, anyone over the age of 55 now had to prove they were a millionaire before being allowed to enter Australia; the period of stay was limited to four years, after which you had to pay another $20,000 to apply for another four years and so on. You also had to have a minimum annual income of 50,000 dollars, and pay for private medical insurance. For all this input you were rewarded with no right to vote, and no chance of permanent residence or citizenship. It was just part of the range of Australia's baffling immigration policies, policies that stood logical thinking on its head, policies that were injurious to the country rather than beneficial.

However, there was nothing he could do about it. It was a price he was prepared to pay to live in Narooma. He just hoped that Elaine kept her promise and came through with the money from the valuation of the two U.K. jointly owned properties. He had already received a letter from her solicitor stating the valuations, what his monetary share would be, and asking him to sign over his part of the joint-ownership to Elaine. He had done that and returned the documents. Now he held his breath and hoped. He had also been served with divorce papers and had responded appropriately, not contesting the grounds of his adultery on numerous occasions over the period of their marriage.

He quit his work for the day and, before closing down his computer, clicked over to his email site.

Coincidences are more remarkable for their frequency than for their actual content, and here was a case to prove the point. Here was an email from Elaine's solicitor stating that, on the instructions of his client, he had today transferred $993,782 to James's bank account in Narooma. A letter of confirmation would follow. It was $6,000 short of the million, but he could make that up out of his own small savings. His relief was palpable, his kind thoughts about Elaine sincere. Now there was nothing to stop his visa application being successful. He sent an email of acknowledgement and thanks, then closed down for the day.

James couldn't believe his luck. He had the money and he was rid of Elaine; both objectives having been achieved without death or destruction – eventually. This was cause for a celebration. By another happy coincidence his good news came on a Friday, so he would be able to share his celebration with his table tennis friends at the golf club.

They were all very pleased to hear that he intended to make Narooma his home, but were shocked when he explained the terms of the visa. None of them had known that their government operated such a self-defeating immigration policy. They could not understand why their country would want to discourage the type of people other countries welcomed as the best-possible immigrants, and often gave incentives to attract them.

Most of his table tennis friends had a jaundiced view of politicians anyway, and this revelation did nothing to change their opinions, the consensus of which was neatly summed up by Ken when he said 'Stuff 'em, mate' as they gathered around the bar after the games and helped him celebrate with a few schooners of cold beer.

The next day he had an email from Elaine telling him she had been banned from returning to Australia for a period of four years because of overstaying her holiday visa. As a result she had appointed Max as her representative in Australia, with the job of seeking out aborigine art for eventual sale in her London gallery; this being in addition to the paintings Sam would be supplying. Why she had told him this he had no idea, and he had no intention of spending time wondering about it, but he found the thought of a guaranteed Elaine-free Australia for four years quite comforting. Surely that wasn't her intention.

Three days later, satisfied that the work was complete, he clicked his mouse and transferred his latest, and probably his last, book to his agent. Inevitably, he let out a deep sigh, and stared into space for a long time. The completion of a book was always a mixture of relief at attaining the objective, and sadness at letting go the thing you had created and nursed for so long – almost like letting a child go. He didn't like the image of his work, of writing, being reduced to thousands of electronic impulses disappearing into cyberspace, so he always imagined it as 300 sheets of paper, each flapping its wings, flying like a flock of birds, across the continents, arriving over London, gathering, then slanting down, coming together and whooshing through the open window of his agent's office, landing in sequence, by page number, neatly and silently in her in-tray. That felt better.

James shut down his computer and felt a stir of excitement as he swivelled his chair so he could look out the window. This was it – this was the first day of his new life – a new country, no wife, and now no work. All he had to do was go out and enjoy everything his eyes could see. What a wonderful feeling. What a happy prospect.

He had decided to stay in his rented house not only because its convenience and location were hard to beat and he had grown fond of his feathered neighbours, but because he was concerned that, if he bought a house, in four years' time he might not have sufficient money to meet the visa renewal requirements.

That afternoon, with the weather cooling to just below 20C, in its so-called autumn phase, and the fishing starting to slacken off, James went to play golf.

So started his life of leisure in the Australian outdoors, under a blue sky, in the glow of a gentle sun. For a few weeks he wallowed in the simplicity and freedom of his new life – golfing, fishing, walking, table tennis, shopping, cooking, reading – though he was still involved in tying up the many loose ends of his life in Britain, and coming up against the practical problems of setting up a permanent life in Australia with a temporary visa that most authorities were not aware of.

But, inevitably, as the honeymoon period ran its course and a feeling of routine started to emerge, he began looking for new outlets and interests. He looked at all the clubs he could join – fishing, rambling, sailing, swimming, diving, rowing, surfing, bowling, and he finally decided to join the Art Society and the Photographic Society, both of which allowed him to renew his old acquaintance with paint and brush and composition, as well as make new friends. In Narooma most of the action took place out of doors, taking him to new places, new vistas – all beautiful. The pleasure of spending all day under the shade of a tree, with an easel in front of him while he attempted to capture the beauty, was enhanced by the fact that he started to sell a few paintings in the Art Society's shop in the main street. He had not lost the ability to reproduce what was in front of him, but he could see little sign of any improvement in his lack of flair.

Every time he took his easel to a beach, whether alone or with the group, he thought of Claire. Their first tentative meeting came flooding back. And then the other meetings at the beach house. The watercolour nips on her arms. Her delicate, willowy features, her wind-blown hair. The sound of her voice when she said 'dear'.

It was at times like this that he felt lonely. It wasn't the general feeling of loneliness that all single people feel at some time, but the specific absence of Claire – just Claire. He felt as he had when his father died, as if he was missing a limb. But there was no self-pity involved. He was not one to cry over spilt milk. He loved his life in Narooma and he would count himself lucky if this was to be his permanent future. Some Mozart and a beer usually chased these melancholy moments away, then it was back to the wonderful distraction and pleasure of Narooma. By now he had given up hope of Claire returning next summer. He had recently seen a photograph of her and a well-known Hollywood film star, a George Clooney look-alike, on the front cover of a glossy magazine, which caught his eye in the newsagent's shop where he bought his weekly 'Narooma

News'. A massive headline, 'Blake and the Heiress', covered a picture of them immaculately dressed in evening wear, obviously attending some major Hollywood function. The star, Blake Gardner, was clearly the centre of the magazine's interest with Claire playing a supporting role. He was pleased to see her looking so well, but puzzled to see her in such company and in such showy circumstances. This was not the quiet, retiring Claire he knew. Or thought he knew? What *did* he really know about her? A few short meetings while on holiday were but a scratch on the surface of her life – on anyone's life.

What he did know was that he could not compete with rich, handsome Hollywood film stars. And so he had mentally written off the likelihood of seeing Claire again. After all, it had been her infamous husband who had started their holidays to Australia, for the game fishing; she had just tagged along. No doubt Blake or somebody like him would eventually persuade her to tag along to their idea of holiday paradise, and Narooma and the Englishman who started sentences with 'sorry' would eventually become a distant memory for her; a fond one, he hoped.

Two months later she made the headlines again. This time on the front pages of serious newspapers and on television and radio news broadcasts. The word 'heiress' was used often, reminding people that she had inherited the businesses and fortune of her late husband. She was announcing to the world that most of her husband's personal wealth was to be handed over to charities dealing with people struggling with drug addiction. And 90% of the personal income she made from the many legitimate companies she had inherited would go to the World Wildlife Fund to help preserve endangered species. 'Future generations will curse us if we leave them a lifeless planet,' she said during the announcement.

That's my girl, James thought fondly as he read about her and watched her on television, this time dressed in plain, casual clothes. *That's the Claire I recognise.*

The next day a major earthquake captured the attention of the world's media and Claire and her announcement quickly faded from the limelight.

Approximately six months after Elaine had flown back to England, on a quiet 'spring' day, James returned from his morning walk to find a large envelope sticking out of his post-box on the front lawn. It contained notification that the divorce had been granted, the decree absolute signifying the absolute end of his marriage.

It felt strange being *absolutely* single again. Up to this point he had always had a vague, almost abstract, feeling of being connected to somebody. Now he felt as if he had been cast adrift like a street kid in a big city, like a small buoy in a mighty ocean. He wondered if his new status would manifest itself in any way. Would his demeanour change? Would he start wearing outlandish clothes and buy a sports car to attract the opposite sex? He had been getting one or two encouraging glances from the membership secretary of the Art Society, a gentle soul with a face like a cocker spaniel, and some definite 'come-ons' from the merry widow of the Photo Society, an ex-model with skin like tanned leather. Time would tell; it would be interesting observing himself.

During the 'winter/spring' period, when the fishing was relatively quiet, James had started to write letters to newspapers, and the occasional article, highlighting the strange and mean-spirited aspects of Australia's immigration policy as it affected people over 55. This had resulted in him being contacted by others with the same visa as himself, and together they had formed an on-line self-help group intent on making a concerted effort to get the government to change their harsh visa conditions. He found this absorbed him in lengthy, but worthwhile, activity, which satisfied some of his itch to keep writing.

As the 'spring' developed seamlessly into summer, the only change being a rise from 21 to 24C, the fish, in all their glorious varieties, started to come into the inlet and patrol along the beaches, and James wound down the days he played golf and increased the days he went fishing. He went to Cemetry Beach only once. He found the sight of the shuttered beach house, and the memories it held, overpowered the feelings of innocent happiness he had previously associated with the beach. The revelation of this level of sensitivity surprised him.

He also started to walk in the evening as well as the morning, to counteract his spreading waistline. In typical lazy, single-man fashion he had begun to eat the easy way – takeaways and microwave ready meals. He didn't like the result and was determined to lose some weight.

His walk was a three quarters of an hour circuit – down the hill, through the forest to Bar Beach, along the beach, on to the boardwalk, along the boardwalk, up into the forest again and back home. Sometimes he did it in reverse. It was a walk of great beauty and interest, particularly along the boardwalk, and he never tired of it. In the evening the boardwalk was relatively quiet. Narooma, like most Australian towns, shut down early by British standards. The daytime, sun-time, was for work or play. Evening and night was for relaxing, mostly drinking. Sometimes he played golf in the evening and found he had the beautiful course to himself, something unheard of in Britain.

He was walking along the boardwalk one evening when a procession of three stingrays came gliding along, all of different sizes and colours. He had tried to learn which was which but found differentiating among the many species difficult. A small greyish one led the way, followed by a larger brown one, and bringing up the rear was the big black 'stealth bomber'. This was his favourite because of its extra size, its sense of threat, its other-worldliness, its effortless grace. He walked along with them, then stopped as the black one paused to rummage about on the inlet bed. He leaned his arms on the handrail and looked down into the clear water, feeling privileged to see such a creature only a few feet away.

'Beautiful isn't it,' a woman's voice behind him observed.

'Yes it is,' he replied without turning, knowing that another tourist simply wanted to share their pleasure of discovery.

'Mahler's fourth, the slow movement, would be appropriate accompaniment, don't you think?'

James spun round. She was smiling.

He didn't often see the membership secretary of the Art Society smile; she tended towards a frown usually. 'Yes…Mahler's fourth would be perfect,' he said eventually, trying to hide his disappointment, waiting for his pounding heart to calm down. She was taking her dog for a walk. It was a cocker spaniel. They exchanged pleasantries, James careful not to make any encouraging signals, then she went on her way. James continued walking in the opposite direction.

He was passed at great speed by two boys riding bikes, temporarily kicking their addiction to their PlayStations. They rang their bells in warning and shouted 'Hi' as nice country boys usually did.

Next, he walked past a tall woman who appeared to be deep in thought, her head down, the wide brim of her hat hiding her features.

'James?'

He turned.

The woman had turned. The light was dimming. She was hesitant. 'James?'

Her voice. 'Claire?'

They retraced their steps and stood facing each other in the centre of the boardwalk.

'You're back,' he said.

'Yes.'

'How long?'

'Depends.'

'Holiday?'

'Depends.'

'Where's Blake?'

'Who?'

'Blake Gardner.'

'A friend of a friend. She owed him a favour. I owed her one. His ratings were slipping…he needed some publicity.'

'You're alone?'

'Yes.'

'Can we spend some time together?

'Did Elaine turn up?'

'Yes, but she's gone. We're divorced.'

'Then we can spend a lot of time together if that is what you would like.'

James offered a tentative left hand towards her. Claire took it with her right. Suddenly they were in each other's arms, taking part in a feeding frenzy of love, intent on satisfying their long hunger in one sitting. Lips, cheeks, foreheads, eyes, necks, hair, ears were kissed, and then they went round again. Their bodies trembled with urgency.

Passers-by smiled, looked embarrassed; one applauded.

'Definitely not the wife,' a fisherman quipped to his mate as they squeezed past with their rods and tackle.

They both heard the remark and they broke apart laughing, still holding hands.

'Have you come back to me?' James gasped, still not certain.

'No, I came back to return the pen I borrowed.' She was getting the hang of English humour.

'So, where is it?' James played along.

'At the beach house. If you want it you will have to come with me.'

'Let's go,' James laughed.

They set off walking along the boardwalk, arms around each other like teenagers.

After a few metres, James said, 'So this 10% you're keeping. How much is that?'

'Oh! Just a few million a year,' Claire replied.

'You'll do,' James said.

As they neared the end of the boardwalk, the sun started to slip behind Mount Gulaga. The air stopped moving, as though the earth was holding its breath. Wagonga Inlet became a mirror. The birds were silent. Narooma was saying farewell to another perfect day.

James whispered, 'Better ending than the movies, this.'

'I thought it was a beginning.'

'Are we having our first argument?'

'Looks like it.'

'I hope we have lots more.'

'So do I.'

They stopped and wrapped their arms around each other and kissed.

There was a sound of distant rumbling, and then thudding. The boardwalk shivered slightly beneath their feet. They broke away and looked back along the boardwalk. A large man, wearing vest and shorts came pounding towards them. As he ran past them, he shouted, 'Best bladdy sunset in the world that, mite.'

End

Bibliography:

Pacey, Laurelle, *Narooma's Past*. Narooma N.S.W.: Published by Laurelle Pacey, 2005.

Fiction:

This book is a work of fiction. References to real people, events, establishments, organizations, or locales are intended only to provide a sense of authenticity, and are used fictitiously. All other characters, and all incidents and dialogue, are drawn from the author's imagination and are not to be construed as real.

Fishing:

When the first settlers arrived in Australia they gave some of the fish they found the same names as fish in British waters – e.g. salmon, bream, whiting etc. However, they are not the same species. An Australian salmon, for example, is a member of the perch species and bears no relationship to the Atlantic salmon.

Narooma:

To see some of the locations described in the novel you can visit: narooma.org.au

About the Author

Michael Wood has combined a career in industry with that of a writer. His first novel – The
Fell Walker – achieved wide acclaim. He has
lived in England and Australia.

Acknowledgements

Thanks go to members of B.E.R.I.A. (British Expats Resident In Australia) for an insight into the problems of over-55's retiring to Australia and other Commonwealth countries.